Pro

The Protective Series

Book 1 Protective Instincts

Book 2 Protecting Melissa

Book 3 The Cost of Deception

Protective Instincts
The Protective Series
Book 1

Mary Marvella

Cover Design	Gina Dyer
Images by:	Depositphoto
Interior Design:	Melba Moon
Editors:	M. Barfield

Dedications and Thanks
Dedications are hard to do. This book is dedicated to my critique partners Connie, Melba, Pam, and Sharina and to a lovely lady I met at a writers' conference fifteen years ago. Linda, we're still at it and we're having more fun than those literary writers.

Special thanks to Georgiana Fields, Gina Dyer, Carol Shaughnessy, and Jackie Rodriguez, who make me feel I can do anything!

Chapter One

"Oh, hell," Brit Roberts groaned when the ringing phone on her kitchen wall stopped her in her tracks at seven AM. No, she'd let her machine take the message from whoever called so early in the morning. She turned away and reached for the doorknob then paused at the second ring. *What if the call is important, like Julie in a panic, a sick car, or a family emergency?* She opened the door.

Dammit all! She cringed at the third ring. On the fourth ring she slammed the door closed. Why make this call the first she left to her machine? Curiosity would have nagged at her all day, anyway.

By the fifth ring Brit snatched up the receiver.

"Hello." No answer.

"Hello?" *Not another one.*

"Look, this is so bothersome!" She pulled in a long deep breath then slowly exhaled. "Could you *please* check your number before dialing again?" Her voice rose.

A dial tone droned in her ear. *Another hang up call.* "Damn!" She slammed the phone down and, grabbed her purse and keys. *Mental note–replace battery so caller ID works again. I'll just put a stop to this aggravation.* Anyone could dial a wrong number, but anyone who couldn't at least apologize was just plain rude.

Now, I'll be late starting parent-teacher conferences. Just what I need. Parents could be late and she'd smile and bear it, but her first appointment wouldn't be so forgiving. She'd start her day with a too-busy-for-words mother, a lawyer whose time was worth more than that of a measly teacher or even her own son.

She rushed out to her car and threw her cloth tote bag and purse onto the front seat. After she punched the garage door opener she revved her engine—twice for good measure. *Slow, deep, calming breath! Another!* She still didn't feel calm.

Warm Georgia temperatures nurtured pale green buds and shoots of spring flowers in her yard. Brit was in an ill mood while she backed her old Mustang from her driveway into the tree-lined street. If she hadn't been so tired from lack of sleep she'd have enjoyed these signs of renewed life.

She'd awakened before her alarm buzzed, thinking about Tommy. He'd have been thirty-five today, if he hadn't been killed in a hit and run accident. Her stomach still knotted when she thought about how much she missed him after three years.

Having your husband die stinks. If the man who'd killed her husband had returned to the scene of his accident to get help or turned himself in closure might have been easier for her. The Butlerton City Police still hadn't found the driver. They told her each time she called that they didn't expect to, but she wouldn't stop reminding them. Tommy had mattered too much for her to let the police off easy. There had been plenty of witnesses to the hit and run. She owed him that much. She owed herself that much.

***

Sam Samuels rubbed his stiff neck. He'd removed his tie and unbuttoned the top button on his dress shirt. He'd left his sports coat in his truck, but he still felt over-dressed. By now he should have shed his business attire for worn jeans and a tee shirt.

He'd put in a long day. His notebook page was full of ways the school security system needed to be improved. It had taken years to get the board to agree to look at a plan and proposal for his company to do the job. Small town-folks in

Georgia weren't into change, but recent violence in so many schools, even small-town ones, pointed to the need for caution everywhere.

Sam had waited until after his regular calls to begin this part of his plan. His son was a student here and he'd make it a safe place for Sean, even if he had to cut his price to the bone, past cost. This wouldn't be the first time he had cut his price to put a good security system where it was needed. The one at his parents' church and the community center had been donations, pure and simple. Nothing was more important than taking care of family.

Sam's mobile phone startled him.

"Samuels here."

"Samuels here, too, Dad. Coach said to remind you I need my physical exam papers and your permission slip by next Wednesday or I can't continue Spring practice."

"Well, Samuels, your doctor's appointment is Friday at four, I've already signed the permission slip."

"Oh, yeah. Got a library stop after supper with Bill and his parents, then some of the guys wanted to ---"

"Don't be late."

"But I don't have school tomorrow."

"Not one minute after eleven. You know the rules."

Sam grinned as he broke the connection. Sean always made curfew at the last minute. One mess-up, one speeding ticket, or even one bad grade and he'd lose the Corvette his mother bought him. He'd lose the car and football. For a traffic offense he'd surrender his driver's license, his mother's rule. Shared custody had worked well, especially with her travelling on business a lot since the divorce.

He rubbed his five o'clock stubble then started on his second page of meticulous notes. His cramped handwriting made his eyes hurt. He shouldn't have left his glasses in the truck.

Clicking heels on wood distracted him. The footsteps sounded small but businesslike, in a hurry. He glanced in the direction of the feminine sound. The lady wore navy hose and a navy skirt. He smiled and nodded at Ms. Roberts as she passed him on her way to the parking lot. "Good evening," he said to her back as she barely slowed her exit, leaving a light floral scent to wrap around him. He liked skirts and hose, call him old fashioned.

Her impersonal nod toward him could have been meant for anyone.

"And a good evening to you, too," he muttered to the closing door. *Typical for her.* She wasn't the friendliest woman he'd ever met. Most women at least gave him a smile when he spoke to them.

Suddenly his gut cramped. He glanced around the deserted hall. Pressure built in his head. He felt a premonition attack coming on. Why now? Why when his son's teacher had just passed by? He didn't need an attack now. He hurried to the school parking lot to catch up with the cause of his discomfort. He'd finish his figures later.

Sam had figured he'd probably see Ms. Roberts here sometime before he left, but he hadn't planned to do more than nod to her as he always did. She was attractive but standoffish. Sean had mentioned she was a widow. Maybe that was why she seldom smiled.

His mama's training in the ways of a gentleman prodded him toward her and the old Mustang. He'd follow her tonight. He had no choice. *Maybe these premonitions are about car trouble. Probably.* It wouldn't be the first time he'd rescued someone from being stranded.

Sam was so preoccupied he didn't think about the possibility he'd startle Ms. Roberts.

She whirled around to face him. "Are you following me?"

That sounded like an accusation. "I'm Sean Samuels' father."

"I know, but why are you here at my car? Isn't that your truck, over there?" She tilted her head toward his truck.

"Sean's always talking about your Mustang, '65?"

"'64 1/2."

"I had a '66 way back when." He ran his hand along the back fender. "Restoring it?" He pointed to sanded areas.

Her raised eyebrow made him feel like he was intruding. It couldn't be helped. The hairs on the back of his neck were still at alert. "Does it run well?"

She smiled a teacher-humoring-the-boys smile. "Two-eighty-nine, high performance engine, four-barrel carburetor, automatic, and I never drive it above 85 mph." Despite the way she seemed to parrot the response, a small smile played on her lips.

Sam's hands gravitated to his pockets as he resisted the urge to reach for her keys and unlock her door. Now, that would be pushy. Standing close enough to share body heat and inhale her subtle wild flower fragrance, he noticed she barely came up to his shoulder, even with her heels.

Pain lanced through Sam's head. His reactions were stronger. If only he could get an idea about the source of the danger. But then he'd have to work on using the pesky *gift* he hadn't wanted, one he couldn't ignore.

He couldn't let her leave alone. She'd think him crazy if he told her he sensed she was in danger.

"Ma'am, I know it sounds like I'm being forward, but do you have a cell phone for emergencies?" She gave him a look that said she did think the question was forward.

"I've never needed one." She put her key in the ignition and started the powerful engine, gunning it more than was necessary. "Why, are you selling them?"

"No, just acting like a parent and a man who makes his living keeping people safe."

She needed a reason to let him help her with a problem she didn't know she had, especially when he couldn't tell her the truth.

"Your engine sounds a little rough. You have a couple of worn tires, too. Mind if I follow you home, to be sure you get there okay? Can't have my son's teacher stranded on the road at night. I do have a cell phone." Lame, he sounded lame.

"I don't see any need for you to follow me home, Mr. Samuels."

Probably thinks I'm hitting on her, which I wouldn't.

"I'm tired. I'd just like to go home and put up my feet and relax. It's been a long day." She adjusted her rearview mirror then stretched her seatbelt to secure it.

"Please, humor me. Every woman needs a cell phone. I'm a security specialist and my mama raised me to watch out for ladies and it's... Oh, Hell, it's practically on my way and..."

"Fine, whatever, Mr. Samuels. Knock yourself out."

Even in the parking lot light he could see the dark smudges beneath her eyes. She must have had a hard day.

"Sure thing." What else could he say after he'd badgered her.

"I'll try not to drive my old clunker too fast for you." *Smart mouth and humor.*

"Good evening, Mr. Samuels."

She reached for the floor gearshift and pulled the T handle to reverse.

Sam hurried to his truck. Personally, he'd have preferred a manual shift on that hot old car.

***

Douglas Drake watched the teacher talking to the character in the school parking lot. Damned binoculars weren't enough help. *Who the hell is the man? Didn't know she had a boyfriend sniffing around. Too bad I can't hear what they're saying.* Maybe he'd bug her car if he didn't finish his business tonight.

Douglas followed the Mustang and the man's black Ford muscle truck. *The jerk better not interfere. I hate it when people mess with my plans.* Douglas had work to do. Preparation was the most important element in his job. He was nothing if not professional, and he'd been paid a hefty deposit to off the teacher.

***

Brit was bone tired after the first day of explaining to parents that no homework, plus no class work, plus poor or failing test scores equals a failing grade. She was ready to shed navy heels and the pantyhose that were more binding than supporting. They helped her leg muscles but could be a bother. Conference days created more pressure than regular teaching days did. She loved teaching, but some parents could be demanding. Three months before graduation was late for high school seniors' parents to finally become concerned or defensive, as a few always did.

Sean's dad was a handsome pain in the rear, but a pain, none the less. He'd seemed determined to follow her home tonight. Over the year they'd had a nodding acquaintance. He'd ask about Sean's progress in her class. She'd comment. Lately Mr. Samuels had been at school a lot. Before tonight he hadn't initiated a personal conversation, but she had noticed him staring at her.

He'd always smiled at her. The man's "serious father" look slipped when he laughed at something one of the kids said or did. She hadn't been paying attention to men for a long time, but it was hard to miss his deep laugh or his fatherly way of mussing one of the boy's hair or the way he hugged his son's shoulders when he did well. He was the kind of father her Tommy would have been if he had lived. He and Tommy probably would have been friends.

He and Tommy would probably never have met. She would not have met Mr. Samuels if she hadn't lost Tommy, if she hadn't applied for a teaching job at Julie's insistence. Teaching and her best friend had brought her back into the world.

At times she'd glanced Mr. Samuels' way longer than she'd meant to. His deep green eyes were framed by laugh-lines. When their gazes locked she was always first to look away. She didn't want to give him the wrong idea. Sean and his crowd talked about his dad a lot. He sounded like a perfect parent.

Brit pulled into her drive, thankful for the remote door opener. She eased into her garage, then closed the wide door. She could see Mr. Samuels' truck through a window in her garage. The man was about as subtle as a bear in Sunday School. Too tired to keep watch from there, she unlocked the door and entered her kitchen.

Startled by the loud ringing, she hesitated before answering her phone. *Please, not another damned hang-up.*

Mr. Samuels' baritone, bedroom voice from the answering machine sent heat to Brit's face. Foolish to let a little thing like a few hang-up calls scare her.

"Come on, Mrs. Roberts, please answer your phone so I'll know you're okay," he insisted. He sounded worried.

13

Brit grabbed the phone. "Mr. Samuels, I didn't know I'd need to check in with you. You were just going to make sure my clunker made it home." She sighed and rested her elbow on the yellow counter. "What if I'd thought you were one of the bad guys?" She cocked her head and smiled. As an afterthought she asked. "Still concerned?"

"Well, uh...glad you're okay, ma'am, I didn't mean to worry you. Bad Guys?" he asked, as though he had just realized what she'd said. "Someone been bothering you?"

Could he possibly know about the hang-up phone calls? Nah! Besides, it was none of his business, unless he'd made them. He'd never seemed the type of man to hang up instead of saying what he wanted. *What does he want?*

"Mr. Samuels, my brothers keep my car running and in good repair. The tires are fine, too. Now, tell me why you really followed me then go on home." Brit wasted no effort to disguise her annoyance, rubbing her neck to ease a day's worth of tension. She'd almost sell her soul for a good massage or even a bad massage.

"Maybe I was planning to be in your neighborhood. I wanted to be sure you got home safely? Maybe I hoped you'd invite me in for coffee." She could almost see the grin she heard in his oh-so-masculine voice. She should've guessed. How long had it been since a man had flirted with her? Would she have noticed?

"In your dreams." She smiled. "I'm fine, so go on home."

"I really was worried about your car."

Brit interrupted, "Mr. Samuels, I'll talk to you about your son tomorrow in our conference." She almost hung up on him. As an after-thought she added, "While I appreciate your concern I've been looking after myself since my husband's death. I can fix almost anything about my Mustang and I even have *two* spare tires, a heavy-duty jack, and my own tool chest. Good bye, now."

Seconds after she hung up she heard the loud engine of his truck as he passed her house.

She popped a frozen dinner in the microwave and poured a glass of Georgia grown wine. The nuked low-fat *culinary delight* would be ready when she finished her soak, surrounded by scented candles.

She was looking forward to a quiet Wednesday night, a night with no interruptions or wrong-number calls. She could let the answering machine take her calls. She'd buy fresh batteries for her phone tomorrow, instead of Monday. If her caller ID worked she might know which caller to tell to go to Hell! Should she report the nuisance calls to the police? Nah! Too much trouble. Maybe the pest would become bored before she had to chase him or her down with caller ID. Pulling her cell phone from her purse, she grinned. She didn't know why she hadn't told Mr. Samuels she had one.

Sipping Muscatine wine from a stemmed glass, Brit headed for her bathroom. Kneeling beside the claw-foot tub, she secured the stopper and turned both taps. Forehead against cool porcelain, she relaxed for a minute to the sound of running water.

Returning to her kitchen, Brit stripped the baggy, soft sweater and tossed it on a chair before checking to be sure the door to the garage was locked. A woman couldn't be too careful, even in this small town. Only two hours from Atlanta, Florence was like being in a totally different world.

She noticed the marks left by her bra pushing into a little excess flesh. Since Tommy's death she hadn't taken such good care of herself. Once she'd rejoined the world of the living, meals for one had led to junk food. Time for a real exercise program to go with the sensible meals she planned to adopt soon.

***

Sam had made the trip from the teacher's house to his, with a stop for Burger King take-out, in fifteen minutes. Sean was still out. Sam had felt foolish following his son's teacher home. He'd felt even more foolish calling her from his car to be sure she was safe. Though he felt responsible for taking care of others, he'd never been so strongly compelled to see after someone who wasn't even family.

Never again would Sam ignore feelings that someone was in danger. Not since he was twelve had he done so. His friend had become separated from the group on a camping trip.

If Sam hadn't insisted on going back to find the boy he'd have died from a snake-bite. Sam had tried tonight to ignore his spooky premonition, but it had grown inside him until he thought he would burst.

His premonitions were too strange to discuss. He couldn't explain why he had them. It wasn't like he was psychic. Circumstances and people triggered the symptoms. Some could be attributed to natural instincts, like times he'd awakened in the middle of the night to find Sean sick.

The night he'd called to wake Adrienne, his ex-wife, from a sound sleep she'd been ready to skin him until she'd smelled gas and realized she might not have awakened ever again if he hadn't called. Thank God his premonitions didn't happen often.

Sean's English teacher was always full of piss-n-vinegar. She'd stood up for students and their needs at PTSA meetings. She'd stood her ground when coaches had suggested she give passing grades to athletes with key positions on school teams. They'd lost football and basketball games while key players were ineligible because of grades in her class. Sean respected her.

Sam's decision to follow the teacher tonight had been spur of the moment. He'd had to follow her home. He hoped the age of her car was the reason his premonitions acted up, but he couldn't take a chance. The gut ache had faded. The hairs on his neck stopped bristling.

After the burgers and his second beer he fell asleep in his worn recliner in front of the television, where he waited for Sean, the most important person in his life, his joy.

***

Brit's soaking bath would be delayed. She couldn't believe she'd ordered flowers for herself. Well, why not? She deserved them. Tommy, darling man that he was, had always given her flowers on his birthday to celebrate the anniversary of their first date. Flowers and a meal delivered to her door should go a long way toward dispelling her gloomy mood. A soft, blue, fleece sweat suit allowed her to answer the doorbell decently covered. Grinning, she opened the door.

"Ohmigosh!" She'd never seen anything like the arrangement of expensive looking flowers obscuring the deliveryman. "You've got the wrong address," she blurted. Glancing past the uniformed man she spotted the florist truck.

"No, ma'am, I don't. These are for you. Says so on the order." He shifted his heavy load to thrust a paper toward her.

Stepping back, she motioned for him to put the heavy looking arrangement of flowers on her table. Foxglove and belladonna blooms hung on long stalks. Pink throated Stargazer lilies and white Casablanca lilies dominated a vase suitable for a hotel table centerpiece. Calla-lilies stood out on their graceful long stems. Delicate blossomed freesia and flowers she didn't recognize provided color to the mostly white arrangement.

"These aren't my flowers. I ordered a dozen roses, not a garden." She was punching in the number of the florist as she saw the deliveryman heading toward her door. "Wait, you have to take these back. Someone will be disappointed when you take my dinky bouquet of roses to the person expecting these."

The man shrugged, waiting for her to set the record straight. "But I ordered..." Brit tried to explain, pacing back and forth in front of the tall, antique telephone table.

Arguing to no avail, she shrugged at the deliveryman. "Well, I am *not* paying for this fortune's worth of flowers." Using her read-my-lips tone, she slowly enunciated into the phone, then hung up.

Brit reached for the five-dollar bill she'd put aside for the tip, an appropriate amount for the flowers she'd ordered but ...

"No, thank you, Ma'am," he called over his shoulder. "it's covered."

Her dining room was redolent with fragrances from Stargazers, Casablanca lilies, or the blooms she couldn't identify. Good thing she'd had the deliveryman put the arrangement on the dining room table. Again she moved to answer the doorbell. The food delivery?

"What the...?" she blurted at the two tuxedoed men standing on her porch. The one in the lead clicked the heels of shiny tux shoes in salute. Too weird.

"Your dinner, madam."

"All this for one meal delivered?" She stepped aside to allow the small, formal army access. She reached for her phone. "Wait, what are you doing?" she asked the crew setting her dining table with a white lace table cloth, candelabra, and expensive looking dinnerware.

While she argued with someone at the restaurant she'd called earlier, waiters transformed her dining room into a romantic, candlelit dinner table setting. Tantalizing aromas teased her senses and had her stomach growling.

"I didn't order all this," she repeated. "I don't understand." She shook her head. "Well, be prepared to send out another meal like this when the person who ordered this one doesn't get it."

The phone barely rested back in its cradle when a waiter escorted her to her seat at the elegantly appointed table, the one she planned to refinish during spring break. The glare from delicate, white china, gleaming crystal, and polished silver reflected candlelight in the darkened room. The two tuxedos stood along one wall of her dining room while she ate, moving to serve her every need.

Could she be dreaming all this? Where was the handsome man who would come in to tell he'd admired her from afar for an eternity? Maybe a shadowy hulk would materialize and tell her he was an ugly beast who would transform into a prince if she could love him. Brit wove a romantic movie fantasy around the pampering. Soon she'd wake with memory of this dream.

She enjoyed the succulent lobster, a special favorite, and the salad made with more tender leaves and other ingredients than she'd ever seen in one bowl. Asparagus tips and baby carrots tempted her taste buds. Potatoes swam in delicate white sauce.

The sinful dessert was made with chocolate, nuts, whipped cream, ice cream, and cake and had to have at least a zillion calories. She'd need a priest for confession, though she was thoroughly Baptist. Within seconds of her last taste of sin on a plate, the room was cleared of the evidence of an expensive error. She was almost glad for the mistakes in delivery and that the waiters refused her puny tip, which would have paid for what she ordered.

Finally the tuxedoed men had cleared the carnage. They had departed but the aromas remained, mixing floral fragrances with that of freshly perked gourmet coffee. Now she was ready to take that bath. What was left besides a soak in her tub and a hot guy?

Candlelight cast a glow around a freshly run, now steaming tub. Aroma-therapy tonight included Chamomile and lavender. Stepping into the hot water Brit felt chill bumps appear on the exposed flesh, so she quickly immersed her body. "Ah!" She sighed, "Heaven."

Reaching over the side of the high tub she retrieved her wine glass from the faded blue linoleum. Sipping the fruity flavor, Brit stared into the bubbles surrounding her, decadent, lightly scented, soothing bubbles.

As she lounged in a hot, foamy bath, staring into the steamy haze, bittersweet thoughts of Tommy relaxed, comforted, and saddened her. Mostly, they comforted her. Each day the pain diminished, but only a little.

Tommy had been her best friend. He'd always been there for her. It was so hard to lose her best friend and her sweet, gentle lover. Memories of two happy young people flickered past. He had taught her to love, but he had not taught her to live without him. There were wonderful things they'd done together, so many things they'd discovered together, so many things they had left to do together, but there'd be no more together for them.

Her parents were supportive when she could only hide within her memories. There had been no quick or easy cure for the bewilderment and loss that held Brit in its icy clutches. No magic spell.

The driver of the truck probably hadn't seen him step between parked cars onto a busy street. He had sped away after robbing her of the chance to grow old with her love. Witnesses at the scene said it had been Tommy's fault.

She hadn't wanted to remember that they'd had one of the few arguments of their six-year-old marriage the morning of the accident. He'd been taken by surprise when she'd suggested he might be the reason they hadn't conceived. If only she'd saved her request that they go for tests for an evening when they could've talked things out. Had she sent him out too distracted to pay attention to what he was doing? Could she have been at least partly to blame? Her doctors had said they should both be tested.

"So sorry, my love," Brit whispered. Her hand relaxed.

Water splashed her face, her glass now floated in her bath water. She hadn't realized she'd let it slip from her fingers.

She rose from the tub, shivering as she toweled dry. Pulling on Tommy's old bathrobe, she took comfort in the extra length. His scent had long been washed away, but she could pretend. Clutching the worn terry robe closed she opened the bathroom door and headed for her bedroom and sleep.

She tied the belt to her robe and crawled into bed. Pulling the covers over herself, Brit thought about the green eyes of the man who had followed her home tonight. Why had Mr. Samuels needed to follow her? Why on earth had he called her to make sure she made it inside all right? Was it really because he was worried about her car? Had he acted on a whim, or had he really felt she needed to be looked after?

He attended every ball game, every event, and every parent-teacher meeting. He wore age and fatherhood well. She remembered things she hadn't thought she'd noticed, besides his knowing green eyes, like his midnight black hair, or his air of confidence.

He looked like the kind of man a woman could lean on. For the first time in years she'd noticed a man. How dare he intrude on her bed time blues? Tommy was the love of her life.

***

Half asleep, Brit reached for the ringing phone. She was disoriented from a dream that had left her breathless. She'd seen Tommy's body fly over the hood of the truck that hit him. She'd heard herself scream. Then she'd seen a masked man staring at her, his look menacing. When he'd started toward her she'd turned and run 'til she couldn't catch her breath.

Now cloying, oppressive, the fragrance of the garden sized arrangement in her dining room had permeated her bedroom. She glanced bleary-eyed at the luminous clock. Two o'clock? Who'd call at this hour but family with an emergency? She snatched up the receiver.

She cleared her throat and gathered her wits about her. "Hello."

"Havin' a real nice nite, Sugar?" The voice was raspy, deep, and very southern. It made her skin crawl.

"Whom are you calling?" She tried to sound reasonable. "Wrong number? Please check your numbers before you call again. You keep getting me instead of whoever "

"Did you enjoy the little romantic surprises, Darlin'?" His voice was a cross between a caress and an insult.

"Surprises?" she asked. "What surprises?" At that moment she realized. Her chest constricted. She bolted upright in bed so quickly her head swam.

"Aren't the flowers gorgeous? Beautiful flowers for a beautiful lady. Intoxicatin' fragrances, huh?"

"Who are you? Am I supposed to I know you?"

"Not as well as I know you, lovely lady."

"Why–how did you change my order? Who *are* you!"

"You deserve beautiful things," he purred.

"But you shouldn't send me gifts. I mean it." She didn't recognize his voice or the lazy southern drawl. "The flowers were extravagant. The food was way past too much." She hit her pillow. "You have no business listening in on my phone calls."

He seemed to ignore her. "You need a new robe, silky, sheer, and black, Sugar. That's some sexy body under all that terry cloth, smooth, sweet, warm from sleep. Are your beautiful, white breasts aching to be touched?"

Brit gasped, yanking the bed covers to her chin. Someone had been in her house, had invaded her space. Her expensive dinner, the one he'd had sent, threatened to come back up. "Look, whoever you are---"

"Is the sweet place between your thighs wet, Darlin'? Bet you're wanting it as much as I do." A long pause was followed by, "Oh-h-h, Sugar, love the old claw foot tub. I can wash your back for you. Then your rosy nipples and work my way down your belly to..."

For seconds she had been frozen. She'd hoped to learn who the pervert was by using her head and staying calm. *Don't let him get to you.* She swallowed hard before she could speak without choking. "I'm really too tired for this," she said as she started to hang up. She'd hit star--whatever, then call the police. Maybe she'd use a neighbor's phone, so he couldn't listen.

"Bet your heart's just pumpin' away, *ma bella*. See you soon. Think about me, Darlin'. See you in my sweet dreams."

My God! The pervert watched her sleep? The idea made her shiver. He knew too much about her. The police, she'd to call the police.

Brit slammed the phone, ready to snatch it back and leave it off the hook, when it rang again. "Damn!" It might as well have been a snake. She wasn't answering it this time.

The answering machine picked up. "Pick up your phone. I know you're there, Ms. Roberts." Mr. Samuels was calling at this hour? "Aw, come on, Teach. Your line was busy, I know you're awake."

Brit wanted to answer the phone, she really did. She wanted to carry on a sane conversation with a real person, someone she knew. But she couldn't bring herself to touch the cursed thing.

***

Sam was ready to climb through the phone line. Something was terribly wrong. He'd known it just before he woke in a cold sweat, his gut in pain. The memory of her frightened amethyst eyes haunted him. Why had he dreamed about her? Why had she seemed so upset? He'd speed dialed Ms. Roberts' number before he realized he'd picked up the phone beside the recliner where he'd fallen asleep. All Sean's teachers' numbers were programmed into the phone.

"I'm comin' over." Sam rose from the chair as quickly as his sleep-stiff body would allow. The phone was still in his hand when he heard her answer.

"No! No, don't come over here."

"Something's wrong. I know it is." Still half asleep, Sam held the phone between his chin and his neck as he shoved his feet into the shoes he'd discarded before dozing off.

"Everything's fine," the woman told him. Why would she lie? He knew she had, because his premonitions were never wrong.

"So, why didn't you answer your phone?"

22

"I was half asleep. Do you know what time it is?"

"Yes, but I'm worried about you. I'll be at your house in ten minutes," Sam had his keys and wallet in his hands. "or less. I'll explain, but I really need to be sure you're all right, please."

He replaced the phone, then checked Sean's room. Sean was sprawled across his bed, blond hair mussed, his hand dangling off the edge. Grabbing a sheet of paper, he scrawled, "Son, back soon. Don't worry. Gone to check on a friend."

Sam felt foolish. He raced across town, hoping he didn't get stopped for speeding. The streets were deserted. Good fortune had put each light on green or flashing yellow. He didn't think he'd have stopped if there had been one red light. The eerie feelings weren't as strong as when he'd awakened, but they wouldn't go away until he checked on the teacher.

Her house was dark, except for the porch light and a warm glow from a window facing the street. The lady probably thought he was a lunatic. Sam didn't care. She faced him from the other side of the screen before he could touch the doorbell. The teacher looked fragile, clutching the large white robe at her throat. Her auburn hair was in disarray and she was beautiful.

"Please, let me in for a minute. I need to be sure you're really all right. You sounded so strange over the phone."

"I was trying to go back to sleep when you called. As you can see, I'm fine." She acted like she hid a yawn. No way. He knew people and he had a teenaged son. She was hiding something, and she looked too shaky to be sleepy. He had to get her to talk, or he would get no more sleep. She probably wouldn't, either.

"If nothing is wrong I'll go away. But you look like you'll break if anyone touches you. Has this anything to do with the bad guys you mentioned earlier?" Her flinch told him he'd made a hit. "I won't stay long. Please, just let me in for a minute."

She let him in. Mr. Samuels represented a familiar face. He seemed so genuinely concerned about her. The likelihood she'd go back to sleep was non-existent.

"I was only kidding about the bad guys earlier to see if you were paying attention." If only she'd known there really was a bad guy. She shivered. God, she needed to talk to someone.

This man's masculine presence filled her hall, which seemed to narrow when he entered. He was so close Brit wondered if he could hear her heart beating double-time. Black hair looked as though he'd run his hands through it a lot. His clothes looked slept in.

The light hanging from the ceiling of the entrance hall cast him in soft shadow. Sharp cheekbones and whisker dark hollows tempted her to touch him. He was large and should have been intimidating, but his eyes showed concern and vulnerability.

His gaze moved slowly from her face to her bare feet then back to stare into her eyes. Brit felt as though he'd examined her, reassuring himself she was unharmed. Why had he insisted on coming here in the middle of the night?

"Mr. Samuels?" she asked after what seemed like forever.

"Call me Sam, please. It's late at night for formalities, especially with you in that robe." His half laugh sounded nervous when he inclined his head slightly to indicate her robe. "Are you going to keep me in the hall, or could we sit down while you tell me why you invaded my sleep tonight. You were frightened in my dream, then on the phone, and I have to know why."

The man seemed so earnest she knew she'd have to give him the reassurance he needed or he'd never leave. "Come into the kitchen. I was about to make hot chocolate." He'd been dreaming about her? Strange, since she'd gone to sleep thinking about him.

Sam noticed little about her house as she led him to her remodeled old-fashioned kitchen. A heavy floral smell made his nose twitch as they'd passed her living/dining room area. That same smell followed them to her bright, airy kitchen. The combination of odors was heavy, oppressive, not one he would have associated with this woman.

Sam studied Brit while she stood at the old, large stove. Her delicate hands shook as she struck a match and lit the gas

24

burner. With deliberate movements she turned the knob to lower the flame.

She was still upset, and he needed to know why?

"So, you were dreaming about me, huh?" she asked without turning to look at him."

"Yeah," he wished he hadn't mentioned that. She'd need some kind of explanation.

"Some of my students say they have nightmares about me, but few parents mention having them." Her hesitant laugh sounded nervous.

Time to change the subject. He couldn't explain the reason with her back to him.

"Real milk and cocoa in that chocolate?" he asked. *Wonder what she's wearing under that worn robe.* He could distinguish no lines. *Shouldn't be looking for lines.* But he was. Her rounded hips moved beneath the robe when she stirred.

"No, half and half." She shrugged. She reached to a shelf beside the stove and took down a large can of cinnamon.

When she brought the saucepan over to pour the bubbling liquid into cups he noticed her hands shaking. Those small, pale hands looked like he could hide them in his. Her innocent, fresh-from-bed look tugged at his need to protect.

"Um, Mr. Sa..., ah, Sam?"

Her soft plea brought him back to the reason he'd come to her so late. She was offering him whipped cream to top the chocolate treat, his favorite as a boy.

"Yeah, might as well go all the way." Had he actually said that? "Sean and I always drank real hot chocolate when he was younger and needed to talk over things at night. It seemed to help him get his worries off his chest so he could sleep."

"I know what you mean." She stared into her cup. "Daddy and I spent a few after date hours over cups of the real thing. He believed in real, fat-laden comfort food when there was a problem to discuss."

Why was she telling him about her past? Maybe it was his understanding dad manner. Maybe she could tell he really cared. Maybe nerves were making her ramble. He did care, and he wanted to hear all the little things he'd already know if they were friends.

In the light of the kitchen he could see shadows under her eyes. She hadn't been sleeping well. "You might as well tell me what's been keeping you awake nights. Maybe I can help."

"How did you know?"

How could he tell her he'd sensed danger around her that evening when he'd followed her home? How much should he explain?

"If you're on the phone at two in the morning you aren't sleeping," was his non-committal answer. "Why? Something frightened you. I saw you and your fear in my dream."

"I don't understand why I was in your dream. I just had a crank call." The robe slid down on her shoulder as she reached for her cup.

The man at her table was staring at her as though he could read her thoughts. Did he realize how attractive he was in rumpled clothes? It had been a long time since she'd sat across the table from a man.

It had been a long while since she'd noticed a man on a personal level. He was a very physical presence.

She might as well tell him why she was awake at this ungodly hour. She needed to talk, and he seemed determined pull the truth from her. Staring into her cup she exhaled heavily.

Gathering her courage, she looked into his eyes. "I had several hang-up calls this week. Tonight I had an obscene call. The caller probably finally said something. That's all. I was startled when he actually spoke." How could she verbalize what the pervert had said to her? Taking a deep breath to calm herself, Brit continued. "It wasn't as bad as some I've heard about, just unsettling."

"No threats?" Sam asked, trying to remain calm. He drained his cup, keeping his gaze on her. She looked pale and vulnerable.

"Not really. It was just a call. Now he's had his say, so he'll probably leave me alone and pester someone else."

"Don't count on it. Call the police and report the calls, now." Sam stood and reached for the phone. "I'll dial."

She hesitated too long. He dialed information then the police station. By the time Brit made her way to Sam's side a deep voice called from the instrument she had begun to hate.

"Florence Police Department, Detective Johnson speaking."

After clearing her throat several times Brit spoke into the receiver, "Hello, my name is Brittany Roberts and I -- I need to report an obscene phone call and maybe a break-in."

"You didn't mention a probable break-in," Sam mouthed.

She shushed and waved him away. Brit answered more questions than she put on true-false tests for her students and hung up the phone.

"I'll explain about the break-in, but I've got to get dressed before the police get here."

She escaped to her bedroom to put on slacks and a bulky sweater. When her doorbell rang, she walked down the hall, carrying a brush.

"You can do this," Sam whispered. He held out his hand palm up.

When she placed her hand in his he squeezed hers gently.

The doorbell rang again. Brit bit at her upper lip, squared her shoulders, then walked her toward the front door.

"Coming," she called. "Be right there."

Officers Briggs and Jacobs were straight out of a television cop series. Briggs wore his uniform and his short haircut with a pride that made the military types look slouchy.

Introductions were quickly made. Jacobs seemed to take the reason for Sam's presence in stride, as though there was nothing out of the ordinary to find a father visiting his son's teacher hours after midnight. Briggs acted less accepting.

Brit hated to talk about her naïve acceptance of the food and flower order mix-up. The officers looked skeptical. She should have been suspicious, but Florence was a quiet little town.

"What makes you think there might have been a break-in and when?" Jacobs looked like he could see if she lied.

"He said some things when he called this morning."

"Just tell us as much as you can remember, please," Briggs said.

"It was all so awful."

"We have to know before we can evaluate the situation."

Brit heaved a long sigh. "He mentioned my claw-foot bath tub and my robe — and what he wanted to do with my body." She repeated as much as she could, avoiding looking at Sam or the officers when she spoke of the sexual threats. And they had been threats.

"Has anyone been in and out of your house but you?" Jacobs wrote in his notebook. "Any repair men around?"

"No."

"Have you noticed signs of forced entry?" Briggs asked.

"I haven't looked yet, but I haven't had time to think, really. There was no reason to before tonight."

"Ms. Roberts," Briggs asked. "have you noticed anyone who seemed to be hanging around when he shouldn't be?"

"No." She shook her head. "I haven't really noticed anyone suspicious, but I haven't looked for anyone who didn't belong."

Jacobs nodded his graying head as he wrote carefully in his notebook. "Anyone follow you around in the grocery store? Offer to help you with your groceries?"

"No one, Officer."

"Come on too strong, maybe not take 'no' for an answer?"

"No," Brit toyed with her sweater's hem.

"Maybe you flirted with someone who misunderstood, thought you were offering more?" Briggs suggested.

Sam moved from the protective position he'd adopted, advancing on the offensive questioner. "Officer, I fail to see the reasoning behind your suggestive question."

"A lady can smile at a man and make him think she's interested, even if she isn't. Some men get strange ideas these days." Briggs posture remained stiff, his gaze riveted on Sam's face. "What were you doing when Ms Roberts got the call?" he asked.

"Sleeping. At my house, near here."

Briggs frowned. "So you rushed over when the lady called?"

"I called her." Sam flushed. He cleared his throat. "I had a nightmare about her being in danger and couldn't shake the feeling something was wrong." Sam wished he could take back those words. He didn't want these *Keystone cops* to think he was sleeping with the teacher. He hadn't breathed a word about his premonitions in more years than he had fingers and toes.

Both cops handed Brit and Sam business cards. Briggs reached for the door now to leave. "Call either of us if you remember anything else, ma'am. Not much we can do about the phone call. We should stay posted for a stalker or a break-in."

Sam stayed after the boys in blue had finally gone. He touched her shoulders with his large warm hands.

"You did just fine," he said. Brit looked ready to drop, but he wanted to make sure she would be alright alone.

"Stay for one last cup of chocolate? I can nuke it."

Sam joined her for a last cup of hot chocolate for the road. The kitchen was old but well remodeled.

"So, who did your remodeling?" He liked the way it was cluttered with racks of utensils and copper-bottomed pots hanging like decorations. "You use all those things?"

"Yes, I love to cook." Her smile wavered. "I sanded and painted and did most of the work on this room. It's good therapy." She stood and started to leave the kitchen.

"You need caller ID and a thorough check of all door and window locks, and an alarm system. This house is old, but we can fix any areas for easy forced entry."

Looking toward the door as a direct hint, she smiled wanly at Sam. "I'd already planned on it. Now go home. I have to face more parents tomorrow."

Daylight would break soon.

Following her down the hall to her front door, he thought again how appealing the lady looked sleep-rumpled.

***

Douglas was disappointed to see the police so early, but that could work in his favor. Breaking in and attacking the teacher tonight had been tempting. His plan wasn't written in stone. The fear in her voice pleased him. The actual executions he'd performed over the years had given him a rush but never this kind of high.

Setting the stage was as important as doing the deed. Only a master at his craft could create a diversion so clever. By

29

the time he was done with this job no one would know who was responsible.

The plan this time offered the aspect of entertainment. Once she told her blonde friend about the calls there would be a trail to a non-existent stalker. No one had fingered him yet. No one ever would. Nothing would get in his way. He wouldn't allow it.

The man in the black truck had shown up twice. Was he the teacher's lover? For weeks Douglas had watched and noted her every move. There had been no men at her house until tonight. He'd need to learn more about this possible problem.

***

Before Brit left for school the next morning she worked one of those makeup miracles after almost no sleep. She'd pulled out all stops and used every trick in her repertoire. Around noon she bolted down a sandwich and teacher's lounge coffee. Checking her mirror before her next parent conference assured her that her concealer and foundation had lasted the first half of the day, barely. They were beginning to wear thin, as was her patience. The soft pink eyeshadow still looked good.

Around three that afternoon Brit sensed the presence of Sam Samuels before she looked up from her notes to enjoy the sight of him. His no-frills Old Spice scent was only part of the aura that was all strength.

She heard him clear his throat from the doorway across the room. Could last night be responsible for the new closeness she felt toward him? Surely it was about the protection he offered. His relaxed stance exuded confidence. His smile set off fireworks in her system.

"Please, come in and have a seat." She glanced in the direction of desks directly in front of hers. *Take control of the meeting. Tell the other person where to sit*. She'd need all the help she could muster for this conference.

"Let's talk about Sean," she instructed with an in-charge manner.

"Yes, ma'am." His deep voice sounded amused.

She was so distracted by the memories of his charge to protect her she had to look away from his face. Eye contact wasn't a good idea. Her pulse seemed a little fast and her chest tight.

He, however, seemed to have forgotten their late night meeting. He hadn't mentioned it or even asked how she was. He looked casual in a long sleeved, white dress shirt and jeans. Sam Samuels looked like he should be in an ad selling beer or whiskey, or maybe boots. His thick hair looked as though a stylist had done it.

She seldom become distracted when discussing a student's grades. It was unusual to be facing the man who had suddenly become her protector, the man who had shown up on her doorstep after two in the morning, looking like he'd dragged himself out of bed to come to her. How would it feel to wake up beside this man?

The undercurrents were strong and new.

"My son talks about your class all the time." Sam shifted his body in the too small student desk. He seemed all energy, like a man who seldom sat still.

"Sean's grades have improved greatly in the past month. His crush on Angela, you knew, of course?" At his nod she continued. "Well, it seems to be working in his favor. She's an excellent student in language arts and he wants to impress her."

"Yeah, I know." Sam grinned. "For the first time I've had to limit his telephone lounging."

"Telephone lounging?" she asked.

"Uh huh, long periods of silence interrupted by monosyllabic responses. He lounges on chairs, his bed, or the floor, looking like he'll go catatonic."

"Oh, yes, I remember relaxing in positions my body won't even do anymore. My parents were sure I'd hurt myself or freeze in those positions. Today I definitely would."

"Me, too. Old football injuries."

She needed to end this conference before she started imagining Sam in lounging positions. Too late. She took a sheet of paper from a neat stack and reached across her desk. "Here is a list of assignments every student needs to complete during the month. Remind him so he'll keep his grades as good as they are now."

When she'd handed him the papers he reached in his shirt pocket for a pair of glasses. She'd considered him the jock type, rugged, virile. The wire-rimmed glasses made him so very appealing.

"Have you always wanted to be a teacher?" Sam glanced up from the assignment list.

"Oh, yes, since I was in pre-school, at least." She grinned so hard her face hurt. Her chest tightened. "Oh, yes. Have you always wanted to be a security specialist?"

"I wanted to be either a professional football player or a school coach. Halfway through college I decided against either."

"I see."

"Sean's car is being serviced and he should be through with football practice. Guess I'd better go." Sean's dad stood, twisting to remove his man-sized body from the student-sized desk.

Brit smiled. His awkwardness made him seem almost normal. She was reluctant to let him go, but she was ready to finish her conferences so she could get her stuff together and head home to her private space that had been violated.

The police were supposed to go by this morning and check all outside doors and windows for signs of forced entry. They had promised to send an officer by the school to tell her if they had found anything suspicious. No one had been by and she hadn't had time to call the station yet.

She was tempted to ask Mr. Samuels to follow her home, but if he had to take Sean home that might alert Sean to her problem. He'd want to help. She didn't need a student involved in this, whatever it was.

Brit stood and extended her hand as she had each parent before him. His hand was callused, and strong, and warm. Her skin almost gleamed in its paleness against his tan. When she looked up to his face the tension of his jaw spoke volumes. His eyes left no doubt he'd felt the intimacy of their clasped hands.

He removed the glasses and slid them into his shirt pocket.

"Bye, now," he said, then turned and left.

32

Two hours and three conferences later she had to rub her palm against her legs when she thought of heading home after five o'clock. Would Mr. Samuels be in the parking lot to offer her an escort home tonight? She probably wouldn't give him an argument this time.

He'd looked about to say something personal. Their conference should have been simple. It would have been if she had been able to say what she needed to say. Sean was doing well. Simple enough. Time to pack up and head out to her Mustang. She needed rest.

***

Sean and Sam sat in Sam's truck, ready to leave the Florence High School parking lot. This had been a long day, and the parking lot lights had come on.

"Dad, can we have pizza tonight?"

"After the practice you put in you deserve it. I'm not sure I can handle it, though." Sam felt gut punched, pole-axed, wrung out, hung up to dry. He'd met Ms. Roberts to discuss Sean's grades and found his mind on *Teach*, frightened and vulnerable. Should he offer to follow her home tonight? So far, his premonitions were quiet and it was still daylight. Maybe she had been right about the caller having made his point, but he doubted it.

Her gray silk blouse today had reeked of good taste and modesty. The way it draped over her curves had him wanting to caress the soft fabric. Wisps of ginger toned hair had escaped her French twist, all business but soft. He liked the tousled look. He'd wanted to touch her hair last night. He had needed to keep her safe and secure.

"Dad, Dad?" Sean interrupted Sam's daydream. Oops, he must have missed something.

"Yes, son?"

"I need to go to Ms. Roberts' room and get a book for my project. If I get an A on this project I can make an A for the semester."

"Do you have to get it now?" Sam didn't think he'd be able to look at her violet eyes without thinking about the fear he'd seen in them. He didn't think he'd be able to leave her

33

again with his cool intact. He certainly didn't need Sean watching him.

"She's probably gone, anyway." Sam's hand was on the door handle, his keys in the lock already.

"No, Dad, her car's still here. That real old Mustang over there is hers. Tough, huh?"

"Yeah. She wasn't happy when I followed her home last night to be sure she made it."

"Dad, you didn't!"

"Well, it looks like car trouble waiting to happen."

"Dad, she's had that car since she was in high school."

"She basically told me to mind my own business. That she could take care of herself. But she didn't even have a cell phone in case of any kind of trouble." Sam left out mention of the late night visit and the reason for it. There was no reason to worry his son with information the teacher might not want spread around.

The hair on the back of Sam's neck was suddenly charged. Stupid feeling. His gut hurt. He was light headed. Damn! This time he was near panic. This premonition was a bad one. Oh, shit!

"Come on, son," Sam called over his shoulder as he headed back toward the school building. "Let's get that book and see that she leaves with us. She doesn't need to be here alone this late."

Sam didn't slow down when Sean called to him. "Dad, there are coaches and football players parked on the other side of the building. She's not really..."

Chapter Two

Brit was so tired she could hardly see straight. She stared toward the chalkboard. The smells of chalk dust and pencil shavings usually made her feel at home. Finding the old board hadn't been easy! Of course she had the usual dry erase boards and bulletin boards.

She could swear the Sam's scent lingered. Her stomach churned. "Guess I'm just too hungry. I should've gone to supper with Julie. She'd have waited 'til I finished my last conference," Brit mumbled. *"A relaxing, long, cold strawberry daiquiri or two would taste wonderful, with extra whipped cream."*

Julie was the reason they were teaching at the same school. Her best friend since childhood had drawn her from her depression. There hadn't been time to tell Julie about last night's order changes, or the call, or even about Sean's dad following her home. Julie wouldn't believe the strange story about the gifts, or the obscene call, or about a man showing up on Brit's doorstep so late.

The last parent had been a *My-kid-has-always-been-a-good-student-and-I-don't-understand-how-he-can-be-failing* parent. Only a look at her grade book and his most recent test score had made even a small dent in the mother's attitude. The parent had left with a copy of the same list of assignments Brit had given each parent, with a deadline for completing the make-up work.

At a sound in the hall Brit glanced up as Mr. James, the custodian stuck his head in the doorway to warn her to wait for him to escort her from the building. She pulled the old window shades down to the lowest window, shutting out much of the parking lot lights. Standing behind her desk, Brit lifted her purse from a cabinet drawer.

After checking her desk drawers she glanced up as the lights went out, leaving her room almost dark. Who would've cut off the light when she was visible from the door? She glanced up to see the large silhouette of a man standing in the lit doorway.

"Mr. James? I'm still in here and I still need the light, so could you please cut it back on for a minute?" Brit asked. The silhouette was silent, looming. "You're not Mr. James. Who are you?"

The dark figure moved silently toward Brit. She could read menace in his stance, the predatory way he moved. Her throat seemed to close for seconds as danger stared her in the eye. No one else should have been in the building this late.

"Who are you?" Brit repeated, her gut churning. She could see part of his harsh, handsome face but could not recognize him. She glanced around the room. Not a weapon in sight. She tried to keep her voice calm and authoritative but loud. "Look, you'll have to come back tomorrow if you need a conference. It's after hours."

"Don't you even know who I am?" a petulant, low-pitched voice murmured. "I'm disappointed, Sugar." He arched a bushy blond eyebrow.

Brit was certain he was toying with her. She moved from behind her desk, grabbing her purse and tote bag. *Please, God, let Mr. James be back soon.* Would anyone hear her if she screamed or would it just make her tormentor angry? *Show no fear. Show no fear.* Her brothers had taught her to defend herself against stronger opponents. She could stall this man until she could get past him.

"After the gifts I sent you I expected a warmer welcome. I went through a lot of trouble to please you," he drawled. "You weren't very friendly last night." He crossed muscular arms across a broad chest.

"Why would you send me gifts? I don't know you." She tried to sound reasonable. If she could get him to talk maybe he'd let her go. "Maybe if I could get to know you?"

He shook his head. "You called your boyfriend and then the cops. That wasn't nice of you. A woman should show appreciation when a man does romantic things for her. So, here I am, m*a belle donna*, to collect my appreciation."

There was no mistaking the threat in the term of endearment as the stranger moved. He didn't act like he'd heard what she said. She chewed her bottom lip so hard it hurt. He stopped just in front of the desk. She eased away from the only protection in her room. If she could just get around him to the door. He stared at her while he wrapped the end of a handkerchief around a large, hairy hand she could now see well.

He was still too close for her to get to the door. Brit raised her voice and ordered, "Leave, or I'll call..."

"Don't bother, Sugar," the man purred. "Too late. We're all alone, at last. I can finally do all the things you've wanted me to do but were too shy to ask." He chuckled. "Nobody's gonna disturb us now. That old man's not coming back. I saw to it. We got the place all to ourselves."

Brit screamed as she dashed toward the door. Pain shot through her left arm as a vise-like grip jerked her back. Her purse fell to the floor. She swung her tote toward his head but he snatched it and threw it across the room, spilling its contents. Now there was no way for her to get to her keys and use them as a weapon.

"You aren't going anywhere until I'm done with you," Brit's attacker snarled in her ear. His good guy mask back in place, he shook his head while he stroked the place he'd grabbed.

"Look what you made me do, Sugar. You shouldn't run from me. It brings out my mean side." His eyes narrowed, his kind expression changed. "Now why don't you shut the hell up! Women who don't do as they are told make me hurt them. I can shut that smart mouth."

Pain clouded her vision. Should she beg? Should she pretend to go along with him, just 'til she could try to get away?

"I'll bet you're good with those luscious lips. Just thinking about the things you could do with that sharp little tongue makes me harder than a rock. I might give you something to

37

tempt your taste buds before we're through. Are you wet for me? I know you ache as much as I want to be inside you."

Revulsion filled her as the assailant whirled her and yanked both hands behind her, pushing her trembling body flush with his. She knew the fear must show, but she brazened it. She had to.

"Get your filthy hands off me!" Brit yelled in his face. She tried to twist away from his hateful grasp but was rewarded by a slap that left her head ringing. If she could push away enough to lift her knee to his crotch she might be able to escape. God, the man was strong.

"I warned you, slut! Don't cross me again," he sneered. "You can't get away." His fast breathing and the grinding of his erection against her belly sent a bolt of fear searing through Brit, a fear like none she had ever known before. When she tried to kick him he dodged her efforts like he knew where she'd aim. He laughed at her.

This cannot be happening. Things like this happen to other people. I'll wake up in a minute wishing for dreams of protective Sam.

The hateful voice broke through the protective fog. "Don't stop fighting me now that we're beginning to have some real fun." With his free hand he grabbed the front of her blouse and squeezed. "Nice tits, the kind I like, white, soft, a good handful."

"No-o-o!" Brit screamed. She wanted to vomit from the humiliation and pain and pure fear. No one had ever handled her roughly, much less with such cruelty. She had to get away!

Gripping her skirt waistband, he yanked, popping the front buttons loose and tearing buttonholes.

He pushed her down to the top of her desk, sending books and papers crashing to the floor.

"You're gonna like it so well you won't wanna stop."

She tried to kick him, but his weight held her.

"You're like the other whores, pretending you don't want it. Bet you spread your legs for the boyfriend who came to your house last night. Did you really think it would help to call the cops?"

She twisted beneath his weight and fought cruel hands yanking her blouse up, mauling her breasts. Holding her down with the weight of his sweaty body, he turned loose aching breasts to grab her hands. Raising them above her head he clamped them with one hand to give him freedom to run the other one over her body. Bile nearly choked her.

He forced her legs apart, shoved one leg between hers. "Spread 'em, Bitch." She heard the sound of his zipper. Oh, God. He was really going to rape her. He turned loose her wrists to grab her jaw as he lowered his face toward her mouth. Grabbing the hair hanging over his forehead, Brit yanked and was rewarded with a stunning blow to her head, knocking her to the floor. He was on her again before she caught her breath.

He bellowed, "You don't learn! The teacher isn't so high and mighty now, is she? You're all alike - just waiting for a real man to do it to you!" His pale blue eyes gleamed with madness.

Stunned, she couldn't give up. She would fight as long as she was conscious. Suddenly Brit's flailing legs struck nothingness. The body of the attacker rose and sailed through the air. Someone had turned on the lights.

"Help her, son!" Sam, thank God.

Sam pounded the assailant. Brit was shocked by Sam's murderous expression. Then his eyes softened in concern for a second before he was caught by surprise by the man he tried to subdue.

Two combatants scrambled as Sam tried to grab the escaping man. With the strength of desperation, the assailant escaped Sam's grasp and stumbled to the door. He ran down the hall.

Following him to the door, Sam looked back to see Sean covering Brit with his jacket. "Just get him!" Brit pleaded. "Go, Sam! Hurry!"

Sam threw his own jacket toward Sean and raced down the hall, shouting. "Don't let the son-of-a-bitch out the door! Stop him!"

Sean slid his dad's folded jacket under her head as a pillow, but Brit tried to rise. "Please don't move, ma'am," Sean whispered. His blue eyes were wide with shock and fear. He reached into his back pocket for his handkerchief. Awkwardly he wiped blood left by the blow to her mouth. "Dad will get help."

"Thanks, Sean." Still shaky, she clutched her blouse closed. "No broken bones. He didn't get the chance to h-h-hurt me m-much, thanks to you and your father," Brit reassured him.

She tried to rise, but stopped when the jacket Sean had placed on her lap slid to expose the lack of a skirt or slip. "Oh." She looked away in embarrassment to see a small pile of shiny fabric on the floor near her legs, her torn slip.

"Thanks, Sean."

"Dad!" Sean exclaimed, looking toward the doorway.

"Sam!" Brit was so relieved to see him back she almost cried, but she wouldn't let herself break down yet.

"Brit." Sam took Sean's place, sending him downstairs to watch for the police and the ambulance. "I didn't get him. I'm sorry! He was too damned fast. He pushed Mr. James down into my path. I almost ran him down. Are you all right?" Sam rambled, as though he didn't know what to say. Brit sensed his fear and anguish, his frustration at failing to catch her attacker! "If he hurt you, I'll kill him. Did he..."

"I'm okay, I think. And no, he d-didn't." She took a deep calming breath. "You and Sean got here in time." She shook her head to clear it. "Why were you here at this hour?"

She interrupted before he could say the words that would make the experience too real. Her body shook. One more word and she'd be stuttering from delayed reaction.

Sam swore under his breath. If he answered her question she missed the answer. He sat down on the floor and took her in his arms, re-covering her with his jacket. "Teach, if anything had happened I would've... Maybe I'll kill him anyway, dirty bastard!"

The comfort of Sam's arms around her all but stopped her trembling, replacing fear with the warmth of safety. Leaning her head against Sam's chest felt so good! If she could stay here a minute she would be strong enough to face the questions the police would ask.

"Sam, how did you and Sean find me when you did?"

"We saw your car in the parking lot as we were leaving. Sean needed to get some book he had to borrow. I can't explain, but I got this strange feeling you were in danger."

She tilted her head to look into his eyes. "Like the ones you had last night?" she asked.

Sam nodded. His gentle hands rubbed her back. "Kinda. We didn't think you should be here alone so late. We didn't think about Mr. James waiting for you, and I'm glad we didn't! If we'd not come back, if we'd been a minute later. God knows, I don't want to think of the what-ifs!"

"Are you psychic, or something?" she asked.

"Or something." He shrugged. The friction of fabric against her cheek released his masculine scent.

"Sam! You didn't call an ambulance? I don't need ..."

"Shush. You should be checked for injuries. Anyway, while I chased the son-of-a-bitch into the parking lot, Mr. James called 911. They're sending the police and an ambulance."

"But, Sam," Brit looked up to see two police officers, followed by two paramedics carrying a gurney.

"Sir? Ma'am?" Two policemen advanced, followed by a man and a woman in white and Sean and Mr. James.

"Dad?" Sean blurted, startling Sam and Brit, as Sam started to rise, then thought better.

"Sir?" A policeman came forward, signaling behind to the two paramedics who advanced with the gurney and a blanket.

"Oh," Sam rose with Brit in his arms and placed her on the gurney. He raised his hands to gently remove her arms encircling his neck. Keeping her hands in his, he held them, comforting her.

It was all he could do to keep from gathering her back into his arms and holding her again. He couldn't believe he was thinking like this when she had been merely his son's teacher before last night. Could his premonitions be responsible for the way she made him feel? He wanted to protect her. No, he *needed* to protect her.

He'd never wanted to kill anyone before he'd found that SOB trying to hurt the teacher.

"Officer, could we get her to a hospital before we put her through questioning?" Sam asked.

"Sam, please." She gripped his hands like a lifeline. "Officer, it was a harrowing experience but I'm not injured. I can answer questions now and get them over." She hoped she told the truth. The shock could set in at any moment and blow any coherent thoughts from her head.

"Officer, she needs medical attention," Sam snapped.

"Sir, we need to know what happened so we can begin our investigation immediately." He held a small, black notebook open. His partner had taken out a small tape recorder and inclined his head toward her in question. When she nodded, he pushed the button.

Brit began. "I had completed my last conference and was preparing to leave... "Her voice, strong at first, wavered as her fear was relived. Sam's arm slipped around her shoulder, his eyes glaring at the men for putting her through the torture of re-living the near rape.

She continued, "I t-tried to outrun him..." When Brit paused to take slow breaths to regain her composure, one paramedic entered with a glass of water and handed it to her.

Sam watched his son leave the room, knowing by his expression where he was going and why. It sickened him to think of that filth putting his hands on such a gentle woman or any woman, for that matter. Sam wanted to take the animal apart with his bare hands but that wouldn't help Brit. He and Sean would have a talk later about tonight. Sean was a good, sensitive kid who'd had little or no experience with violence in real life.

Teach needed the most support.

After several swallows of water she continued. She saw an EMT guy in white leave the room. "Poor Sean," she whispered, then tried to continue, "He slapped me and..." Brit swallowed convulsively and turned her face against Sam. If she could just burrow in and hide!

"Ms. Roberts, please describe your assailant? Distinguishing features?" Officer Smythe was business-like but kind.

"He's tall, over six feet. Blond hair, icy blue eyes." Brit shuddered and swallowed convulsively. "He is m-m-muscular and has a strong s-s-southern d-d-drawl."

"Had you ever seen him before, maybe hanging around here?"

"No, officer, he did mention he'd changed my order for flowers and a take-out meal last night."

Officer Smythe looked puzzled. Had she explained about last night? She was doing well to remember what she had to tell him about what she had just experienced. Her eyes hurt with unshed tears. She swallowed, trying for calm.

"That b-b-bastard has seen my bath tub, my robe, and God knows w-what else."

"Officers, I'll tell you about the attacker's invasion of her privacy and telephone harassment and his obscene phone call last night." Their puzzled expressions said they hadn't learned of last night's incident. "We reported the incident. I'll also tell you what I saw when I arrived, but this injured woman really must have medical attention!"

Blood had dried on her lips where she'd been hit. Scrapes and fresh bruises marred her cheeks. Sam opened and closed his fists at his sides. The urge to slam his fist into something was unbearable.

Sam turned to the woman paramedic. The tall paramedic who seemed to be in charge turned toward the policemen and nodded. The other paramedic, who was just returning with a white faced Sean, signaled his partner who moved toward Brit on the gurney.

Sam waved the man away. He placed his arms under her arms and knees, ignoring the gurney and the hands extended to help. Sam carried his bundle from the room, down to the ambulance.

43

Sam put Brit on the gurney in the ambulance before turning to look out the door. Sean looked up at his dad with a timid smile. "I can drive your truck to the hospital. You should ride with Miz. Roberts. She probably needs a familiar face and a hand to hold."

Sam pitched his keys to his son. "Damn, that's one great kid," Sam said to the young EMT cleaning the blood from Brit's lip. He turned to the woman who would need someone she knew to hold her and let her cry or even give in to hysteria if she needed to. She would need help to handle the ordeal.

***

Well, shit! Douglas Drake never failed. Shit! Shit! Shit! He'd had his hands on the damned teacher. He'd been hard and ready to stick it to her.

This time had been different. Something had taken control of the calm, cool killer. He'd become the rapist he'd planned to make people think was responsible. He'd enjoyed the attack too much to just kill her quickly. He had taken too long and been caught before he finished his job. He'd been seen with very little to disguise him. Fortunately, there would be no mug shots and no way to match his prints, if there were any. Maybe on the light switch?

Damn! It would've been over if the man and the boy hadn't shown-up. All the days of watching the woman had gone to waste.

He'd set the scene so carefully with the food and the flowers last night. The teacher had been scared, the way he liked his victims. He liked the taste and scent of fear. Just listening to her reaction to the hang-ups calls was enough to get him hot. With the "bugs" he'd planted in her house, he'd listened to her report to the police last night. He'd scared her good when he'd let her know he'd been inside her house.

In the weeks he watched the woman, he'd never seen the man with her. Who the hell is he? There had been the kid, too. *Now I'll have to wait 'til things die down to get at her again.*

He hated complications. He'd watched the ambulance arrive. Now it was leaving. He hadn't hurt her enough for an ambulance. The hero of the day was riding with her. How sweet.

The cops should be leaving. He'd never come so close to being caught before. He really needed to sneak in and wipe the light switch. Shit! He had failed to follow his plan and execute his victim on the first try. It would never happen again. He'd just wait to get her alone again and finish the job. This time he'd do it right.

Chapter Three

It was only ten o'clock in the evening but it seemed much later, like a whole day had passed since...

During the past three torturous hours Brit wondered if she could answer even one more question about worst and second worst experiences since she'd lost her husband.

The doctors examining her had been gentle, considerate. She'd been mortified anyway. Photographs recorded bruises that had begun to darken on her fair skin on her writs, groin, and her face. Studying her harried reflection in the mirror in a dressing room, Brit noticed the beginning signs of a black eye. She looked down at the borrowed nurse's scrubs. They had been well laundered and felt soft against her skin. At least she didn't have to sit around in an open-backed hospital gown.

Her clothes had been placed in a plastic bag to be searched for hair samples and would be held as evidence when they caught and tried the man. She had to hold onto her control until she could get home. Tears had threatened to overwhelm her as she tried to fill in the blanks left from her interview with the investigating officers. They'd even cleaned under her nails for skin or blood samples from her attacker.

A rotund man had shown her pictures of facial features as she tried to help him create a likeness of the maniac who had violated two places she considered safe and hers. She hadn't been able to put together a likeness.

How would she tell her parents about the events of last night? Worse, how could she tell them of the horror of this afternoon? She didn't want to upset them tonight, but she could hardly keep the enormity of her fear and revulsion to herself. She'd need their help to get past everything. And her attacker was still loose.

She'd call her parents in the morning, after a good night's rest and time to distance herself enough to tell the story without bursting into tears. They'd imagine things worse than what had actually happened. Things could have been so much worse. She could have become a statistic, and she didn't even know why anyone would want to hurt her.

If only Julie were here. Sam and Sean had been wonderful but there were things only a woman could understand. A choking sound alerted Brit to look past her pitiful reflection to the startled reflection of Julie. Had she conjured up her friend?

"Brit? Oh my God, Brit, honey." Julie's voice quavered. "What did the bastard do to you?"

Though Julie hand covered her mouth, her horror was evident in her eyes. Biting her lip to delay her tears, Brit whirled around to move into Julie's comforting embrace. She wouldn't cry. She wouldn't.

"I'm all right, now," Brit assured, stepping back from her friend's support. Her attempts at a smile failed miserably. "thanks to Sam, Sean's Dad. He and Sean were w-w-wonderful. I --- don't know what I would've d-d-done if Sam hadn't c-come in when he did." Her voice faded as she swallowed past the lump in her throat.

"Hon, I couldn't believe it when Mr. Samuels called to say you were in the hospital. He said you'd been attacked and to come quickly - like I wouldn't have rushed here anyway. How did he know to call my number?"

"I'm so glad he did. Sean must've told him we're friends. We do hang out together a lot, especially at school. You're in the phonebook, like I am."

Julie brushed Brit's hair behind her ears as she had many times before. If Brit could have chosen a sister, she'd have chosen Julie.

"Have you called your folks?" Julie asked.

"No, I'll call tomorrow morning, after I've rested. You know how I'd break d-down if I tried to tell them what that m-monster did." Brit shook her head. "They'd assume the worst and rush here now. Daddy was scheduled for a full day of surgery today and tomorrow. It wouldn't be good for either of them."

"So, pal, when do you escape this place?" Julie put her arm around Brit's shoulders.

"Soon." She jumped at the deep voice. The young doctor who had examined Brit pushed the curtain aside and approached. "The police want to make sure the photos we took of your injuries are okay. I'll be back with something to help you sleep for the next couple of nights."

"Thanks, but I don't take sleeping pills." Brit spoke to the retreating back of young Dr. Blake.

"Take 'em anyway, girl. You might need 'em after all that has happened." Julie said. "I'll take you to my place. You can sleep in the guestroom I just redecorated after I got rid of that no good Bill. My nightgowns will fit you."

"No," Brit said too quickly. "I have to go home to my own house! I won't run." She took Julie's hands, squeezing a little too hard. "I've taken care of myself since I stopped hiding from life in my parent's home. I bought that house, took a job, and built a new life. I can't let a monster chase me from my home, I just can't."

"Shush, honey." Julie hugged Brit. "It's okay, I'll stay at your house with you."

"But I can't ask you to do that."

"You don't need to ask. I'm coming home with you. I'll stay as long as you need me. We'll face this together." Julie rubbed her friend's back, comforting her.

Brit pulled away, sniffing. She took the package of tissues Julie had found on a table. "Thanks."

The good doctor didn't make it from the room. He stopped and turned back to the ladies.

"Mr. Samuels has been pestering me to let him in here to talk to you, Ms. Roberts. He's been pacing like an expectant father."

"Tell Sam I'm decent. He and Sean may come in, if they wish, but this room isn't really party size.

"Did I hear you call Mr. Samuels *Sam?* On a first name basis, are you? You and I are in for a long talk."

Brit started again at the sound of another deep voice, one she recognized quickly as belonging to her rescuer and new hero.

"We've seen too much of each other in the past twenty-four hours to stand on ceremony, haven't we, Teach?"

"What?" Julie and Sean chorused.

"Tell you, later," Sam and Brit answered in unison then stared at each other, startled.

Sam wore his wire-rimmed glasses and held his tablet. The neon bandage strip above his lip could not diminish his blatant look of strength. With his torn shirt and bruised chin he was a welcome sight.

***

Brit winced as she eased down into Julie's white Thunderbird. The digital clock on the dash read twelve o'clock. Sam squatted beside the open doorway to look into her eyes. "I wish you'd go home with Ms. Devereaux." Sam's voice was gentle, concerned.

"Call me Julie, please. I tried to talk some sense into her," Julie said. "She's too stubborn for her own good."

"I need to go to my own house," Brit insisted. She needed to feel as though things were almost normal. She wouldn't be run from her own home. Dammit all, she wouldn't! She'd lost a husband and now her sense of safety in her safe places, but she wouldn't give up her independence.

"It's okay." Sam patted her hand in her lap. "I don't have any right to tell you what to do. Well, then, I'll take Sean to his grandparents' house to spend the night and I'll be at your place as soon as I can."

"No need, Julie will spend the night with me."

"I'll be there." Sam rubbed his neck. "The pains in my gut are acting up again, nothing would keep me away."

"He's having gut pains?" Julie asked. "Why is he sharing this personal information?"

"Don't ask, just take me home so I can have a long, hot, relaxing soak, please."

***

Douglas watched the teacher get into the T-bird with her blonde friend. They were always together. The hero and the boy showed up everywhere. Must be his kid. Too bad he hadn't been prepared to off them tonight. Nah, one kill per job and one per town. If he started killing for the sake of killing he'd be taking unnecessary risks. He'd never killed for free before. He watched a cop car pull in behind the old T-bird.

***

Brit's head was less than clear from the light sedative she had been persuaded to take. Julie's car was so quiet Brit could hear herself think. She'd rather not think, but what was there to talk about? She couldn't think of a thing but the police car following them since she had insisted on going home.

Two police officers examined doors, locks, rooms, closets, and the grounds around Brit's house. Julie even checked under beds before they could relax. Trust her to do anything she thought might help.

***

Sometime around two a.m. Brit had time to relax.

Julie ran hot water with lavender and chamomile oils and Epson Salts in the guest bathroom and sent Brit there. She took a sedative, as if she could sleep after everything that had happened. Soothing hot water and bath oils soaked away the aches in Brit's muscles. The sedation fuzzed away some of the terror, dulling horrific memories. Domestic sounds and quiet conversation in the house assured Brit her friend was changing sheets on beds and washing them. Had her assailant handled them?

What had he touched when he checked out her bathroom, her robe? The doorbell chime roused her from her steamy stupor. Hearing Sam's deep voice so near reassured her. He and Julie spoke in quiet tones. Were they afraid they'd wake her?

She heard something about Sam's being glad there had been no ambulance chasing reporters at the hospital. She hadn't even thought about that. She'd had her fill of nosey reporters after Tommy's death to last a lifetime.

Julie cracked the bathroom door enough to pass a fluffy robe, Tommy's big robe into Brit's hands. *She's warmed it in the dryer. How sweet, how like Julie to know what I needed.*

Brit floated through her bedroom toward the hall. She'd say good night and send Sam back home. She and Julie would be just fine.

"Thanks for coming over, Sam, but..." Whatever she'd intended was lost as she stared into his eyes. "Lost that thought. Must be the drugs." Or because she breathed in his comforting Old Spice that robbed her of thought? "Well, night, Julie," she said, "You, too, Sam." She turned on her heel and found her way to her bed, barely.

Sam wondered when Sean's teacher had wormed her way past his defenses. He'd seen this woman neatly dressed and all business. He'd seen her mussed from sleep, he'd seen her roughed up and vulnerable. He'd wanted to protect her, to beat the hell out of her attacker. He couldn't afford to dwell on the rage that had gripped him when he'd seen her on the floor, fighting for her life.

Teach wasn't the cold woman he'd overheard local men suggest she must be. Though she was the newest woman in town, none of them had even persuaded her to go out for coffee or drinks. She didn't date, they had said. No one had seen her out with any man. Ms. Devereaux seemed to be her only friend in town.

Sam's gut was acting up something awful, she was still in danger. The gun he'd picked up at home would stay within reach, in case he needed it. Did she have a weapon? Did she know how to use one? He'd be glad to take her out to his parents' farm and teach her. She'd sign up for a class in self-defense. He'd see to it. He'd stay tonight.

Julie had been shocked when he told her about what he and Sean had found in Brit's classroom. He sat on Brit's sofa and brooded until Julie went to a spare bedroom.

When Sam was sure Julie slept, he crept into Brit's bedroom where he sat next to her bed, watching her sleep. When moans or thrashing about told him she was reliving a painful memory he lay on the bed on top of the covers beside her and talked until she quieted. That had always worked for his sister Esther when she'd had nightmares as a kid and hadn't wanted to call their parents.

He'd comforted Sean the same way on many occasions, especially after the divorce from his mother.

Something about this woman made him want to slay dragons for her. His latest attempt hadn't gone so damned well, had it? How would he feel about her once she was safe? He'd wait and see. What choice did he have?

Sometimes he dozed, but he made himself leave the warm bed. He'd only meant to comfort Brit but, well…he got some much-needed sleep.

***

Brit ran from a monster. She felt breath hot on her neck, smelled her own fear as he gained on her. Her heart pounded so hard it made her chest hurt. Her lungs ached. She couldn't get enough air. She ran until she feared she could run no more. Her legs were lead, her feet dragging like in deep sand. Without turning back she could still see his horrible face. A clawed hand griped her shoulder. She screamed. Sam, the knight in armor shining brightly, rode in on his white steed to save her.

"It's all right, Teach." She heard his kind voice. "Just sleep." He chased the monster away, then he lay beside her and held her. This was some dream. The warmth of his big body soothed hers. She felt herself drift into peaceful sleep.

Brit heard a scream. Someone was terrified. Who? She was afraid to wake up, but she had to. How else could she erase the threatening face, the vile, degrading things the horrible man uttered. She had to wake from the nightmare before it was too late.

Her eyes finally opened. Sam held her in his comforting arms. He was really good at this. He should have a wife and daughters.

"It's okay, Teach, it's okay." His warm, callused hands rubbed her back and arms. "You're safe now. You were having a bad dream. I won't let anyone hurt you."

Brit felt the trembling subside. Her breathing calmed.

Julie stumbled, bleary eyed but concerned, into the bedroom. Through a yawn she asked, "You alright, Hon? I heard you crying." She raised an eyebrow and smirked. "Hi, Sam. Looks like you beat me to the rescue. I'll leave you to your nightmare chasing in a minute."

Sam stood and stretched. He watched Julie offer medication and water. Brit swallowed the pill and drained the glass.

Brit tried to clear her mind. The fog remained.

52

"Can't remember." Her throat was raw.

"You can remember later. Rest now. Sam will stay with you for a while," Julie reassured, patting the hand of her best friend. "I'm in the spare room." She smoothed the soft brown hair from Brit's forehead, pushing it behind her ears.

***

Brit drifted in and out of sleep. *Who made the warm body go? Sam? Felt like Sam. Smelled like Sam or kind of like her daddy but not. Hurts to think. Strange dream. I liked the ones with Sam holding me, whispering kind words. Nice. What can't I remember?*

***

By morning Brit had awakened several times. Around six thirty Julie called Brit's parents.

"Hi, dad Simpson," Julie said. "Could you put Ms. Ellen on the other phone so I won't have to explain twice?"

"Sure, Julie, girl." She heard his deep voice calling his wife. "Get the other phone, mother, so we can both listen to Julie."

"What's wrong? Is Brit sick?" he asked.

"No, S-S-Sir, not exactly." Julie waited for the sound of a second phone being lifted.

"I'm here, Julie, honey. Now take a deep breath. What's wrong, honey?" She nearly lost her composure when she heard Ma Simpson's soft voice. Maybe she should have called her own mom and had her go tell these kind people. No, she could do this.

And she did with only a few stammers and stutters. She tried to ignore sounds of Ellen crying softly or she'd cry, too. She'd thought she had shed enough tears in the privacy of the shower. Who would hurt someone as good and caring as her best friend?

"Oh, Julie," Dad Simpson said. "We're so grateful you're there."

"She's had a hard time, but she'd handling things, okay."

"Are you sure we don't need to come now? I can cancel my appointments or get someone to cover for me. Ellen can't drive yet after her surgery, or she'd be on her way as soon as we hang up."

"Brit said she wanted you to do your surgeries today. So, you can wait to come here and bring ma with you. Brit should sleep most of the day. She's worn out."

"Who'll stay with her if you go to school?" Ellen Simpson asked, her voice tremulous.

"Well, Sam, Mr. Samuels, will until I get back from School."

"Mr. Samuels?" Dr. Simpson asked.

"Yes, sir, the man who saved her. He's security and can help her feel safe. He said he'll call his mother to come by to help make her comfortable. She's thirty minutes away and has doctored her own four kids through everything imaginable. Brit's in good hands."

"You can just go on to school and do your conferences, honey, I'll call later and talk to this Samuels person. We love you."

She'd arranged for someone to cancel Brit's appointments, then rushed home to change for school. Keeping her mind on talking to parents about their kids and their math progress all day wouldn't be easy, but there was no help for it.

There was nothing she wouldn't do for her friend. She and Brit had always been closer than sisters.

***

Sam had been alone with Brit for two hours when he had to grab the phone to keep Brit from awakening again.

"Hello, who is this?" a woman's voice asked.

"This is Sam Samuels. You sound like Brit, ma'am."

"How's my daughter?"

"She's sleeping now. She's had nightmares. Julie and I finally persuaded her to take another sleeping pill. She should be up and around a little bit later today. That bastard, excuse my language, yanked her around and terrified her. She's sore, but she can go to school Monday, if she feels up to it."

"Mr. Samuels, her father is driving us there this evening as soon as he can finish his last surgery and clean up a bit. We'll leave around six and be there in a couple of hours. I had surgery and am not allowed to drive yet," Ellen explained.

"You be careful now, ma'am," Sam said. "Julie'll be here as soon as her conferences are over. I'll be just a phone call away. My mama promised to come by in a little while."

"Her daddy and I thank you for all you've done for her, Mr. Samuels. We don't know what we'd have done if, well you know, if anything had..."

"Sam," he said. "Just call me Sam."

Sam slipped quietly into Brit's room and sat lightly on her bed. She looked so young in sleep. Dark lashes fanned against porcelain skin. Red lips moved softly as she breathed. He couldn't stop staring at her peaceful face. She'd have one heck of a shiner, but the bruising could have been so much worse. Damn that bastard!

"If the cops don't catch him and put him behind bars, I'll take care of that maniac, myself. I promise you." She slept.

Sam's call to his office caught his foreman replacing the night office person. All systems had proven clear, no break-ins for any of his clients. After giving instructions to start proceedings to burglarproof Brit's house, Sam started a pot of strong coffee.

After a shower in the guest bathroom Sam dressed in clothes Sean delivered on his way to school. The boy insisted he would be better off at school, helping in the office 'til time for football practice than sitting at home or hanging with his grandparents. Besides, he didn't want rumors to panic or confuse his classmates, when he knew the truth.

"Sam, what are you doing here?" Brit asked. He looked wonderful in his pressed, blue dress shirt. The open neck revealed dark chest hair curled crisply on tanned skin. His callused hands slowly caressed her forehead and stroked her hair. He smelled so good, freshly showered. When he brushed a lock of hair from her face his hand lingered on her unbruised cheek.

"I'm here to feed you, Lady. Mama brought a pot of homemade chicken soup. It's waiting on your stove, I'll heat it."

"No, thanks, I'm not hungry." Brit frowned. "You look tired." She commented on the dark circles beneath his eyes. He looked so worried! "Oh, Sam!" Memories of that horrible man pinning her to her desk hit her like a carousel out of control. She shook.

Without even thinking, Sam pulled her onto his lap so he could hold her and shield her from memories of yesterday's horror. He felt her tears wet his shirt while he rocked her like he would a child after a nightmare. But this nightmare wasn't over. It might not be over any time soon. *That animal will pay for what he did to this kind creature!* The moisture in Sam's eyes burned.

"I'm here, Teach," he whispered. "I'm here. He won't hurt you again, I promise. Go ahead and cry, you've earned it."

Peace surrounded the two until Brit raised her tear-stained face from Sam's chest. "Sam, uh, I---I, uh. " She blushed as she whispered, though they were the only two people in her room.

"Oh, Teach," he said when he stopped laughing. "I can't believe you're embarrassed about a little thing like that." He rose from the bed, scooping her soft body up in his arms and taking her with him.

Before he made it the bathroom Brit spoke. "Don't laugh at me. Put me down. I can walk. I just meant for you to leave the room since I'm not dressed. Besides, I can't do anything with you waiting around."

"Don't let it bother you, Teach. I've tended to my mama and my sister when they were sick. I won't look."

He set her to her feet close enough to grip the door jam.

"Get out so I can...you know..." she instructed. "Get out."

"Sure you don't need any help in there?" he asked. She was still a little groggy but she shooed him away. He could see most of her lush body through her gown. He should've realized she'd need a robe. He needed for her to have on a robe. This was no time for him to notice the dark area at the juncture of her thighs or her rosy nipples. Raising his gaze to her face, he realized she was speaking.

"Leave me alone or you'll mop the floor! I'll tell Julie. On second thought, Julie wouldn't help me. She thinks you're a hunk!"

Laughing, Sam turned and started for the door. "Just don't tell my mother, she thinks I'm a nice boy. I'll get your soup."

Sam felt the heat of more than the stove as he heated the soup. He'd thought he could look after Brit. He'd tended his brothers and sister and, of course, Adrienne, Sean's mother. This was way different. He hadn't had to worry about resisting Adrienne since he'd been married to her. Was Brit forbidden fruit? Had their shared danger caused his over-the-top reactions?

Thirty minutes later Brit had eaten, despite her protests. She'd missed supper and refused to eat at the hospital. Relaxed, she was drifting back to sleep. "Thanks, Sam," she murmured. "This doesn't mean anything, you know?" She left the thought hanging.

Oh, yes. It meant a lot to him. After so many years since his divorce he'd finally found a woman who touched his heart. He wanted time to explore what she made him feel. She was real and she made him feel things he had forgotten he *could* feel. Did he really want to risk feeling again? Maybe the feelings would go away with her danger.

***

That afternoon Julie found the two sleeping, side by side. Brit lay snuggled under the faded, patchwork quilt. Sam lay on top of it.

Sam awoke. "Don't say a word! What time is it?" Sam growled in a scratchy voice.

"It's three-thirty and I'm back from school. My last conference cancelled, thank goodness. Time for a tired hero to go home to his son who, by the way, is a brave young man." Julie laughed. "He worked in the office, showing parents to rooms.

Sam yawned and stretched. He glanced down at Brit, then eased from the bed. "Brit's parents will be here around eight. Let me know if you need anything. Have a good night, Miss. Julie." He left Brit's room. He turned when a thought grabbed him. "Oh, has Brit mentioned anything about getting crank phone calls or obscene calls?"

Julie's grin became a frown. "Why, has she had more wrong numbers while you were here?"

"Not exactly. Does that happen often?" Sam asked. Julie's shrug told him nothing.

"She didn't say. Just often enough to make it hard to sleep when they called at all hours, day and night. The caller never says anything. Who you gonna call, the wrong number police?"

"The night before last the caller went too far." Sam didn't smile. "He knew entirely too much about this house. Let her tell you about him. He was stalking her before last night's attack. Sicko! Do you know of anyone who would have it in for her?"

"No. How do you know so much about that night?" Julie asked.

"Long story. Ask her when she wakes up."

"Is she safe here? What if the cops don't catch the bastard?" Julie asked.

"They're watching her house and she's about to get a decent security system. I'll even send some of my men to watch if I have to. Does she like dogs?"

***

Brit slept quietly most of the afternoon. Julie dozed until loud knocking woke her. She rose to unlock the dead-bolt lock Sam installed earlier. Security lights streamed around window blinds, reminding her to peek through the new, eye-level diamond of glass before punching the code to unlock the door. Brit was gonna hate having to mess with numbers to memorize and all. She opened the door to mom and dad Simpson.

"How is she?" Ellen asked, enfoldeding Julie in a comforting, motherly hug.

"Yes, how is my girl?" Joseph awaited his hug.

"She's sleeping, but she should wake soon. I know she'll be glad to see you," Julie assured the concerned parents she loved almost as much as her own. "Mr. Saxon, our principal, was upset something like this could happen at our school. We were so lucky the media missed it."

The Simpsons slipped quietly into Brit's bedroom. She looked so small and vulnerable her mother almost cried. The bruise near her mouth had begun to color.

Julie said her good-byes and pointed out phone numbers for Sam and the doctor who had seen Brit the night before.

"I hate to leave, but I have papers to grade and I have to be at school tomorrow. I'll call you from school to check on Brit."

Julie gave both parents a guided tour of the new locks and security codes. Then Joseph walked with Julie to her car.

"I'm so glad you're here, Pop."

She hugged him and kissed his cheek.

"You did a good job, Julie, girl. We're proud of you."

It felt good to have someone hug her. She loved that he watched her get into her car as he would Brit.

"Buckle up and lock up."

"Yes, sir."

He waved to her as she drove away.

***

"Mama?" Brit whispered when she opened her eyes. Her mother's light floral fragrance penetrated her sleep. "Oh, Mama!" Brit raised her sleep-heavy arms and shoulders to meet her mother in a tearful hug. Joseph moved silently across the room to enfold his girls.

"Baby," Joseph whispered with his teary voice.

"Julie said to tell you that your Mr. Saxon called from the school and said you were to call him if you needed anything, like extra time off," Ellen said.

She treated Brit to a body rub. It was good to have her mama here. Brit told some of the story and found it barely easier to face than when it happened. They had to know.

Morning found Joseph returning home, once he knew Brit wasn't seriously injured. He could leave his wife to tend their daughter.

Brit and Ellen shared a light breakfast, using TV trays in the bedroom. They had a good, long, heart-to-heart talk about what had happened. It was easier to tell her mama the details than it would have been to tell her daddy.

Mid-morning Brit's mother answered a knock at the front door. When Brit shuffled into the living room she watched her mom look out the window toward the driveway then speak with a man.

"Who was that?" Brit asked.

"Mr. Samuels sent him over. His truck had the sign Sam said it would. His name-badge photo looked just like him."

"Who, Mom?"

"Jacob McAllister."

"Mama."

"Honey, Mr. Samuels stopped by early and told your daddy and me he owned a security firm and he'd send people over to finish installing security stuff here. Didn't I tell you?"

"No, Mama, you didn't."

"We thought it would be a good idea, since you know him."

Later workmen who arrived to put up a fence and wire it to her house current. Then more workmen disturbed her quiet. The men presented work orders signed by John S. Samuels, owner.

Someone else installed security lights.

Brit called the number Sam had left. Presumptuous men made her see red, and she had some heavy anger to unload on someone. He hadn't even discussed his security measures with her. She was a grown woman, capable of making her own decisions. Protecting people was his business, but he should've given her choices, damn it. Saving her life didn't make him her keeper. He had no authority.

"Mr. Samuels," she said when she was patched through to him. "What the hell did you think you were doing? There have been strangers with work orders building fences, and putting in wiring, and making changes I didn't order. They're making my house feel like a high security prison."

Sam sounded weary. "Protecting you, maybe?"

"Did I ask you to?" There was a pause. "Security locks, an electric fence? What other decisions have you made for me?"

"I spoke with the police, and I discussed my plans with your father this morning and when he stopped by my office on the way out of town."

There was another pause from Brit's end. The man was too logical. Not fair! Of course she'd have needed time to ask questions and get people out here to put in a system, once she'd researched her needs.

"Still want to shoot me?" She remembered his cocky smile.

"Mr. Samuels, you should have discussed your plans with me. I'm an adult and it's my house and I..."

"Ms. Roberts, someone made threatening calls to you. I found him attacking you last night. I failed to catch him."

"But, Sam, that wasn't your fault."

"I plan to protect you, at least until the bastard's in custody for good! That's not negotiable, Teach. If you have no more questions, I have work to do. I have to replace an antiquated security system in my son's school. That will protect you and a lot of other folks."

"You win." She hung up.

"Brit." Her mom's voice was gentle but scolding. "You didn't even thank the man."

"I will, maybe."

***

Wearing a sweat suit, Brit answered her door. She couldn't stall seeing people forever. Through the peep window she saw Sam holding his hands behind his back.

Her mom rushed from the kitchen, wiping her hands on a dishtowel as she cautioned Brit.

"Look through the new peep hole first."

"I know, Mom. It's just Sam."

"Well, then, why don't you let him in?"

"I forgot the code."

"Honey, you didn't set the alarm."

"Oh, yeah. I forgot."

"Come on, Teach. I've got a surprise for you."

Chapter Four

Against her better judgement Brit opened her door to Sam. Even through her screen door she had to suppress the urge to touch his still damp hair. His smug expression made him look like a kid pleased with himself. From behind his back he produced a bouquet of daisies.

"Hi, Teach." Sam cleared his throat. "For you."

Brit opened the door and reached to take them.

"Thanks," She smiled and turned to take them inside. "they're beautiful, but I'm still not happy about the high-handed way you took over my life."

Mrs. Simpson took the bouquet from Brit and motioned Sam inside. "I raised her better," She shook her head. "but she's stubborn."

"Thanks, ma'am. But there is something else." From out of Brit's view Sam retrieved a bag and handed it to her.

Brit opened it with caution. "A dog bowl and cans of dog food? Sam-m-m-, I don't have a dog," she said.

Sam snapped his fingers. "I know, but I found Monster here," A Doberman materialized by his side. "and he needed a home. He's a trained guard dog and he needs a new job."

"Sam, that animal looks more like a horse than a dog." She stared at the Doberman now standing at Sam's side. What would she do with such an animal? His lines were sleek, and he looked at her like she was supper. With a sigh Brit turned and went inside. She didn't need the responsibility of a pet, even one trained to earn his keep.

Once inside, Sam began to explain the proper care and feeding of a guard dog. Monster followed his new owner, who reluctantly put her hand on his head.

"Teach, I don't think you should ..."

Sam's warning came too late. A sloppy tongue wet Brit's hand as Monster rubbed against her, nearly pushing her over. "Don't give me that look. I don't need a dog."

.

Monster's big eyes watered as he sat on his haunches, begging. "Don't start with me, dog." Monster whined and licked her hand again. "Sam, I appreciate the thought, but..." Brit backed against the wall when large paws bracketed her shoulders and a lick wet her face. "Monster?"

"Teach, sorry about that. Monster was supposed to be trained to protect you, not love you to death. I'll take him back for a better trained one."

Monster whined and put his big head on her shoulder.

"I'd say Monster has found a home." Mrs. Simpson laughed.

"I think you're right, Mom. Maybe if you open the bag with his food I can get free."

Julie arrived shortly after monster stole Brit's heart.

"Omigod!" she exclaimed when she saw Brit sitting on the floor, nearly hidden by the huge animal. Its head took up her whole lap.

"Julie, you'd better be careful. Approach Monster slowly," Sam advised, quietly.

"Why?" Julie asked. She clapped her hands in delight.

"Monster's a guard dog," Brit answered. "He's trained to attack anyone who threatens me."

"Well, he is," Sam said.

"What a sweet baby you are," Julie crooned as she knelt at Brit's side. Monster turned liquid brown eyes toward Julie. He whined. "Monster? He's a sweet boy." She rubbed the large doggie head. His tongue bathed Julie's face before she could dodge. "Where did you get this sweetheart?"

Sam harrumphed. "I brought Monster to guard Teach. I didn't expect him to love her to death. I offered to swap him for a scary dog."

Julie rubbed between Monster's eyes, putting him into a trance. "You wouldn't!" She glared at Sam. "His coloring is like King's."

"I thought so, too," Brit said. "He's as sweet as your King was. How long has it been since King went to doggie heaven?"

"Oh, about five years. He was old, but he still looked pretty scary, like this big ole baby here."

Monster carefully roused. He rose to all fours and moved toward the door. His growl shocked everyone in the room. "Think he needs to go for a walk?"

The doorbell chimed. Monster stood at attention. He looked capable of going through the barrier to get the person on the other side. Sam gave a sharp command. Monster growled more.

Julie brushed past the guard dog to peek out the peephole. She turned back to Brit, who stood and moved to put her hand on Monster's head. "It's just Sean."

"Let him in," Julie reached for the doorknob. Monster looked like he could make Sean his snack.

"No, Monster," Brit said. "Mama doesn't want you to hurt Sean. He's a friend." Julie opened the door, leaving only a screen between Sean and a killing machine.

Monster started to growl low in his throat. His lean body shook with restrained tension.

"No, be good, Monster!" Brit warned. "Stay. It's okay, Sean. Come on inside."

Sean entered while Julie held the screen door. "Come meet Monster."

He stood quietly. "Are you sure?"

"Keep your hands out, palms up," Sam instructed. "Monster will sniff them. Don't grin or show a lot of teeth."

"Monster, say hello to Sean." Brit removed her hand from his head. "Go ahead. He's a friend. He's Sam's son."

Monster looked like he understood. He moved to Sean. He sat on his haunches and the trembling quieted. Sean stood still as the dog checked him from feet to head. He licked the upturned hands.

Julie and Mrs. Simpson left the room through the swinging door to the kitchen.

Sam shook his head. He'd never seen such a friendly guard dog. More dog shopping to do. At least the animal looked mean. He also seemed ready to protect the ladies.

"Where did you get this big boy?" Sean looked to his teacher.

"Your dad brought him to guard me." Brit laughed. "I think he's a bit disappointed."

"Whatcha got in the sack, son?" Sam asked.

Sean held the bag to Brit.

"Not more dog food, I hope." Brit smiled at Sam.

"It's from your students." Sean rubbed the head of his new friend sitting contentedly by his side.

Brit had to fight tears when she pulled the oversized cards from the bag. They'd been made and signed by students and teachers.

"Sean, how did you do this? School wasn't even in session, today."

"It was no big deal." He blushed. "I was helping Angie in the office for a while before practice and some of the kids came by to make the cards. The coaches gave the football players a few minutes to sign them before practice."

Brit hugged him. "You're a good kid, Sean Samuels!"

"Supper's on," Mrs. Simpson called. She came through the kitchen door carrying a platter of fried chicken. Julie followed with bowls of potato salad and rolls.

"Better be going." Sean started toward the door. "Angie and I'll be working on our project over the weekend."

"You have to stay or Ma Simpson will be hurt. You, too, Sam."

"That's right, wash up and get back here. Monster, sweet boy, come on." He followed her through to the kitchen.

"Where's Monster?" Sean asked when he held a chair for Julie.

"I gave him his own food. We don't want to torture him by making him watch us eat or spoil him with table scraps yet."

"You said you and Angela are working on your project already?"

"Yes, ma'am. We're writing a parody of Hamlet."

"Excellent," Brit said.

"We'll make it modern or in America during the Civil War, maybe."

"If you do that you may be able to use the research for a history project, too."

Conversation continued through dessert and doggie treats. When Sam finally gave up on the idea of having Brit to himself he and Sean headed home.

***

Douglas Drake sat in his room at a cheap, no-tell motel, lying low. As a rule, he didn't drink on the job. He crunched a beer can then tossed it at the trash can. Two points. Hell, most jobs didn't take this damned long. His cooler was only half full. Popping the top of another cold one, he settled back against the wall at the head of the bed. Damned pillows weren't worth shit.

Even three didn't cushion his back. The picture on the TV had ghosts and snow. There was no cable and the pay for movies box didn't work. He took a long swig of imported beer. Probably imported from Alabama. At least his small cooler kept the beer cold.

Not one single television news report or paper had even mentioned an attack on a teacher in her classroom. Had no one reported it? Did he want someone to report it? An anonymous call could send someone to the police station to check out reports.

He didn't think anyone knew who he was or where he lived, but he couldn't take the chance of going home. He'd thought the teacher's company would be around all night. There weren't a lot of places a man could hide to watch a house being watched by security folks. He'd spotted them easily.

Another long draw emptied the can. *Don't put much in these damned things. Like everything else worth having, the crooks shortchange a person, put in less and charge more. This job should've been easy.* They'd removed his bugs from her house. *Damn! Can't re-bug the place 'til Monday, if the teacher leaves the house to go to school. The security boyfriend made things difficult, but I'm a professional, a pro-fes-sion-al. I'll get inside and set things up again.*

He was being paid to kill one bothersome woman whose inquiries were making his employers antsy. Their source in the police station reported she wouldn't let the matter of her husband's *accidental* death rest. *Too bad I can't get her and*

66

her mother. Mothers! Bet she's like my bitch of a mother. Nothing's ever good enough for her. Lying bitch.

Now the teacher's got a damned dog, too. Hate to have to hurt the mutt, but I will if I have to.

He popped another tab, well on his way to getting stinking drunk. What else was there to do? He'd rather spend time with the teacher's blond friend. She'd been nice to him when they'd run across each other in the grocery store. What would she say if she knew he planned to kill her friend? He couldn't afford to get close to anyone, even for a prime piece of tail.

***

It was only eight-thirty on a Friday and Sam was exhausted. He slept long and hard, dreaming about the lady who was the opposite of the women he usually chose.

Brit wasn't tall and slim or blonde like Adrienne had been. She wasn't sleek or sophisticated like most women he'd dated. She was vulnerable and almost innocent, as Adrienne had been when they'd fallen in love so long ago. She seemed so unaware of her natural beauty. She used makeup, but he'd seen her with none.

She was the most trusting person he'd ever met. Who else would have assumed the phone calls were student pranks? Well, he remembered pulling his share of harmless pranks in his youth. Teach was just the right mix of innocence and mischief.

Maybe he was just attracted to that innocence, to her need for his protection. Maybe the attraction would ease when she was no longer in danger. Brit and Adrienne were both career women, but he'd bet Brit would never give up family life for a job. She was older than Adrienne had been when she'd become a mother. It was his fault they'd married before she'd graduated from college, pregnant.

What if he and Adrienne had been able to wait 'til after they'd married to start a family? Would they have stayed together? Would they have married at all? He wouldn't trade anything for Sean.

In his fantasies Brit was confident, alluring, and sexy as hell. Her lips tasted of passion and need. They drove him to the edge of need, then pushed him over. He ached every place her body touched his, everywhere. He woke hot and aching, as he hadn't in more than fifteen years. Maybe his years of abstinence since he'd decided to save sex for serious relationships was responsible. Maybe Teach tempted him so much because she was off limits since she'd been hurt and scared so recently.

***

Brit felt so much better by Sunday she called her dad to take Mama home. Julie spent the night at Brit's to keep her company. Brit was thankful Julie wasn't leaving her on her own just yet. There was little chance of that with Sam calling every few hours to check on her. If Julie hadn't stayed, Sam would have or he'd offered to call his own mother. The woman had brought soup over but she'd been asleep and missed meeting her. She seemed like a nice lady from Sam's and Sean's accounts, but she was still a stranger. She wasn't ready to meet Sam's mother.

All things considered, it hadn't been such a bad day. Brit was tired and ready for her mother to stop fussing over her. Julie helped without hovering.

Julie had made her smile with talk about a shy guy she'd talked to in the grocery store.

"Tell me about him," Brit asked, as if Julie wouldn't if she had found him interesting.

"Oh, he isn't really my type, but he was kinda cute. You know, short blond hair, blue eyes. I've seen him a couple of times. Usually he just nods at me. Today he asked questions about keeping lunch meats and deli food fresh. Like he was looking for something to say."

"Where does he live?"

"I didn't ask. I think he's new in town. After all his questions he had bought beer and chips and crackers."

"Not your type huh?"

***

Monday morning Brit had to make herself get out of her Mustang in the parking lot at school. She and Julie had driven separate cars, but they'd parked side-by-side. Together they started toward the doors into the building. Putting one foot in front of the other took every ounce of courage Brit could muster.

Friendly faces greeted her, but she barely registered their identities. The walk to her classroom seemed to take an eternity. Once inside the room she choked up, amazed by the colorful posters on the walls. Someone had gone through a lot of trouble to change the room. Desks had been rearranged so she could look out windows at the sunshine.

Her own desk stood as a reminder of what had happened to her there. Her breath caught in her throat. Again she felt the hard wooden edge digging into her back when she'd been pushed against it. She was once again prone on it, frightened. She couldn't breathe.

"Mrs. Roberts, Mrs. Roberts?" She whirled around to see several students and the custodian standing just inside the door. *Breathe slowly. Deep cleansing breaths. He's not here. It's broad daylight, and you're not in danger. You are not in danger.*

"Do you like the changes?" Sean asked. "We all worked on them.

"I painted the walls Saturday and I'm trying to get you a new desk," Mr. James said. "Hope you don't mind."

"I thank you all."

A bell rang, bringing in hordes of laughing teenagers.

Teaching will get me past the nightmares. Her hand was less than steady when she wrote on her one chalkboard. The in-box for late assignments filled as students brought in makeup work. She needed to reschedule the conferences she'd missed Thursday and Friday.

"Could we get a better substitute teacher next time?" someone asked

"Shush!" The warnings stopped the banter that would have seemed normal on any other day.

She welcomed the sounds of discussion as small groups circled desks to read their essays from the weekend's homework. She seldom had to settle arguments about grammatical errors, punctuation rules, or form. Hearing her students so passionate about their work grabbed her teacher's heart. A few times she saw an error about to be accepted by the group as a whole. Those groups she had to guide a little.

At the end of each class she reminded everyone she expected to have all project final drafts on Tuesday.

People stopped by to wave or to walk with Brit at breaks and on the way to lunch. No one mentioned the attack, thank God. At odd moments during the day she thought she sensed Sam watching her from outside her door, but she refused to look.

At other times the air she breathed hurt her lungs. Her head felt ready to explode. Nausea grabbed her stomach. The feeling of menace would pass.

During her planning period someone just happened to bring cookies to share with her. Though they tasted like dust, she ate them and smiled.

After school Sean and Angela, who was often near him, brought notes on the project they were doing for her class. The two blond heads were close an awful lot. They worked in a corner and asked her a few questions to make it seem less obvious they were baby-sitting her. Having company was good.

The room became too quiet. Brit tried to grade papers. She could hear the ticking of the large clock over her desk. She usually loved that clock and rebelled against having a digital clock in her classroom. She sat at a student desk to grade papers. Not once had she sat at her own desk. She couldn't! Her concentration was completely blown when a car backfired outside. Her heart raced and she needed to go to the restroom, but she couldn't face the deserted halls alone. Her hands shook while she stuffed rubber-banded stacks of papers into her tote bag. Suddenly she had to get out of this room, out of this building, now.

"Time to go, Ms. Roberts." Mr. James stuck his head in the room. "I'd like to walk you to your car, if that's okay."

It was more than okay. "Ready," was all she could make herself say.

"We're going, too," Sean and Angela said. They stood quickly. Although Sean was barely taller than Angela, she looked so dainty beside him. "Thanks for the help." They left just ahead of their teacher.

Her Mustang looked so alone in the parking lot. Mr. James waited until she was inside with the doors locked, then he waved her on. "Home, baby, let's go home," she said.

Sean drove Angela home, by way of Brit's. He didn't even pretend he wasn't following her.

***

Douglas was not a happy man. He'd watched the teacher for so long he felt he knew when she farted. His listening equipment wasn't that good, but he knew an awful lot about her habits. Planting listening devices in her schoolroom, the teachers' lounge, and the ladies' room had been almost fun. He'd walked into the school dressed like a maintenance worker, and he'd done his work. Planting cameras would have pushed his luck. The grey beard and shaggy wig were a touch of genius. No one had even asked to see his forged paperwork. Neither teacher had recognized him. The interfering boy hadn't either, of course.

His mother had been so wrong when she'd said he would never make anything of himself. He had enough money in the bank to keep the old lady in a good nursing home. Too bad he had her in a cheap one. She'd cuffed him enough when she was spouting her scriptures about the wages of sin. The whole time she'd spread her legs for the preacher. Bitch!

The teacher had to die soon. Douglas did not fail! She was turning into her driveway. There he had cameras. The one he'd mounted on a telephone pole gave him a good view into several windows. The security system and the big dog posed problems with getting inside, but he'd just have to get around them. He'd never met a security system he couldn't by-pass with a little studying.

***

Brit's house was quiet inside. The daylight lightened her mood. Her devoted guard dog greeted her at the front door with so much affection she ended up on the floor laughing and hugging him. For a short while she forgot to be afraid. Maybe after she changed into jogging clothes she'd let Monster take her for a walk.

Her house was the same, but it wasn't. She must be paranoid. There was no way anyone could be in here. She still checked in closets and under beds.

By four-thirty Sam arrived, hoping for time with Brit. He felt their relationship had changed. He didn't want to rush her. He just wanted to hold her and show he cared. He wanted to be more than just the parent of a student. He wanted more than her gratitude, maybe a friendship, for now.

Brit had snapped Monster's leash to his collar when her doorbell rang. Monster strained toward the door. "Gotta look through the peephole." Monster acted excited, like the ringer was someone he knew.

"Just Sam," the deep voice called. No wonder Monster was excited.

She opened the door. Sam's face lit with his sexy smile. His bedroom eyes threw her. He probably looked that way at all women. He'd certainly charmed her mother and Julie.

"Gonna walk Monster?" he asked.

"I think he's gonna walk me," Brit said. Monster gave Sam a welcoming hand lick and nudge, then he strained toward the sidewalk.

"Mind if I walk with you?"

"Ask Monster." Brit laughed when her guard pet pulled her down the sidewalk. "I don't think he'll mind. He likes you."

Tempted as he was to follow Brit so he could watch her cute backside, Sam set his stride to bring him even with her. He took the leash handle she held in both hands. He still had a hand free to grasp one of hers. She didn't object. Holding her hand made him feel strong and humble at the same time.

When Monster finally slowed to investigate flowers Sam asked. "So, how did it go today?"

"Okay. I did all right, mostly."

"I'm glad. I stopped by the school a couple of times. I kept getting funny feelings."

"Oh?"

"Not as strong as before. I ..."

Sam touched the yellowing bruise on her cheek. He felt her wince beneath his fingers. "Does it still hurt?

"Not so much, now."

Conversation halted when Monster tugged at his leash, ready to walk Sam and Brit again.

She looked good, more relaxed.

They had to persuade Monster to head back home. Sam had worked up a sweat and he could hear Brit's raspy, open-mouthed breathing.

"Julie will be home soon. Would you like to come in for a while? I have some of Mama's cookies left."

"Sure, Teach, love to."

Inside, Monster headed for his water. Sam had worked up an appetite for more than water or cookies. He settled for cookies and coffee.

Just as he and Brit sat down to a cup of coffee, Julie breezed in with news of a therapy group she wanted Brit to check out. That discussion occupied the women so much that Sam had no more private time with Brit. Modern men discussed relationships and feelings with women. He wanted to be a modern man. But it wouldn't happen tonight.

He checked his watch. Time to head home.

"Teach, Julie, gotta go. Sean's fixing supper and he hates for the sandwiches to get cold."

"Aw, Sam, I'll bet Sean is a good cook." Brit laughed.

"Yeah, he makes great sandwiches." Sam placed a light kiss on her soft cheek.

"My turn, hero." Julie stood on her tiptoes and gave him a sweet friendly kiss.

"You ladies be careful." He opened the front door and walked out. Only after he heard the click of the lock did he leave the porch. Something about the attack and the phone calls hovered at the back of his mind while he drove home. He couldn't put his finger on it. He'd call his brother Drew, an Atlanta undercover cop and talk things through.

***

Julie spent the night there, as planned. Their time grading papers and watching sit-coms together seemed deceptively casual, like it was a normal thing, like it was just one more pajama party.

"Julie," Brit asked. "am I being paranoid to feel like someone is watching me?"

"I think it's natural after what happened to you."

"I can't shake the feeling that someone sees too much. I'm almost afraid to go to the bathroom alone." Brit shook her head. She banded a set of graded papers and put them into her tote.

Julie's fingers stopped tapping the keys on her calculator. "I know what you mean. That's something you should mention at the group therapy session. Maybe talking to other victims can help you get over that concern. I think it's just a normal reaction."

The spare room given to Julie was across from Brit's, with its own bathroom. Both bedroom doors stayed open. When the women went to bed Monster slept on a quilt beside Brit's bed.

It had taken forever for Brit to get to sleep. Now she tossed and twisted to escape the huge hands mauling her breasts. A rough hand covered her mouth. The hand grabbing her between her thighs hurt.

"Not again!" She tried to scream. She tried to bite the hand hurting her mouth. She twisted from hands grabbing her, so many hands.

"You want it," the gruff voice growled. "You all want it!"

"No!" She clutched desperately at the cruel hands, scratching, trying to bite them.

Julie heard monster's whine before she heard Brit's whimper. Her friend was having a Nightmare, so she rushed to help.

"It's just a nightmare, Brit. It's just a nightmare. You're safe." Julie held her friend, patting her back, crooning words of comfort as her sobbing finally slowed. "No one's gonna hurt you." Monster licked his mistress's hand.

***

Sitting in his hotel room alone, Douglas rubbed his crotch. Two half-naked broads in bed together. He'd enjoyed the fear causing the nightmare for his target. He could terrify her without even being there. He planned to terrify her more when he got her alone again.

The blonde had a body that made a man ache. Her breasts were large and her waist small. She'd be so hot. Such a sweet ache. Too bad there wouldn't be a real show. Hell, he could've sold the tapes if the teachers hadn't been straight.

So the math teacher thought he wasn't her type, huh. He hadn't meant to be noticed. He'd learned a lot though. Maybe when his job was over he'd dress like his real self, put on some attitude, and give her another chance. Or maybe not.

Shit. A man with his looks and money shouldn't have to jack off in a cheap motel alone. He just couldn't risk having a woman recognize him later. Maybe he could wear a disguise? Nah, he didn't screw around during a job, unless it was part of the job. He'd had his heart, such as it was, set on raping this woman and killing her.

Too many beers and too much hiding time made him crazy. His employers hadn't been pleased when he reported he hadn't killed the woman yet. They were in trouble neither their hired cop nor their *mouth-piece* could fix. Their attempts to expand outside of their little town had brought them to the notice of the big boys. Organized crime in Atlanta could buy better cops and bigger trouble.

Lately the teacher kept asking too many questions about her lawyer husband's *accidental* death. His employers' dirty cop had threatened to off Douglas and then her. *Like that dope could kill me?*

The teacher's husband had been the best at lawyering but hadn't been for sale. The lawyers these small town crooks hired now could be bought but weren't so good. This would be his last job. He'd take his money and go where the weather stayed warm and the women wore little clothing and were willing to accommodate a man with money.

The problem was that Douglas had taken money for a job he hadn't done. Now it wasn't just about the money.

Finishing any job was a matter of pride. He wouldn't go out as a failure.

***

Tuesday night Brit drove to therapy group. Sam had wanted to take her but she had to do this on her own. It had helped to talk with the other victims, to share her feelings without upsetting her friends with her fears. With a lot of effort she managed to hide her paranoia from those close to her. The feeling of violation was hard to explain to anyone who had not experienced an attack, sexual or otherwise, in her own space, where she had always felt safe. It was hard to take.

She'd even signed up for the self-defense class the policewoman had recommended. The week had gone well and the weekend was upon them.

There had been fewer hang-up phone calls. Each time she checked her caller-ID and reported the number and time of the call. She even called a few back, pretending to get wrong numbers. Hang-ups were not a new phenomenon. Only when they had become frequent had she minded. Since the one obscene call every call had become a cause for fear.

***

Julie and Brit stood at the sink, clearing breakfast dishes. They'd had a lazy Saturday morning meal like Brit's mother used to fix after a slumber party. Their routines had been a comfort to Brit since the attack. Brit cooked suppers and often Sam dropped by. After meals Julie washed dishes and Brit dried them. Julie made a good roommate since the attack and a great friend, but she wanted Brit to go out tonight.

Brit dried and put away a cup. "No, thanks, Julie. I'll just hang around and clean house. But you go ahead."

"Aw, Brit," Julie pleaded. "It's Saturday night and I can't go to Mustang Red's by myself. I'd look desperate going to a bar alone." She rubbed her nose with her forearm as she fished a glass from the soapy water. "It'll do us both good to get out."

"I don't think I'm ready for a night on the town."

"This place is new and everyone says it's great. You'd love the Mustang memorabilia there. If I can't go with a date, I need to be with a friend, at least. Two women wouldn't look so

76

much like they're looking for guys. It'll be better than sitting at home."

Julie looked pitiful. "Please! Pretty please! How can you turn down your best friend in the whole world? *Mr. Right* could be there. It could be the only chance I'd have to meet him. But would you care if I miss my one chance for happiness? Huh? Huh? How could you refuse the person who kissed a frog for you?"

Monster moved from the corner where he'd been basking in the light streaming in through the window. He nuzzled Brit then Julie. Absentmindedly Brit rubbed his head. She narrowed her eyes at Julie, who seemed unfazed. "Con-artist. You said the frog might be a prince in disguise and you *double-dog* dared me."

Monster pushed against her leg. She glanced down him. "Not you. We know you're not a dog, you big baby." She looked back at Julie. "You only kissed the frog because I said darers go first."

Julie dried her hands on a dishtowel.

"I won't make you kiss any frogs tonight." Julie grinned. "It could've been a prince, you know. Some friend you are. Besides, you need to get out of this house. You go to school, to self-defense classes, and group therapy." Julie touched Brit's hair. "You see Sam, and me, and the folks at school. You haven't even been to the grocery store alone. Let's have a little fun. If you're too uncomfortable, we'll come back here."

Brit stood facing her best friend in the whole world. She threw her hands up in defeat. "I give up! I'll go."

Julie hugged Brit with an enthusiasm that was all Julie. She took Brit's hands in hers. "I'm going to my place to grab a few things. I'll be back in time to finish my laundry. Then we can take the baby for a walk before we leave him."

Julie had been gone about an hour when the phone rang. Brit stared apprehensively at the instrument. Her new caller ID showed Sam's number. Relieved, she answered.

"Hi, Sam."

"Hi, yourself." His baritone voice was comforting.

"So?"

"So, I just wanted to tell you I'd be at my family's farm today. You have my mom's number if you need to reach me."

"Sam, you don't need to check on me every day."

"But I like hearing your voice, Teach."

Brit was glad Sam couldn't see the flush she felt heating her face. That man said the sweetest things. "You don't need to check in with me, either."

"How can I be your hero if you can't find me when you need me?"

"Sam, you always seem to know when I need you. Something tells me I wouldn't have to call you."

"You and Julie have plans for today? You could come visit my family while I work."

"Thanks for asking, but Julie and I will probably spend the day catching up. We'll take Monster for a walk later." She didn't know why she hadn't mentioned Mustang Red's. She'd probably chicken out anyway.

"Well, gotta go. Dad and my brother, Luke are expecting me."

"Have a good day. Bye, now." *Have a good day? Brilliant.*

By the time Julie returned Brit was feeling the peace and quiet too much. Would she ever be comfortable alone in her own home again? The people in her group sessions said it took time. How much time? She couldn't believe that crazy bastard had taken her security away so easily. At least now she was finally learning to protect herself. She'd get kick-ass strong and regain her confidence. She could do it! She'd dealt with her husband's death and she could deal with this.

Julie had suggested taking her car to the club. She'd commented on Brit's white knuckled grip on her purse. She also noticed Brit's blank stares.

By seven Julie's T-bird drove close enough for them to spot the newest joint in town. The parking lot had nearly filled and Brit was thankful for the distraction of the front of the place. The walkway to the front door led them past a restored, red Mustang. The sheen of its paint was blinding, as though it had been waxed that day. Someday Brit's Mustang would be the golden-bronze it had once been. Above the hood of that gleaming classic machine were the hooves of a magnificent white horse. Its marble body with thrashing hooves and flying mane and tail radiated energy, bringing to life the statue representing the wild and powerful namesake of the automobile.

Julie studied the rapt face of her friend and grinned. "Wait 'til you see the inside of this place. Everyone who loves old Mustangs has raved about it. They say the owner isn't bad, either."

"That is a sight to behold," whispered Brit. "But wait 'til my car is ready. You haven't seen anything yet."

The women walked away from the statues of the adversaries, machine and animal. A man of giant proportions greeted the women at the door. Brit felt a second of hesitation at meeting a strange man, even in such a public place. He was an imposing man but non-threatening. She sensed gentleness about him. His auburn hair and beard, both reflecting golden-red highlights, left no doubt as to his ownership of this place. His proprietary smile welcomed his guests when he gazed at each in turn.

Guess he has a thing for blonde hair. Brit watched Julie blush at the open admiration of the fine specimen of manhood. Knowing Julie, Brit was sure she had taken a mental measure of his impressive biceps, triceps, and any other 'ceps' visible in the form-fitting shirt and snug trousers. The sleeves of his white dress shirt were rolled up to his elbows, displaying tanned forearms to tempt any sighted, breathing female.

Julie's look of undisguised admiration traveled from the ruggedly handsome, tanned face to the wide hand Red extended to her. She was breathing, but barely, as she took that hand in hers. Brit almost burst out laughing as the two looked into each other's eyes and fairly melted on the spot.

"Welcome to my establishment. I'm honored to have such lovely ladies here." He would have looked natural sweeping a cowboy hat in salute. "I'll see you inside soon. Drinks are on me."

"Drinks on him sounds great to me. Anything at all on him sounds delicious," Julie whispered. A grin reached all the way to her eyes.

"Down, pervert. Wipe the droll off your little chin. Something tells me you're going to embarrass me before this night is over." Brit laughed at her companion.

The decor of Red's was a surprise, yet not a surprise. Hanging on the wall by each booth was a photograph of a Mustang automobile, one per year since 1964. The walls not lined with booths sported murals of Mustang herds, capturing the untamed spirit of those wild creatures. Barstools resembled bucket seats while booth seats looked like Mustang back seats. Doors leading from the entrance to the bar proper looked like Mustang car doors.

A small stage stood empty, but music and flashing lights from a jukebox lured people to donate their quarters. A few people danced on the small dance area in front of the stage. The room was filled with welcoming talk and laughter.

Here goes nothing. Brit considered. She took in a deep breath and exhaled slowly. Then she did it again for good measure. It's now or never.

"You ready?" Julie poked her ribs.

"As I'll ever be." She and Julie entered the crowded bar. The room smelled of new leather and testosterone.

***

Sam had wanted to relax for a few minutes. He'd stopped by to see the bar his old friend had opened recently. *Old Jesse has done all right for himself.* Seeing Brit and Julie walk through the double doors startled Sam. Whose idea had it been to come here? Teach looked scared to death.

While he'd done chores at his parents' farm he thought about the way he'd been drawn to the teacher since the first time he'd met her up close. Even before his premonitions had kicked up he'd thought about getting to know her better, but she'd always seemed so unapproachable.

All day he'd helped his dad and brother repair fences and paint. He'd tried to work himself hard enough to forget how much a certain woman aroused him. The strain of wanting to approach her on a physical level and knowing how inappropriate that would be strained his control.

In the shower, after he'd worked up a good sweat this afternoon, he'd thought about her soft, red lips and pink tongue. His body betrayed him when he imagined kissing her. Even after he'd turned the shower to cold his mind left him hot. While he ran his Saturday errands he saw her face everywhere. *And here she is now, in the flesh*.

In his mind she was in the flesh. He hadn't forgotten his view of her charms when he'd helped her to the bathroom after the attack. He hoped she hadn't been aware of his view. And now he sat in the shadows, watching Brit feel her way back into the real world. He needed to let her do this without his help.

A body builder type who introduced himself as Jack stopped by Brit and Julie and ordered drinks. "Whatever these ladies want, okay?" he tossed an order over his shoulder to the bartender without taking his eyes from the ladies.

"Phony," Sam muttered, watching broad shoulders shake and hearding deep, loud laughter at something one of the girls said. "Probably thinks he's a comedian. Wonder which one he plans to take home to bed."

When the hunk finally asked Julie to dance, Brit breathed a sigh of relief. "Howdy, ma'am," she heard as a lanky, red-haired man greeted her. "I'd be proud if you'd dance with me."

"How kind of you to ask, Jeremy." Brit smiled up at the baby face of the young man who often helped her with her groceries. He was harmless, but there was still the initial panic reaction. *Keep smiling*. "I don't feel up to dancing, tonight."

"Oh, yeah, I didn't think about, well, you know."

"I know. Thanks for asking." The thought of standing close enough to dance with a man had frightened the hell out of her.

Only monumental effort kept Sam in his chair. Even across the room he'd felt Brit's panic. She'd done well. Sam's neck itched again. He glanced around the room but saw no one who resembled the man with whom he'd fought. Something was wrong, but he couldn't grasp what.

He rose and strolled around the room. He didn't want to give himself away to Brit. She didn't need to think he was checking up on her. She was such an independent, stubborn woman. Since Julie and his buddy were so wrapped up in each other Sam wanted to be aware of any problem, in case Teach needed him. He sensed she would. There was that familiar pain in his gut. Not a good sign.

As the young man walked away, Brit sensed eyes boring into her back. She had that funny feeling that goes with being watched. She glanced around the crowded room but saw no one who seemed to be staring at her. She nearly jumped out of her skin when a voice sounded by her ear.

"Having fun?" Julie asked Brit, who had not realized Julie had returned from her last dance.

"Oh, yes, a real blast," Brit answered. "Are you? You'd better be. You owe me for this one."

"I'm about to, my friend, and I really do owe you if this works out." Julie beamed like Christmas lights while the owner of the place approached her. "Wish me luck!" she murmured.

After greeting Brit Red looked at Julie like a man planning to make a move. Neither Julie nor the man seemed aware of anyone else.

Brit started to order another drink, when a heavy hand landed on her shoulder. Just before she swung at the intruder she whirled around to see George Wilson grinning at her. As Tommy's roommate and friend, he'd gone along on double dates. They'd taken him on picnics and played touch football with the gang at Mercer University. They stayed in touch, getting together for visits in Macon. George had held her when she'd lost Tommy. They'd been there for each other.

Looking into George's kind blue eyes, Brit dismissed the unsettling feeling of danger and relaxed. It would be good to talk to someone about the time they had shared. She did love George.

"Remember the time we---?" George laughed.

"I remember your taking my husband-to-be and getting him bombed the night before our wedding. He had a headache when we said our vows," Brit complained good-naturedly. "By the way, what are you doing in town?" Brit asked.

"This is one of my new territories. I inherited several new accounts right here in town. I'll be coming through here about once a month to service 'em," George explained.

"You'll have to let me know when you plan to be in town next time so I can have you over to supper. I'll cook lasagna and you can make your famous chocolate soufflé. Lord, but we put away some good meals together. You'll have to bring beer for you and Marge."

"Marge'll be jealous I saw you first. She's giving up beer for a while. I'll bring her after she gets over morning sickness. She doesn't travel now." George grew taller in his pride as he shared the news.

She had begun to relax as she and George caught up on old times. She was startled when Sam spoke behind her.

"Hi, Teach, how's it going?"

"Hi, Sam." Her smile was tremulous. Damn. "Sam Samuels, meet my friend, George Wilson. George and I have been friends forever."

The testosterone level was palpable, plenty of male protection.

That malevolent feeling was thick enough to cut. Exhaustion kicked in. She could barely keep her head up or her eyes open. The room spun. She must have stumbled. Though her vision cleared, she was ready to drop. Sam's hand was on her elbow and George's expression showed his concern.

"You okay, Brit, honey?" George asked.

She nodded. "Sam, I'm ready to go home, now, please. George, I'm in the book. Call me."

She turned toward the bar doors and nearly ran. She needed air.

Sam placed a gentle hand on her arm and escorted her to his truck. Once inside he pulled his mobile phone from his pocket and called Julie's mobile number. When she answered he said simply. "I'm taking Brit home. I'll wait 'til you get there to leave her. Have a good time with Jesse. He's a great guy."

Sam disconnected his cell phone. He turned to Brit, who seemed to stare at him. "So, what happened in there?" Sam asked. He didn't care for the lack of color in her face.

She took a deep breath and let it out slowly. "I just...I just couldn't breathe. I felt like someone was watching me, willing something bad to happen to me." She hesitated, gnawing her bottom lip. "Does that sound crazy?" Her voice was small and frightened.

Sam touched her face gently. He touched her cheek, then her nose. "You're asking that question of the man who gets weird premonitions? No, Teach, I felt something, too. That's why I was watching from across the room. I'd have noticed if anyone had made a move toward you." He stirred in his seat and glanced in the rear view mirror of the truck. "I had my own reactions. My premonitions were acting up."

She nodded in understanding. "You think he was inside?"

"I couldn't spot him, but, yes, I think he might have been in the bar." Sam turned the keys in the truck's ignition. It came to life with a roar. "Still want to go home?"

She nodded. "Please," she whispered. She clutched her hands in her lap for the short drive. The silence surrounding them was palpable.

When they arrived at Brit's house Sam pulled slowly to a stop. He reached across the seat to take her hands in his. The truck was warm. Her hands were like still ice. She turned her head to look at him, fear in her eyes. He hated the man who put fear there.

"Wait here 'til I get back," Sam instructed. "I just want to take a look around. Lock the doors."

She clutched at his sleeve. "No, I'll come with you. I'm not staying in this truck alone." She slid up against him and followed him out on the driver's side.

Before they were off the driveway all the security lights Sam had installed came on. No movement followed. The steps leading to her porch creaked with the weight of two people, Brit in the lead and Sam closer than a shadow. At the front door

Sam reached around her to slide the mailbox aside to reveal an alarm board pad. The red light blinked.

"No one set off the alarms." Brit wasn't sure she believed him. Alarms were going off in her head. If only she could let this man be close. If only she didn't need the security he offered. If only...

Sam unlocked Brit's door before she could fumble for her own key.

Inside, they sat on Brit's comfortable old sofa with Monster curled up at Sam's feet and waited for Julie's return.

Brit fell asleep leaning against his shoulder while they watched an old Bob Hope movie. Her exhaustion took her out.

***

"Goddammit all!" A lot of good listening in to the teacher and her friend had done Douglas. He'd watched and waited patiently at the bar. He had been so near the woman. He'd have spoken to her if her boyfriend hadn't moved in on her. *I could've snatched her in the parking lot and killed her. It would still have looked like a sex killing.*

The parking lot was large and he could have used his van to take her away before anyone spotted him. By the time someone found her body dumped somewhere he'd have been long gone. She attracted men like shit attracted flies. Probably spread her legs for 'em. He'd have his turn soon. He might have to take the hero guy out before he got a chance at the teacher. She was a real challenge. The man was a real nuisance.

***

The week that followed passed quietly. With each day Brit gained strength. She'd even stopped at the grocery store on the way home from school. It had felt good. She was gonna get past the fear.

Julie had been so dependable and helpful Brit insisted Julie accept an invitation to spend Saturday with Jesse James Stewart, the hunky owner of Mustang Red's. Jesse had called Julie every night since Saturday. The *billing and cooing* over the phone had been so cute. She had given him a ring on her cell phone.

How could a best friend not notice how excited Julie was about the prospect of a date with a man who seemed to respect her, unlike Julie's last boyfriend who'd cheated on her? Saturday morning Julie was out by ten o'clock, in Jesse's shining, red Porsche, headed for a secret destination. Brit stayed alone to putter around in her house.

The phone rang. She had forgotten about the hang up calls. The long silence reminded her. "Look, you, if you need help finding out which number you need, look it up, or write it down. How hard can it be to dial a phone number correctly?" The caller seemed to stay on the line longer than usual. "You could at least apologize." She slammed the receiver when the dial tone sounded in her ear. "Jerk!"

She recorded the number on her caller ID, probably a payphone.

Chapter Five

It had been two weeks since Brit's life had been turned upside down. Some nights she still woke up in a cold sweat. She could almost smell the ludicrous flower arrangement and feel the choking sensation she'd experienced when she'd learned someone had been in her house.

Julie had awakened her at least once each night when her attacker had invaded her dreams. Thank God Julie had offered to spend her nights with Brit until she felt safer alone.

Monster's barking reminded her he'd been outside long enough. In the past two weeks Sam and Monster had become part of her everyday life. The man invaded her day-dreams and dominated her thoughts, confusing her with memories she couldn't be sure were real. The endearments and promises must've been her imagination.

Brit was rubbing Monster's tummy when the ringing telephone broke into her reverie. Now who?

"Hello."

"This is Sean, could you use some help working on your Mustang? I can change the oil and *Bondo* rust spots."

"Sean, how thoughtful." Relieved, Brit wound the cord around her finger. "Rust spots on my car? They're all that's holding it together." She laughed then paused. "Did your father put you up to this? He has taken over as my guardian angel."

"Uh, no, ma'am. Uh, Angie and I wanted to know if we could come to your house to work on our project. We can't work at her house 'cause her parents won't be there for the afternoon. They don't want her at home alone after...you know... They don't want us alone. Oh, I didn't think to ask if you had plans."

"No, I don't have plans. Come on. Any time after two will be fine," Brit assured him. "Oh, and Sean, I have oil and filters."

At two o'clock Brit opened the door to Sean standing on the porch, balancing a stack of library books and a box of note cards. She opened the door wide after unlatching the chain then showed Sean to the living room to put his load on a coffee table.

"You don't need the chain lock if you use the security code."

Brit hadn't set the alarm. She'd put on the chain as soon as Julie left the house earlier. She had to get in the habit of punching in the code and peeping through the hole in the door and being suspicious. Sean was talking to her.

"Angela's mom's taking her shopping and will drop her off here around four."

"Come with me and I'll show you where I keep the oil and filters. We'll be through before Angela gets here."

Three-thirty found Sean under the Mustang checking for oil leaks and Brit sanding rust spots. It took a lot of elbow grease but was good therapy for her tension. The area she sanded sometimes became the face of her attacker. She had to work to avoid rubbing too hard.

A deep voice startled Brit. She looked up into emerald eyes almost close enough to touch. She could swear she felt the warm breath of the man in question. His lips were within kissing distance. She could smell his clean, manly scent mingled with Old Spice.

Sean scooted from under the car. "Hi, Dad. Angie's coming over to work on our English project."

"I thought you two would be at the library or at her house." Sam did not look pleased to see she had company.

"Her folks didn't want us working alone at her house, and the library's too quiet for us to discuss things while we work."

Sam would have no privacy with Brit. After Angela arrived she and Sean worked in the living room. Brit seemed as jumpy as a cat on a stove burner. They talked about her therapy sessions and her self-defense classes. They talked about Sam's call to his brother, the cop in Atlanta. They discussed the local police detectives' theory that her attacker had given up and fled the area.

"Drew says your attacker is probably lying low 'til things cool off. You'll need to be careful. Obsessed psycho types don't give up easily." Sam wanted to hold her close and tell her everything would be fine. She probably wouldn't let him.

Having the kids come in to share apple pie didn't help Sam's need to get closer to Teach.

"I have apple pie and whipped cream or ice cream."

Watching Teach eat reminded Sam about the erotic dreams he'd had lately. Brit had played a starring role and he'd made love to every inch of her. Every time she put a bite into her mouth he wanted to share it. Every time the spoon passed between her lips he wanted to taste them.

When Sean and Angela left to study, Brit cleared the table.

"I'll help you do that later, Teach. Come keep me company,"

About to toss scraps into the garbage can, Sam froze. Seething. he removed a bouquet of dead weeds. They definitely didn't look like flowers. She hadn't mentioned them at all. "These come with a card?" he asked, waving the offending bouquet toward Brit.

"Probably just a student who needed a better grade but lost the card." She shrugged. "They were probably pretty before they stayed on my porch overnight."

"Probably." Sam didn't sound convinced.

Not every little thing could be traced to the attack.

Sam pinned her with his gaze. "We need to talk about—"

"Just let me clear these things. I hate to leave a messy kitchen, and it won't take long." She was not ready to approach the subject of what had passed since the night of her attack or the times she'd awakened to find him on her bed or the sweet words she thought she remembered hearing him say.

Brit stood at her sink with her hands in the dishwater and her back to Sam. The hairs on the back of Brit's neck stood on end just in time to warn her Sam was close. She sensed his silent movement across the room before warm hands touched her shoulders to caress and massage the tight muscles. His voice, deep and husky, slipped beneath her skin like liquid, hot liquid.

"Relax, Teach. Let me help you get rid of your tension. Old Sam's hands will work their magic," Sam murmured in her ear, his hot breath causing her to shiver.

"Now, Sam, there's no need. I'm fine, really." Brit shivered like a leaf trembling in a gentle breeze. Heat and cold attacked her body when his hands moved to her neck, using his thumbs to fill the hollow at the base of her skull.

Sam's magic hands moved back to her shoulders before traveling down her arms and up again. The relaxed state she had reached kept her body immobile and vulnerable. His warm, strong hands moved from shoulders to collar bone. The calluses abraded sensuously.

Brit wanted to tell him to stop. The kids were only doors away and could come in. *I'll make him stop in just a minute.*

Her knees turned to water while she stared at the ceiling. Leaning her head against the wall of his chest, she inhaled Sam's familiar scent. His mouth at her ear whispered endearments she could barely hear or understand for the breathiness of his voice.

Sam knew he should stop before he went too far, but her hot, soft skin felt too good beneath his fingers. The pressure he felt building in his lower regions had begun to control his brain. He'd heard about men thinking with their penises, but had not expected to be one.

He put his arms around her and just held her close. A shred of sanity kept him from turning her in his arms where she would feel all of his arousal. She was responding to his gentle touch, but she had almost been raped, so he couldn't rush her.

Sam buried his face in her hair. The faint scent of wild flowers enticed him. He moved to her shoulder and nipped through the fabric of her shirt. God, he wanted her! "I have to go," he whispered harshly. His throat ached. Something else ached more. "If I don't leave soon I might disgrace myself." He laughed ruefully. "How could we explain this to the children? I'll be back later, I promise."

Sam let himself out the back door quietly while Brit tried to compose herself. Her breathing slowed to almost normal, but she feared she would never be normal again. She believed the memories of her attack would fade with time and therapy. Not so with the way Sam made her feel alive and feminine. Could she ever enjoy what he could give her?

Washing her face with a damp cloth in the bathroom helped cool the fever lingering, even after Sam left her. A fresh ponytail and a bit of lipstick made her presentable on the outside, though she was still a mess on the inside. How far would she have let him go before fear made her stop him? Could she have made love to Sam? Should she make love with him? Stupid question.

When she tried to make love with him would he be disappointed? It had been so long since a man other than Tommy had held her, since she had loved a man. She wasn't into casual sex, but she definitely wasn't ready for love. Would she risk loving and losing again? Did she deserve another love after she hadn't taken care of her first? She'd been greedy for a child and maybe expected too much of Tommy.

***

The hot water beating down on Brit's arched neck felt like heaven. Sean and Angela had left a couple of hours ago. The house was quiet and almost everyone had checked to be sure Brit was all right. When Julie called to say she might be out later than planned Brit had told her loyal friend to stay out as late as she wanted. She had taken the phone off the hook so she wouldn't be disturbed by any more wrong number calls. It was time to stop stalling and get her number changed. Maybe she'd tattoo it on her hand. She had to have it unlisted or changing would do no good. So many people would have to be called if she decided to go that route.

Strangely, Brit hadn't felt afraid to be alone. Monster was in the kitchen, nibbling his supper. The big dog was such a dainty eater. This was her house. She had her guard dog and she was securely locked in. The group sessions and self-defense classes made her feel stronger, more empowered.

Now, in the shower, she let her mind go blank. As she raised her arms to shampoo her hair the shower spray beat down on her breasts. She rinsed her hair, trying to erase the erotic feelings slipping into her mind. She imagined Sam's strong hands, gentle, and callused, roaming over her heated skin. Her nipples ached to be caressed. She ached to be loved. Time to get out. She'd steamed her brain.

As Brit cut the water taps off she thought she felt cool air move the still-closed shower curtain. She paused for a second. Hearing no noise, she squeezed excess water from her hair. She reached for the curtain, only to have it pushed toward her. Wrapped in the wet curtain, she was yanked from the shower.

She tried to scream while the attacker dragged her, dripping wet, to the bedroom. Her heart raced. She kicked and twisted, trying to escape. Strong arms and the element of surprise overpowered her.

"Shut up, bitch, stop fighting!" a raspy voice snarled. "It's going to hurt more if I beat you up before I do it to you. That pretty hero and his scrawny kid aren't here to save you, so you might as well relax and enjoy it. Some women *get off* on it. Oh, and don't worry about your dog. I took care of him. Great watchdog he was."

The hateful voice that had been in her worst nightmares in the middle of the night was in the room with her. She was awake, wide awake! Her heart stopped for a second, paralyzing her. When it started back she struggled to get away, hampered by the curtain. A blow to her head slowed her frantic movements, allowing the man to fling her to the bed, plastic curtain and all. He yanked the curtain from her body, leaving her wet and cold atop her covers. She rolled to the side nearest the door to flee, only to trip on something on the floor.

"Damn, you're a stubborn one. The more fight, the more fun." His laugh froze her blood in her veins. He grabbed her wrist and yanked her. She landed hard against his body, knocking the breath from her lungs. He grabbed both wrists pushing them together. Wrapping a cord around her wrists, he pulled her to the bed and threw her onto it. "Stay the hell where I put you, or I'll slap you around some more."

The southern accent was gone. Brit couldn't believe this was happening again. There was no one to save her but herself. She wouldn't be a victim again. There had to be a way to get away. She shuddered at the ranting of her attacker. His faded bluish eyes were cold and cruel. His expression was hard to read because his pale brows were difficult to see without her glasses.

"I'll squeeze those white tits till you beg me for it." He squeezed hard. "I'll touch you all over, then I'll give it to you good," he threatened. "Do like I say, I won't hurt you too bad."

Brit frantically watched his every move to catch any chance at escape. Her breasts ached. *I am not going to take this lying down. Funny. What a time for a sense of humor.* The rasp of a zipper brought her to full attention. Gathering more strength than she realized she had, Brit used the hand she had worked free to slam her palm upward into his nose as she kicked at his groin area. She rolled from the bed. He was between her and the way out.

The attacker swiped out with one hand while his other one held his injured nose. "Shit!" Blood seeped through his fingers when he turned toward the door to chase her.

"Brit, Brit, honey! Where are you?" Sam's voice sounded frantic. "Where the hell are your watchdog cops?"

"In here, Sam," she yelled.

"Bitch, you stupid bitch. You broke my Goddamned nose. I'll kill you and your boyfriend." Obviously blinded by the pain, her attacker moved just enough to clear her way to the door.

Brit flew to the door. *Escape.*

She grabbed the knob and pushed it open. A broom stood beside the door. She grabbed it and slammed it into the man stumbling after her.

Brit flew past Sam in her dark hall.

Sam's anger nearly blinded him. "Where is he? I'll kill that bastard when I get my hands on him. We don't need to wait for the cops. I'll kill him with my bare hands."

His gun in his hand, he tripped over something large. A man with his pants down around his knees and briefs covering his vitals.

"Sam?" Brit's voice quivered. "Sam, what do you see?"

"Scum, that's what I see, and I'd like to erase it from the earth. I could kill him before he wakes and get it over."

"Sam." Brit looked around Sam and saw the body on her bedroom floor. "While you stare at him and plan his demise, I can tie him up so he can't get away." Brit stalked past Sam. She came up short when his arm snaked out to yank her back.

"You don't think I would let you near that SOB, do you?" Sam asked. The naked woman had dignity. "I'll tie him up. Stay put."

"Monster? Sam, he said he 'took care of' my dog."

"Asleep, honey. I nearly tripped over the dog when I came in the back door. He was just drugged. His breathing seemed normal. Call the police and see what's keeping those idiots," Sam added. "Then we'll check on the puppy." Taking his attention from her wasn't easy, but he couldn't have that bastard coming to and staring at her. "And put something on, Teach."

"No need to call," Brit answered.

Wrapped in a tablecloth she'd grabbed from the table as she passed it, she stopped the charge of uniformed police officers. Two came from her kitchen and two from the front door they'd crashed.

"Brit, have you called to find out where those idiots are? I called them on my car phone when I didn't see any surveillance vehicle. My gut still aches. I knew something was wrong before I reached your block. Where the hell are they, anyway?"

"They're here." Turning to let them pass, she pointed down the hall.

"That way," she calmly instructed. Shock numbed her. She sat down in the large blue chair by the matching sofa. She tucked her bare feet under her and waited. *Breathe in, breathe out. Breathe in, breathe out. You can do this. Stay calm a little longer.*

Two male officers shoved the trussed man through the hall and out her front door, reading him his rights. Brit noticed that someone had pulled his pants up. *Nothing like getting caught with your pants down. They should've left 'em down. Let him try walking with his pants around his ankles. Would serve him right.* Something else caught her attention. He looked different. His hair was short instead of longish. Had he worn a wig to attack her?

The other two officers came back to the living room where Brit and Sam waited. "We have to ask you some questions."

Brit heard the words but barely registered the speaker. "Sure," she murmured. "Might as well get it over while I can speak." Adrenaline still pumped through her veins. That would end and she'd crash or lose it before long.

Another pair of plainclothes detectives appeared carrying cameras and a brief case. "He attacked the lady in her bedroom," Sam volunteered. "The backdoor lock was broken and the alarm disabled."

"Thanks." One detective headed toward the bedroom.

"Who's he?" the other new detective asked, inclining his head toward Sam.

"Mr. Samuels is her friend. He helped capture the perp."

"The bathroom, too." Brit's voice quavered.

"What?" The man with the camera stopped. "Ma'am"

"Oh, yes." She thought a second. Her mind wanted to blank out. "Look in the bathroom, he was there, he found me in the shower."

One of the policemen with Sam and Brit opened his well-worn notebook and perched on the sofa arm nearest Brit's, to question her. He was disheveled and she wouldn't have been surprised to see him lick a pencil, like the old series *Colombo*.

"I'm so sorry, ma'am," he began.

He pulled a pen, not a pencil stub, from his pocket. The pen had no cap and she would bet there would be an ink spot on his pocket.

"We had a robbery reported several blocks from here and had to pull the car we had parked across the street, to answer it. The caller reported shots. We moved quickly, and in force."

A policewoman entered the room, carrying a plastic zippered bag of evidence, an opened knife showed through. Brit had been so frightened she had missed the knife. Sam followed the cop.

"Did you get the break-in person?" Brit asked.

"Uh, no. We woke up the occupant instead. He wasn't being robbed at all. Someone called in a phony report."

"It figures. I don't believe you numskulls left this woman unwatched, after what happened at school. Her family and friends have tried to make sure she had moral support, but we believed she had your protection in case that piece of trash showed up."

"Sam, please, let's just answer their questions. I'm tired and would like to get it over before the shock hits. Please."

The officers occupied the sofa, so Sam marched over to Brit's chair. He draped the robe over her shoulders, then stood beside her.

"Go on, officers. As you can see, the lady needs rest." She shivered despite the robe, so Sam left to get a blanket.

The three intent men listened while she told of fear and determination. "H-h-he said some of the other women enjoy it rough, so I guess he has done this before... I ran from the room still n-n-naked." She gulped, "I hit him across the face with a broom handle. Mr. Samuels came and—and I grabbed the cloth from the table and here I sit."

"You must have been scared," someone commented.

"So scared I'd have wet my pants, if I'd had any." Her nervous laugh would've fooled no one. "But I was more angry. I couldn't let him have his way without a fight. I just couldn't."

Bless Sam! He'd squatted beside her chair and held her hand. He was trembling as much as she was. When she turned to look into his eyes she wanted to erase the anguish she saw.

"Was the attacker tonight the same man who attacked you at school?" an officer asked.

"Yes!" Sam and Brit answered together.

"And you still don't know who he is or why he targeted you?"

"No," Brit answered.

"Have you thought any more about why he would want to harm you?" the Columbo lookalike asked.

"No, I can't."

"We'll spend some time with you after we interrogate him. Maybe we can figure things out if he doesn't tell us. They sometimes brag and give themselves away."

"Your story, Mr. Samuels?" one of the officers asked.

"I was on my way to check on Mrs. Roberts when I got a call from my headquarters. Her security system wasn't sending the right signals to the main board. There was no surveillance vehicle outside. I used my cell phone to call the station to see why and was told someone would be here to check things out."

Sam rubbed her arms to ease her trembling. Feeling her calming, he continued, "I tried to get in the front door, but found it locked. I went around to the back door and found it standing slightly ajar.

"The lock was broken, so I slipped in. Teach, here, had won the battle with that maniac. His pants were around his knees. He was unconscious. She wouldn't let me go ahead and kill him, so-"

"Sam!" Brit admonished.

"So I tied him up to wait for you. You finally got here."

"Thank you. Once again, we're real sorry about the mix-up. Where will you be staying? Ma'am? We need to know where to reach you."

Sam rubbed his jaw. "Guess it wouldn't look right for you to stay with me, but my parents' house isn't far away and they have room."

97

"No," Brit answered. "I appreciate your offer, but you can't understand how I feel. I let my husband take care of me until he died. When I lost him I couldn't deal with things, so I let my parents take care of me.

"When my friend Julie told me about the job here I realized it was time to pull myself together. I got the job and bought the house. I took charge of my life, and I'll be damned if I'll let a crazy man take my life away from me. I'm staying here. This is my home. Besides, you have my attacker. Why shouldn't I be safe?"

The crew from her bedroom appeared and left quickly.

Her interviewers were finished, too. "We'll call you on Monday to make sworn statements at headquarters, Mrs. Roberts, Mr. Samuels. Good night." The officers let themselves out, promising to keep a car on watch until they could send a man to fix the locks in the morning.

"Don't bother," Sam said. "I'll do it. I want it done right."

"Don't be so hard on them, Sam."

"Is Julie coming home, I mean here?" Sam asked.

"She called after the kids left. I said I was locked in securely," Brit shrugged at Sam's raised eyebrow. "Julie explained that she and Jesse were planning to drive to the lake."

"I'll put you to bed in the guest room and I secure the doors the best I can, and then I'll leave Sean a message to let him know I'll stay with you. He can call here if he has questions."

"Sam, I need another shower. I'll use the guest bath and then turn in. I think I'll sleep in the bed Julie's been using."

"Want some help washing your back?" he asked as she retreated toward the guest bath.

"What?"

"Just kidding. I'll check on Monster."

Sam secured the doors with heavy chairs propped under the knobs and checked to be sure the cops were parked outside. He called his office to leave word to send someone out in the morning.

Brit stepped from the guest bath feeling secure that Sam would protect her from intruders and too tired to wonder who would protect her from her need for Sam or from herself.

Unable to face going into her own room yet, she slipped into one of Julie's gowns. She pulled back the covers and crawled into the bed. Monster padded slowly into the room and licked her hand. He looked groggy but all right. She was soon asleep.

Sam had cleaned the mess in Brit's bathroom and bedroom. The cops had left dark dust on doors and every hard surface. Brit didn't need to see this mess! They must've taken the shower curtain. He wiped up the puddles of water, using the towel on the floor.

He stripped the bed and rummaged around to find clean sheets and remade it. He could sleep there and still hear Brit if she needed him. Sam slipped past a sleeping Brit to shower. This was the third shower in one day. As he tiptoed past the sleeping woman Sam heard the rustling covers and Brit's screams.

***

"No! No! Not again!" The knife to her throat cut a thin line.

The gruff voice hissed. "Bitch! You want it! You know you do!"

Brit wanted to twist away from the knifepoint pressed into her throat. He was going to rape her. She couldn't protect herself in her own house. He peeled his face and hair away like a mask. She screamed.

"Brit. Brit. Wake up." Slipping onto her bed, Sam spoke gently, trying to make her hear his voice through the fog of sleep. "It's all right, baby. It's just a bad dream. I'm here." He lay atop the covers and tried to hold her in his arms. Rubbing her back, he talked until she settled in his embrace, breathing slowly on his chest. Sam was sure he would not sleep a wink, but both occupants of that bed were dead to the world by midnight.

Sam awoke, puzzled to feel a fanny pressing against his hard-on. He didn't remember getting under the covers. The fanny wiggled again, causing Sam to let out a slow breath. He wasn't ready to wake Brit. He'd realized who the body was the second he caught her delicate scent.

Sam carefully shifted to put his very much awake penis farther away from the squirming fanny and moved close enough to plant kisses on her shoulder. The woman beneath his lips turned toward him. He couldn't resist kissing her. His kiss was gentle, soft.

Never before had Sam wanted to give so much of himself to any woman. Not even Sean's mother had caused such an all-consuming need to possess, to claim. He kept his touches comforting. He couldn't seduce her now. What if she awoke angry that he had taken advantage of her in her sleep? There would be better times to show her how good they could be together.

He whispered, his voice raspy, "Sleep well."

Brit returned slowly back to the reality of the man holding her. Apprehension tried to surface to her brain, but she pushed it back. Tommy had been the man she loved, so she had never expected to find a man she would let take his place in her life or her heart. But Tommy had never caused the fear of losing herself in another person. She would not give in to the fear of losing control to this overwhelming man.

"I don't want to need you, Sam."

Chapter Six

This time Brit wasn't lucky enough to be ignored by the media. She'd been hounded by reporters from Atlanta, as well as the local papers. *The Macon Telegraph* had treated the case as local news since Florence was only thirty miles away. On the night of the attack someone had been in the police station when her attacker had been taken in and identified as one Douglas Drake. Sunday papers plastered his picture on the front page.

Sunday afternoon Julie had called from her mobile phone. "Brittany Marie, why didn't you call me? I can't believe I had to read the paper to learn my best friend was attacked. I should have stayed with you."

"If you had he'd have hurt you. I didn't realize the papers would cover it since no one called me until this morning. I wouldn't tell them anything, but I called my folks as soon as I got the pests off the phone. We had to leave my phone off the hook and use my cell.

"You didn't call me, though," Julie complained.

"I tried but couldn't get through. What could you have done, anyway? You needed that time with Jesse."

"I'm so sorry."

"I know, I know. At least you were safe."

"Oh, I forgot to tell you. The picture of the man who attacked you looks a lot like the man I told you about, you know the shy guy from the grocery store."

"Damn!"

"I'm on my way."

"I take it you had a good time."

"Oh, God, you won't believe how wonderful Jesse is. We talked all night and I fell asleep in his arms."

"No sex?"

"No sex."

***

By Monday the reporters hadn't found anything on him. How could a man so vile have no record of previous arrests? He didn't even have a traffic violation.

After the first week the news headlines and detailed articles had moved from page one to shorter articles buried further inside. News reports mentioned her in passing.

Day after day Sam had been to Brit's house on some pretext or another. He had repaired her front steps and her porch swing. They had repaired every squeaky door and replaced bathroom tiles. With the longer days their walks with Monster stretched longer and longer. Brit was relieved when people stopped asking questions about the attacks and offering their condolences.

Two weeks after the capture of Douglas Drake, Sam arrived in his truck. Of course he had called first, as usual. "Come on, Teach, you'll have a good time. You've been doin' so well these past weeks. Today will be a good next step. You'll meet my family. My brother Drew is interested in what has been happening to you."

"Why would I want to talk to him? What good would it do? Sam, I don't see the point. The man is in jail and he was caught in my house with his pants down, literally. The authorities are matching the finger print from the light switch in my classroom and fibers they vacuumed."

"He has experience in police work. Maybe we can learn something about why the jerk chose you. What if you weren't his first? He has no traceable history under his current identity. So far he isn't telling anything about himself. I told you that, I think.

"Besides, it's time to get out and have some fun. You never go anywhere but school or self-defense classes or group therapy. If you aren't comfortable I'll bring you home. Bedsides, Monster would love the freedom to run loose at the farm."

"All right, you win. We'll make Monster happy." Monster slurped her hand. Sam kissed her cheek. She could do this.

She had finally agreed to meet the Samuels clan. Maybe it would be good to be around people who weren't as paranoid as she had become. Monster would have plenty of running room. He was too attached to her to run away very far.

***

The white farmhouse was all Brit had expected and more, with its wrap-around porches and red shutters and doors. The yard was a profusion of both wild and cultivated flowers and shrubs. Spring flowers in Georgia could make most Yankees jealous, but Mrs. Samuels and whoever helped her had outdone anything Brit had seen so far this year.

A white picket fence surrounded the house and yard, separating the residence from the larger farm. Outbuildings sported shiny, white paint and the same red trim as the house. Within the white fencing around the entire farm were sections marked by wire fences, decorated by shrubs and more wild flowers.

Monster's snout nuzzled Brit. His whine was pitiful but fake. He was always trying to get by her with his begging.

"Soon, boy. We'll let you out, I promise." Monster thanked Sam with a generous doggy kiss.

Sam stopped the truck as four horsemen neared. He stepped out and hurried around the truck. As soon as he opened Brit's door Monster bounded over the seat and out. Sam caught Brit before she slid out by herself.

His hands at her waist sent heat through the fabric of her jeans. She clutched his shoulders to steady herself while she slid down the length of his hard body. The dizzying effect of his touch brought warmth to her face. She pushed against his chest. She couldn't let him feel how she reacted to him. She wasn't sure she was ready for that.

The boy astride the black horse sat tall and straight. "Hi, Dad!" Sean yelled. "Hello, Miss Roberts. I'm glad you and Dad are here, finally. Hey, Monster." His blond hair captured the sunlight. His blue eyes gleamed sapphire.

Beside Sean, an older man tipped his Stetson as he looked at Brit. A smile multiplied crinkles around his eyes. He was all masculine charm sitting on his copper horse.

"I'm Sam's daddy, John Daniel. Everybody calls me Pop." The green eyes twinkled with the same devilment Brit had seen in Sam's. Gray streaks threaded the thick, black hair so much like Sam's.

"I'd be honored to call you Pop." Brit felt welcome, almost able to forget her problems.

Sam seemed to gain his voice. "Teach, the guy with the pony tail is my baby brother, Drew."

"Pleased to meet you, Drew." She had to reach up to shake Drew's hand. His tall gray was a beautiful horse.

Drew released Brit's hand. "Meet Luke, the oldest brother."

"Pleased to meet you, Ma'am." Luke smiled down.

Pop's voice boomed. "Let's get this woman to the house and have some iced tea."

Sam led Brit back to the truck, placing both hands on her waist to lift her up on the high seat. Watching her climb would have been ungentlemanly and torture. Touching her was exquisite torture with her charms practically in his face. God, they were charming and lush!

Brit's hands instinctively moved to Sam's shoulders when he lifted her. Her mouth went dry as she looked into his eyes. Their gazes held for heart-stopping seconds.

Brit's skin warmed. Finally tearing her eyes from Sam's, her gaze stopped as his lips parted to kiss. Her own lips parted involuntarily.

The blush on Sam's face was instant when a loudly cleared throat reminded him they were not alone. He grinned while Brit's blush deepened more than he had thought possible.

Closing her door, Sam ran around to the driver's side and climbed in. Cranking the truck, he pointed toward the house and proceeded to outrun the horsemen and Monster, who followed Sean.

Brit was silent while the truck made its way to the house. Hormones could be dangerous in adults. Sam's being so sexy didn't help. Maybe if she just said nothing, Sam wouldn't either. She needed space and a chance to relax for the day. It was

Protective Instincts

difficult to face Sean in class, knowing he must hear the nonsense his dad whispered over the phone. Where were Julie and Jesse? They were supposed to be here.

After the truck pulled up to the white gate at the sidewalk to the house, Sam jumped out and hurried to open Brit's door. She jumped out and landed flush against Sam, who held her chest to breast, eye to eye, and lips to lips. Sam gave in to temptation. He felt that kiss all the way down to his booted feet, a kiss that made him want to make love to her here and now.

Monster ended the kiss as he tried to join in. Maybe that was a good thing, since his passions ran deeper than he could understand, more than a healthy man's attraction to a beautiful woman.

"Here come the ladies," Sam warned. "Hi, Mom. I brought her, see? Rachel Samuels, meet Brittany Roberts. She's right pretty when she's awake and coherent."

"Welcome to our home, Brit." Sam's mother rushed down the steps. "We're so glad you could be with us today."

Following Rachel were Jesse, Julie, and two women Brit had not met. She knew immediately that the raven-haired beauty must be Sam's sister. She had Sam's dark good looks.

"My sister Esther." Sam draped an arm around the woman who so closely resembled him.

Esther's handshake was firm and reassuring. "I'll give you all the dirt on my brothers later."

Rachel's brown hair was streaked by gray and sun. The azure hue of her eyes, so similar to the blue of Sean's and Luke's eyes, was startling. Her build was pleasantly generous in a soft, motherly way.

For seconds Brit allowed herself the luxury of imagining herself with kids, hers and Sam's? Why not, as long as she was imagining?

Well, he certainly made her hormones simmer. Would they have green eyes? Would they have violet eyes like hers or maybe even hazel ones?

Talk about jumping the gun! If she and Sam made love there would be no children. She hadn't conceived during the

105

years she and Tommy had tried. But she could allow herself fantasies. She shook herself to push such thoughts from her mind. Reality wasn't so bad for now.

Following Esther was a woman whose petite frame made Brit feel of normal height. Esther reached for the woman's hand and pulled her close. "Becky keeps Luke in line. Meet our sister-in-law."

"We've heard so much about you from Sam and Sean, Ms. Roberts." Becky took Brit's offered hand. Her voice was as soft as her fresh "Irish Spring" look. "You're so much braver than I could ever be. I'm glad you're here. You'll enjoy this terrific family."

"Please call me Brit, everyone."

Brit gazed at the group surrounding her.

Sam's mother reminded Brit of her own. "Let's go have a picnic," Ms. Rachel ordered.

Deep, booming laughter came from the men who left their horses to be fed and watered at the stable nearest the house. The picnic baskets, coolers, and tables were now in the back of Sam's truck. Brit sat nestled between Becky and Esther in the back seat of the Samuels' Lincoln with Daniel and Rachel in the front, leaving Sam to ride with Drew.

The ride to the creek was just long enough for Sam to fill Drew in on the gory details of the two attacks and the strange hang-up calls, as well as the dead weeds with no note.

"How'd he get past your alarm system?" Drew asked.

"He went in through the back door after breaking the lock. Either Brit forgot to set it or he tricked the system."

"Big brother, this man's not just some wacko obsessed with raping the teacher. He's a professional killer."

Sam glanced from the dirt road ahead to stare at his brother. "Drew? Do you know something you're not telling?"

"I asked a few questions at the Florence Police Department. They haven't been able to trace the guy's prints in the statewide system. Not a good sign. No driver's license or car registration, nothing. We accessed the FBI system, too. Nothing there."

"Meaning?" Sam asked.

"Meaning, someone wants the lady dead. This guy is a pro."

Sam dodged a rut in the road. He could practically drive this route with his eyes closed. "Damn. Now what, little brother?"

"Now we dig in her past for someone who would want her dead."

"What could she have done?"

"Or what does she have or know might be more like it. Her husband was a lawyer who was run down about three years ago? Roberts - Peter, - no, - James?- Oh, Thomas Roberts? Hmmm," Drew mused. "I'll check the computer for information about the husband in the system, maybe call Washington. Could be he was dirty. They lived in Butlerton, was it?"

"You've already been checking into things."

"She graduated from Mercer University in Macon, where she met Tommy Roberts, moved to Butlerton where they lived for six years. He had a small law firm and she taught school, language arts. A truck hit him and kept going. Driver never found."

"That's a shame," Sam said.

"Atlanta newspapers covered his death, so their accounts might give us insight." His eyes narrowed as he stroked his chin. "Maybe a list of his clients would give us clues. I haven't gotten much information from the Butlerton Police. I just may need to go higher up. In a town that size there might be a connection with a big city crime organization. Seems the crooks want to live in the suburbs, now. And big city crooks like to branch out into new territory and give the *good ole boys* a run for their money. Big business buys out or runs small businesses out of business."

Sam's attention left the dirt road while he watched his brother map out a strategy for an investigation he hadn't considered a possibility. "You think the 'accident' might not have been a real accident?" Sam glanced back at the road.

"Jesus H. Christ! That means she might be a target for worse than rape?"

"Maybe there's nothing more than cop's imagination." He shrugged. "I'll call you as soon as I've checked into things. There's probably nothing to it. Maybe this sicko guy is a rapist who has nothing to do with her husband's death. He could be a serial rapist. She could be a random target."

Drew didn't look convinced. His had a mind like a steel trap. Sam would bet his last dollar Drew suspected way more than he was saying

"Talk to her, warn her about the possibilities."

This shaded place beside one of the farm's creeks had always been a family favorite for picnics. Before the afternoon ended someone would give in to temptation to test the waters, even this early in the season.

Sam made sure to stay close to Brit, as he always did, once they reached the picnic site. He liked being close. He pitched in and helped the ladies unload and unpack the food. There had to be enough food in the hampers to feed an army.

Sean brought her a chilled can of Coke Zero. "Is this okay?" He asked. He shifted from one booted foot to the other. He glanced down at the ground, then back at Brit. "The kids at school think you're awfully brave to keep teaching and everything. Everyone wants to help." He blushed. "I just wish I'd stayed with you instead of going to Angela's the night, you know ---"

"Sean, you have been a big help." She touched his arm. "Now I know why everyone has been so good, lately. I keep wondering if the *Body Snatchers* have taken over my students."

"More likely the Pod People." Sean laughed.

Sam's approach stopped the conversation. "Taking good care of the teacher, I see."

"He certainly is," Brit answered.

"Drew flashed a Frisbee and he and Sean entertained Monster while they sauntered along the creek away from the bustling women. Luke and Pop Samuels had already walked in the opposite direction to set up fishing poles.

Sam led the way to a row of blankets spread on the ground. "Was Angela invited or is there trouble in paradise since school ended yesterday?" Brit asked.

"Sean asked her, but her family had a reunion to attend. The kids are too young for Sean to be included in an out-of-town thing."

"You're right. Boys can be so much in love or lust at that age."

"Or at any age, dear teacher." Sam took her hand. He kissed each finger slowly, gazing into her eyes. "At any age." His smile was slow and damned sexy. Brit felt her insides melt when he sucked her pinky finger into his hot mouth. She was struck dumb.

"Come on, everyone," Esther called. "You, too, Sam and Brit." No second call was necessary. Brit wanted no more attention.

Trestle tables held food and ice tea pitchers. Rachel had outdone herself with fried chicken, sliced meats, potato salad, and more. Sandwich fixings included sliced tomatoes and lettuce as well as all kinds of condiments and breads. Baked beans and bean salads added vegetables to the bodacious spread. Chocolate pies and banana pudding vied with chocolate and coconut cakes as favorite desserts.

Monster settled between Sean and Drew.

Brit took her food and sat down between Esther and Becky. She was sure there wasn't room for anyone else. Her smugness fled when Sam sandwiched himself between his sister and her. Esther scooted over to give him more room, but Brit had nowhere to scoot. Scoundrel!

The spring sun beat down, warming everything. But the sun wasn't the reason Brit was too warm. Sam sat so close their legs touched from thigh to knee. Every time he moved Brit felt the play of his muscles against hers. The fabric of their jeans might as well have been non-existent, for all the good it did. The rat kept making it a point to brush elbows with her, looking at her to see her reactions. She hoped he couldn't see her panic. It would be best if he couldn't see the flush that warmed her face, or the pulse beating wildly in her throat, or the rising of her chest as she gulped air.

She caught very little of what was being said. Concentrating on eating, instead of the man beside her, took more effort than Brit would have thought possible. *If I could think about anything but this pest, I could enjoy the company of these people.*

Everyone did some serious eating. Sam barely tasted his food. All he could think about was the woman beside him. He loved the way she stopped chewing when he touched her. He'd move his leg to touch her, then look to see her eyes dart to look at him. It took all the effort he could muster to look innocent. God, she was tempting when her skin took on that soft, pink glow. She looked as skittish as a frightened bird with a cat watching its cage. When she breathed hard, like she'd been running, he wanted to pull her to him and catch her parted lips. He'd give her air.

Lord, I gotta stop this line of thinking. If my jeans were any tighter, there isn't a person here who wouldn't know just what I'm thinking. Think of something non-arousing. Uh, a dip in the stream, cold eggs, liver, cold French fries.

His imagination betrayed him and moved back to dangerous territory. *I wonder if she is wearing French cut panties under those jeans, lacy ones, satiny ones? Shoot! Good going, Sam.* Even thinking about the dangers Drew had suggested was difficult here in the country, surrounded by friends and family.

"Mom, chicken's great. Looks like Jesse was hungry. Jesse, 'member the time we ate ourselves sick with plums? I thought my belly would never stop hurting. Your aunt thought we'd poisoned you and gave you a dose of castor oil." Sam rambled to ease his arousal.

Eating had never been so sensuous for Brit before Sam. She found her gaze returning to him. Each time his tongue whipped out to lick food from his lips she licked her own. It was like sharing. She imagined that he was licking her lips and she was licking his. There was a spot of chocolate beside his mouth. She wanted to lick it off, chocolate and Sam, a tasty combination. He even swallowed sexy!

Each time his Adam's apple moved she wanted to press her lips to his throat, then his chin, working her way to his lips. Heat pressed from all sides, threatening to smother her with thoughts about the exasperating man. Conversations around her faded. Her eyes felt heavy as she blinked, trying to force her vision to clear. God, it was hot!

"Don't you agree, Brit?" Becky asked.

"Huh? I'll have to think about that," Brit hedged. Brit hadn't the foggiest notion what Becky was asking, but Sam was grinning at her. He looked so smug she was sure he knew what she'd been thinking, what he was likely thinking, judging by his grin.

"What do you think, Sam?" Becky asked.

"Uh, you're probably right, Becky. I always take your side." Sam had no idea what to say. He was watching Brit, wishing he could lick the speck of chocolate from her cheek. *Chocolate and Brit would be delicious. She might really blush if she knew what I'm thinking. I'd like to remove every stitch of clothes from her body, then spread meringue all over her. I'd slowly lick it off... Stupid.* Sam fought his way to the conversation around him.

"You look tired, Teach," Sam drawled in that sexy, bedroom voice that made her melt. "Want me to take you home and put you to bed?"

"Yes, indeed, son," Rachel insisted. "That poor girl looks all tuckered out. Take her on home, unless she wants to lie down at the house. We've plenty of rooms."

"That's okay, I'd rather go home and take a shower and relax, but I do want to help you clean up, first," Brit insisted.

"Never you mind, now. We'll clean up. You just rest."

The ride home was quiet, except for the snoring of the tired Monster. Finally, Brit spoke. "Your family is nice. Growing up with them must have been great. Have you always lived there?"

"Yeah, Dad bought the land and house from a man who was too old to tend to it. The guy's first wife had died years back and he was ready to move to a retirement community. He was looking forward to living close to people and enjoying his remaining years. He died on the golf course at the age of ninety-seven."

"Are you serious?" Brit asked.

"Yes," Sam grinned. "He made love to his new thirty-year old wife that morning and went straight to the big tournament. The old guy was almost at the end when he keeled over onto an opponent's ball. He died smiling. They called off the game out respect and he won." Sam shrugged.

Brit's incredulous look made Sam grin even more. "You're making this up. You can't be serious," she admonished.

"Sounded serious to me. Golfers are serious about their games. No one wanted to move the body so his ball could be hit. They couldn't have finished for a while, anyway. There were paramedics and an ambulance to haul him away. You know, no one was in the mood anymore. Rumor has it he became a daddy, posthumously."

Sam had wanted to make Brit laugh. She wouldn't smile when she heard what Drew had suggested. A vision of a very pregnant Brit stunned him. His pants became tighter again. He was too old to be a Daddy again, or was he? It could be fun, especially making the babies!

Sam wanted her to keep talking. He loved the sound of her husky voice. The mixture of Georgia raising and education made listening to her a pleasure.

Sam had been very quiet as Brit told him of her family. Her smiles made it clear how much she cared for them. "Why didn't you stay with them when your husband died?" he asked.

"I did, but it was too easy to dig myself into a rut and let them take care of me." Brit shrugged. "My family is supportive, maybe too much so. Everyone took care of me, even my niece.

"She shared my pain and took me out of myself. She was the person I first told about Julie's suggestion that I apply for a teaching job here. The kid gave me good advice. In some ways the loss of her mother made her grow wise for her twelve years. My family loves Julie and knew she could help me. And she has!"

They had been sitting in Sam's truck, in front of Brit's house for a while, but neither wanted to break the comfortable mood. Sam didn't want to leave Brit, and she was afraid he would want to go inside and she wasn't sure she could refuse him. Together, each started to speak—

"Sam--"

"Brit," Sam offered. "I would like nothing better than to help you with that shower, then tuck you into bed."

With his pulse racing, Sam slowly kissed every inch of Brit's face, thinking of the earlier wish to lick chocolate from her cheek. The rush of heat that swept his face should have warned him to stop, but he preferred to listen to the voice of desire, which outtalked the voice of reason. His mouth dragged from her cheek to her parted lips and moved hungrily over them. He nipped at her sweet lower lip.

Brit had realized Sam was going to kiss her. She didn't want to stop him. After all, how much trouble could they get into in broad daylight? As his mouth seared a wet path to her mouth, her gasp allowed his tongue inside to rub its velvety surface against her teeth and gums.

The burst of desire turned her brain to mush and set her body aflame. Her arms wound around his neck, almost choking him as he tried to slide from under the steering wheel. Heat traveling from her thighs to her belly threatened to consume her with pent-up desire. Only his pained groan allowed her to break the mind-numbing kiss.

"Sam?" Brit whispered, frightened by his pained expression.

"It's okay, honey." He winced. "I strained my back stretching the wrong way. I hate to stop when we're having fun. I want to stay and make love to you for hours." Sam smiled. "We almost gave your neighbors a real show. If I hadn't strained my back..."

Brit teased. "I don't neck with old men, especially in broad daylight." It felt wonderful to feel good. Sam did look odd. She sobered. "But I will let you in for a drink."

The pained expression returned to Sam's face.

"What's wrong? Does you back still hurt? Sam? Sam?"

"Not this time." He rubbed his neck. His belly hurt and he felt nauseous. Not those damned premonitions, again. Likely something he ate. Brit's attacker was in jail. How could she still be in danger?

"How about I check the place for you, just for good measure. I won't stay long."

"But you've installed all those state-of-the-art security measures and the attacker is put away in jail. And I've got my guard monster."

"Humor me, please." Sam looked determined enough to keep her in the truck if she didn't humor him.

"Fine. We'll do it your way." She leaned over the seat to shake her dog. "Wake up, Monster. We're home again. Brit called as Sam got out of the driver's side of the truck.

Brit unlocked her door and punched in her security code.

"You're not safe, bitch! You will die." Brit heard announced from her now unnecessary answering machine.

Chapter Seven

Not again! Would she ever be free of whoever wanted her dead? "Why, why, why?" Brit clutched her temples, paced from the door to the answering machine. Monster glued himself to her side, when he wasn't running to the back door, scratching and whining.

"Okay, Monster, we'll come with you in a few minutes. Calm down, boy." Brit patted her dog. "Stay."

"Honey, your attacker is probably a hit man. Whoever hired him isn't likely to give up just because he's out of commission. They can hire someone else." Clasping her shoulders, Sam stopped her frantic movement. "We need to check your messages. We need to call the police. Then you and I need to figure what threat you could possibly be to anyone."

She slowed her movements. "I can check my voicemail."

"Listening to the machine might be easier for both for us."

"Right. Rewind the machine and let it play all the way through. No, wait, let me get a glass of iced tea." Her glass shook as she dropped ice into it. "I'd prefer a shot of something stronger, but I need a clear head." She grabbed the plastic pitcher from the refrigerator. "Want anything?"

"You're right about the clear head. Tea for me, too," Sam called after Brit.

"Fresh water for you, baby," she said while she filled Monster's bowl with tap water. She hadn't left food or water out since the last attack. He paced between his bowl and the back door, whining. "I know. Drink your water. We'll check outside soon." She'd let him out after they'd gone through her messages. When she could stall no longer, she went to join Sam in her living room.

Fortified with glasses of iced tea, Brit and Sam stood beside the answering machine. He punched the play button and put an arm around her.

One hang-up. Dial tone.

Brit let out a pent-up breath.

One sales call. Dial tone.

Brit took a long swallow of tea.

One credit card protection offer. Dial tone.

Sam smiled and squeezed her shoulders gently.

An angry voice, she recognized too well. "Think you're safe, don't you? Well, you're not. It's time." Dial tone.

Monster actually growled at the voice.

Brit held her breath so long she nearly fainted. "Oh, Sam. Now what?"

Hang-up call. Dial tone.

Monster licked Brit's hand. She absentmindedly stroked his head.

"Check your back porch." A gruff voice. Dial tone.

"Wait," Sam warned. "we don't want to disturb any evidence. The cops should be here anytime now." Sam pulled Brit into his arms and held her, stroking her back. "We're in this together. Drew is checking things in Atlanta. He knows how to access all kinds of computer files. I don't think this a local problem."

"What are you saying?" Brit pulled back to look into Sam's eyes.

"Have you ever witnessed a crime or testified against anyone?" Sam asked.

"No. Sam, I can't possibly be a threat to anyone. I don't *know* anything about anyone."

"Drew suggested the killer may be connected with one of your husband's cases."

"What?" Brit turned at the sound of the doorbell. "Let's let the police in."

"Check, first," Sam reminded.

"Yes, Sam, I did," Brit called as she opened the door. "Officer Briggs," she said, letting her favorite policemen in. "So good to see you, again."

"Mr. Samuels, you must spend a lot of time here."

"Someone has to look out for Mrs. Roberts," Sam responded to the implication.

"I'd like to hear the answering machine tapes. Mr. Samuels said there were more threats?"

Brit cringed as the messages were replayed. Her policemen made notes, commenting occasionally. "Better check the porch," he said. "I'll go around from the front and check things out."

"Why not just go through the back door?" Brit asked.

"It could be a trick. The door may be booby-trapped," Briggs answered.

Brit hadn't considered that possibility. Good thing Sam hadn't let her go out. Good thing she didn't let Monster out.

"Holy Sh—!" a voice crackled from the small radio unit Officer Briggs pulled from his coat pocket.

"What is it?" Briggs asked.

"Sick! We need the camera and extra help. Don't let Mrs. Roberts out."

"Stay here," Officer Briggs ordered. "Keep her inside." He started to open the door. "What is the code?"

Sam reached around and punched the numbers.

Opening the door let in a stench. Briggs let himself out. Sam peered out the window beside the back door. "Oh, shit!"

The porch was covered with garbage. A dead cat hung above the steps. The paper tied around its neck glared white in the afternoon sun. As soon as these small-town jokers were gone he'd call Drew. Then he'd arrange for his security to install perimeter cameras and wiring to watch her and her house.

"Teach, can you get me your camera?"

Brit tried to see around Sam. He wouldn't allow it.

"Please, wait 'til the cops finish their work, then I'll let you see."

117

Looking through the digital camera lens, he described what was happening, trying to soften the shock. Monster whined and paced. He was as anxious to see what was happening as Brit was.

Within an hour Detective Briggs came inside to assure Brit and Sam that most of the mess was bagged as evidence and taken to the station.

"Are you sure you don't know who would have a grudge against you? Maybe someone made a threat against your husband and is taking it out on you."

"Not that I know of," Brit answered.

"There was a note. It was more of the same. This time Mr. Samuels was mentioned. We'll send someone to check your home, sir, if you want to go with me.

"Thanks, but I don't want to leave Mrs. Roberts alone," Sam protested. "Let me check my messages." After listening to his messages from his cell phone Sam shook his head. "None so far."

"What about Sean?" Brit asked. "Is he in danger?

"Nah, he's spending the weekend at the ranch. He has plenty of company and protection."

Officer Briggs took the tape from her answering machine and placed in one of the unending supply of zippered plastic bags he labeled. All but one man left to check out Sam's house. A new team arrived to bug her house and phones.

They had barely replaced the old tape when the phone rang again. The new tape-recorded a laughing tormenter. Caller ID showed that the caller was too shrewd to use home phones or the same pay phones. *Unavailable.* She hated that one.

Sam placed gentle hands on Brit's shoulders. His warm fingers stroked reassuringly through her blouse. His eyes were so green she felt she would drown in them. His look was so intimate she almost forgot the police had invaded her home to do their work. What the hell?

"Teach, while you still have company I'm going home to pack my overnight bag. You and I are going to spend the night in a hotel. I need to get you away from all this and the officers have more work to do here."

She couldn't argue with Sam's idea.

***

Douglas would have laughed if he'd been anywhere but in jail. It had cost him a small fortune to arrange the phone calls to the teacher. It was amazing how easy it was to get to phones in jail. Using a calling card purchased by another inmate's mother should screw up the caller ID thing. Arranging the trashing of her yard had been a stroke of genius. The men he'd called to get that job done owed him big favors. According to the digital images they'd sent him they were just about even.

He'd hated that his employers and their lawyers hadn't been able to get him out on bail. The judge hadn't been amenable since he'd been as good as caught in the act. At least he had an alibi for this last little harassment of the teacher. The guards carried big sticks and stun guns. But they were also dumb enough to let him make his calls in private.

He'd spread around a few bucks and gotten the favors he needed. He'd even made calls from the infirmary. Now all he had to do was find a way out of this dump. When he made it out of here he'd go for the teacher and kill her, slowly, painfully. He'd make her watch him kill the man and the blonde friend first.

***

Sam returned to Brit's house and found her sitting on her sofa with her canine protector. When she rose to greet him he took her into his arms and made a suggestion. "I've called my brother to book us into a hotel on the way to Atlanta." He kissed her temples gently. "We can sneak out now."

"Yes. I don't think I could sleep here tonight," she murmured. "Let's go away, anywhere."

Sam helped her pack a small bag for her and one for Monster. He put their stuff in his truck and drove to a large hotel forty miles away.

Brit watched Sam handle the truck like a part of himself. Attempts at conversation fell short. What would they have discussed? Her thoughts were not to be said aloud. She wanted to be held by this strong man. She wanted to feel wanted and alive. She wanted to forget she was in danger. She needed Sam.

The bench seat of his truck beat bucket seats, but the seat belts were confining. What the hell difference did seat belts make when someone was trying to kill her? Without the constraints Brit would've been all over Sam. She'd have probably caused an accident. She was adult and could wait a few minutes more. Maybe.

Registering as a couple, using phony names, and paying cash at the multi-storied hotel felt illicit. They'd stopped at a gas station to call their parents to let them know not to call home that night. Sam's mobile number or Brit's would let them be reached in case of emergency. A stop at a restaurant had been wasted, since neither had any appetite for food. The picnic food was only one reason. Take out boxes would insure Monster's supper.

She remembered little about the hotel lobby, but it seemed tastefully furnished. Drew must have had great influence to get the hotel management to allow Monster to stay with them.

The suite was more than two people needed. Monster settled down on the lush beige carpet in one bedroom. Sam placed their baggage in the large bedroom. Brit stood at the door watching him.

"Sam." Her voice was thin.

Instantly he was at her side, taking her face in his hands. Her arms circled his waist, her hands pressed into his back. She loved his strong gentle hands. His touch warmed her clear down to her feet. His moist breath tickled her skin. His lips touched her cheeks, her eyelids, her nose.

When she thought she could not wait another second, he touched his moist lips to her own in a chaste kiss. With parted lips he kissed her again, slanting his mouth, licking and tasting. When one hand moved to touch her breast she felt it swell to fill his palm. Her hunger blossomed with a vengeance.

She was starved for his taste. Parting her lips, she slipped her tongue inside his mouth. With a moan he moved both hands to her bottom, pressing her against him. She wanted to feel his touch all over her body. She wanted all he could offer now!

Sam loved the feel of Brit in his arms. In his dreams he'd made love to her in many ways. Just seeing her aroused him, but holding her was so sweet his chest hurt with the need to protect.

As much as he needed to take charge, he sensed he should let her take the lead. It would break his heart if anything he did made her remember her horrible ordeal. Could a wrong move make her feel pressured? Would he sense any hesitation or fear soon enough to avoid damaging her trust?

He'd remained celibate by choice for the last few years. Now he wanted this woman who might be forever haunted by violence. God, he hoped he would do the right thing.

She trembled in his arms. "Brit," he whispered. "Scared?"

Her cheek brushed against his chest. Her moist lips brushed his throat in a caress. "No," He felt her breath against his skin. "not as long as you hold me."

Sam's groin tightened so hard he hurt when he felt her hands move gently to unbutton the top button of his shirt. Her hot lips branded his chest then his neck then his chin. His arousal grew. His heart ached. The fragrance of her hair was fresh and subtle and innocent.

"Make love to me, Sam."

"Not so fast, Teach." Sam touched his lips to her forehead. "Take it easy, Love."

"But I need you. I need for you to make love to me."

"We have all night."

Brit shivered again. "But what if I can't? If I wait too long, I might lose my nerve. What if I can't, what if I panic?" What if I disappoint you?"

"We'll take things slow and easy. If you need to stop, we'll stop," Sam's voice rasped. "So, sweetheart, take charge.

Make love to me. Take me, take me now!" He flung his arms wide and grinned. "I'm all yours."

Brit chuckled against his chest. When she looked up at him he nearly drowned in her eyes. At least she was smiling at his antics. "You got it, Bud, I'll take you to heights you've never been before."

She kissed his throat again then unbuttoned another button. With each button she released, Sam felt his control slipping. Each wet kiss tested his endurance. His heart wanted to beat itself from his chest. Her hot tongue on his nipples was almost too much for him to bear without grabbing her

He needed for her to slow down. He needed her to speed up. He didn't know what he needed except that he needed her. Tunneling his hands through her silky hair he tilted her face up. Lowering his head, he kissed her slowly, gently, thoroughly.

Brit needed this man. Sam was so different from Tommy. Was she disloyal to want this man so much? Surely not! She needed to feel alive and clean. She needed to enjoy a normal sexual experience with someone who cared. She needed to know she could stop whenever she wanted to.

Kissing Sam was wonderful. He made her feel cherished. He made her feel he needed her as much as she needed him. He was handsome, manly, sexy as all get out, gentle, in control, and caring. *If Sam can't help me through this, no man can. I can do this. I can. I must.*

Sliding her hands inside Sam's shirt, Brit absorbed the rough texture of springy chest hair between her fingers, against her palms. She gasped into his mouth when he picked her up and moved to a couch. Without breaking the kiss Sam seated them, with her in his lap.

Kissing Sam, nipping at his lips, Brit tried to stoke his passion. She wanted him to make love to her, but he held back. Why was he waiting? If he would just make love to her she would know she wasn't scarred for life.

Changing positions, she became more aggressive. She straddled his legs and faced him. "Too many clothes." She yanked his shirt from his jeans. Gliding her hands up his chest and over his shoulders, she exposed his sculpted torso.

Gripping the bottom of her blouse she yanked it over her head. Heat and moisture spread through her loins pressed against his thighs by the stretching move. Sam's eyes glittered. She knew she was tempting him. His heat burned through their clothes.

Emboldened, she slowly unclasped the front catch of her lacy bra, freeing her breasts to press against him.

Sam felt his control slipping more. He could hardly swallow around his dry tongue. She might just kill him.

"Come to the bed and lie with me," he pleaded. "We need to slow down, honey."

"Why? I need you now." Snaking her arms around his neck she pressed her breasts against him.

"Hang on." He rose with her. "Lock your legs around me." Making his way to the bedroom wasn't easy while she kissed his face and rubbed against him.

When Sam reached the large bed Brit leaned over to grab the satiny coverlet and toss it back. He toppled them onto the bed.

He lay on his side, facing her. He had to give her the chance she needed to stop anytime. He kept his touch gentle. Her pale skin felt smooth beneath his rough fingers. Pebbled nipples begged for more than his touch. Dipping his head, he stroked his tongue over a nipple, then its mate. She tasted so sweet. Her response was all he could have wanted and more. Her hips moved with each pull from his mouth. Her stomach muscles clinched beneath his hands. She was close, so close.

Brit clutched Sam's shoulders as he suckled. *Will a baby ever suckle there? Would it be Sam's? Too damned slow.* Tension built to an unbearable peak. When Sam's hand moved between her thighs, touching her through her jeans, she felt heat spiral to her core. Her world flashed then went dark. She was floating and she wanted him with her. Before she could act on her need he pushed her over the edge.

The dear man hadn't even taken his own pleasure. If she could just rest for a few minutes she would show him real earth-shaking pleasure.

***

Brit moved her cheek to ease the tickle. Moonlight slipped through the curtain of the hotel room to paint the naked chest beneath her face. Sam's scent triggered her memory. What he had done for her last night had been wonderful, selfless. She owed him. His slow breathing moved his chest gently.

Had she fallen asleep atop the man or had she moved in her sleep? Shifting slowly to avoid waking Sam, Brit slid a naked leg along his hairy one. Even in sleep he reacted to her. She didn't remember removing her jeans, hadn't expected to fall asleep.

What I could do to him while he sleeps. She slid her hand down his taunt stomach. Moving the sheets, she enjoyed the feel of him beneath her hands. From the indentations where his legs joined his torso she moved down muscled thighs.

Spying his morning arousal, she wondered at what she'd missed by falling asleep. Not this time. Her chest tightened when she moved down to his bulging calves and back up toward his growing hard-on. Thoughts about what she wanted to do to this man were interrupted by a deep rumbling from his chest.

Working her way around his arousal she smoothed her way back up a firm, flat abdomen, following the line of dark, curling hair as it fanned out to cover his nipples.

"Oh, God." Sam's voice was hoarse.

When Sam's mouth was in sight she moved to straddle his waist and kissed his beard-stubbled face. When he would have claimed her lips she bypassed to kiss each cheek, the corners of his mouth. When her tongue made contact with the seam of Sam's lips he opened and captured her questing mouth with a hunger to match her own.

Sam wasn't sure he could wait for Brit to join their bodies, but he'd promised himself he would, even if it killed him, which it might. His body was so awake he feared he'd explode too soon. Heaven poised over his arousal.

With a slow, deliberate move she sheathed him inside her. His moan escaped into her mouth. She was so hot and wet he knew how much she wanted him, needed him. Her muscles clinched around him, setting him on fire. His hips became alive. Her body moved above him, fluid and lush. At the moment he was certain his head would fly off, Brit shuddered above him.

"Sam, oh, Sam," she cried.

"Yes!" was all he could hiss as he filled her, losing control and his sanity. She'd literally ridden him to completion, a first for him.

There was no doubt the woman hadn't been ruined by her bad experience, unless she'd always need to be on top. Maybe he could learn to live with such a hardship. "Take me, take me, now," would become his favorite words. Her contented sigh matched his feelings of satisfaction, for a while at least. Drifting back to sleep Sam wondered if he could make love to her next time.

***

Jail. Douglas wanted to let loose, but he couldn't allow that. He had to stay in control to be safe.

His mother would probably laugh and say she'd told him he'd end up this way. She threatened him with beatings when he was young and with an eternity in Hell when he'd become too big to hit. Well, age and nature had put her in a mental hell, and he'd helped by putting her away in a cheap nursing home.

He'd used the pay phone twice to call the teacher bitch. Either she wasn't answering her phone, or she'd taken off. She was probably with the interfering daddy! She should be scared shitless by now. She should be hiding from the world.

For the first time he had failed not once but twice. He had to get out of this dump, surrounded by losers. He'd go crazy locked up for much longer. He had a reputation to save.

So far he'd been able to fend off the jail animals so horny they'd screw anything or anyone. A couple of the guards looked bad enough to do just about anything. There was one stupid bastard who'd left him alone with a telephone in the clinic but he'd looked like he expected something personal in return. The suggestion that he had something contagious had made the guard willing to accept money instead.

The cigarettes he'd bought with money from his lawyer had been a good investment. Some of these jerks would sell their souls for a smoke. Nasty habit!

He nearly gagged at the odor of the food tray. He shoved it to the floor. Damn! The food in this hellhole was pig-swill and the place was a dump.

Pacing the perimeter of his damned cell wasn't helping, but he'd managed to convince the other men around him he was a loony. Anger, frustration, and hate were his companions, and they made it difficult to think straight enough to plan his escape. He had to get out of here. He had work to do!

***

Morning came all too soon. Brit awoke slowly. Sam's arms and body enfolded her. His arm around her waist was heavy. His hand on her breast was hot and brought back memories of wonderful, hot sex. A hairy leg covered hers, trapping her with its weight and security. A hot chest blanketed her back and a hot hard appendage pushed against her bottom.

Brit ached in places she had forgotten she had. It was a glorious morning. If she lived to be one hundred she'd remember the first time she'd made love with Sam Samuels.

Staying right where she was appealed to her until she felt a twitch against her derriere and a hand moving on her breast. Her whole body tingled. Her toenails tingled. Her hair even tingled. Turning in Sam's arms she looked into his eyes.

His cheeks were dark stubbled. He would have looked formidable, but a lock of black hair hung over his forehead, obscuring part of an eye. So endearing, so sexy. Turning her face to nuzzle his neck, she inhaled his musky scent. It was hard to tell where his scent ended and hers began, but the effect was as overwhelming as feeling his chest against her breasts, his legs rubbing against hers, his erection begging for attention. It definitely had her attention now.

Brit reached down to caress its satiny length. Within moments she'd invited Sam inside her body and the glorious morning was off to a spectacular beginning, one of the most beautiful of her life.

***

While Brit showered Sam called room service for breakfast for four. Monster had demanded Sam's attention and was happy since Sam had taken him outside to examine the trees behind the hotel. The big baby was hungry.

Sam watched Brit feed Monster from her plate after he'd finished his own, both of them. "Aren't you a good monster?" She looked so vulnerable with her big dog.

The time had come for Sam to take Brit and Monster home. He planned to have his men over to recheck her security, as well as his and his parents'. Sean would be on a plane to meet his mother within two days. He'd resist leaving if he realized his teacher was in such danger. Sean would enjoy the Spring break with his mother and grandparents in Hawaii. At least Sam wouldn't have to worry about the threat where his son was concerned.

Within an hour Sam, Brit, and Monster paused outside her front door. Her hand shook so much when she retrieved the key from her purse Sam took it and unlocked the door. He opened it slowly and peered into the living room. The police had assured him they'd made a thorough sweep of the inside and outside of her house. The telephone was bugged and a man was assigned to watch the house.

Monster whined and pushed his way past Sam. No frantic barking warned that danger lurked. No pain in Sam's gut, no nausea. Brit peered around him.

The living room seemed normal. Walking toward the kitchen she wondered what she would find in her back yard. Looking from the kitchen window she saw normalcy, no dead animals and no trash.

"Did you call Drew?" Brit asked.

"While you showered."

"And?"

127

They moved back toward the living room and the answering machine. Brit prayed there wouldn't be another obscene message.

Sam's hand rested at the small of her back.

"My gut says we're not done yet."

Monster trotted from the kitchen, carrying his food bowl.

***

Sam sat in Sean's car, waiting for him to come out of school. He'd managed his schedule to allow him to spend a lot of time watching out for the teacher. The trashing of her yard emphasized the danger she still faced.

The sight in the school parking lot Wednesday afternoon at three fifteen caught Sam's curiosity as he waited for Sean.

He was feeling whimsical, strangely enough. He was reminded of some kids tales and some very bad horror movies. Three jean-clad backsides leaning on the front and one side of the faded, brownish Mustang seemed to belong to topless bodies, Mustang leftovers. Sam couldn't believe he was thinking something so weird. Brit would probably think it amusing. The monster car had its mouth open as if to take another bite of the three scrawny, teenage, male butts. A fourth, more padded and feminine fanny looked like a tasty morsel for the car, or a hungry man. Now there was a sight to provoke his fantasies.

Short legs were attached to tiny feet in red, high-heeled shoes and were very visible in sheer, red hose. The legs strained as the heels were suspended in air. One knee bent, bringing a foot in the air, almost touched her backside while its owner worked to make up for lack of height. Was there anything about this woman that didn't turn him on?

Sam's eyes followed the movement of leg upward to see a red skirt covering the top of shapely legs, none too soon. The skirt had scooted up with movement, allowing a tantalizing view of upper leg and lower thigh. The red fanny moved from the car, treating the staring man to the sight of a red sweater scooted up to bare a pale midriff. Sam hoped the teens weren't looking at the display of flesh, however innocently exposed.

Brit was wiping her hands on a rag and instructing her young audience. "Stand back while I try to crank this old girl."

She pulled the sweater down and hiked the skirt up as she placed her backside on the bucket seat and then swung her short legs under the steering wheel. Leaning forward, she placed a cushion behind her back, then straightened to insert the key in the ignition.

The youths stood with their attention under the hood, awaiting the sound of the engine coming to life.

His perusal traveled from the sexy, dainty slipper, up the leg, then continued to the bent knee, and to the upper legs, of which the skirt hid only a short length of slim thigh. Sam imagined running his hands over her thighs, stretching the skirt tight against her upper legs and hips.

A cheer rose when the engine whined then roared to life, snatching Sam's attention. His sweaty palms and dry throat were not caused by fear the car wouldn't start, but by thoughts of what he wanted to start.

"Hey, Dad! Didja see that! The guys couldn't believe a lady teacher could show 'em about cars. Billy's gonna ask her to see if she can start his '68 Mustang. Dad? You asleep? You got my new tires!"

"Sorry. I was thinking. Didn't you hear wheels turning? It takes a lot out of us geezers to concentrate," Sam apologized. *You don't know the half of it, my boy. Thank goodness you don't! Boys probably think their fathers don't get horny.*

"After school Miz Roberts' car wouldn't start. She got out and raised her hood. I didn't know a woman would know what to do. Well, Billy, Jon, and I headed over to help. By the time we got to her, she was taking the breather cover off and checking the butterfly."

"She did that herself?"

"Yeah, she sure did. When that didn't work she put a screwdriver to hold it open and she started the thing. We put the cover back on for her and screwed it down so she could go home. Wait 'til I tell Angela. She won't believe it! Dad! Are you listening?"

"Yes, son, I'm impressed." *To think I used possible car trouble as an excuse to follow her home. Well, she had trouble, but she fixed it herself.*

"Could we ·go home, Dad? I'm hungry and I got homework to do. You can daydream at home."

Chapter Eight

Brit was breathless when she grabbed the phone. Caller ID showed Sam's mobile phone number.

"Where were you, woman?" Sam's voice exploded through the phone. "It's after seven and starting to get dark."

"What?"

"I called and the machine took my message," he complained.

"Bad answering machine. I'll have to fire it," Brit laughed. Monster licked her hand.

"No, I mean, it's not self-defense night or group counseling night and you hadn't mentioned plans to go anywhere or I would have come to take you."

"Calm down, bodyguard." Brit rubbed the big dog's head. "Even though we had the most wonderful sex I've ever experienced you don't have to know my every move."

"Sorry."

"I know. Monster took me for a walk. He's been so good and I really needed to walk some kinks out. I also took five minutes to water my lawn and flowers. So shoot me."

"Don't even joke about it. Someone wants to do bad things to you. I worry about you. Why don't you let me move into your guestroom as soon as Sean leaves? I promise to behave."

"In your dreams, pal." Brit laughed, holding the receiver between her shoulder and chin. She washed her hands then opened the freezer. "Sam, I'm fine." Monster nudged her as she dropped ice into her glass. She glanced out the window, hiding behind the curtain, as she often did. Strange noises made her jump more than was normal for her. Something she'd never admit to Sam.

"What about staying with my folks. At least there would be two men to guard you when I can't."

"Oh, right, we can put your folks at risk, too. I don't think so."

"At least let me take you to dinner."

"Sam, I told you this would be a busy week." She poured Coke Zero over the ice in her glass "I don't have time to go out or have company. I have papers to grade. We let Sean leave early, but Spring Break doesn't start for me for another couple of days."

"Come on, Hon, you have to eat. I'll just bring over take-out and leave as soon as we have eaten," he promised.

"I'll just have a sandwich and keep working. I don't have time for more," Brit muttered to the dial tone. *The man hung up on me.* "I won't let him in!" She took a swallow of Coke Zero.

Thirty minutes later Brit sat on the floor in her living room, surrounded by stacks of folders. There was too much to do and too little time. Monster lay on the carpet with his chin on a stack of reports. Thankfully she hadn't heard from the stalker lately. No nasty notes, no garbage on her porch or in her yard and no threatening phone message. She had been careful to let her machine screen her calls before she answered them.

So far her attacker hadn't graduated to using her email yet. How long would it take for him to start that? Could he get her online address at home or at school?

Sam's visits to school didn't help her sanity any more than his nightly phone calls did. Even after he was gone his image was not. The teachers' lounge buzzed every time he or his offerings appeared at school. The roses he had delivered at school caused a stir. A handsome man like Sam visiting her on campus and bringing candy caused an even bigger stir. She knew he was just watching out for her, making sure she was safe. Memories of their time together kept her mind in turmoil and her hormones near the surface. She needed some measure of control over her life.

Monster raised his chin off the reports then bounded toward the front door. "Damn!" Brit said as the doorbell rang. "I'll ignore him. I told him not to come. Now he's banging on the front door." She lifted folders from her lap and scrambled to her feet.

"Ohhh!" she moaned as her stiff muscles resisted her attempts to make them move smoothly. She'd been sitting on the floor too long. "I'll shoot him!"

A peek through the peephole told her what she already suspected. Opening her front door, she faced the long body leaning against the doorframe. The lazy grin on his face would've warmed Brit's heart if it hadn't already stirred her blood. *God, whatever is in those bags smells better than any sandwich I could make. The man just doesn't play fair.*

Monster was doing a begging doggy act, welcoming Sam with generous slurps.

Sam waved one sack in front of her nose and lifting it just below his eye level. He extracted a ham bone from another sack and tossed it toward the kitchen. Monster caught it in mid-air. Opening the food bag, Sam peeked inside then gave an appreciative whiff. "Well, if you're not hungry, maybe I should take this delicious smelling food home. I could save or throw away whatever I can't eat."

"You don't need to go that far," Brit said reluctantly. "All right, we can eat in the kitchen, but you promised to eat and leave, and I plan to hold you to your word."

Grinning, Sam followed "the warrior teacher" as she marched from the room. Her ponytail swished with the determination of a soldier while the fanny in her gray sweats swayed in a manner too feminine to fool Sam. She was the first woman who could turn his body hard and his mind to mush without even trying, even in a baggy sweat suit and glasses.

Brit turned and almost got a nose full of paper bag.

"They gave me utensils at the restaurant. I knew you were too busy to wash dishes. Sit while I get everything ready."

It was difficult to keep from smiling at him, especially when her growling stomach announced how hungry she was. She opened the refrigerator and withdrew two Cokes.

"Cokes?" he asked as they sat down to the feast in boxes he had spread out on her table.

"Caffeine and sugar to keep me awake." She shrugged.

Sam sat in the chair beside her and opened the container of Hot and Sour Soup. Stopping her hand from reaching for a spoon, Sam dipped the spoon he held and filled it with the delicacy before heading it toward Brit's mouth. She opened her mouth to taste. Though neither spoke, tension began to build as he watched her lips caress the spoon. Her tongue darted out to lick a stray drop and met Sam's.

The jolt Sam felt at the sensual contact made him swallow, almost convulsively, as his eyes met hers. The deep amethyst he saw pooled there told him she had felt the same desire he had. As he opened his mouth her lips parted to welcome his kiss.

"Good soup!" she commented when he released her lips.

"Best I ever tasted!" Sam drawled, one thick dark eyebrow arched wickedly. "I haven't tasted the soup by itself."

"You should try it," she suggested. "The soup, you idiot." Brit laughed as Sam waggled both brows. Grabbing an egg roll she bit off a hunk and began to chew. She supposed it was good but could only think of trying to get the exasperating man to concentrate on food instead of sex. She had to make herself think of something besides seduction.

Pleased he had pulled Brit from her angry mood he let up. He really was hungry and knew she was, since her stomach had announced the fact only moments earlier. "Have some cashew chicken and rice." Watching Brit eat was making Sam think of other things. His promise was hard to keep, but he really intended to let her work in a while. How could eating egg rolls look so sexy?

Brit had never thought eating could be this sensual, but she thought back to the picnic and what she had wanted to do with the chocolate cake. She remembered several suggestions Sam had made earlier about delicious things they could do for dessert.

People could do strange things with food! The growing warmth between her legs was no help. Squirming didn't help, either, especially when she looked up to the devilish eyes studying her. The blush warming her face had to be a dead give-away. Sam must realize what he was doing to her libido.

"Sam, were you really hungry when you ordered all this food or were you planning to feed an army?" Brit asked, leaning back in her chair. Her eyes must be bulging she was so full.

The hand that unconsciously rubbed her tummy did not go unnoticed. Oh, dear, green eyes stared at that area. Why did I do that? Why do I care that he's staring at my stomach? He can't be hungry after all he ate, not even for sex. I know I don't have the energy for that kind of activity. Liar! *Go home Sam! Please!*

"You must've been hungry, Teach. You ate your share. Of course we'll probably be hungry again in a couple of hours."

"Thanks for supper, Sam," she said. "Now you really must go so I can get back to work. I'll be up for most of the night finishing these papers." Grabbing his arm with both hands she tried to steer him toward the hall. He followed her into the dimly lit hall only to stop suddenly and pull her into his arms. His sudden move caught her off balance and gave him an edge. Her mouth opened in surprise and Sam moved right in.

Even if he had intended to ravish her in the hall, the feel of his muscular arm beneath her hand was torture after the meal they had spent watching each other. His hands seemed hungry for the feel of her. They were touching to their fill. His mouth devoured as his tongue ravished her mouth.

Brit had really meant to push him away, but somewhere inside a chemical reaction closed off the passages needed for her body to respond to the messages from her brain. It had to be a chemical reaction or a lack of oxygen. Her body refused to listen and her hands explored as her body clung to the wall of heated flesh and bone and hard muscle.

The loud ringing of her phone finally made itself heard. Monster pushed at Brit and Sam. He ran to the phone then back to Brit. She was still slowed by a cloud of desire. Breathing so hard she had trouble answering.

"Hello," Brit was barely lucid. "Julie?"

Julie's voice was strained. "Is something wrong? I'm coming over right now!"

"No, nothing's wrong."

"Well, you sound funny." Julie knew her too well.

"I was getting something from my car. I ran in from the garage when I heard the phone." Watching the way Sam leaned back against the wall was a distraction. He raised his eyebrows and batted long, thick, black eyelashes as he mimicked.

"I was wondering if I left my red sandals at your house. I can't find them here."

Brit wanted to smack Sam when he held a hand to his ear while gesturing with the other hand. "Your red shoes? I don't know. I'll look and bring 'em with me tomorrow if I find them."

"You'll let me know if they aren't there?"

"Yes, yes, I will."

"You'd let me know if something were wrong, wouldn't you?"

"Sure thing, Pal. Bye."

Brit's eyes still felt heavy, like a woman ready to make love, but her resolve had returned. The pesky man grinned when she tried to swat him. He took both of her small hands into his large callused ones. He turned both palms up and placed a kiss in each. When he began to nibble on a finger she tried to free her hands.

"I know. I'm sorry, sweetheart. I don't know what came over me. My horny body took over. Couldn't help myself. You shouldn't be such a sexy eater. Your tongue kept inviting me to taste, and my hormones egged me on."

Putting both hands in the air with palms toward Brit, Sam signaled surrender. "I'll go peaceably, officer, but I do plead guilty of wanting to stay." Sam had backed to the door and placed his hand on the knob.

Brit held her mouth straight and used her best teacher frown to show him she meant business. She just hoped it worked as well on Sam as it did on her students. If it didn't she was in trouble. Her resistance was definitely low.

"Bye, Sam," she said as she pushed him out the door. "Thanks for supper and *dessert*. Monster, tell the nice man bye."

She leaned against the doorframe, watching him walk backwards to his car. Her arms were crossed as she hugged herself to keep from feeling the loss of his warmth. It didn't help much, but she let him go and turned back into her house to watch his car pull away. From inside the screen door she watched the red glow from his tail lights disappear.

She locked the door and punched the security code. Back inside she returned to her place on the floor where she had left the papers. *Now, if I can get my mind back on my work.*
***

Douglas had a plan. He'd complained about stomach pains all day. He just had to convince the guards and the doctors in the infirmary he was sick and helpless. He'd need help to get away, but he could do it. He'd thought about enlisting the help of one of the inmates, but they were all too stupid. Any one of them would screw up and get them caught.

The men who'd paid him to kill the teacher were not pleased with him. It didn't matter that this was his first problem hit. They were in too much trouble themselves. He'd had a visitor today. His employer had threatened to hire another killer to off the teacher. That wasn't good. That killer would also try to kill him, as a loose end.

Soon they'd begin to sound like his bitch of a mother.

"You're just too stupid, Douglas," his mother had said so often. "You're just like your stupid father."

No, he wasn't like his father. Or at least he wasn't like the man his mother had said was his father. She probably didn't even know who his father was. The man who'd deserted him had been weak and stupid and had left them. He shoulda planted his fists in her loud, lying, filthy mouth.

Heart pounding, Douglas leaned over the open toilet in his cell and wretched and cried, which he never did!

137

***

The week before Spring Break was as hectic as Brit and Julie had feared. The students acted just as anxious to get away as the teachers were for them to go. They'd planned activities to keep order, but each day was tiring, like trying to hold the water in a dam with one finger to plug two holes.

The test on Tuesday kept her students quiet for a while. The play on Wednesday was a Godsend. Thursday she returned book reports and quizzes and explained the correct answers, which kept the attention of the classes only because the material was guaranteed to be on the exam. By the end of Thursday Brit felt like she had been rolled over by a bulldozer. She grabbed her purse to head to the teacher's lounge to commiserate with her fellow suffers.

***

Thursday evening Sam gripped his phone so hard his fingers ached. "Okay, Drew, I'll calm down." Sam took a deep breath then let it out slowly, but he still wanted to tear someone apart. "Look, Bud, I can't spring something like this on her over the phone. I'll pick her up after school is out tomorrow. We'll have a nice dinner out. Then I'll sit down with her and tell her what you and I discussed. If she's upset about this as I am we'll need to sort things out calmly."

Sam finally stopped pacing and sat back in his desk chair. He let out a long slow sigh. "I'll have the next ten days to find out what she knows."

"Maybe she has information she doesn't know she has." Drew had always been the voice of reason, even as a kid.

"Yeah, I'll ask her if she still has any personal notes of her husband's packed away."

"If she has anything, and I do mean anything, let me know immediately, Sam. Don't tell anyone else, even the local law."

"I'll have her call you."

"Anytime, day or night."

"Thanks little brother, I owe you one." Sam sat staring from his office window. He didn't expect to sleep well tonight.

He'd thought seeing Sean and Adrienne off to Hawaii for a whole week for spring break would make him feel better. He and Brit needed some time when he didn't have to worry about sending the wrong messages to his son.

At least Sean would be having a good time instead of worrying about his teacher and getting in the way trying to help. On the drive to Atlanta to Hartsfield Airport Sean had been beside himself with excitement. Adrienne had booked them first class tickets. Sean had taken his exams early so he could leave two days before the break began officially.

Sean and Adrienne had promised to let him know when they arrived in Honolulu and then at her parents' house.

Should he worry about his son's safety when he was so far away? Probably, since no one knew much about the people who wanted Brit dead. He and Sean had seen the attacker. Though he was in jail, God only knew about the scope of his employers' influence

***

Friday afternoon had finally set students and teachers free of school and each other for a whole week. Brit didn't think she could have stood one more day of pressure.

"Let's go, Brit," Julie urged. "I'm ready to hit the road and *blow this burg!* You have everything out of your car. It'll be fine in the garage 'til you get back. Monster's in my back seat on his bed and ready for a ride. Mom's expecting me for supper and yours will be waiting at the door for you."

Closing the door of her Mustang, Brit locked it and patted it good-bye. Opening the door of Julie's red T-Bird, she slid into the seat, trying to act excited. "Well, what're you waiting for? Let's go."

Julie backed from Brit's drive into the street.

"Well, girl, what did Sam have to say when you told him you were coming home with me this week? Bet he was disappointed you'd be gone while he is <u>baching it</u>, huh?"

"I didn't tell him." Brit shrugged.

"Bri-i-t, I can't believe you did that. Sam was so excited about having some time alone with you. The poor man has been driving everyone crazy and you didn't even have the guts to be truthful with him."

"I know! I'm chicken. Part of me says he's just another man and I can enjoy his company, but the other part is afraid he'll charm me into a relationship I can't handle. I dream about him. I think about him when I'm awake. He's too potent. If they could bottle his *essence of virile male*, a fortune could be made. Wimpy men wouldn't have to be alone."

"Why don't you relax and let things take their course? Let it happen if it's going to. You can't fight fate, you know."

"I don't believe in fate. Besides, even if I did I would not stand in front of a speeding car and tempt fate to step in. I don't believe you'd give in to fate, even if you knew tomorrow was to be your day to go. You'd fight it all the way, and I am fighting for my life!"

"Brit, you ninny, we're not talking about death, or a fate worse than death. We're talking about being loved by a wonderful man, a chance at lifelong happiness, at the most, or at the least, an incredible affair with a sexy man. How can you lose?"

"You don't understand. I had a *'til death do us part* love, and death did us part. I don't think I can take another one. Besides, Sam's so good with kids. What if he wants marriage and more family?"

"Don't jump to conclusions. He has Sean. What if the problem was with Tommy? What if you can have children?"

"What if I can't!"

"You can't hide from life just because the worst could happen. You could miss the best that could happen."

"Could we please talk about something else. I slipped off to get away from that man. I need breathing room." Brit turned so she could watch her friend's expression. She neglected to mention that she'd had another threatening call this morning and a note slipped into her house, like one straw too many. "I've been thinking."

"Terrific." Julie grinned. Brit's serious expression chased the grin away. "What is it, girl?"

"Tommy's home office and personal papers are still packed away in boxes at Mama's house. Matt packed his computer away, too. Wonder if it still works. I hadn't the heart to use it so I just kept mine." Brit took in a long breath. She held it so long her lungs hurt by the time she let it out. She hadn't come close to crying this time. Was Sam the reason?

"You *have* been thinking." Julie glanced at her a second.

"I think it's time I spent some time going through the papers. I can probably throw away a lot of stuff, but there are special things I'll want to keep. I think I'm ready to sort things out." Her eyes were pleading as she chewed her lower lip.

"You want me to help?" Julie offered.

Chapter Nine

Sam fumed. He'd called Brit from his car phone when a trip around the school parking lot hadn't revealed her car. When he called her home he got her answering machine. She hadn't answered her cell phone. What good would it do her if she didn't leave it on? Anxious, he drove to her house to wait for her. She should've been home long before now. He'd been waiting for over an hour.

"Where in the hell is that woman? She's not at school or here. Her car's still in the garage, but no one seems to be home," he muttered.

He went to his car to phone Julie's house. *Maybe the girls are together.* "Please, Lord, let them be together."

He dialed Julie's house and found himself speaking to her voicemail. He slammed his hand against the dash as he waited through the message. She hadn't said she'd be unavailable for a while.

"Didn't Brit realize I'd worry about her after the attacks and the yard mess-up?" he muttered to the phone he held.

So what if the SOB was in jail? He'd never told Brit about the fears that had kept him awake long after he was in bed every night. If Drew was right, someone had hired Douglas Drake to kill Brit. What if they hired a replacement for him? What if they decided to kill off their hired killer, the one who had failed, before he could trade information to implicate them?

The woman he loved could be in danger and he didn't know where she was. *I do love her. I really do love her.* That wasn't so hard to think, but could he say the words to her? He hadn't expected it, but he felt good. In love. Yeah.

There was no sign of Monster in the yard or peeking through a window at him. He could usually hear the dog before he even knocked on the door. He'd have to get her mother's number from his house. Damn! The alarm system light was visible from the window in her door. It was on, so he couldn't break in to check things out without going to the office for master codes to the alarm system. This time she'd remembered. *Where the hell is she?*

***

The ride down I-75 raced by. Julie put the pedal to the metal, waving at the trucks she passed. The truckers hit their horns and waved back. Free spirit Julie did some strange things She never bored Brit. Brit worried enough for both of them.

They'd only stopped once for a walk around a rest area with Monster. He covered a good portion of the back seat of Julie's car. Once his blanket and favorite toy had been placed over the seat he'd settled down.

Leaving the busy expressway had put them only fifteen minutes from New Britain, a town as picturesque as any in Georgia. It was like a town time had forgotten, a one horse town, but there were no horses on the street.

There was still a town square with a steepled, brick, three-story courthouse. The huge clock was an hour behind. Brit absentmindedly noticed the "Five and Dime" store and Stephen's, a quaint drug store, with its poster-board, handwritten list of soda fountain specials displayed on the large window.

On her mother's quiet street trees budded and tulips bloomed in every color. One hour and forty minutes after leaving Brit's house, the red T-Bird pulled up in front of a brick, two-story house. Its covered porch ran the length of the front and sides.

Ellen moved out of the large, old, porch swing and down the six wooden steps before Brit could unbend her legs and alight from Julie's car. Brit closed her eyes and savored the warmth and love in her mother's arms.

Monster nosed mother and daughter, rubbing against Ellen for his hug. Ellen bent down so she could rub the big dog's tummy when it rolled over. "Grandma has a special doggy treat for Monster. Yes, she does."

143

The big dog licked his chops as though he understood. He explored, "greeting" the trees and bushes in male dog style, making himself at home.

At the sound of Julie clearing her throat, mother and daughter pulled slowly apart. Ellen opened her arms and Julie moved into them. Julie hugged her, giving her an extra, quick, hard squeeze. "Mother Simpson, you look spiffy. Looking good."

"Julie, dear, I'd invite you in to visit, but your mother's anxious to see you. We had lunch together yesterday." She turned to Brit. "I can't believe I have you here for a whole week!"

"Thanks, Mrs. S. Well, gotta dash. Mama'll call looking for me again if I don't get on home." Julie winked at Brit, then she left with an impressive tire squeal.

The Simpson women walked side by side up the walk to the porch steps, each carrying a black, leather suitcase. Brit slung the garment bag over one arm. She'd leave with more luggage if her mother had anything to say about it. Glancing from the swing hanging from chains to the metal glider at the other end of the porch, Brit made her choice, the glider. The brightly covered cushions looked like a flower garden with splashes of color. The paint was shiny and pristine white.

Ellen nodded and confirmed what Brit figured. "Yes, Matthew repainted it last weekend. He was afraid it would rain if he waited. He hasn't forgotten his favorite oldest sister's favorite place to spend a summer evening."

The manicured yard made a welcome view from the glider. Purple and yellow Irises lined the porch. Clusters of Azaleas bloomed in bright, pink matching the glow in Ellen's cheeks. She and Brit sat moving back and forth when Brit's foot pushed against the floor to keep the bench moving. Peace and quiet here, coupled with many restless nights, lulled Brit, who was about to drift off to sleep.

"Sweetheart, why don't you go upstairs and take a nap before supper. There's time before everyone gets home." They lifted the suitcases from their resting places and headed through the screen door. Up the familiar, picture-lined staircase daughter trailed mother, who opened the white door at the far end of the hall.

Lavender curtains fluttered on a fragrant spring breeze. Everything from curtains to matching comforter and dust ruffle had been freshly laundered, mixing the fragrance of detergent and fabric softener with that of flowers. *Heaven must smell like this. especially with the smell of cinnamon and spice hanging on from the morning's baking.*

The garment bag was slipped from Brit's arm and hung in her closet before she had put her suitcase down. Funny, she'd expected the usual bitter-sweet memories of her recuperative months to be stronger, but they hung quietly in the back of her mind. Hmmm.

Same curtains and bed coverings, same furniture, same lamp and even a stack of paperback novels she had left on the bedside table. The dresser scarf matched the chest-of-drawers scarf. Very little about the room had been changed, but so much seemed different. Maybe she was different.

"Mama, the room looks fabulous. You certainly have been busy. You didn't have to go to so much trouble washing and ironing everything, though." Brit hugged her mother again. "How did you know I'd be here? I hadn't planned to come."

"A mother knows," she said. "We washed everything this morning. Your niece helped a lot. Alicia adores you. She almost didn't go to softball practice this afternoon, but she had to since the first game is tomorrow."

Ellen had begun to hang up Brit's clothes. "She's so excited she could talk of little but the game and her favorite aunt. You'll be so proud of her. You can help protect the umpire from the most enthusiastic parent in the bleachers. Matt makes enough noise for two. He out yells his father and me."

"You, Mama?"

"Yes, me. You know I get in there for my children."

"No, I mean does he really out yell you?"

"Smart aleck, I'm not that bad," Ellen said. "And you're not too old to spank, young lady."

145

"Right." Brit laughed. She couldn't count the number of times she had heard that announcement, but she didn't need five fingers to count the number of times she had actually been spanked. It wasn't that her parents weren't believers. Other methods, like separating her from Julie, her usual partner in crime, had been more effective.

"Mama, is there a good light in the attic? I'm thinking about going through some boxes of stuff Daddy put up there for me. Maybe I'll check 'em out while I'm home this week."

"There should be plenty of light up there. I'll have your Daddy check tomorrow. Going through Tommy's things?" Ellen asked. "I'll help if you need me. Just let me know."

"I think I'm finally ready to start sorting things out." Brit sighed at the thought of facing the ghosts of her past. *The time has come.*

***

Brit's nap lasted only an hour, but it was long enough. The shower relaxed her less than she would have liked. That damned, dark haired Sam had no business insinuating himself into her shower in her mother's home. His smoldering eyes watched as she soaped her body, especially as she circled her breasts with the wet wash cloth. She remembered vividly how Sam's mouth had felt at her nipples. She could just see the smirk on his insolent face. Only Sam was miles away.

Forcing herself to stop her erotic daydreaming, she finished her shower, willing the face that haunted her to disappear before she started thinking about his wonderfully sexy body and the ways she had come to know it intimately. She had left him so she could find breathing space to sort out her feelings, to gain perspective. He was the kind of man she didn't need. He'd keep trying to protect her. He'd expect too much.

The nap and shower had revived Brit. She almost bounced downstairs to greet her family. Alicia stopped setting the table to run and hug her. The twelve-year-old was a tad taller than her aunt. Both wore ponytails and looked like sisters.

"Aunt Brit!" Alicia exclaimed, looking Brit in the eye. Then she hugged her again. "I missed you so much! Daddy, I mean Dad says we might get a horse once softball season is over and I promised to take good care of it and keep my grades up and," She finally took a breath break. "you look great, you know that? I have so much to tell you." She squeezed Brit again.

"I missed you, too, squirt. You look like you've grown six inches in the past two months. Look at you, you're taller than your old aunt. I guess I'll have to stop calling you squirt."

"Everyone's taller than you." The girl giggled. "I'd better get back to setting the table or Grandmaw'll skin me."

"I heard that, young lady." The response came from the kitchen.

"Watch it, smarty, never make disparaging remarks about your elders. I'm still tall enough to whup up on you," Brit threatened good-naturedly over her shoulder as she pushed open the swinging door to the kitchen.

"Good evenin', Mama. May I help?" The mingling fragrances in the kitchen set Brit's stomach grumbling.

"You may put the salad together. Everything's on the counter." She turned her head to her right near the double sink. "You look rested."

"Yes, Mama. When I was a kid you sang the praises of a nap as a cure to everything. I wasn't one for taking them."

"You didn't want to miss anything, and you weren't old enough to wish for one. You and Matt kept me so busy when you were small that I would've given my eye-teeth for time for a nap. You two were a handful, especially after Amber came along."

"You must not have been *too* tired, since Jared wasn't so far behind Amber, less than two years," Brit teased.

"I said I didn't have time for a nap, not that I didn't have time for anything." Ellen laughed. "Besides," Her face crimsoned. "your father was to blame for that. That man always was frisky!"

"Was?" Brit questioned.

"Now you're being too nosy, young lady," Ellen cautioned, blushing even more.

Brit smiled while she finished tearing lettuce leaves into a large bowl. Would she be blushing years from now while her daughter teased her about sex? Would she even have a daughter? Could Sam possibly be the man who could keep her happy for thirty years or more? Nah, not likely.

The phone rang twice.

"Could you get that, honey?"

"Sure, Mama." *This is New Britain, not my house where a phone call could mean a threat to my sanity.* The phone rang a third time before Brit answered it. "A dial tone." No*t here, too?* Had they followed her?

"Honey? Who is it?"

"No one." Brit hoped her voice sounded normal.

"Probably Mrs. Bates." Ellen laughed and shook her head. "She gets the wrong number when she doesn't wear her glasses. Poor thing gets us instead of her son."

"She needs a phone with built in memory."

"She'd push the wrong buttons." Ellen covered the corn she had stirred. "She won't get rid of her old rotary phone."

Brit had just chopped a tomato and was scraping it from the cutting board when her father slipped into the room. She cut off the greeting she was about to voice while he crept to her mother bending over the open oven door. Father and daughter smiled as her mother re-arranged pans in the oven and straightened. Her dad turned Ellen into waiting arms. A quick kiss surprised Ellen when Joe playfully grabbed a handful of derriere.

Brit's grin grew when her mother half-heartedly smacked him before he turned toward Brit, who needed no encouragement to move into his embrace. Her cheek was pressed against his chest. His Old Spice mixed with his natural body chemistry to create the familiar scent that was Daddy.

She hoped he'd never change to a newer scent. She'd know his scent in the dark, and it spelled security, especially during those long, dark months after Tommy's death when he had just held her while she had cried in his arms. It reminded her of Sam. Funny they wore the same after-shave.

"Still frisky, I see." Brit grinned cheekily.

"There's too much company in this kitchen. You two go visit while I finish up in here." Ellen's face was still glowing from the oven's heat or from the conversation, probably from the conversation! "Everything will be ready in five minutes. Matthew should be here any minute. We can eat as soon as he gets here. Now scat, so I can get this meal ready."

Brit's oldest brother, Matt, met Brit in the dining room and swung her around. He felt a little thin. Looking into his grayish-brown eyes, she saw love and exhaustion. Lines at the corners spoke more of worry than too much sun. Her gaze traveled down his beloved face to notice his gaunt cheeks.

"Working too hard or partying too hard?" she asked.

"Working."

"Wash up, supper will be on the table in one minute!" Ellen called when she brought two steaming bowls of vegetables to the dining room table. With Brit and Alicia as helpers everything was on the table in one minute.

It felt good to share a meal with family, even with Amber and Jarred missing. *Mama always cooks all the food I don't bother to cook for myself.* Brit smiled. *I can't believe she cooked both butter beans and black-eyed peas tonight, with everything else.* Bet Sam would enjoy the cornbread. Sam? *He's always in my thoughts! Always!*

"Aunt Brit," Alicia broke into her thoughts. "Are you going to my softball game tomorrow? It'll be our first real game. We're playing last year's girls league champions. Coach said we should play the team we fear most and get it out of the way."

"Sure, I'll be there. I can't promise to out-yell your father or grandmother, but I'll do my best. Who's your coach? Should I know him?"

Matthew grinned. "Yeah, you should know him. He's none other than *Zeke the Geek* or should I say *ex-geek.*"

"Coach Zeke used to be a geek?" Alicia frowned. "No way!"

"Some of our classmates called him that because he was a wizard with inventions and shy around girls," Brit explained. "He was really very nice!"

"He was in love with you, Sis." Matthew looked at Alicia. "He used to stand across the street and wait for your aunt Brit to go outside so he could see her." He grinned at Brit.

"I can't believe he coaches girls' softball. Does he have a daughter on your team?"

"He isn't even married," Alicia answered. "You should see the way the moms make eyes at him. It's ridiculous."

"He doesn't have a daughter? How'd he get roped into coaching a league team?" Brit asked.

"He teaches a computer class at the YWCA and we ran out of fathers to ask," Alicia explained.

"I'd have volunteered to help you if I hadn't agreed to take over some of Mrs. Ricker's classes. Teaching can take its toll on a person without adding evening classes."

"That's true," Ellen confirmed. "He spends too much time studying, even on weekends. That's why he's so thin and tired. It's a good thing next week is Spring Break."

"Second that motion!" chimed Alicia.

"Third it," sighed Matthew.

Now she knew the best reason her brother deserved her thanks for painting the glider for her! It was just like him to make time to do something special for her, no matter how tired he was.

"Baby, we're glad you decided to spend this time with us. I'm not on duty at the hospital at all this weekend, so maybe we'll have some time to visit and talk. I want to hear more about your capture of the intruder." Joe's voice shook.

Brit just nodded. Alicia's open expression said she didn't know the whole story. The murderous look in Matthew's eyes told her he did. Could she keep the worst of her problems away from her family? It might be best if she did what she needed and headed back home, back to Sam and danger.

After supper Brit helped her mother clean up and shared girl talk. Alicia went with friends to a movie.

***

Sitting in the glider and watching the stars soothed Brit. The warm spring night washed over her. As a teen, Brit had spent many an hour sitting in this very spot, reading and daydreaming about handsome knights rescuing a certain amethyst-eyed damsel.

Sometimes her rescuer had golden hair that shone in the sunlight like a halo or a crown. Sometimes he had auburn hair like her adored older brother. But more often than not, his hair had been dark as the night. She hadn't seen his face or the faces of any of the heroes, but she felt an eerie shiver when she tried to forget how at home Sam seemed in girlhood daydreams she conjured from the past.

Matthew plopped beside her. They sat in companionable silence as the glider resumed its back and forth motion. A heavy arm moved from the back of the seat and settled around Brit's shoulders. "I would've killed that bastard if I'd been there!" Her brother's voice, rough with emotion, startled her.

"I know you would have. Sam tried to catch him. He was afraid I was hurt. He saved me by arriving when he did."

"Who is this Sam fellow? Mama likes him, and she's usually a good judge of character." Matthew looked at his sister as if trying to read her mind.

"He's the father of a student. They were in the parking lot and had come looking for me because they saw my car was still there. Thank God they did!" Brit's voice came as a harsh whisper when she turned her face into the shoulder her brother offered. He just held her for a while, then he asked again.

"But who is he to you? Is there something you want to tell your big brother?"

"No, we enjoy each other's company." She couldn't tell her brother that she and Sam suffered from *late hormone* problems or *lust* or *sexual attraction* or whatever!

"I just want you to be happy, little sister. I know how lonely you can be after losing the person you love more than you love your own life. You and I both need to find someone to love. At least I have Alicia, but she needs a mother. I know Beth would want me to love again but---."

"I know, believe me, I know. Maybe it's still too soon." Brit felt her brother's tears dampen her hair. Her forehead rested against his chin. The ache in her throat made it impossible to say more. She hadn't seen him cry since her sister-in-law's death. Brit's hurt was already lessening. Beth had been gone for five years. Maybe Matt would find someone who would make him forget some of the pain. He deserved another chance at love.

***

Pain erupted in Sam's gut, matching the stiffness in his neck. Something was bad wrong and he couldn't ignore it. If only he could see or hear something. The premonitions didn't give him any ammunition.

Sam was on his way back to Brit's house two hours after he'd found her missing. She hadn't called. He wanted to wring her neck. *Please, God, let her be hanging out with someone instead of hurt and unable to respond to the phone or let me in.* He'd rather forgive her shutting him out if he had the chance. His premonitions hadn't kicked in, but his panic button had. Panic was unlike him. He'd always had a cool head in a crisis. He wanted to protect her. Love had done this to him.

He got his address book and called Brit's mother.

"Hi, ma'am, this is Sam Samuels. How are you?" He tried to keep his voice normal.

"I recognized your voice, Sam. How's that nice son of yours?"

"He's spending a week visiting with his mama and her family in Hawaii for spring break."

"I'm sure he'll have a great time. I'll bet you want to speak with my daughter."

Sam held the mouth piece away from his mouth. He exhaled a long sigh. "I just called to make sure she got home all right."

"She's in the shower. Shall I have her call you?"

"Oh, no thanks. I'd love to surprise her."

They worked out a plan. Now he needed to find out how she could have up and left him without a word. She should've realized he'd be half out of his mind with worry.

One good thing about the security system he'd installed for her. A visit to his office had netted him the key to her front door and the information he needed to get into her house and disarm the alarm system. Something had made her run scared. Maybe the answer was there.

Getting inside her house hadn't taken long. He was proud of the system. Without his tools he'd still be waiting outside.

He looked for notes she might have left. Nothing lay out on tables or counter surfaces. He found no notes in wastepaper baskets or near the top of her trashcans.

Her answering machine. He'd check it. The phone rang as he reached for the play button. "Hope you enjoyed the redecorating we did in your backyard. Did you get our message? We'll soon stop toying with you. Did you really think bugging your phone would help? Stupid bitch! Enjoy life while you can. Our friend botched the job, but we won't. Kiss the boyfriend and his kid goodbye. They're next. Trace this."

After the dial tone had died down Sam reversed the machine to check for messages left earlier.

Message one. "I know you're home and I have a poem for you. *Roses are red. You'll soon be dead. Your spring break is gonna be fun. I'll be out soon to see you, hon.* Ha! Bad rhyme but true, I'm gonna get you."

Damn. Had Brit been home to hear this one when it came through or had she found it when she got home from school. Sam wondered why he hadn't had a warning belly-ache or other symptom. The caller certainly sounded serious. Surely her attacker hadn't been able to call her from jail. The trial would be soon but not soon enough.

Time to go back home and pack a bag. Adrienne had promised to have Sean call before bedtime tonight. At least his kid was away from danger.

Sam needed to try to get some rest and head to New Britain in the morning. Wouldn't Brit be surprised? Why hadn't she at least called him to let him know she'd skipped town? Didn't she trust him to take care of her?

***

Saturday morning couldn't have been any better for softball if it had been ordered. By noon the balmy temperature had reached the low eighties and shorts and sleeveless shirts were in order.

Having slept late, Brit wandered downstairs to find Matthew still in his pajama bottom. It was strange to see him lazily scratching the thin pelt of reddish brown hair on his pale chest. By now his skin should have been shades darker and he should've been working outside. He must be as worn out as she was to sleep so late. Of course she'd slept fitfully.

Her nightmares had followed her. Last night she'd dreamed her attacker was here. He'd followed her and was now a threat to her family. Sam tried to get to her, but the attacker shot him. She'd cried in her sleep! Her pillow was wet when she awoke.

Matthew had come to her rescue in the dream and saved the family, but she couldn't risk putting the people she loved in danger. She'd head home as soon as she finished going through Tommy's things tomorrow. For now, she had to put up a brave front for her family.

"Aunt Bri-i-it, make Dad get dressed so he can toss a few balls with me. I gotta warm up before the game," Alicia whined. The uniform shone like new. The white shorts were bright enough for a detergent commercial and the shirt was fire engine red. The red visor topped sun-streaked, brown hair, which hung in a French braid. The shiny baseball glove wasn't a hand-me-down, either, and looked like it needed more seasoning.

"Let me have a piece of toast and I'll be out with you," Brit offered as she gulped down a glass of orange juice.

"Oh, I was hoping Dad would be out soon."

154

"I'll be out in three minutes, slave driver," Matt said over his shoulder when he stood and stretched then sauntered toward the basement apartment he and Alicia had shared for the past five years. "Don't sell your Aunt Brit short. She throws pretty well for a girl."

"Chauvinist pig!" Brit called out after her brother. "I throw well for a girl or boy." And she did, too.

Chapter Ten

Lunch at one o'clock was rowdy with the adults eating huge sandwiches while Alisha was too nervous to do more than nibble.

"Can't you eat any faster? You'd think this was the last meal any of you'd ever have. Come on, I don't want to be late!"

"We have plenty of time," Matt assured her.

Brit laughed when Matt grabbed the car keys and invited her to go with him and Alisha to the field. The kid nearly danced to all the way to the car.

What would my life have been like if I'd stayed here to teach instead of going to Florence? Would a crazy man have attacked me? Would I have met someone like Sam? Not likely.

Shortly before two o'clock brother and sister watched the excited twelve-year old race to the baseball field where four other red-shirted, pony-tailed girls bounced in anticipation.

By two o'clock Brit stood stock still as Zeke stepped from his navy blue sports car. His auburn hair was wind-blown and his tan dark. His physique was nothing short of fantastic. The waist was slim, but his shoulders and chest were anything but.

He faced the girls on the field, his fists rested on his hips in a militant stance that stretched his red coach's shirt taut across his chest. Dark sunglasses covered his eyes, making them unreadable despite the determined set of his mouth and jaw. White shorts showed enough well-muscled, hair-dusted leg to catch any female eye.

The hero stood with the twelve admiring adolescents awaiting his instructions. Brit grinned watching her old friend in the limelight. "Go get 'em, Tiger," she muttered. Her grin stretched. *He is one absolute hunk.* She noticed him pause in his instructions when carloads of blue-shirted girls invaded the home territory.

The girls had barely left his side when the man was attacked by a female about to burst from her short halter-top and leaking cheek from her red shorts. *That much cheek should never be seen on that end*, especially in public. The gushy woman grabbed one arm just as another woman reached for his other arm. He looked like a wish-bone about to be pulled. They looked at him like he was God's gift and it was Christmas.

Brit's breath held when Zeke's auburn head raised. His hand rose to his glasses. Piercing blue eyes gazed over the tops at an untinted sight of Brit from across the field. They stared for seconds before grinning like long, lost friends. They both waved and Brit moved toward the field when Zeke broke from his female bonds and strode toward the stands. Nearing, he stuffed the glasses into his breast pocket.

Brit's arms wound around his neck when he swung her at a dizzying speed. The kiss he planted on her lips caught her by surprise. He'd learned something in the past fifteen years. The man could really kiss. *What else has he learned? He did have a crush on me, and I was fond of him, and he's one sexy, male.*

"Hi, stranger," a deep, husky voice whispered against her ear. "it's been a long time, too long, and I missed you."

"You're a sight for sore eyes yourself!" Brit smiled. "Don't you think you should let me down before the town has us married or at least sleeping together?"

"Good idea, but without the town. Dad's still a judge and could do the honors," Zeke teased. "Besides, if I let you down we could be embarrassed. I don't think my players will notice but an adult might."

Knowing he referred to the arousal pushing against her, she grinned. "I'm sure every woman would, especially the two who were about to use you for a wishbone, but we can't stay like this all day. We'll stand here until things are back to normal."

"After the game, Lady, I'll see you." His voice was rich with meaning. He saluted her by dipping the bill of his red cap.

Brit thought her face would never cool and was sure of it when she looked back to where Matt had been joined by the rest of her family. "Oh, my God!" She nearly fainted at the sight of the man standing beside her mama, fury in his green eyes.

This can't be happening! What's he doing here? Can't I get away from him for a few days? Maybe he's an apparition and will disappear if I close my eyes. She closed her eyes in desperation. Before she could count to five, she felt strong, warm hands banding her arms as Sam's anger changed to concern.

"Are you okay? You look like you've seen a ghost."

"I have," Brit muttered. "How did you get here?"

Sam's arm held her up, steering her to the seats near her family. "Your mother told me you were here when I called last night. I couldn't believe you left town without telling me. Why didn't you call? I was worried sick about you."

"Sam, between my attacker and the harassing threats I'm being smothered to death. I know you mean well, but you make me feel like I'm drowning. I worry about me. I worry about you. I just had to get away."

"I saw you and the jock." Sam's arm moved from her shoulder as he faced her. "I thought I'd explode when I saw him grab you. If your mother and sister hadn't stopped me, your niece would have needed a new coach."

Her hands on hips pose mirrored his while the two glared at each other. "Look, bub, just because we, you know...you don't own me, and I'll not have you assaulting my friends. Do you hear me? You don't own me."

"Yes, I hear you. Everyone in the park probably hears you. You don't have to shout. I'm right here," Sam said quietly.

"But you don't act like you hear me. I speak but you don't seem to understand." Her voice was low, her frustration evident.

"So I won't beat him up if he keeps his hands off you."

"It's not up to you, you idiot. Besides, we're old friends who are glad to see each other after a long time. He took me to my high school prom. We haven't seen each other since we both went away to college," Brit explained.

Sam's reasonable expression didn't fool her when he looked her in the eye. "That was not the kiss of a friend, honey," he explained. "That man wanted to throw you down on the ground and screw you, right here and now."

"You are so crude." She couldn't deny that since she had felt the evidence of his desire, but she wouldn't give Sam the satisfaction of affirming his accusation. "Not all men think with that part of their anatomy. Zeke is a good man who cares for me as a friend after all these years. Besides, you presume too much, Mr. Samuels, you just can't..."

The sound of cheers and clapping signaled the entrance of the players on the field. The red shirts were in the dugout, except for the one player who stood bravely at home plate.

The first inning ended with no runs. Sam and Brit forgot their argument to cheer Alicia's team. Well, Sam did want to cheer for the team not coached by the red-haired jock, but he couldn't. The Simpson clan would've killed him, if Brit had left anything.

Brit forgot everything but the game, except when Zeke would sneak a glance in her direction. Funny how Sam seemed to anticipate those glances in time to grab her hand to stake his claim. Zeke had no way of knowing about Sam unless her family had told him, and she could think of no reason for them to.

It was the third inning, Alicia stood at bat. The Simpson family held a collective breath as she swung hard at the first pitch. "Aw-w-w." The next pitch went as a ball. The third pitch made two balls and a strike. Every member of the family stood, except Brit's sister Amber who held one sleeping twin while the other rested a curly blonde head on her thigh. On the next pitch Alicia swung. The thwack sent the crowd to their feet.

"Go! Run, baby, run!" Shouts erupted from the bleachers when the ball grounded past second base. By the time the ball was recovered and in the pitcher's hands, Alicia stood at second, brushing red dust from her shorts and her filthy leg.

The ear to ear grin on the girl belied any pain she must have felt from the slide to beat the throw from first.

"Do it, girl!" yelled Brit.

"That's my granddaughter!" yelled Ellen, who was jumping up and down, clutching Joe's arm for dear life.

Sam and Matt slapped each other's backs, exchanging yells.

Jared jumped with the sleeping twin he grabbed when Amber half rose to her feet.

There was enough yelling to be heard in Atlanta, more than a hundred miles away. They silenced when Zeke and the umpire looked to the stands so they could resume play.

A batter struck out for two, with a runner on second. When the next batter, a tall, slim blonde, reached down to dust her hands and then spat in them, silence reigned, followed by pandemonium as she whacked the ball and raced toward first.

"Go, Alicia!"

"Run, Brenda!"

"Move! Move!"

Brenda's rooting section was as vocal as Alicia's.

When the ball was overthrown, Brenda moved toward second base, vacated by Alicia, now at third and ready to head home.

Alicia looked toward the stands and the dugout as shouts of "Go! Go!" "Stay! Stay!" roared through the stands. She watched the first baseman and a fielder scramble for the ball. The yell of "Go for it!" she heard in a man's booming voice triggered her into action and she responded to it at a dead run. The ball sailed wildly toward the pitcher, who caught it and threw it home as Alicia slid.

"Safe!" The crowd cheered. Yelling loudest were Joseph and Ellen. Brit clasped Sam's arm. He swung her around then soundly kissed her. Her pulse raced as Sam tried to obliterate any memory of the jock's kiss. It was one more in a long string of kisses she would need a lifetime, no at least two lifetimes, to forget.

When he finally ended the kiss, a dazed Brit was thankful no one appeared to notice anything but the girl being congratulated by her teammates. Brit removed her arms from their firm hold around his strong neck.

During the fifth inning Brenda homered. Alicia made no more runs, but she struck out only once. The game ended at three-two.

Fifteen red visors landed on the ground as fifteen girls danced around the three players who scored runs. Zeke's auburn head stood above the crowd of screaming adolescents. His teeth flashed in the grin he hadn't relaxed since Brenda followed the runner she knocked in to end the last at bat for her team. Parents began to rush onto the field to hug or console.

Brit broke away from Sam to congratulate her niece, who was passed from one hugging relative to another. Sam reached for Brit too late to keep her from an embrace by the winning team's coach.

Zeke's adoring fans whisked him away again.

Brit just smiled when Sam muttered, "You'd think he made those runs himself. He looks like a peacock, preening and strutting for the audience."

"He's proud of his girls. Most of them are new and they just beat last year's champs. He was never a jock, by the way."

"Humph!" He took Brit's arm and steered her toward the borrowed Lexus. He expected to take Brit and her horse-sized dog back with him. Esther, good sister that she was, had offered her nice car for his use. She was driving his sports car since she had her own truck and didn't need his. Trusting her with his high-powered, man's toy was only fair, but she'd probably have to flirt her way out of a dozen tickets since she knew only one speed, faster.

Sam forgot to be jealous of the coach when Brit allowed him to take her home. She had really enjoyed the game. He guessed she'd needed to get away from her problems for a while. Her skin had a touch of that sun kissed look. He hadn't liked the way the jock had behaved worth a damn. Had Brit let him kiss her to prove a point to herself?

"Sorry I yelled at you, darlin'." Sam glanced at Brit. He slapped the steering wheel with his palm. "I was worried. I panicked, pure and simple, but I can see you needed to get away from the craziness. I couldn't believe you'd go away from me."

"I know. I should've let you know I was leaving town. I meant to call you last night. I wanted to pretend the other life didn't exist and life here was real for me. With my family I felt safe. The rest of the threatening world seemed so far away."

"I forgive you, but don't ever scare me like that again. Kiss and make out?" He grinned.

"Don't you mean kiss and make up?"

"Were we fighting? Okay, let's do both."

"You idiot." Brit laughed at his not so innocent expression. "Oh, I forgot to ask about Sean. Have you heard from him? How was his flight? Is he excited?"

"Slow down, he arrived on time and had a good flight. He and another boy his age visited the whole way. He and his dad will be staying near Adrienne's parents' place. It seems the kid's mom died of cancer last year and this trip is the first time they've had to get away since she became ill two years ago."

"Poor baby!"

"He's as old as Sean, honey."

"Poor baby, losing his mother at any age. Alisha had a hard time when her mom died. She wasn't much younger that boy."

"Guess you're right. Sean would be devastated if anything happened to Adrienne."

"And you?"

"It would be like losing a dear friend." Sam glanced at her. "But we'd have you to help us, wouldn't we?"

"Yeah. And your wonderful family."

"Maybe we can persuade him and his dad to visit this summer."

Sam nodded. "Good idea, Teach." He liked that she'd said *us*. Were the two of them *an us*? Or maybe the three of them. *Can't leave Sean out of it.*

162

Protective Instincts

Soon they arrived at the Simpson home where the rest of Brit's family joined them, except for Alicia and her dad who had joined the victory celebration, a round of ice cream and drinks. Everyone noisily discussed plans for Sunday dinner at the Simpson's favorite restaurant.

"Sam, will you be staying in town tonight?" asked Amber.

"He didn't come all this way just to leave right away. He's anxious to spend some time with your sister. You will stay, won't you?" Ellen asked.

"Mama, I'm sure Sam is too busy to stay," Brit protested, ignoring her mother's puzzled expression.

"I'd love to stay, but I won't put you out, ma'am." Sam grinned smugly at Brit. "I appreciate your offer. Treat me like family. I'll be glad to help with any chores."

"Then you'd better behave like family," Amber warned, "We try to get out of doing chores."

Sam was enchanted by the family. They reminded him of his own. "I'll help enough to make a good impression."

Brit ducked her head and announced. "I'll just slip upstairs and shower some of the dust off."

"I'll help," Sam whispered in her ear. "I can scrub your back and save water."

"No," Brit swatted his arm in warning. "My mother wouldn't like it. Help her or get ready for your own shower."

"If your mother needs help with her shower I'll help her but I thought that was your daddy's job. Won't he mind?" Sam asked. He just loved to bait Brit and watch her get her back up. He owed her a grave conversation about the last two messages on her answering machine. They also needed to discuss Drew's theory that her husband's death had something to do with her recent attacks. They'd have a serious talk soon.

"You're incorrigible. Go talk to Daddy and behave." Brit headed upstairs. She needed the shower to re-group.

***

Teacher, teacher, where's the stupid teacher? Is she spreading her legs for the daddy? She hadn't spread her legs for Douglas. Douglas is good looking. Douglas can please the ladies. Douglas can show the stuck up teacher what a real man's like.

Douglas hums. Five steps right and five steps forward. One step left and two steps back. Four steps right and five steps forward. Two steps left and one step back. The jail cell dance, his own creation. The others don't know my dance.

Douglas must kill the bitch! Douglas hates being cooped up in a hellhole of a prison cell with the riff-raff and the dregs of society, the small time crooks, not even one lawyer or stockbroker to keep him company! This place is not dark like the closet Douglas hated but he needs to get away or he'll go crazy. Douglas will get out and make the teacher ver-r-y sorry!

Chapter Eleven

Brit hummed, brushing her fingers through her hair while she dried it in her room. She stared through half closed eyes at an image in the mirror. Tommy had always loved to watch her dry her hair. He'd offer to help her and wind up helping her into bed. She smiled. Strangely, her memories made her feel more comfortable than sad.

The fluffy, blue towel wrapped around her hid very little, but there was no one to see anything. At least there was no one until a half-naked man knocked on her door and opened it before she could warn him she wasn't dressed.

"What do you think you're doing in my room? I'm not decent, and you shouldn't be here." Brit switched off the small hairdryer she held.

Sam twirled a non-existent mustache. "On the contrary, dear Teach, you're better than decent and quite appealing in that costume. There's no better place for me than where you're not dressed." The door closed with Sam inside the room, which seemed to shrink with his presence.

Sam's jeans hung below his tan line, barely covering the thatch of hair she knew was at the end of the trail to the bulge at the base of the zipper. The least he could do was button the jeans so they would cover a little more of his flat stomach. Sam had the body of a Greek statue. But Sam was a lot warmer.

He was so alive and so hot. The blush staining Brit's face spread and she willed her eyes up. The trail of hair led back up to his broad chest. The matted, damp curls let his flat nipples exposed. The power he had to make her want him was nothing short of criminal. She could hardly speak for her dry throat. She swallowed hard.

"Sam, you and I are not going to sleep together in my mother's house. You might as well leave this room now," she warned. The hand she had been raking through her hair fisted on the towel to keep her only covering intact.

His strong hands gently grasped her shoulders, pulling her close. The hand that grasped the towel pressed against his bare chest. She flattened her free hand against his warmth. She'd intended to push him away, at least she thought she had, but the feel of his smooth, damp skin beneath her palm tempted her too much. His hands were work roughened, but the rest of his skin was soft as a baby's

"God, but you're beautiful, woman." Sam cupped her chin, tilting her face for better access to her mouth. His tongue touched one corner of her mouth then the other. It moistened the outer edge of her upper lip then the outer edge of her lower lip before bathing both trembling lips. "I missed you," he murmured against her mouth. "Didn't you miss me, at least a little bit?" As her soft lips parted for a sigh he darted inside to touch her welcoming tongue.

His free hand cupped her breast, massaging through the towel. The other moved from her chin to caress the other breast. She cupped his neck. Abandoning the tuck in her towel, her hand roamed up a muscled arm to a taut chest shuddering at her touch. When the towel slipped Sam pulled her naked front flush with his.

One denim-clad thigh pressed at the juncture of her thighs while the evidence of his arousal pulsed against her hip. His hands cupped her derriere to pull her close enough for him to taste pouting nipples. One seemed to beg his tasting. His hot tongue laved the nipple, savoring it as Brit opened her eyes to see his naked back reflected in the dresser mirror.

She saw part of her own nude front and the face of a woman aroused. She could feel the heat between her legs grow as a strong hand moved behind one knee and raised her leg to rest her foot against his thigh. Sam's hand moved to her heat, sending a shudder through her body as all thoughts beyond the couple in the mirror fled. She could not stop now, even if ... *Damn! What if my mother walked in right now?*

Before Sam could realize her intent, Brit balled up a fist and punched his shoulder as she pulled a reluctant breast from his mouth and yanked the foot from his thigh.

"Brit, Honey?"

"You sneaky, rotten, no good scoundrel, you sex maniac, you...you..." Brit grabbed the damp towel, inadequate as it was. Realizing how little it covered, she snapped it at the bewildered man and she turned her naked back to him. She scrambled for her robe. "My mother could've walked in." *And it would be my fault as much as his! But he's so sexy! Not fair! Better to be mad at him than at myself and my weakness for him!*

"Love, your mother's a married lady who must've learned about lovemaking when she created four children. Surely she realizes that you would know about it, since you were married." Sam tried to joke with the fuming woman who was having trouble stepping into black, lace-trimmed, satin panties.

"But she's my mother, for Pete's sake. Besides, it could've been anyone, my daddy or my brothers. They'd have shot you on the spot!" Brit punched him again, this time on the other shoulder.

She continued to grab clothes, turning her back on the obnoxious man as she slid her arms from the sleeves of her robe, through the straps of her bra, and fastened the front clasp before letting the robe fall. She was as angry with herself as she was with him, but she wasn't about to let him know it.

I don't know if I can watch this. Sam recovered from the loss of arousal caused by the sudden change in Brit. He cleared his throat.

If she puts on a garter belt and black stockings to go with those scraps of lace she has on, I don't think I'll taste a bite of food at supper tonight, just knowing what she's wearing. Watching her dress aroused him as much as undressing her did. He couldn't stop watching her.

"Your father and brothers know about the birds and the bees, sweetheart. I don't think they'd be so shocked. They might've made you marry me and make an honest man of me, but I don't think they'd have called me out or shot me." He grinned. "How can you call me a sex maniac? You're the only woman I like to watch dress and undress."

He saw the shimmer of tears in her eyes. *Damn!* "I didn't come here to seduce you, but you make me forget my brain." He sat back on the edge of her bed.

She had stepped into black slacks and was buttoning the waist when she paused for a second. Then she grabbed a black blouse with filmy sleeves.

"You, jerk, Alicia could have walked in. What if she had? How would you have explained that, huh? How?"

"Look, I'm not sorry I was making love to you. I am sorry I upset you, Love. Alicia isn't even home. Anyway, maybe I can leave now without embarrassing myself or compromising your virtue. Wouldn't want anyone to see what you do to me, would we? See you at supper. By the way, I like the black lingerie. Promise you'll wear it for me?" Grinning, he reached for the doorknob. He unlocked it, smirked over his shoulder, and let himself out. He closed the door behind just in time to miss the hairbrush that bounced against the other side.

Damn his arrogant hide. Another couple of seconds and we... Who was that woman in the mirror? I'm not sure whether I'm more sorry we started or that we didn't finish. The flush returned as Brit remembered Sam's mouth on her nipples, the desire pooled between her legs, the feel of his hand as he touched her, the feeling of abandon that gripped her while she watched their actions in the mirror.

Sam stuck his head back inside. "We need to talk about your husband. I heard the last message on your machine and one came while I was looking for clues to your whereabouts in your house. I was afraid something bad had happened to you."

"Can we get into that later, Sam, please?" How could she let herself be so immersed in sexual feelings for one man when she had loved another so much? She shouldn't have let Sam worry about her, even though she'd never given him the impression he should keep up with her. She couldn't help his tendency to take responsibility for everyone.

The knock on her door broke into her daydream. She swallowed to clear her throat before answering, "Come in."

The door opened and her father poked his head around it. He'd changed from the jeans and sweatshirt he had worn to the ball game. His gray slacks and gray and white striped polo shirt looked youthful. His hair was slicked back from a shower and he looked downright hugable.

"Wow, don't you look spiffy, little girl!"

"Not as spiffy as my daddy." Brit hugged him.

"How about a drink before supper? My treat. I've got cold strawberry daiquiris ready. I used fresh strawberries, too. Sam's already downstairs, helping your mama. He's quite a charmer."

"He's a charmer, all right," Brit murmured.

Father and daughter descended the stairs together.

Ellen looked fresh in a blue pantsuit, with her hair smoothed and tied with blue ribbon. The look that passed between her parents did not go unnoticed when Sam gave Brit a knowing smirk. Her mother's flush affirmed that her parents had been too busy to walk in on Brit and Sam. There had not been time for them to take separate showers, but they both looked fresh.

Well, I'll be darned! Still frisky! And so dear.

She couldn't endanger them by hanging around while someone was after her. She'd go through everything in the attic tomorrow after church. She had to know if Tommy had left a clue to whoever had it in for her.

"Hello, gorgeous," Sam called out to Brit. He held the swinging door open for Ellen, who followed him from the kitchen.

"After you, madam," he bowed.

"Go on with you, Sam." Ellen laughed, blushing. "Such a nice young man your mama raised."

At that Sam blushed. He carried a platter of meat to the table. "Why, teacher, that's some fancy outfit for supper at

169

home. Maybe we can find somewhere to show it off after later. Ellen says there are places we could dance."

Sam had changed into real clothes. He looked no less devastating than he had been in jeans and no shirt. He removed the frilly apron she recognized as her mother's. Her mother must have taken him up on his offer to help. A teal, open-throated, chambray shirt reflected his eyes, showing his early tan to perfection. Black, denim slacks hugged his hips like a second skin. He looked like sin and just as irresistible. He handed Brit a daiquiri glass, letting his fingers brush hers when she took it.

"Did you know Daddy makes the daiquiris light, with real strawberries and low on alcohol."

"So he said."

Their gazes locked over the glass rims.

Joseph returned from the kitchen with a large bowl of potato salad and put it on the dining room table set with matching festive paper plates, cups, and napkins. He turned to take the plate of sliced tomatoes and lettuce from Ellen. Picking up two glasses from the table, he handed one to her.

"To victories and those who are still celebrating them," he offered as a toast.

"To victories to come," Sam offered, looking over his glass at Brit.

"To knowing what's important in life," Ellen responded.

"To cool drinks on warm evenings in Georgia," Brit murmured, rubbing the chilled glass across her forehead.

"Let's eat," Joseph suggested. "I might manage to finish a meal without an interruption. I can't believe the Stanton babies waited so long to come. They'll probably decide to cause their Mama labor pains in the middle of the night. I wouldn't want to tempt fate with the good luck I've had so far this evening." Ellen blushed as their eyes met across the table.

"Dinner is served. Everything's on the table. Just have a seat by me so we can talk, Sam." Ellen nodded to the chair to her right.

"I'll sit next to Daddy." Brit took the chair across from Sam. The men held chairs for the ladies. Brit was glad Sam wasn't holding her chair. She didn't need him so close. Hell, she didn't need him across from her, either! Even adding a leaf to the table wouldn't put Sam far enough away to suit her.

"The beef and ham are both good, Mama."

"I cooked them yesterday before you got here. Your daddy sliced it for me with that nice meat slicer you gave me for Christmas. It's a money saver when I make so many lunches. I gave the ham bone to Monster when we left for the game.

"Bet he loved that, but he'll make a better watchdog if you don't give him extra treats."

"He's on vacation, too. And besides, he's in a new place and he's been so good," Ellen explained.

"You wouldn't have leftovers if Sean and I ate here," Sam complimented. "Sean and I don't cook and I can't sponge off mama every night."

"We're glad you're looking after Brit, Sam," Ellen said.

"It seems she needs more than the city police to watch out for her." Sam's sarcasm made his anger apparent.

"The man's in jail, so I'm perfectly safe now," Brit reminded her parents, as well as Sam.

"Yeah, well..." Sam stammered. He wasn't so sure about that. He hoped that he and Drew were wrong.

"You're not to blame, no one is, so let's just forget it," Joe suggested. "My daughter says you acted admirably, for which we are grateful."

"She now has a warning system, at least."

"Ellen told me about your son. Nice young man, she said. How is he?"

Sam's pride made him glow. "He's spending Spring Break with his mama and grandparents in Hawaii."

"That's some trip for Spring Break," Ellen said.

"My ex's parents are living there as part of his job. He lectures at the University of Hawaii."

"I figure to take Ellen there some day."

"Maybe for our second honey moon."

Here they sat, not two hours away from where she had been attacked, with their windows and doors open to let in the cool, fragrant air of spring.

As Sam used his special humor telling parts of the story about how they met, Brit allowed her mind to drift. She'd need to check her answering machine before she went to bed. The police tracer should call if there were more threatening calls.

The doorbell chimed at seven o'clock. Joe answered the door with an enthusiastic, "Come on in, Zeke, son. It's good to see you. You don't look any worse for the wear. Alicia and Matt aren't home yet. How did you beat them?"

"Good evening, Dr. Simpson, Mrs. Simpson." Joe clapped Zeke on the back as they shook hands. Ellen gave him a big hug. "They were headed for the mall to buy something Alicia wanted. Matt is proud enough to buy her just about anything."

The man who joined Brit in the living room definitely did not look worse for the wear. The blue shirt fit his chest like it was made for him and poured on to shrink. It was just slightly lighter than the navy slacks, which looked tailored and freshly creased. Drop dead gorgeous did not even come close to describing his blue eyes. Even the weak-eyed look that told Brit he needed to put on regular glasses did not detract from his handsome face. How had he remained single this long? He was a fine catch. He'd make a good project.

"Hello, Brit. You're looking fine tonight." His smile weakened a little when Sam stepped beside her.

"Hi, Zeke. I'd like you to meet my friend, Sam. Sam, meet my dear old friend, Zeke."

The men shook hands like adversaries taking measure. Despite smiles, Brit was sure each used an extra firm handshake. There was no questioning the arms crossed across the chest pose or the daggers shooting from Sam's eyes.

"So, tell us, how did you become *Zeke the hunk* and a softball coach?" Brit asked.

172

Zeke blushed. "At O.C.S. they thought I needed muscle. They said I would become a man, and they weren't kidding. When I decided eight years was long enough to serve Uncle Sam I left to work in industry."

Joe led everyone to the den.

Sam grunted. Brit gave him a dirty look. "Your girls played well, coach," he said.

"The league was going to disband their softball team if they couldn't get a coach. These girls didn't want to be absorbed into other teams where they would be extra wheels. I don't have much experience with kids, but I couldn't leave them to a winning-is-everything type who'd squelch their spirits."

"Well, you were right, Coach Zeke." Grinning, Brit tapped his shoulder with her fist. "They are winners, even if they don't win another game this whole year."

"Oh, yeah, remember Julie? You need to call her mom's house. Julie's visiting her mom, too. She'd love to see you."

"Yeah," Sam added. "Bet you two have lots to discuss about old times."

What he didn't say in so many words was that Julie didn't have a man visiting, like Brit did. He shouldn't have to. Zeke's did not get the message and leave.

The jerk took one of Brit's hands in both of his. Sam wanted to rip her hand free. Sam wouldn't mind ripping Zeke's hands off.

"Maybe the three of us can get together before you leave. I want to hear all about you." He grinned like a jerk. "And Julie, too." He looked too smug. "I'm sure Sam would be bored with our talk about old times."

"Never bored. Wouldn't miss it."

Zeke stayed an hour and then left. He'd expected her to go out with him after their meeting at the ballpark. She'd have enjoyed talking about old times. He hadn't known about Sam. As much as Brit wanted to hear all about her friend's life, she had a lot on her mind tonight.

When the house was finally quiet she wandered onto the porch and headed for her glider, her island. What must Tommy think? Would he approve of the wild passion she had with Sam?

The night was so still and felt so remote, so like a secret place, so safe. The only light came from the street light at the corner and the moon. The glider was shaded from the street light. Brit plopped down onto a large soft cushion and was rewarded by a grunt. "You finally came out."

Brit gasped then punched Sam's chest. "You scared me. I told you not to do that."

"Some goodbye kiss you gave ole Zeke at his car."

"You were watching?"

Sam nodded. "Couldn't miss it. So, the jock used to be a geek who had a crush on you. Does he still?"

"That's none of your business."

"Is that a yes?"

"You'll never know."

"I'll bet he couldn't make you feel the way I do." Sam's finger reached to stroke her cheek."

She trembled. "Mind your own business." She could barely breathe. She needed distance from this man so she could use her brain again.

"Get off my porch and out of my life! You're too much trouble and you confuse me." No one had ever made her feel the way Sam could.

"Can't. Not gonna happen, Love."

Brit jumped from the special haven now invaded. "You - - ego-maniac, you --, you --, smug pain in the ass"

"Temper, darlin'! Sweet dreams." Sam smiled. Thoughts of his woman in another man's arms had bombarded him all evening. It had been all he could do to resist punching the guy out. He knew the look of a man who was hot for the sack, and that joker was hot to make it with his Brit.

I don't know why she can't just admit she's in love with me. I know she couldn't make love like she does if it doesn't mean something special.

174

They should have been able to sit together while they visited with her parents. He'd wanted to pull her into his lap and sniff her hair or kiss her cheek or hold her hand. He'd have to help her get over her self-consciousness around her parents. Maybe when they were married she would be different. When they were married? God, he had it bad.

"Brit," Sam finally found his voice as well as his brain. "did your husband ever talk to you about his work, any of his clients?" He rubbed a hand across his mouth and chin in an attempt to appear far more nonchalant than he felt.

"No, not really." She drew her eyebrows together. "Why do you ask?"

"I was just thinking," he said. "Sometimes married people talk about things they wouldn't discuss with anyone else. Did you have a lot of your husband's paperwork to go through after his death? Maybe he had a dissatisfied client or found out something he shouldn't know."

"Sam, you're scaring me with these questions." She frowned. "If you want to know something, just ask outright."

"Honey, I spoke to Drew again this afternoon about your situation---"

"You what?" she interrupted.

"I've kept him informed since the hang-up calls and the dead weeds you got before the second attack. He and I have discussed just about everything that has happened," he explained. "Since he is a detective, an investigator, I wanted to get his opinion about the way the Florence cops were handling things."

"And?" she coaxed.

"He wondered if you were the target of more than a rape."

"More than a rape? What do you mean more than a rape? Sam, now you're really scaring me." Her insides churned.

"Honey, your husband must have handled cases involving some unsavory characters." Sam let out a slow breath. "Maybe he ticked someone off."

"Sam Samuels, Tommy was the most honest man you could have met. He would never, *never* do anything..." Her voice shook.

"I didn't mean he did anything wrong. What if he learned something threatening about a former client or someone else?" He held her shoulders, looking into her startled eyes. Though he didn't want to frighten her, they had to know as much as they could about her husband's contacts before his death. "Could you still have notes that were not part of his official papers at work?"

"Sam? Sam, are you trying to say someone had him killed? Does Drew know something about Tommy's death?" Her voice caught. "Oh, my God! Does he think Tommy was murdered? But what does that have to do with the attack at school?"

Realization dawned with such a vengeance she trembled in Sam's his protective arms. She didn't want to move her face from Sam's hard chest. She rubbed against it as though to erase the possibilities creeping into her brain. Raising her head enough to be heard, she asked, "Why would they want to kill me? I don't know anything."

"Maybe they think Tommy might've told you something. There could be a notebook, or file, or tape, even a thumb drive that would incriminate them. Drew said he thought one of Tommy's clients was freed of a charge years ago but he has been charged with worse things now."

Brit shook her head.

"Maybe your husband was onto something he couldn't prove. Maybe they killed him because they thought he'd cause trouble." Brit sobbed against Sam's chest. He'd have cut off his arm rather than hurt her. But someone did want to hurt her.

When her crying subsided he used his handkerchief to wipe the tears still glistening in her eyes. He had to ask her. "Did you or anyone go through or throw away his personal notes?"

Brit shuddered as she tried to find her voice. "I have a boxes of papers from his home-office. Does Drew think we should go through them? Oh, Sam!"

Brit just wanted to crawl into bed and pull the covers over her head. She pulled away from the warmth and confusion of his comforting embrace.

"Night, Sam." Brit took several steps toward the front porch door. Turning back, she spoke. "See you in the morning."

***

Sam waited until Brit went inside. By now she'd be in her room, safe from him and his need to hold her and comfort her and make love to her. Rising stiffly, Sam headed inside to the room he had been assigned. It was time to call it a night or early morning. Sleeping just doors down from Brit wouldn't be easy.

Drew had said there might be papers or notes, maybe threats against her husband's life. Going through her dead husband's things would be rough on her. There had to be some clue to track down his enemies. His death probably hadn't been an accident.

Chapter Twelve

Sam couldn't sleep. He thought about the woman in bed just doors away. He ached just thinking about the way she'd looked and smelled so fresh from her shower. Visions of her making love with him in the hotel room after the trashing of her yard had left him breathless and heart-sore. He dreamed about caressing her silky skin. They had been as one body moving together in sensuous abandon. Brit had to realize they were meant for each other. He needed to get her home.

Brit checked her answering machine messages. Three messages came through.

Message one set her teeth on edge. "You betta come home soon, Sugar. Miss ya."

How had the man had the opportunity to make such a call from jail? "See ya soon."

"Not if I see you first," she muttered. She could do this without Sam's help.

Message two was no better. "You're out late, girl. The boyfriend was looking for you. Don't you tell him where you're going? Maybe he's not the only one you're givin' it to. Gonna share it with me when I get out of this hell hole, Bitch."

Brit shook her head. Who was keeping him informed?

How many people were watching her? She had never chewed her fingernails before, but she had to snatch her thumb away before she gnawed it to the knuckle.

Message three was the worst. "I'm gonna get you soon. You'll look around and I'll be there. And I'm gonna have me a good time hurting you. Think about it, dream about it."

Brit watched the shadows of her curtains dancing in the night breeze. Her digital clock changed time with agonizing slowness for an hour before she drifted into a fitful sleep.

She awoke in the cloying dark, shaking from her first nightmare in weeks. Tommy darted in front of the truck. She tried to warn him, but he didn't seem to hear her. The truck sped toward him as she had seen it do many times in the nightmares she had for the first years after his death. It always went the same way. His strong, healthy body flew through the air, landing in a lifeless, crumpled pile yards from the point of impact.

Brit bolted upright in her bed, her throat aching from the scream that woke her. Forcing herself to breathe slowly and deeply, she turned her head into her pillow, certain she wouldn't go back to sleep. She did, finally. She had better dreams this time.

She was having the strangest dream. Strong hands moved over her body, touching her skin, heating it like a fever. Her moan awakened her in time to hear her mother's quiet knocking at her door. She opened her eyes to the daylight. "Come in," she croaked with a voice thick with sleep.

As Brit arose from her bed she remembered that she and Sam were going to bring down the boxes of Tommy's personal papers and stuff. Maybe that was the reason the nightmare had visited again. Would she and Sam find something to help explain Tommy's death and her own danger? What did she hope would happen? It was one thing to know her husband died as the result of an accident, even a stupid accident. The possibility that he was murdered was hard to even consider.

In the Simpson's cheery kitchen Sam settled his gaze on Brit. She obviously hadn't slept any better than he had. Taking a bite of eggs, he asked. "Did you check your telephone messages?"

"Yep, I did."

"So?" Sam held his fork beside his plate.

"He's back." She took a sip of coffee.

"Want to tell me about it?"

"Not really." Brit glanced pointedly toward her mother. Surely Sam didn't expect her to talk about something so awful in front of her mama.

"Later?" He shrugged.

"Why don't you just let him listen to the messages? You didn't erase them, did you?" Ellen asked. "I'll bet the police have already checked into them."

Sam and Brit looked at the woman who had made the suggestion as though she offered them napkins or more juice.

"Well, they are bugging your phone, aren't they?" Ellen asked. "They certainly should be."

"Mama?"

"You really don't need to pussyfoot around me. I know more about the world than you realize. I've been around a long time and I'm not a hermit. You could let me help, too. There must be something I could do."

"Just being here when I need you is enough."

"How long will it take for you two to get ready for church? You are going aren't you? Matthew took Alisha in early for Sunday School."

Brit stared at Sam, who shrugged. She hadn't even
thought about church but
Maybe she could use a little divine guidance.

"I can be ready in fifteen minutes. Sam, you don't have to go just 'cause..."

"Think I'd let you go anywhere without me?"

"I'm leaving in twenty minutes. Your daddy'll meet us there when he can."

***

The attic was a large walk-in type. Bare bulbs dangled at ends of long cords. Afternoon light streamed brightly through bare windows.

"These large boxes are my things," Brit called to Sam.
"I'll check the contents
since I'm not sure what Mama packed in them."

"Here, use my knife to cut the tape." Sam offered, hunkered down beside her. "Wait, this one says clothes."

Smiling at her mother's neat magic marker printing on each box, Brit pushed the first one aside before pulling a second box closer to Sam. "PAPERS- TOMMY'S DESK-DEN," she read. "We could start here."

A bundle of cards tied in pink ribbon were from Brit. A stack tied in twine were from other family members. Other bundles were from friends and business associates. "He was a sentimental pack rat, see these notes I sent him when we were in college."

She smiled. "Here's the program from the play we did together. That was how I met him, you know? It was his last play as a pre-law student. He knew there wouldn't be time for outside activities once he moved into law school fulltime. Here is a napkin from a fraternity dance. He belonged but he didn't really belong, since he didn't care for so much drinking. He wasn't a prude, but he was into law and order even then, very conservative, very Republican."

Sam felt like an intruder watching Brit shuffle through mementos of her time with the man she'd said was her first and only love. Sometimes she seemed to forget he was there, even when she spoke or commented on another piece of a history he would never share. Would someone in the future find his personal memories packed away with Brit's? He hoped so. God, how he hoped so!

"Sam! Look at these," she exclaimed, pulling out a stack of small notebooks and appointment books. She held her breath as she passed them for his inspection. "Should we go through them now or should we call Drew?"

"I already spoke to him. I called him before we went to the restaurant after church to check on his progress and to tell him what we planned for this afternoon. He should be here soon," Sam answered. "We could take these downstairs or we could have him come up."

"We'll be more comfortable downstairs. Let's check the other boxes before we take these down." Brit carefully placed the stacks of cards and memorabilia back into their box.

"What is it, Baby?" he asked, touching a tear travelling from her shimmering eyes to her cheek. "Need a hug?"

In an instant she was in his embrace, holding on for dear life. He placed a kiss on her head. She felt his breath hot on her hair. She shivered then sighed and pulled away.

"I am glad you're here. Thanks."

"Any time, Sweetheart, anytime."

There was one other box of papers with envelopes and scraps of paper with notes about appointments. It seemed easier to take that whole box downstairs to her room for sorting.

"Sam, would you look at this." She held up a desk calendar with notes scribbled on some dates. *"See Costello about inconsistencies in testimony* was written on a square three days before Tommy's death.

"Who is Costello?"

"Tommy represented a Bick Costello. Tommy was awfully quiet after the first day in court with that case."

Sam pointed to the next day. "Send Brit to spend a few days visiting her parents."

Brit frowned. "He did suggest I come home for a few days, but I had classes to teach."

"Check the month before his death," Sam suggested. Notes about people to call or see seemed routine until they saw the note. *Everyone is entitled to a defense. Why me?*

Beside the day of Tommy's accident Sam read, "Call GBI about Costello, then resign from case."

The most shocking thing they found was large manila envelope containing a wrinkled envelope bearing Tommy's bold scrawl. "No sale!" Brit's voice quavered. On the outside someone had scribbled fifty thousand, down payment. Inside there was a stack of hundred dollar bills and more.

"Sam," Brit whispered, "this doesn't look good. Tommy was too honest to be bought. This means someone killed him before he could return it, doesn't it?" Her voice broke. "Damn!"

"I'd say so, but we'll need to show everything to Drew. Maybe there'll be finger prints besides Tommy's on the bills or even the envelope."

By the time Drew's black truck pulled up to the Simpson house Brit and Sam waited in the porch swing. The dark man approaching the porch steps sent Brit into fits of laughter. His worn, tight jeans looked like they had been washed too many times. His black tee shirt was so tight it molded to his muscular chest and showed fine-honed, tanned upper arms. His longish black hair and beard were enough to send small town neighbors running to their phones and set small town law officers to checking wanted posters.

"How nice of you to get all dressed up just for us," Sam teased as he reached for his brother's hand. "Didn't you have anything casual to wear?"

The tug of war that began when Drew took Sam's hand ended in a back slapping, bear hug. "Where's your motorcycle?" Brit asked when Drew turned his brother loose and hugged her. "Mama'll love this. Especially the spider earring. I'm glad my niece isn't here to fall madly in love with you."

Ellen wiped her hands on her apron as she pushed the screen door to greet the stranger on her porch. "So, you're Sam's brother, Drew?"

"Yes, ma'am."

"Come have some supper," she said without blinking an eye. "I've just put food on the table."

Sam and Brit lagged behind Drew and Ellen, who took his arm to lead him through the door. They exchanged shrugs, following the unlikely pair to the dining room table.

Matthew stopped dead in his tracks at the sight of his mother leading the "Hell's Angel" look alike, so out of place in her neat, conservative house. To his credit he said nothing to show his shock at the appearance of the man introduced as Sam's brother.

Supper went well, considering the anticipation plaguing Drew, Sam, and Brit, and quickly.

Brit smiled at her dad when he arrived just after everyone sat down to eat. He took the introduction of Sam's brother in stride, showing no surprise at the addition of the scruffy guest. "I'm running short on time," he explained, reaching across the table to shake Drew's hand.

"Sorry I have to eat and run, but I have a mother in labor and twins that should arrive in a couple of hours. They don't

183

care if the doctor's hungry or tired. Their poor mama won't appreciate it if they show up early and I'm not there."

And he did eat quickly, finishing just as his beeper signaled he was needed. "Glad to have met you, Drew. Gotta go help two stubborn babies get here."

Both Matthew and Ellen warmed up to Drew, despite his appearance. Neither knew the real reason for his presence. It didn't pay to have too many people privy to that kind of information. An intelligent man, he could keep up his end of a conversation without giving away too much.

When the three conspirators sat down with the boxes of papers in Brit's room no one expected to discover even more than Sam and Brit had found earlier.

After an hour of reading and discarding notes to the not relevant to this situation stack, Drew let out a long whistle. He pulled Sam aside near the window before he blurted under his breath, "Jesus H. Christ, Sam! This is it! Look at these comments. The week before her husband was killed he had an appointment to see a Charles Russo about a rumor he heard. Look, it says here that he planned to discuss his concerns about several warehouses belonging to a Peter Salvo."

"We have to tell Brit."

"Yeah, these warehouses are known now for being sites for drug dealing, among other illegal activities. I know of more than one bust there."

"That is unbelievable. He was definitely a target then. I'm sure Brit had no idea."

Flipping the page, he spotted notations dated the next day. "The big man had refused to meet him. He sent flunkies to warn nosy lawyers off things that didn't concern them."

Brit had put down the letter she was reading and joined them near the door.

"Oh, Tommy, what did you get yourself into?" Shaking her head, Brit covered her face with her hands. "He never said a word to me about this."

"He couldn't involve you. I didn't hear you come up." Drew tried to reassure her. "He couldn't go to the police until he had more evidence to go on. Without proof he'd be in trouble."

The room was quiet, except for the turning of pages and an occasional hmmm or wow! "We need to know more about Costello, too. And I'll check the records of our Mr. Drake's visitors in his special quarters, courtesy of the state. Where can we get copies of these papers made?" Drew asked.

"Not here this late on a Sunday," Brit answered.

"We need to get this information to Atlanta, but we need to hide the originals. With what we have learned in the past three years we can use these notes to nail the lid on at least one crook's coffin." Notebooks and papers were being neatly stacked in Drew's backpack. "Since I'm a special investigator I can get an interview with the scumbag who attacked you, Brit. I'll get him to tell me who sent him."

Brit paced. The more real the danger seemed, the harder it was for her to sit still. Drew stood beside her. Taking her hand in his, he explained. "Once I convince the right people that the attacks weren't isolated rapes, we can get real protection for you and your family, if necessary."

"Won't you be in danger, Drew," she asked. "since you'll have the evidence?"

"Not for long. I didn't see anyone following me, so this line must not be tapped. No one is likely to think a cop visited you today." Drew laughed at the idea of someone who looked like him visiting this picture-perfect small town. "I think you shook anyone who might have been following you when you left with Julie. No one seems to be watching this place. I checked things out before I came in and again after supper."

Drew followed the instructions Brit gave him to the sheriff's office. When he made a spectacle of himself after running a stop sign he got an escort. Flashing his badge got him to the sheriff, who was more than willing to make copies and offer to keep an extra watch on the Simpson's house. He could do so without looking out of place and he'd notice any strange cars in the neighborhood.

By the time Drew left New Briton, the sheriff had copies of any information that could pose a threat to Tommy Roberts' former clients. Now it was up to him to save Sam's woman. He'd put the scum in jail where they would stay for a long time.

Chapter Thirteen

They'd seen only a few of the sights of Brit's hometown, but it was time to leave. Sam and Brit headed way back to Florence by ten o'clock, after breakfast. ETA in Florence, noon. The tension between them during their time in New Briton had taken its toll.

Between worrying about what she would learn about whoever might want her dead or who might have wanted Tommy dead and her need to make nonstop, sweaty, loud, mind blowing love to irresistible Sam, Brit was on the way to being batty and frustrated as Hell.

Going through Tommy's things offered the closure she'd needed. No one would ever take away the memories of her life with a wonderful man, but that life was over and now she could move on. Tommy would have told her to go for love again, if he could have told her anything. Maybe he was trying to tell her.

She and Sam were definitely moving toward a relationship, but what kind? The man was handsome, sexy, a great father, and sensitive, and nearly perfect. He was kinda pushy and too much a take-charge man. Would he expect to take over her life if they became close? She wouldn't allow that. She had become so much stronger in the past year.

I'll be glad to be back in my own home, strange calls and all. We certainly can't stay here much longer, anyway. If the bad guys trace us here my folks will be in danger.

The Lexis Sam had borrowed from his sister was a godsend. Monster would never have fit in his 'vette. Why hadn't he brought his truck?

They were on the road toward I-75 when Sam's cell phone rang. "Drew? You find something already?" Sam slammed his palm against the steering wheel. "What do you mean he wasn't there?"

"Sam?" Brit asked. Not good. What on earth could make the always calm Sam so upset? "What's wrong?"

He looked ready to strangle someone. Surely he wasn't angry with his brother. Sam's forehead was so furrowed his brows nearly crossed. He slowed and pulled onto a grassy shoulder.

"Son of a bitch!" he muttered. "How the hell?" He paused. Brit motioned to get his attention, but he waved her off. He held out his hand to tell her he'd tell her in a minute, but she wished he'd tell her now. The suspense was killing her. "What dunderhead let that happen?" He shook his dark head. "Where?... When?... Okay, okay, I'll tell her."

Brit nodded. *Yeah, tell me*!

"Call you when I know where. Thanks, buddy." Sam disconnected his cell phone. He turned to Brit.

"Sam, you're scaring me, just spit it out. What did Drew say?" If he didn't explain now she'd strangle him.

"We're gonna spend the rest of the week at a motel."

"We are?"

"Yeah."

"Yeah? Why, Sam? I have a perfectly good house, haunted though it is. You have a house, which I haven't seen before and your son is out of town. We could go to Julie's, I have a key and she wouldn't mind."

Sam shook his head. "You don't want to bring the haunting to your house?" she asked.

"That's not it." He shook his head and looked away at the traffic passing them.

"You aren't comfortable making love at my house, warts, and spooks, and all?"

"No, Ma'am," Sam's grin when he looked back at her was positively wicked. "I could make love to you anywhere."

"Well?"

Why won't he just tell me the reason for the change in plans, about what Drew had said to set him off? "What happened? Spit it out"

"He's loose. That bastard escaped on the way to court."

Brit thought her breath had stopped in her chest. Surely her lungs had stopped working. She didn't need to ask who escaped.

"Drew thinks Drake'll go to your house to finish what he started. I don't know if he's taken the time to chase me down, but he'll surely do that if you don't show up at your house. We need to alert your family and mine. Who knows what he's been able to learn while he was in jail? What if Julie's on his hit list? If he knows she's close to you he might look for her if he can't find you. We don't even know if he's a computer hack, or if he knew your husband, or anything except that he's a sick bastard with connections."

Sam felt as though he couldn't stop talking. Brit looked at him with utter trust in her expression. If they stayed away from their homes for a day or two, maybe the police could find the menace and get him back in jail. Right. The keystone cops couldn't hold him. They probably couldn't capture him. Drew would be better, if he could get the necessary authority.

"Sam, I should go home. If he comes there—"

"No!" Sam interrupted. "No way will I let you—"

"Let me?" Brit enunciated. "Let me?" She looked magnificent in her anger. Her eyes flashed. She seemed to vibrate with energy. "You don't *let* me do anything."

Sam wasn't exactly feeling calm, himself. "That's not what I meant. But what about when your friendly neighborhood attacker shows up at your house?" The very idea made Sam's teeth hurt. "You know he will. What if he slips by the security system again and attacks before we can get to him? It's the best system I could get, but no system is perfect and this guy is good. And what if he is already there, even as we speak?"

Her arms were crossed in a definite close-out-any-logic pose. The stubborn tilt of her chin made him wish they were in a hotel room already. He'd do his damnedest to convince her he was only thinking of her safety.

"Sweetheart, let's just find a place to think things out while the law looks for the guy. They can make sure he's not at your house and set up a stakeout. We'll talk about it."

Monster whined. Sam let him out and clicked his leash on his collar. He walked away from the car.

After he returned, Brit said nothing while they drove toward Florence. Sam didn't for one second believe he'd won this round. He had some heavy convincing to do. She was ready to kick-ass! He thought he could stop her?

***

Douglas was pleased. He'd outsmarted the guards and policemen. The teacher bitch won't get away this time. The man in the courtroom restroom hadn't wanted to swap clothes with a prisoner. Too bad!

With a bit of reconnaissance, he'd found the perfect house in the teacher's neighborhood. The family was out of town. There were signs. The grass was overgrown for the neighborhood in which other yards looked immaculate. The mail truck passed the house without stopping. No junk mail? Strange. He could learn a lot about people from their junk mail.

Dressed as a workman, Douglas had driven into the driveway and parked a newly acquired van. He'd spent time clipping shrubbery to watch the teacher's house.

An hour after Douglas had started his stakeout a neighbor drove into the driveway next door. She checked her mail and newspaper box then walked to check the mailbox and newspaper box at the end of the drive where Douglas worked.

By the time he'd been working six hours he was impatient. How long would he have to watch for her? Either the teacher was sleeping away from home or she wasn't answering her phone. She had to come home sometime.

He had his story ready, but no one had bothered him. His disguise made him look like he belonged. Too easy!

***

Nearly two hours later and five miles outside of Florence Sam stopped at a Hilton. Its column decorated front was a tad much, but it had all the luxuries, including suites with Jacuzzis. Sam handled the check-in while Brit took Monster for a walk. The dog's protective attitude proved he felt his owner's tension.

Monster had watched them unload the car with the help of a uniformed bellhop. The dog cowered in the elevator, leaning against Brit and quivering. Poor, big, old baby. Was he afraid of close spaces or just elevators? Sam carried the doggie bed.

Brit, Sam, and Monster had barely made it inside the room to check out the accommodations when two more bellhops arrived. One carried a large bowl of fruit, the other a vase of red roses. Each ceremoniously placed his obviously VIP offering in a place of honor then helped unload the luggage cart. The story behind the special treatment had better be good. They refused tips and left. When Sam and Brit were finally alone Brit took the time to look around the suite.

She said nothing while she walked around the expensively appointed, parlor-type room. The furnishings screamed money and taste. The place had the feel of a classy apartment.

The red door to the bedroom should have warned Brit about the main piece of furniture. The opulent bed was fit for a sheik and large enough for a harem. Its hangings and coverings were yards of plush white and gold fabric. There were enough pillows to support an orgy.

At the images that thought evoked, Brit felt her body heat and her pulse accelerate. She could imagine Sam's muscular body lounging on the bed. His green eyes would reflect the gold. His familiar dark eyebrow would arch in expectation. His body would beckon to her need.

Remembering she was supposed to be annoyed, she sauntered to the bathroom. Surprises awaited an unsuspecting guest.

"Holy sh...?" she uttered. The large Jacuzzi sported gleaming gold handles and spout. Surrounding it were gold candelabra and fat candle holders. Lights from the overhead chandler reflected in the mirrors, sinks, counters, more porcelain than she'd seen outside country club restrooms. The biggest surprises were the mirrors over the tub and the bidet.

"What have you done?"

"Would you believe it was the only available vacancy?"

"Not on your life." Brit pushed past Sam to leave the room designed for sex and decadence.

"Look, Love, I thought it would be a perfect cover. No one would look for us here unless we told them to."

"Did you ask for the honeymoon suite?"

"I hinted we were honeymooning." Sam grinned.

"Sam." Brit was gearing up for an argument again. "This suite is an unnecessary expense when we have perfectly good places we can stay free."

"When did you last check your answering machine?" He offered her his cell phone. "This phone is traceable, but its location isn't." Maybe there would be a clue as to what to expect from the man who threatened her existence.

The man now feeding her dog in the foyer of this suite presented a threat to her independence. He was too masculine, too dependable, too protective, too easy to need by far.

Her phone messages should be rated X for violence. The things the bastard had suggested doing to her body were the kind seen in bondage movies. The intimate acts were not sexy. Knowing the police had listened to them, probably more than once, was humiliating. She couldn't go home. She didn't know where she could go without endangering whoever lived there.

"Sam, can you put me in touch with Drew?"

"Sure." He punched in the code and handed the phone back to her. "Should I leave?"

She shook her head when the dial tone ended and Drew answered. "I need your help. Could you ask Esther to select a hair color and makeup colors to change my look. Tell her I want to look totally different."

Sam watched as she paused. He wanted to know what his brother said, but Brit listened so intently he didn't interrupt. She chewed a hangnail. Her face flushed when she spoke again.

"I need for her to find a couple of bras, size 34." She glanced down at her chest. "Size 34 and padded enough for a

D cup." She laughed. "You didn't miss anything. We'll fake it. I'll need big sunglasses and slutty earrings. Ask her to help outfit me with tops and slacks. I can give her a credit card number, but it would be easier if I get cash and pay her back."

Sam guessed where she headed. When she asked Drew to outfit him, too, he admired her cunning and quick mind. He pictured himself wearing a fake mustache or beard, maybe a different hair color or long hair like Drew's. Big, dark rimmed, Clark Kent glasses would be good.

Padded clothes to make him look heavy would be interesting. Drew would surely find a good disguise for him, too. He had no intentions of letting his Teach anywhere near danger, but he didn't want to spoil her fun. No way would the cops let her near her house or Drake. He'd let them tell her.

He'd been at large only a few hours. The police would find him and put him back where he belonged. He'd show up at Brit's house sooner or later to finish his job. They'd get him.

Chapter Fourteen

"Sit," Brit ordered, pushing Sam toward a large armchair. She punched the disconnect button on his phone. She dialed her number. After responding to the necessary prompts she handed the phone to Sam. He watched her trying to follow his reactions to the first message.

The first message could have been from a lover, albeit a perverted one. "Hey, honey, I'll be home soon. I want you to get out your sexiest outfit. I'll enjoy taking it off with my teeth, one piece at a time. I'll lick you all over before I nibble each sexy inch. A bikini wax would be a good idea. If you're good I won't bite hard."

Sam jumped up to pace, but Brit pushed him down again.

"Hmmm, you'll taste so good. I'm so horny just thinking about how you'll enjoy the little hurts. Maybe I'll tie you to the bed and beat you with my belt. You'll like the pain. Bet you're getting so wet thinking about it. Oh, shit! Oh, yes! Thinking about you is too much. You're my little slut, teacher. Can't wait to teach you a lesson."

Sam couldn't believe Brit had listened to that without throwing up. She looked peaked as she relived the call.

Call two was worse. "Where the hell are you? I escaped to see you and you haven't been home. It's been hours. No one has come in or out of your house. I've been watching. Didn't you get my message? I'm gonna have to teach you a lesson, bitch. I'll bring my rope and tie you up. I had planned to be gentle, but I've changed my mind. We'll use all your holes. You'll service me every way I can think of, like the whore you are."

Sam felt the blood leave his face. He felt so cold then so hot he thought his head would explode, but there was more.

"Been giving it away to lots of horny bastards? Are you still with that Daddy and his pretty son? I'll have to leave him a message, too."

Sam would have stood to pace if his legs hadn't been too weak. Brit had listened to this crazy, perverted monster. How could she keep her cool? He looked at her, wanting to offer her comfort. He hurt for her.

"Maybe I'll borrow the kid and teach him a thing or two. He might learn something if I let him watch what I do to you."

Bastard, Son of a Bitch. I'll kill him. We won't need the law. "Honey?" Sam tried again to rise, but she stopped him. Her hand on his shoulder was cold.

"Not yet, Sam. I'm still numb. You have to hear it all." Her voice was devoid of emotion.

The awful voice made his skin crawl. "Think he'll like to join us? You can teach him more than school lessons, how to give and receive. You might be the first and last piece he ever gets. Maybe he won't like it with women, after all. He might like a big cock instead. I haven't had me a virgin in a long time. Tell his daddy that and get ready for me. Maybe I'll make Daddy watch before I cut his heart out."

Sam couldn't speak. He had to remember to breathe. Brit moved to him. She pulled his head against her breasts and held him. His face was wet with tears, his tears. The light pressure of her head against his comforted him. Her chest shook as she breathed deeply and slowly. She was crying, too. She needed comfort, but she was offering it to him.

Brit caressed Sam's dark hair. She felt his pain in ways she had tried to ignore when she'd listened to the tape the first time. It hurt so much worse knowing Sam was hearing the filth, the threats to his son. She couldn't go home until things changed. She needed to feel clean again. She needed Sam. His back was muscled and hard beneath her hands when she moved them in circles. His face against her breasts sent need racing through her blood.

"Sam," she whispered. "Sam, take a shower with me, help me wash away the filth for both of us." She leaned back to look at his tear stained face. "Come with me. We could use that decadent, overblown tub instead and soak."

Taking his hands in hers, she pulled him to his feet and led him through the bedroom and into the bathroom. She reached to turn the chandelier on low light. Sam watched her but seemed frozen.

Walking around the Jacuzzi she turned on the shiny handled taps, running the water over her hand until the temperature was warm enough. Selecting decorative bottles from the vanity, she sprinkled a mixture of herbal scents into the water.

Her slacks and panties slid down her legs and she kicked them across the room. She felt his gaze on her pubic hair. His touch would have caused only slightly more need in her. Sam's eyes flickered when she removed her shirt. The front catch on her bra slipped free, freeing her breasts. Sam hadn't made a move, but that didn't stop Brit.

She grabbed his shirt and yanked it open. Buttons flew across the floor. Sliding his shirt down his shoulders and arms she licked his nipples. His chest invited her touch, but she had plans. With effort she unbuckled his belt and removed it. Slowly her hand moved against his crotch to unzip his fly. Her hand moved inside his briefs to caress his penis. He was aroused and beautiful. She could see them in the mirrors around the tub.

When Brit reached around to turn off the water Sam came to life. He kicked off his jeans and stepped close to her backside. His hard cock rubbed against her. If she hadn't needed to wash away the memory of the calls she'd have stayed where she was to see what Sam would do next. At this moment she'd have let him make love to her any way he wanted. They both needed it. Nah, she wanted to do things her way first.

"You first. Get in." Her voice was thick with desire. When Sam was seated in the tub she climbed in and straddled him. Taking the scented soap, she lathered her hands and then washed his chest. Her hands circled his nipples, slicking the thick, dark hair on his chest. She moved her soapy hands over his shoulders, savoring the strength and smoothness of him.

Her heat sought to join with him, but she wasn't ready to allow that, not yet. Sluicing water down her front, she rubbed her breasts against his soapy chest.

Sam had tried to let her lead the way but when her hands made contact with his belly and headed down he pulled her above him. His mouth opened over her slick nipples and blew on them. Sliding her against his body he dipped her front in the water, then raised her again to take a nipple in his mouth.

He took a vial from the selection on the shelf beside the tub and uncorked it. Pouring scented oil into the palm of his hand he anointed her body, all of it.

When Brit could gain her knees again she knelt and straddled Sam's cock. When she felt him move against her she sheathed him as far as she could.

Their joining was fast and furious. Brit needed Sam, but she also needed to vent some of her anger and helplessness. She needed to feel like a woman in charge instead of a victim. She needed to experience beautiful, mutual sex with someone she desired, someone who wouldn't defile her with perversion.

Her body spasmed when she came so hard she fell into the abyss, then she soared. She collapsed against Sam, who he hadn't come yet.

It had taken all his control to hold back the explosion building inside, but he planned to fill her thoughts with him, leaving no room for anything frightening. Sam slowly paid homage to the woman who made him feel like he could conquer the world for her. She made him feel both needy and needed. There wasn't a tasty inch of her body he didn't lick or kiss with reverence. She was all woman, and her responses made him feel all male.

When his strength returned he stood with her legs wrapped around his waist and took her to the bed. Gently he lowered his body to place her on the pile of pillows. Their damp bodies clung to the coverlet and each other. The way her whole body moved against his would have tempted even a saint, and he was no saint.

"Hold that thought, sweetheart" he made himself say.

"Where do you think you're going?" she purred.

"We haven't been exactly careful about using protection. You take away my ability to think. I'm being responsible while I remember what to do."

"Oh, that. Don't worry. I'm safe." She began to stroke that part of him that loved to be stroked. He once again threw caution to the winds. If she wasn't worrying, he wouldn't worry, either. Actually he wouldn't mind if she became pregnant. He'd like a baby brother or sister for Sean. He'd love to hold a baby they had made together, one that looked like her.

Her smooth ankles were delicate in his rough hands. He loved the strength of her calves. Her knees were tempting, especially when he found her ticklish spots. Her thighs begged his attention. Suddenly he went brain dead. He couldn't think anymore, but he felt everything. He felt smooth skin and soft hair. He felt nipples hard as pebbles and a smooth expanse of throat.

Sam wanted this woman to remember his loving above everything else. When she thought of loving she'd remember him. When he slid his hands beneath her buttocks she quivered. His tongue made a wet path up her thigh all the way then slid inside her moist heat. He held her captive until she moved against him. He tasted and suckled. Her ecstasy when she came against his mouth nearly sent him over the edge.

He still smelled the natural fragrances rubbed into her skin and sluiced over her body. The longer they made love the more the heady, sexy scents of their bodies overshadowed others. His brain deserted him, but his body was alert to her desires and his own.

"Sam," she chanted. "Sam, Oh, God!"

While she still trembled he slid up her body and plunged in once, twice and exploded. His shout nearly drowned out hers.

Brit had felt all control leave her somewhere about the time Sam placed exquisite kisses on her belly and circled her navel. Her body had seemed boneless. Her skin was sensitized beyond belief, but she knew little more than the sensations of slick skin caressing slick skin and their joining. At this moment her body was his to do with as he pleased, and he pleased her. God, how Sam pleased her - more than any other man ever had.

When his body covered hers she felt so damned safe. She felt loved and protected.

After a while she could speak, "I should apologize."

"For what, love?"

"For using you to make me forget."

He grinned. "Use away, I enjoyed every minute of it." His grin disappeared. "Besides, I was using you to move me out of shock. I needed your wholesome, honest loving."

"Wholesome?" she asked. "Only wholesome?" She ran her hand down his belly to grasp his shaft. When her tongue slid across his teeth he groaned.

She rose above him to gaze into his eyes. Playful, she nipped the tip of his nose.

Now he laughed out loud. "Sexy, irresistible, mind-blowing, brain-stealing, body-sapping..."

"Don't overdo it." She kissed him then settled against his side and relaxed while her heart rate finally slowed to a gallop.

She'd drifted off to sleep in his arms when his cell phone rang, startling her upright.

"It's probably Drew or Esther with your disguise," he said.

"And yours," she reminded.

Chapter Fifteen

Drew's disguising skill worked wonders. They'd created a new man. Sam in camouflage fatigues would have fooled anyone, especially after the clippers had nearly shaved his head.

"Damn, brother, where did you get these rough duds?" Sam looked tough enough to worry anyone who didn't know him.

"Raided my closet." Drew shrugged. "How do you suppose the women are coming in the bathroom?"

"I don't know, but I don't trust our little sister, do you?" Sam asked.

"Not in a million years." Drew handed Sam aviator sunglasses. "I can't wait to see her face when she sees what I've done to Mr. Conservative. Something tells me Sean will be shocked, too. I'll warn the folks."

"Contact Sean and his mother and make sure they don't come back from Hawaii to the mainland until I call them. This scary situation could drag on past their planned stay. Maybe you could go ahead and book them somewhere else under assumed names. You'll need to tell Adrienne why she has to keep Sean away. She'll keep her baby from coming anywhere near this continent. I'll foot the bill for whatever they want."

Sam had even adopted that feet apart, arms crossed, militant pose to go with the outfit. "You'll do, big brother, you'll do," Drew reassured.

***

"There's no way I'll wear this in public!"

Esther looked Brit up then down. "You'll never be recognized as a school teacher. Isn't that what you wanted?"

"Yeah, but --- I look more like a hooker."

"You look fine. Maybe you can earn extra money working evenings." Esther grinned. "No more stalling, go show the boys."

Brit's eyebrows drew together in a scowl mean enough to melt paint from walls, the one she saved for her worst students. Esther had done a job worthy of an artist. If her mama or daddy saw this getup she'd be grounded, even at thirty-three, or probably committed. Sam was gonna hate seeing her like this.

"All right, let's see what Drew has done to Sam."

Brit opened the door to the bedroom and stopped dead in her tracks, teetering on heels high enough to give her a nosebleed. The man beside Drew looked like he belonged on an Army recruiting poster with his arms folded across his chest molded by the fitted shirt. Camouflage pants were tucked into polished boots. If there was any hair the cap hid it. Where was her handsome Sam?

This man looked battle ready, like someone you wouldn't want to tangle with. His beautiful green eyes were covered by big sunglasses. Only his mouth was the same. He looked dangerous and younger and damned sexy. He also looked shocked. Brit watched Sam take in the full effect of Esther's work. He looked as stunned as she felt, which was a lot stunned, beyond words, actually.

Sam had nearly swallowed his tongue when the black haired siren had walked from the bathroom. The woman with Esther looked like she could sell sex at a high price. Her hair was barely long enough to hide her ears. Her porcelain skin made her look like a china doll. Her red lips were full and pouty. He'd never seen her eyelashes so dark and lush or her cheekbones so contoured.

His gaze glued to the shocking cleavage of her impressive chest. The white, satiny blouse barely covered the essentials but exposed a flesh-colored, lace bra. Her short black leather skirt covered even less. Black hose saved her from exposing her panties, at least he hoped she wore panties.

Thong panties, maybe? High-heeled black boots completed the hooker look. *Holy Mother of God.*

The room was so silent Sam could hear his harsh breathing.

She slowly donned the sunglasses that were indeed slutty and perfect. Even her own mother wouldn't recognize her in this getup. Now they could move around without detection. Sam knew he looked mean enough to get answers to his questions. He wasn't sure how her outfit would help, but the memory of it would keep him awake nights for years to come.

"Well?" Brit asked.

Sam couldn't speak. He wanted to grab Brit and kiss her mindless. He wanted to get her out of those clothes. He wanted to take her standing against the wall.

They had an audience and work to do.

***

"Why the hell hasn't the bitch come home yet?" Douglas was tired of watching the house. He'd had to escape the dufus cops taking him to the hospital. The assholes had believed he was sick. They'd been so easy to lure into the men's room with his sick act. Didn't they ever read or watch the movies? They were too stupid to live, but he wasn't into killing without a contract. Since he didn't kill for free, he'd only knocked them out. One hard slam against a wall for the first one and a slam against a stall door had worked for the second.

Over by the driveway two houses down he spotted the nondescript police stakeout car. When a car parks a long time and no one gets out it's obviously a plant. He could teach the plainclothes cops a thing or two about watching a house. Twice he'd sneaked over and checked things in her yard. Since the teacher had her stupid dog with her no barking warned anyone.

Bringing overalls and gardening tools had been a stroke of genius. No one would expect the escaped prisoner to look like a yardman. The five o'clock shadow would soon become a healthy beard. He hadn't been made yet, and he didn't expect to be.

An unfamiliar car pulled into the teacher's driveway. Silver Lexus, maybe a year old, good condition. Who the hell? *Oh, the sign on the door says Brooks Real Estate Agency.*

What's going on here? Did I scare her away? She gonna sell out? She had left her Mustang in the garage and her answering machine message hadn't even changed.

A young looking man dressed for success in a navy suit and yellow tie exited the driver's side and rushed to open the passenger door. A black haired woman climbed out, exposing a great deal of leg above the black high-heeled boots. He'd never mistake her for a real estate agent. She carried one of those huge bags some women liked. God only knew what she kept in it.

"Ma'am, this house was just put on the market yesterday. It's not listed in the books yet." The suit reached into the back of the car and pulled out an expensive looking briefcase. "We haven't had time to put up a *FOR SALE* sign."

Douglas had chosen a good spot to park his van. He could hear them pretty well with the sound amplification device from Cousin Vince. *Twerp looks like he'll trip on his own tongue.*

"Well, let's see it, then, shall we?" She slung the bag higher on her shoulder and took his arm, like he was some kind of gentleman escorting her. "Does it have modern bathrooms and kitchen?" she asked.

"Not exactly, but you're gonna love the claw foot bathtub." It was all Douglas could do to stay out of sight. The man reached into his pocket and brought out a key attached to a large disk. She's smiling at the twerp like she's sending him a message. *Bet he wants to get into her panties. Bet she'll let him, for a high enough price. Like to get into her panties, myself. Bet she wouldn't charge me.*

Douglas wanted to go closer to the house, maybe peek in the windows, but he couldn't take the chance. Damn, he'd give anything to know where the teacher was. She hadn't moved her stuff, so she'd probably come back before her house sold. He'd had feelers out, but no one had seen her recently.

The black haired broad looks like she enjoys a good romp in the hay. Probably likes it rough. The tits are fine, too.

What if I ring the doorbell and act like a neighbor come to visit? I could... Maybe not. Seems like the dark haired broad would've left, by now, if she didn't like the house. What if she likes it and buys it?

What if the teacher never comes back? Shit! Shit! Shit! She's gotta come back! Never missed a hit yet, no matter how long it took. A contract's a matter of honor. *Never had to try more than once, must be slipping.*

Now what? A jeep pulled in beside the agent's car. The man who got out wore camouflage clothes and sunglasses. He had a look about him Douglas didn't like. *Who the hell is he, some relative or someone else wanting to buy the house? Shit!* He'd have to sneak in and mess it up so no one would want to buy it. This should have been a simple, easy money job.

The bad-ass looking guy looked like he was studying the house and the neighborhood. At least he couldn't see Douglas hiding in the van.

Thoughtful of the neighbors to be out of town this week.

The new guy seemed to pause as he looked toward the stakeout car. He turned back to the house when the screen door slammed and the black haired babe raced toward him.

Oh, yes! She landed on him like an octopus, arms and legs around the bad military dude. *Rated XXX kiss in front of God and everybody.* The neighbors will love this. Husband, boyfriend, lover more likely or sugar daddy. Now he's carrying her up the steps, still wrapped around him. Time to kick out the panty-waste salesman. Bet he's disappointed. Hot pants for sure.

Douglas waited and waited. He was bored and too curious about what was happening at the teacher's house to even take the time away to pee. At least he was out of the stinking prison and he planned to stay out.

Once he was done with the teacher, maybe he'd look up the blonde friend, the other teacher. She'd make a good playmate. Since she wouldn't know who he was he could have a good laugh. He could screw her after he'd killed her best friend.

Then he'd leave the country and leave her wanting. Or he could take her with him. Irony? Good word for a man with barely a high school education.

Chapter Sixteen

Brit had left her house just a weekend ago, but she felt she had been away a lifetime.

She had enjoyed turning the rundown house she had bought cheap into the homey house she had loved so much before it had been invaded by a killer. How had so much changed in only weeks?

Each time she passed a mirror she felt disoriented, like she lived in someone else's body.

"So now what?" Brit turned to ask Sam, who sat down on couch beside her. She shifted her weight and moved closer. The house was different without her dog.

"So, now," Sam said. "we confer with detective Peters."

"He's been videotaping from every window. I've never paid much attention to my neighbors' yards. Are you sure it's legal to video tape people around here?"

"Drew said Peters is the best surveillance agent in the bureau. He'll know what's legal and what isn't." Sam rubbed her hand. "Peters and I'll view the tapes and still photos with Drew to see if we notice anything out of the ordinary. No one'll see tapes of your neighbors, but one might be in danger. Your attacker must be watching this house or having someone watch it. We need to figure out what he's doing and catch him. We might see something that could save a life."

Brit watched Sam's large hand move over hers in a comforting gesture. She turned her palm up and entwined their fingers. Looking up at him, she asked, "But can you use what you find? I couldn't stand it if he got off on a technicality."

"Sweetheart, we're just going to prevent him from harming you and recapture him. He's already an escaped prisoner and the cops caught him dead to rights at the assault point." She snuggled into his embrace. "Detective Peters had better hurry. I can't wait to get you back to the hotel." He ran his fingers through her newly cut black hair. She felt the same old tingle that it intensified with each touch.

"I've been wondering how it would feel to make love to you as this new persona." He gently touched his lips to hers.

She was ready to try out their new personalities. He kissed her again. His lips had felt the same, his body felt the same, but his face looked harder, leaner. She missed his hair.

"Okay, you two lovebirds." The voice of detective Peters broke the spell Sam's chaste kisses had woven around them. "I've set up cameras to watch the outside. I can see the police stakeout car watching your house. Those guys would be lucky to find their backsides with both hands. They were so easy to make I'm sure our man has seen them if he's here."

"Oh, he's here." Sam's instincts were vague, not like when Brit was under attack, but there. Now he wished he really had physic abilities. Maybe they should call in a real physic, if there was such a person.

Peters continued as he set up a tiny camera pointing at the front door and the front room. "I'd like to watch that odd van parked across the street. It seems out of place."

"How many of those cameras did you bring in?" Sam asked.

"I brought four in my brief case and the lady here brought in six." He smiled. "I have two more, one for the kitchen and one for this room. The only places without cameras will be the closets and bathrooms. Drew and I thought you'd like some privacy there. By the time our man could get in those places we'd have spotted him on one of the other cameras."

He moved toward the kitchen, leaving Brit and Sam alone again. "We'll catch this bastard and put him away, I promise."

"I know, Sam, I know." Brit moved to the answering machine to check the messages. Two were from fellow teachers, one from the Youth Foundation pickup up caller. Two more were from her not-so-secret stalker.

Sam swore softly. "He's here somewhere watching. We have men to scope out the neighborhood for surveillance equipment. He'd hardly miss a chance to keep an eye on this house. Just wait 'til he learns you won't be coming back."

Brit moved to the kitchen to check her refrigerator for spoiled food. She emptied milk and several leftover containers. There was no evidence her food had been tampered with, but she'd take no more chances. Sam came into the kitchen. While the men rechecked Sam's sensors and alarms she drifted back to her answering machine. Time for a new message.

"You've reached Brit Roberts' answering machine. I'm taking an extended vacation and will be relocating. All messages will be forwarded so I can get back to you. Thank you."

"That should send him into a frenzy." Brit whirled around when the two men joined her. Detective Peters was packing his tools back into his briefcase. "We'll arrange for a U-Haul truck to move just enough empty boxes to make it look like you're moving out, then in. That should bring him out of hiding."

Brit moved quickly to her bedroom to grab a few things she could stuff into the oversized bag she'd brought with her. The cameras she had smuggled inside it had left plenty of room. She would be back with her new roommates, Sam and Drew's sister Esther. Sam and Drew had refused to let her stay here alone while they did their investigations, and she hadn't really wanted to. Back in the front room she asked. "Ready, guys?"

With an exaggerated wiggle and a grin she moved to the front door. "Enter, stage left, hot mama!"

***

Douglas was tired of hiding. He'd watched the front door for the woman and the two men to leave. *Ahhh, here they come.*

The real estate pretty boy must have a real southern lady for a mother, not like my bitch of a mother. Look how nice and polite he is, working hard for that sale. How sweet, holding the door for the woman and the tough guy. I can hear them again.

"Honey Bear, I just love the house. It's so cute. You wouldn't have to travel far and there's a room for your sister to stay with us until she gets on her feet." The woman's voice was as sexy as she was. She'd get her way a lot, the sex kitten.

Douglas could imagine having her rub against him like that. He'd pull her closer, maybe grab her butt. She didn't seem like she'd object to a little public groping. He'd take her back inside and grab other body parts. Maybe he wouldn't even take her clothes off. He'd just push aside anything in the way and shove it to her. Maybe doggy style.

Yeah, she looked hotter than a bitch in heat. She owed him for the days in the cell with no one for company but horny convicts and for taking over the teacher's house. Women like her were made to take care of men.

"It's okay," tough guy said. "We'll talk about it later, Baby." He led her around to the passenger side of the jeep and opened the door. "Let's get a bite of lunch. Gotta get back to work." He picked her up and put her in the seat.

Douglas had been so busy watching the lovebirds he'd missed the Lexus guy. It would soon be time to check the cameras he'd hidden when he'd worked outside earlier.

***

The hotel room was cool and crowded. "So, how'd everything go?" Drew asked.

"We made the local stakeout car too easily." Detective Peters shook his head. "Video cameras are well placed. I grabbed memory cards so we can view them on our computers."

Brit sat on the sofa and removed her torturous hooker boots. "I know he was around somewhere. I felt like he was watching us."

"He probably was," Drew said. "We should know when we see the stuff Peters shot."

"He was there," Sam said. "I felt him, too. Probably in or near the beat up van across the street."

"So," Brit asked. "what do we do next?"

"Agent Peters will take you there in a couple of days. Tomorrow a truck will pull up at your house. Our men will take in boxes to assemble inside, then lug them back to the truck like they're full. We'll take some heavy pieces to make it seem you are really moving out."

Agent Peters added. "A day or two later we'll move your Mustang to a storage place. That should convince anyone watching that you aren't coming back."

"Oh," Brit sighed. "It feels so strange. I'll be there, but I won't be there. And I can't take Monster home with me."

Sam walked over to the sofa and sat beside her. He took her hand and kissed her knuckles. "Esther will be there during the day, and I'll be there, too, at night. I'll take care of you, Teach. My mama will take care of the Monster baby."

"I know. What about some food? This undercover work makes a body hungry," Brit announced.

***

Three hours later pizza boxes lay stacked up on a table beside the door of the bridal suite. Detective Peters stared at a magnified image on his computer, studying it as though it held the secrets to locate a fortune. He had studied each image from on the memory card.

Beside him Drew viewed surveillance footage on his computer monitor. Occasionally Brit would hear one of the men call excitedly to the other and she'd rush to see what was so important. So far she had seen nothing that told her anything. She wished Sam and Esther would get back with the much needed ice cream. Nothing like a powwow of detectives and security people to put a downer on a girl's mood.

Earlier she had muttered to Sam, "Isn't it a little crowded for a bridal suite?"

"Yeah, I hadn't expected everyone to move in with us." Sam put his arms around her. For seconds she forgot about their company. "Maybe we need to book our own little love nest."

Even now she felt the delicious tingle in her lower belly. Closing her eyes, she blotted out the others in the room. She

210

drifted off into a dream world. She needed the warmth Sam's body always gave her. The detectives in the room could protect her.

Drew's excited voice broke through her semiconscious state. "Come look at this, I think I've made our man."

Brit shot across the room in a flash. Drew pointed to a blow-up of a scene in the video on his monitor. The bent, shabbily dressed figure beside the pointer moved slowly from the old service van. With his shaggy beard he looked more like a homeless person than a repairman. The company name on the van had mostly faded and rusted away.

Brit watched the man shuffle toward the mailbox. Why would he be interested in her neighbor's mail? "Drew, my neighbors are out of town for this whole month. Their mail is being held at the post office."

"Look," Drew nearly toppled his chair. "he's taking out a box. Bet he has his own surveillance equipment in the box."

Drew tried to zoom in on the box, but the man outfoxed them by turning his back on the camera.

"Let's go nail the bastard." Brit started toward her boots. "What are we waiting for?"

"Nail whom for what?" Sam asked. Brit hadn't heard him come back in. She watched him put a large bag on the coffee table and calmly walk over to Drew and Detective Peters. "What bastard does the woman want to nail this time?"

"Yeah?" Esther asked. She took the contents from the bag and spread them on the low table. She motioned for Brit to join her. "Who are we nailing?"

Calmed by their joking, Brit pointed to the men and explained, "Drew and Detective Peters think they spotted my attacker watching my house. I was ready to go for him."

"What if he's really just someone taking advantage of an empty house, maybe a homeless person? That man doesn't look any more like your attacker did than we look like ourselves. What if that box was dropped off by mistake? What if it's something illegal and we mess up a police bust?"

Detective Peters muttered. "These local cops wouldn't need help messing up a bust." He had come to the coffee table to join Brit and Esther. He reached for an ice cream carton and read the label. "Rocky Road, my favorite."

"Here." Esther handed him a plastic bowl and a large spoon. "Go for it, Pete."

Sam and Drew joined the ice cream crowd. Sam reached for a bowl, but Brit handed him one full of chocolate chip ice cream. He grinned at her over the bowl when he took it. "What if I had wanted Rocky Road?"

"I'll give you some of my Rocky Road," Her voice was husky. "if you're a good boy."

Gazing into her eyes, Sam warmed. "We could eat it the bedroom and leave this room to the others," he suggested.

"We could, at that."

Brit looked good enough to eat. He was almost accustomed to her new, short, black hair. "We could share."

"Okay, knock it off, you two," Esther interrupted their exchange. "There are no children present, but young Pete's blushing up a storm. He'd never be able to concentrate, knowing what you're up to just a room away. Drew and I might enjoy watching through the keyhole. We haven't done that in years."

"You've made your point, Sis." Sam frowned. Then he grinned. "Jealous, aren't you. You could never stand to be left out of the fun." He pulled Brit toward Esther and hugged her, brother style.

"We'll find you a honey, won't we, Drew?"

"I've tried." Drew mussed Esther's hair. "She just keeps running them off with her temper."

"Knock it off, you two clowns." Esther growled. "I'm just waiting for the right one to come alone."

Drew joined the group hug. This crew reminded Brit of her family. What would her brothers think if they could be in this room with all the technology? They'd love it, but she'd be sent away. At least Sam knew better than to try.

When she separated from the group hug she saw Detective Peters move back to his chair at the computer terminal. He sipped his coffee like he was thinking between sips.

"Let's eat so we can get back to work, since we can't play." Brit shoved Sam's bowl at him. "Bunch of party poopers."

Legal pads filled with lists moved from one observer to the other. Sam watched each person study images on monitors and note his or her observations. Everyone agreed the man in most of the frames didn't belong where he was. The truck didn't belong, either.

The man had made several trips from the truck, one to the mailbox, one to a shed separate from the house, and one to a hedge near the street in front of the house. Brit had tried to recognize him when Peters would freeze a frame, but the disguise, if he wore one, was good. Even the magnified images weren't any better. He seemed to know just when to turn from a camera angle. He might not be Brit's attacker, but he was up to something.

***

Douglas moved from the van to the hedge, checking the electronic spying equipment. Gadgets and inventing had been hobbies of his since childhood. People had no idea how many gadgets he'd made. Even the guys who hired him thought he was just a killer. Fools. Time to leave another message for the teacher.

Watching all around him, he drove the van past the cop car. It was time for the shift change. By the time he got back the new jerks would be napping like the rest always did.

He found a pay phone he hadn't used before and hoped it worked. The booth faced a park and a gas station.

Three rings, then her message, "Yeah, I know you're running away from me, bitch. I'll find you. I don't fail!" His voice rose. "I do not fail! When I find you, you'll pray for a quick death, but it won't happen!" he shouted. "Think of the worst nightmares you've ever had and they'll seem tame compared to what I'll do to you." He wiped the spittle from his lips.

213

He slammed down the receiver when a man approached. "What the Hell do you want?" He pointed his gun at the man who ran.

Two calls to his contacts got him access to a computer and a hotspot. Did the teacher think he couldn't find her? She didn't know how resourceful he could be. He drove the van to a garage owned by his cousin. He left in a recent model Explorer with tinted windows. It had taken thirty minutes to move his equipment to the new vehicle. The car tag had been altered just enough to fool an observer at a distance. He loved chop-shop shopping.

By the time he had spent an hour on line at the owner's computer he had drawn a blank. He hadn't found the teacher's house listed for sale or a record of a sale.

Time to get back to his watch. He needed to get back inside her house. He needed to find a way inside her neighbor's house, but every window and door was locked and the house was wired. He could give up his motel room if he could get inside.

***

Though Brit ran as hard as she could, he gained on her. Even with his unrecognizable face, but she knew who he was.

"Gonna get ya! Gonna get ya, bitch." She felt his hot breath on her neck as he closed the distance between them. Sam? Where was Sam? She needed him to chase the monster away like he always had. Hands clutched her shoulders, pulling her back.

"Can't get away from me this time. They're dead. I killed them all! Now I'm gonna kill you!" Hands closed around her throat, choking her life away. Sam, dead? Oh, no! No! No!

"Brit, wake up." Esther's voice broke through the haze of sleep." It's just a dream, honey, just a dream."

"Sam? Where's Sam?"

"He and Drew have gone to watch the police watch the bad guy. They wanted to check out the local cops. They also wanted to see what should be done before we move back into your house."

"Oh, are we alone here?" Brit asked.

"Nah, Detective Peters is in the other room reading a book that looks like a romance novel. Don't worry, my brothers will be back before you know it."

"Thanks." Brit settled back on the bed. "You've been a great help. But I miss Julie. I didn't get a chance to tell her we were coming back early. She doesn't know Douglas Drake is loose. I really miss Monster."

"Monster's fine at my mother's house, and Drew has kept your family posted on your safety. We'll call your friend Julie and let her know what's happening. Where should we contact her? The guys need to be sure no one's watching her."

Brit wrote Julie's cell phone number on a slip of paper.

"I've wanted to play cops and robbers since I graduated from college, but my family wouldn't hear of it."

"What do you do?" Brit asked. The woman looked like a model.

"I'm a CPA, freelance."

Chapter Seventeen

Sam had hated leaving Esther and Brit home at the hotel. Hours later he sat in an old model, black pickup truck around the corner from Brit's house. By two A.M. Drew had slipped out from the passenger side three times already. Within minutes the truck door opened to let him back in. The interior light had been disconnected for stealth. "So, what did you see?" Sam asked.

Drew opened the thermos and poured a half-cup of coffee. "Cops are dozing and our man found a way into inside the house where he's been hanging around." He gulped the steaming brew and grimaced. "Strong enough to take the hair off your tongue. He broke the lock off the storage shed in backyard." Drew made a face when he gulped another swallow. "He stashed a sleeping bag and a cell phone. The van has been moved. Now there's a Ford explorer in the drive. I'll check the Explorer next."

"What's he doing?" Sam rubbed his stubble-roughened chin. He skimmed his knuckles along his bottom lip. If he could have his way he'd off the jerk and scare the crap out of the cops who couldn't find their rear ends.

He hated not being in touch with Brit and Esther, even for a short time, and even with their man within their sights. He held the infrared camera to his eye and watched the man he believed was an escaped criminal sneak to the Explorer and slip inside. Every move he made looked so damned suspicious. Drew must have answered Sam's question, but Sam couldn't remember the answer.

"Tomorrow we send a pair of yardmen over to water the neighbor's yard. We'll have them go over to Brit's and water hers, too. If we can wet down his surveillance equipment, that should tick him off."

Drew slipped out again. Within minutes a police car pulled through the neighborhood. When it stopped beside the stakeout car, a uniformed officer exited and rapped on the window, causing a ruckus. A horn sounded and the door opened. The driver stood beside the uniform. Sam watched them argue. The driver showed his ID then got back inside the car and left.

Drew returned as silently as he always did. One minute he wasn't there and the next he was. "Now our man probably thinks he has the place all to himself."

"Looks like you're right, brother." Sam chuckled. "There he goes, bold as brass. Even if he's not our man, he's up to no good."

The shabbily dressed man scurried across the yard where the Explorer was parked, nearing Brit's yard. Sam snapped a picture. The man stopped beside a tree and looked around. Sam snapped. The man crept toward Brit's house.

"Smile, dirt bag, you're on candid camera," Drew muttered.

Sam's beeper vibrated. He showed the digital message to Drew. "Reinforcements are here, we can go back to our headquarters and check out the computer videos from the house." Sam snapped one last frame, then he handed the camera to Drew. He backed the truck from its sheltered place to head away from Brit's house.

***

By the time Brit heard Sam's key in the motel room lock her clock read five o'clock. Sam looked exhausted. Unable to go back to sleep, Brit and Esther had joined Detective Peters at the computer screen. Sam handed the digital camera to the detective who loaded the information into the computer.

Sam smiled at Brit. She moved into his arms. In his embrace she felt safe and cherished. Despite the audience she nuzzled his neck then kissed his cheek. His response was so gentle and warm she couldn't doubt his love. This was not the time or place to explore the possibilities. When Sam rested his forehead against hers she felt his weariness.

"Sit," she ordered, pushing him toward a large chair. He practically fell into its cushioned depths. Leaning over the chair back, she grasped his shoulders. Her hands worked his tired muscles. Her thumbs pressed circles against his taut skin. Within seconds she felt his shoulders relax. His head rested against the chair back. His eyes closed. His breathing slowed.

"Let him have a short nap. Then we'll put him back to work," Drew said.

Brit hadn't mentioned her nightmare to the men. She had warned Esther not to, either.

"We need to step things up and start the move tomorrow. I'll send a truck to cart some of Brit's things away." Drew studied the images saved in the computer. Nothing said the man camped out across from Brit's house was Douglas Drake, the man they wanted. If Drake watched the whole scene they didn't want to alert him.

***

Making the most of her fake persona, Brit stood in the driveway watching a moving company truck loaded with her belongings. Sam, wearing his killing machine look, stood with her, watching the movers.

"Isn't it sweet of the teacher lady to let us rent some of her things 'til she gets settled? I just love her piano and the big old sofa. It's just like my mama's," she purred, rubbing against him. "My mama's sofa has some interesting uses." She tilted her face to Sam's. "Real interesting." She stretched up to whisper in his ear. "Is that guy across the street watching us?"

He nuzzled her neck then whispered against her hair. "He sure is."

"I'm gonna get him. I know he's the bastard who attacked me," she mouthed against Sam's lips.

"I'll help," he answered. "But we can't just walk up and ask him."

She returned his kiss. Pulling away from the show, Brit swung her hips, walking up the steps to the porch.

"Coming?"

Sam grabbed three suitcases from the jeep and followed her onto the porch and inside.

***

Douglas played at trimming the hedge. He got a hard-on just watching the black haired woman. He hoped she didn't have a job, 'cause he'd like to make a visit or two to her house while the warrior guy worked. Maybe she'd know where the teacher was or could find out. If she let 'em use her furniture she'd likely keep in touch. Maybe they had her forwarding address.

He'd peeked into the garage last night. The Mustang was still there. He had to remain calm or he'd blow it and his reputation and get caught.

What the hell? A yard maintenance truck pulled to the curb. The man who got out of the passenger side looked big enough to tear the door off. He moved around to the back and pulled a tank with a hose attached.

The other man got out of the driver's side. He was even larger than the first guy. Shit. They were walking up the drive. Douglas shuffled past them on his way to the sidewalk. Ducking his head, he mumbled, "Nobody home." He shrugged. "What ya doin' here? Ain't nobody here to pay you."

"That's okay," the guy answered. "We already got paid to take care of the yard all month. Gonna spray grass seeds and weed killer. The owner wants his yard to look good when he gets home." Each man walked around the yard, spraying away. "What are you doing here?" the other man asked.

"Just keepin' an eye out," Douglas answered. "The owners said I could stay in their shed if I keep an eye on the place."

"You don't look like a house sitter." The larger man squinted at Douglas.

Douglas wanted to waste the man for being too nosy. What business was it of his, anyway? His voice was humble. "I did some work for the lady of the house before they left and she offered me a place to sleep. Didn't let me in the house, of

219

course. The shed's dry, at least, and better than sleeping in the car. It's all I got left. Lost my house last month."

"Lose your job?" the smaller of the two men asked.

"And my family, too."

"Gotta get to work," the taller one reminded his partner.

Douglas watched for a minute then walked back toward his Explorer. Maybe these guys wouldn't take long.

The sprayers were getting too damned close to the camera and listening device in the hedge. Shit! Oh, shit! There goes the equipment. No! No!

By the time they left the yard Douglas was ready to bust a gut. The new broad was coming from her house. She was motioning for the men to come to her porch. They hurried right over. That was some short skirt.

He couldn't hear enough to tell what they were saying. He'd probably have to replace everything. At least they hadn't messed up the stuff he'd planted in her yard last night.

Each tipped his cap to her then returned to the truck. Good they're leaving. No! The driver pulled the truck onto her driveway.

The jeep left, but the woman didn't.

The moving truck finally closed up and left, but the yardmen sprayed everywhere Douglas had planted surveillance equipment. He'd like to stuff their equipment somewhere they wouldn't enjoy.

Another car pulled up. Nice car.

Could they possibly be spraying the equipment on purpose? Nah, too dumb looking. He approached the larger spray man. "So, why are you spraying both yards?"

"The lady asked us to." He looked like he didn't want to be bothered. Tough!

"We'd have done it, anyway," the other man volunteered. "We always spray her yard. Didn't know the teacher was gone." He shrugged. "Nice lady, the teacher."

"Yeah, I heard she was a nice person."

The equipment had been loaded and the larger man held a clipboard and a pen. "This invoice says we sprayed this yard. Wanna sign?"

"Sure," Douglas signed a fake name.

"Gotta get the lady to sign for her yard. Otherwise we don't get paid." The man with the clipboard walked to the porch. The sex-pot came outside again and signed the man's papers. She sure knows how to flaunt it. His mama had always said you could tell the easy ones. This one had hot panties for sure. He'd check out her panties before he was through.

She had to have some idea where the teacher bitch was. Once he knew he'd have a good time with this one, then he'd find and kill his assignment. He'd kill her slowly. He'd kill her interfering boyfriend and his son and the blonde friend. Maybe he wouldn't have to kill the pretty blonde friend.

The yardmen finally left. Now he'd have to go back to his friend to restock his listening devices. Better check to see if any of his stuff had escaped the green spray. Damn! Damn! This job was costing him. His reputation would be in ruins, his employers would want their money back, and his expenses were escalating as he breathed, or as the bitch breathed! After the truck was gone he hurried to the Explorer. He needed to make sure the vehicle couldn't be traced to him or his friend.

First he needed a phone to see if the message on the teacher's phone had been changed or if she had a new listing. Why did she have to make his job so difficult? She was as difficult to kill as her stupid husband had been easy. He'd stepped in front of Douglas's truck as easy as you please. One hit with the truck and he'd been dead, out of the way.

***

Brit sat at her kitchen table, sipping iced tea from a tall glass. Men had come and gone from her house and their watches and already she was tired of it all. She just wished she could get her dog and settle back in her own house, in her old life. In four days she was expected back in school with everybody else. No one would be safe with her around. The scum had better show up soon so the cops could put him back in jail.

Drew had promised to explain things to her family and Julie before anyone tried to reach her here. Empty boxes loaded in the moving van had been taken away. The yardmen had thoroughly watered and sprayed grass seed all over the areas her enemy could have stashed cameras or listening devices.

The scraggy guy across the street had paced the whole time the men worked outside. He must be the man she needed to see put away for good. He'd be over here before long to check on the woman he'd attacked, the woman who'd sent him to jail.

He disappeared while she was daydreaming and enjoying a glass of tea. Brit ate a sandwich and wandered, waiting for Esther to join her. God, she missed Julie. Hardly a day would go by when she and Julie didn't see each other. The doorbell rang and Brit rushed to answer it. No, she stopped. She checked the peephole and saw Esther. Esther was not alone. Drew had hidden his hair under a western style hat.

"OOOOh you're here, finally!" Brit gushed. She hugged Esther like her long lost friend. "You look so gorgeous," she whispered as she hugged again. "Smile for the camera in case the asshole is watching." She made a point of ogling Drew. "Who's the cowboy?"

Drew stepped forward, offering her his hand. "Just a friend, Ma'am. This pretty lady and I met last night and she told me about your great house."

"Well, come on in and see the inside. It's so cute." She turned to Esther. "Did you bring your stuff so you can stay? There's plenty of room."

Acting the gentleman, Drew went back to the get some of the extra empty suitcases. He followed the girls inside and returned twice to make it look like Esther was really moving in. Once all the suitcases were in he checked each camera then joined the girls in the kitchen.

Brit's old phone line rang and the answering machine went on. "I won't be returning to this number or address but will answer any messages you leave. I'm sorry if this causes any inconvenience, but circumstances beyond my control prevent my leaving any more information." An angry voice came on as soon as the beep stopped echoing. "You don't believe you can run away, do you? I'll find you, you bitch. I'll find you." The dial tone was deafening.

"Nice man," Esther said.

The phone rang again. The message played again. This time the voice seemed so reasonable. "Hey there, we really need to talk about your car. It's time for your oil change and tune-up. Please call for your appointment. Our number has changed to 912-732-1554. Thanks, Joey."

Drew looked over at Brit, his eyebrow arched.

"Not even." She shook her head.

Again the phone rang. Julie's voice followed the message. "What the hell is going on? You'd better call me, Brittany Marie Simpson Roberts."

Drew shrugged, sheepishly. "She and her mother have been out of the house for the past two days. We'll get to her. I've sent a messenger to stake out her house and deliver a very important flower box. It has with enough information about your change in plans that she shouldn't worry."

"Well, if the jerk is listening in on my messages he'll be a believer after that one."

"Sam will call here as himself. He'll also act upset that he can't find Brit," Drew warned. "We need to be careful. Even if the strange character across the street isn't Drake, he sure seemed upset about the spraying. He might manage to replace any ruined listening equipment quickly. If it's someone planted by Drake or Drake's employers he's still dangerous. Whoever he is, he bears watching. I've checked around and no law enforcement agency admits to owning him."

Drew drained the glass of water he'd been holding. "Come on, Essie, girl. Time to see the sights."

Both girls and Drew made a tour of the cameras, still and video. Conversations would require scrambling and coding in case any listening devices planted by the enemy were sophisticated enough to record them. "I think any bad bugs have been killed." Drew explained. "If our man comes in this yard or in the house, we'll know and get him."

***

By the time Douglas returned to his post he had almost calmed down. He set about pretending to do yard work and placing spy worthy equipment aimed where he could keep watch on the house. Cameras recorded each move. Listening was no help since stereos blasted and televisions stayed blasting his ears. The new occupants must be crazy about their gadgets.

He needed information yesterday. Time for a new approach. He slipped back to the shed for a few minutes and returned, dressed in a suit and tie. His hat covered enough of his face to fool a person who had not seen him enter the shed. His first move was to walk down the street like a regular person. He approached the muscle-bound letter carrier and tried to get information. Her face was ugly enough to stop a clock, but Douglas smiled and charmed her. After several minutes of grilling her he finally gave up. Back to the shed.

Carrying a briefcase, he prepared to try again. He walked up the sidewalk to a house near his target. When a tall, slender redhead answered the door he went into his spiel.

"Hello, Ma'am," he said. "I'd like to show you our line of stainless steel cutlery. It's guaranteed to cut anything, from tough shoe leather to rocks." He smiled and gave the woman his most charming look. "May I demonstrate for you?"

"Thanks, but my husband just bought me a really nice set." The lady of the house looked scared. *Liar.*

"I understand, Ma'am. Maybe next time?" He tipped his hat to her and left. He turned back and asked. "Oh, do you know anything about Mrs. Roberts, the teacher down the street? She ordered a set and paid for it. I really wanted to deliver it today, but I can't get her on the phone."

The lady of the house shook her head. "I don't know her very well."

"Well, thanks anyway. You have a good day, you hear?" He left for good.

Under his breath he suggested painful things he'd do to her if he hadn't a job to do.

The rest of the neighbors were away from home at the moment, so he got no help.

He finally approached the house he'd been watching to no avail. Maybe the new people living there knew something. After all, she still got her messages there. He'd tried the number, hoping she'd had it changed with a forward. So far she hadn't. He'd better catch her before she did.

Drawing himself up and pasting on a posed smile, he rang the doorbell. He wasn't sure what he'd expected, but it wasn't the beautiful, dark haired woman who looked like a goddess.

"Yes, may I help you?"

He was struck speechless.

Chapter Eighteen

Brit watched from the closet where she hid. She couldn't risk being recognized or she'd have answered the door herself instead of letting Esther do it. She punched her speed dial to call Sam, who'd call the authorities. They were finally going to get the bastard who'd tried to rape her.

The man at her door looked so normal, but she recognized his voice. What was he carrying in the briefcase? Knowing Esther was trained in self-defense and carried a gun strapped to her thigh gave Brit confidence she could handle herself. Backup support had better get here soon or Brit might shoot the man with the weapon she aimed at the door.

"Good afternoon, Ma'am. I'm looking for Mrs. Roberts." The man at the door smiled at Esther. Oh, yes, Brit would have recognized him anywhere.

"I am sorry," Esther had put on a slight Spanish accent. "there is no one here by that name." Esther shrugged, looking puzzled. She should have been an actress.

"Are you sure?" the man asked. He looked confused. "But I was here just last week and she ordered a set of cutlery." He patted the battered briefcase. "I was supposed to deliver it today. Are you sure she's not here? She made me promise she'd have them in only a week."

"I am sure. My brother and his wife are buying this house from some real estate person. That is all I know." She moved as if to close the door in his face. Brit heard the panic in her attacker's voice. Good, let him sweat. His turn, now.

"My name is Michaels. Maybe she left a message for me, like where she can be reached." Brit could see him shift his weight from his left foot to his right then back again.

"I know of no message for anyone named Michaels. You have to come here when my sister-in-law is here. She maybe would know something." She shrugged again.

Sitting quietly was killing Brit, she wanted to run out to the porch and confront the man and beat the living shit out of him. She and Esther needed to immobilize him, but she would wait for reinforcements. Sam and Drew should be here soon. Esther couldn't let this jerk get away. If he became suspicious and left he might keep on walking.

"Look, if I could just come inside for a second I could leave a message for Mrs. Roberts."

Esther paused as though in thought. "Well, just a second." She moved aside for him to enter. Esther led the man to the dining room table, in plain sight of a camera. She maneuvered him so his back was to Brit, who was ready to slip up and get the drop on him while he was distracted.

Esther smiled at the man. She pointed at the briefcase. "Maybe you could show me the cutlery set? Maybe my sister-in-law would like one, whatever that is."

"Oh, it's a set of knives, you know, steak knives and all kinds of knives fit for a chef." He hefted the briefcase onto the table and slid out a box. Before he could open it Brit was behind him, a gun in her hand pointed at his heart.

"So, you're looking for me?"

He turned to face her. His expression showed surprise. "No, ma'am, I'm looking for the teacher." He nodded toward the gun. "You don't need that thing. I'd never harm a beautiful woman, certainly not two beautiful women." It was clear he didn't recognize Brit.

"So you don't remember me?" Brit stared at him. "I'm insulted."

"You have to be mistaken. You're not exactly the kind of woman a man would forget." He looked almost innocent. "I was just looking for the woman who owned this house. I wanted to deliver something to her. If you have a way to reach her, I'd really appreciate your help."

Brit was enjoying the game of cat and mouse, but she couldn't risk losing this man. "Well, I'd like you to sit in that chair." She pointed to a chair in the kitchen, away from the box he'd led them to believe contained knives. There might actually be a weapon in it.

Esther had been quiet, watching, evaluating. Her voice came out hard and demanding. "Do as the lady says." She pointed a gun at the man's head. "Now."

Douglas sauntered to a chair in the kitchen. "All you had to do was ask." What the hell was with these women? Both were hot looking enough to get any man they wanted. Were they into kinky sex, or had he stumbled onto a couple of criminal types? No matter. He'd play their game. He'd take his turn. "So, what are we playing? I'm into bondage."

"We're playing capture the rapist, the jail escapee," Brit said as Esther whacked him on the back of his neck. She grabbed his hands behind him while he was dazed and handcuffed them. Reaching for the rope they'd hidden, she started to tie him to the chair. When he would have resisted, Esther skimmed the gun along his jaw.

"Don't make me use this."

Her Spanish accent had disappeared. The cold steel traced a line across his skin. These ladies played rough. The tall one had a body that wouldn't quit. He'd like to grab those big, generous boobs. Her hair would be long enough to cover their tops. He hardened at the vision of his face smothered in their valley. If he had the gun he'd run it down her chest to her stomach. She'd move beneath him as he ran the barrel between her thighs. His erection was painfully sweet. Oh, yeah, maybe they'd both use him. He'd like a turn with each of them.

Brit noticed the man in the chair seemed to be enjoying this situation. Outside, a car door slammed. Brit knew it couldn't be their cavalry. They wouldn't be so noisy. Who?

Esther was convincing as she moved the gun to the man's chest, then lower. Damned if he didn't look like he anticipated the gun's nearness to his crotch.

The front door slammed and Julie's voice sounded loud enough to startle everyone.

"Brit, what the hell is going on? Your mama said you'd headed back home with Sam and your machine said …"

Julie barged into the room in time to distract everyone's attention. The man in the chair jerked his hands loose and bolted. The chair clattered to the floor as he grabbed Esther's gun.

"Wha ...?" Esther shouted.

The man must be an escape artist to get one hand free. Brit whirled to point her gun at Drake. He dove to an unsuspecting Julie and grabbed her hair, yanking her into his grasp. The gun in his hand dug into her neck.

"Where the hell is your teacher friend, bitch?" His nice guy voice was gone. "You and the teacher's boyfriend are really getting on my nerves." Julie was speechless. "The party was just getting started. You can join us now."

"And you," He pointed at Esther. "you hit me. That wasn't nice. I liked you. We could've had a good time together. Now you have to pay. Get over here." He kept the gun pressed to Julie. Esther shook her head. "Undo these bracelets."

No one moved or broke the silence.

"Do I have to shoot this one?" he threatened.

Esther looked at Brit. Brit shrugged.

"And put that gun on the floor, now!"

She hesitated.

"Do it now!" He pulled back the hammer on the gun. "Now, bitch! Carefully."

Staring at the man holding her best friend, Brit slowly lowered the weapon to the floor. She refused to break eye contact with the man who had turned her life upside down. "Hurt my friend and you'll wish I had shot you."

"Now," he said, "shove it to me."

Brit pushed the gun toward Julie and her assailant. The gun wasn't what she wanted to shove to him. "You're such a big man. Like to hurt women, do you? Well, there are three of us now."

Douglas laughed. "And I'll handle all three. You'll get your turn." He didn't break eye contact with Brit. She looked awfully familiar, but maybe it was because he'd been watching her the last couple of days. "Bring the key and open this bracelet."

When Esther hesitated again, he pointed the gun over Julie's head and fired. The picture over Esther's head fell to the floor. "Next time it won't be a picture. Get the hell over here."

Esther glanced at Brit. Brit's look of pleading was enough. She moved cautiously to the man she had cuffed earlier. Unlocking the cuffs, she threatened, "They'll get you for this, too."

His fist slammed Esther before she could react. "Now, you sit in the chair," he ordered Brit. "Tie her to it." Brit steeled herself as she sat down. She and Esther still had hidden weapons. Esther grabbed the discarded rope and began to tie Brit's hands.

"Do it right!" Douglas growled. He inclined his head toward Julie. "Now, blondie, where is your buddy?"

Julie glanced at Brit, who sat still while she was tied.

"I don't know where she is. Who the hell are you? And why are you threatening us?"

"He's a rapist," Brit said. "Not a very good one."

Esther finally stopped. She walked over to Julie and her captor. "The teacher got away. You lose."

"I never lose! I'll find the bitch and kill her. This one will draw her here and I'll do her when I'm through with the first one." Douglas's fury simmered. He wouldn't lose this one. He'd kill them all. He'd...have to calm down. He shoved Julie to another chair. "Move, and I'll shoot you all." Waving the gun at Esther, he ordered, "Cuff this one to the chair."

This party was too boring. While the one called Esther worked, he moved to shorter one. "You got a smart mouth, Bitch." He leaned close to her face. Her violet eyes glared at him like he was dirt. He hated that. He backhanded her. "Get that smug look off your face."

He rubbed his crotch. Hitting her had felt good. Having her use that smart mouth on his cock would make him feel better. Reaching down he grabbed a handful of her blouse and yanked. Buttons flew across the room. Her gasp was music to his ears. His arousal grew with the scent of the women's fear.

He'd left one woman loose for the moment. Now he'd put her to good use. "Come over here," he called to Esther. "See your sister-in-law's blouse? I want to see more. Show me her tits."

He pointed his gun at the woman's crotch. "Now, show me her tits or I'll kill her, bit by bit."

Douglas grinned at her gasp. He could tell she was excited when he rubbed the barrel along her thighs. When the breasts spilled from her black bra he noticed they were smaller than he'd expected. So she cheated. They were still a good handful.

Douglas remembered the tapes he'd enjoyed of the teacher and her friend, his thoughts of two women together. He ought to make the free one do some of his fantasies. The one in the chair had acted so hot for the military looking dude she'd probably hump pretty much anything.

With two women occupied, he reached for the tall one with the green eyes. He grabbed her by the wrist and yanked her to him. His arousal was painful. She could take care of him, on her knees. "Down, bitch. Open that red mouth of yours. I'll bet you can show your friends how to do a proper blow job on a real man."

Esther slowly moved to her knees, holding his gaze with her own. He was gonna get a blow-job he'd never forget. One hand unzipped his pants. The other reached under her skirt. She could tell by his expression what he thought she was doing. He trembled when she exposed his turgid penis. She was gonna enjoy this so much more than he was. His gun hand had relaxed. Her gun hand hid between his legs and caressed his balls through the fabric of his pants. He looked ready to explode in her hands. His eyes closed in that instant before climax.

Her gun slid to the exposed penis and hit him. "Bitch!" he screamed.

"Now try to come, you bastard," she said, springing up, hitting his wrist with cold hard steel.

Her knee hit his groin. He grunted. Her head hit his jaw. He staggered back. Her foot kicked up and connected with his throat. He fell.

Esther slid a knife into Brit's hand and the cuff keys into Julie's.

Julie was at Brit's side before she could finish untying herself. "Oh, Brit. Who is that bastard? What have you done to yourself?"

Brit stood and hugged her friend briefly. "I'll tell you everything as soon as this asshole is in good hands.

She moved to help Esther. The asshole was coming back to consciousness. She hit him again herself. She and Esther checked him for weapons, taking a gun from his pocket. Where were Drew and Sam? Where were the cops? Someone should have been here to get this bastard long ago. Grabbing the phone, she dialed nine-one-one. Her high-tech gadgets hadn't been any help so far.

**

Sam left the shower as soon as his neck began to itch. The pain in his belly matched the pain in his head in intensity. That could mean only one thing. Brit and Esther were in trouble.

The towel wrapped around his waist failed to protect the carpet from dripping water. The screen of the monitor filled with images of Brit and Esther and a man Sam didn't recognize at first glance. The panic signal was blinking. Detective Peters was asleep. Sam uttered a curse when he raised the audio to match the pictures broadcast from a camera in Brit's house.

What the hell was Julie doing there? The man in the picture had a gun on the girls and Sam knew. He damned well knew. His pain was no longer from his premonitions. It was fear.

At the curse Peters started awake. "Holy Mother." He jumped from the chair and reached for his phone and his gun. "Oh, God, I'm sorry." His voice quivered. "No replacements came and ---

"Get Drew and the local police." Sam ordered from the room where he'd run. He yanked slacks and a shirt on. His shoes and jacket dangled from his hand. His gun and shoulder holster hung in place. "Tell them what's happened and find out why no one seems to be responding to Brit's signal."

Sam was out the door and on his way to the elevator before Peters could respond. Sam pulled his coat on to hide his weapon. He hopped around on first one foot, then the other. He slid his foot into the last shoe as the elevator door opened.

"Why the hell did I have to take that damned shower?" Sam unlocked the door to his truck. "Peters picked a fine time to finally doze off." He slid under the steering wheel and started the vehicle. Why hadn't someone been sent to spell Peters? Even he needed to sleep sometime. The radio picked up the sounds from his hotel room.

"I made contact." Peters' voice was breathless. "Drew is on his way back from the meeting at the prison and the police have dispatched backups." Sam pulled from the motel parking lot into the street. There was a pause. "I won't fall asleep again."

"I know." Sam skidded around a corner. "Stay on. Patch me in for video." He switched his dashboard computer monitor on. Horns blared when he passed under a traffic signal just turned red.

Pain sliced through his gut. The man was threatening Brit and Esther and Julie. "Sick bastard," he growled. "Oh, hell." He hit the brakes in time to avoid plowing into the cars ahead of him. All lanes were blocked. Firemen helped paramedics load people into emergency vehicles. Four cars formed a jagged line across the street. *Crazy chain reactions!*

Esther tied Brit to a chair. "Damn. Not again." He wanted to scream when he saw Julie handcuffed. Only Esther remained free, but for how long?

Sitting still in traffic, Sam could not tear his eyes away from the scene unfolding across town. *Where the hell is Drew? Where the hell are the police?*

One vehicle was being hooked to a tow truck, but more remained in a jumbled mess. Sirens blared as an emergency vehicle sped away. Red and blue strobe-like lights lit the area like a stadium.

"I'm not believing this," he muttered. "I'm just not damned believing this." He'd bet every cop in town was at the scene of this accident.

Sam nearly puked when he saw the gun barrel touch between Brit's thighs. He'd take the damned shoulder of the road if he could get there.

Sam grabbed his cell phone before the first ring finished. "Where the hell are you?" Drew's voice came loud and clear.

"Stuck in traffic." He watched Esther kneel at the bastard's feet. Sweat covered Sam's body. "No, Sis, no!"

Another piece of the car collage ahead moved onto the bed of a tow truck.

Sam heard Drew's voice. "Oh, shit! Get him, Esther."

The girls had him. Ahead, several cars came toward him. "They're letting cars through," Sam said into the phone.

"Thank God." Sam rested his head on the steering wheel for a second only. Esther turned to the sink and ran water onto towels. She handed one to Brit and one to Esther.

Sam screamed when the man rose behind the women. "Behind you, damn it! Look behind you! No!"

He swallowed bile. Esther went down from a blow to the back of her head. Brit crumpled before Esther hit the floor." Sam heard Drew's hoarse "Bastard."

More cars moved ahead. Sam could finally going to make it through. "Please don't let me be too late."

"You're coming with me, Bitch," the assailant ordered Julie, grabbing her. "You're my insurance." He slapped Julie, then hit her in the gut. "Come along like a good little slut and you might live until your stupid friends find you." Poking a gun in her ribs, he dragged her across the floor to the door. "Make a sound and I'll shoot you and anyone who gets in my way."

Sam lost sight of Julie until she passed in front of an outside camera. He pulled past the crowded accident scene. A Patch-in made his blood run cold. The assailant shoved Julie into a car that sped away. The license plate numbers embedded themselves in Sam's memory.

"All police cars be on the lookout for Georgia license plate number JKL6667JK, Twiggs County." Drew's urgency came over the telephone. Sam had no voice to respond to his brother. "Driver is armed and dangerous. Please send emergency vehicles to 347 Pitt Street."

Sam heard a loud dial tone drone. He sped toward the woman he loved. By the time he got to her, she and Esther would be ready to chase Julie's captor. He had to get there in time to stop them from taking matters into their own hands. The son of a bitch had hit each of them too damned hard.

In the small screen he could see Brit stirring, but he had to watch the road around him. Weaving in and out of traffic required all his attention. Sam saw Esther sit up. Good. Brit moved. Even better. She grabbed the phone and punched in numbers. His phone rang part of a ring. He answered immediately, before the ring ended so there could be a second one.

"Where the hell are you, Sam? You said you and help would be here to get Drake." Her voice made him shiver.

"I'm so, so sorry you had to take care of things on your own. I'm on my way, sweetheart. I love you." He hung up and swallowed the lump in his throat.

Chapter Nineteen

Brit looked out her front window in time to see Sam's truck speed around the corner and into the driveway behind the police car. Drew's truck pulled behind Sam's as Sam raced up the porch steps. She was at the door by the time Sam opened it and in his arms before he could step inside.

"Oh, Sam. He's got Julie and he'll kill her if we don't find him." Brit was engulfed in Sam's embrace.

"I'm so sorry we weren't here to stop the bastard," he said. They moved away from the door.

Brit was barely aware of Drew, who passed them to hug his sister. Esther dropped the icepack she'd been holding against her face. "I'd get you all wet," she explained.

"Anytime, Sis."

"What happened to back-up? Why wasn't someone here to respond to Brit and Esther?" he asked. "They never should have been alone."

Sam's arms tightened around Brit. "I don't know, but there was an awful accident near here," Sam said. "Which reminds me, I thought an EMT was requested."

Detective Briggs came in from the kitchen. "Mrs. Roberts and Ms. Samuels said they didn't need medical assistance. I called and cancelled, since the accident tied up so many of the nearby emergency resources."

"Detective," Sam acknowledged him. "glad you're here." He pulled away from Brit but did not let go of her.

Sam saw Briggs look their way while he labeled plastic bags. "Our men watching the house got the call about the accident. It sounded like a mess. They radioed the station and my partner and I came to replace them. We'd just come on duty."

"It's a mess," Sam told them. "There are as many as six cars and an army of police cars and emergency vehicles. All lanes are blocked." He looked down to Brit. "I thought I'd never get here. I was so scared the bastard would hurt you."

"But he didn't really hurt either of us, not badly."

"And what in the hell did you two think you were doing, Esther Louise Samuels? You let a dangerous man in the house when you women were alone? God damn, Esther."

"Brit needed to get a close look to identify the man. You said so."

"And you, Brittany Marie Roberts. You confronted the bastard? Don't tell me you had to let him see you. Honey, we just needed to be sure who he was under the scruffy look. What if he hadn't been disguised?"

He closed his eyes and hugged Brit again. "I thought Julie was still visiting New Britain. What the hell was she doing here?"

"She was upset she hadn't heard from us. When she called here she got the message I left for the bastard and rushed over to find out what it meant," Brit explained.

Esther stepped from her brother's embrace. "We'd have had him if Julie hadn't distracted us."

Briggs wrote in his notebook. "Why do you think he took your friend?" he asked. "Does he know her?"

"So Sam and Brit would follow him to save Julie, of course," Drew said.

"No, he doesn't know her," Brit answered. "Or at least she didn't know him."

"We'll go after him as soon as we get an idea where he can be." Detective Briggs looked stern at the four people watching him. "This is police work, people."

"I am police," Drew said. He whipped out his ID. "I was at the prison trying to learn how the son of a bitch got messages out of there to keep threatening Mrs. Roberts after he was captured. I was investigating his escape."

"We need to access the cameras to show Briggs and his partner what happened. I was watching it in the car on my way over here." Sam left Brit's side to boot up the computer Drew and Peters had installed. Icon's appeared on the screen so fast

Brit couldn't count them. Sam typed and clicked until pictures of cameras appeared. The screen filled with images.

Brit felt her heart squeeze when she saw Esther at her door, opening it to trouble. Officer Briggs made notes while they watched the video. She could barely watch it without retching. Sam and Drew took turns accessing the views necessary to tell the story. All camera cards would go to the police station.

Sam wanted to punch something. He wanted to punch someone. If only someone had been here to stop Julie from walking into the trap they had set to catch the prison escapee. If only someone had been able to prevent the girls from being injured. If only... *Shit!* The bruise on Esther's face made his gut ache.

Why had he needed to take the stupid shower? Why hadn't he just come back here, instead of going back to check in with Peters? Why take even a short rest?

Brit felt Sam's anger. She knew he'd blame himself.

"We should never have let Brit and Esther bait the trap. We just put them in danger," Drew added.

"Do you really think you could've stopped us from being involved? At least you knew where we were." Brit's fists rested at her hips.

Esther moved to put her arm around Brit's shoulders. "Yeah, we'd have struck out on our own. The only thing that went wrong was that no one warned Julie to stay away. If she hadn't come Brit and I would've taken him ourselves."

"She's right! Now, how do we get Julie back and put the scum away for good?"

***

Douglas drove the stolen Explorer. Luckily he hadn't reinstalled the ruined surveillance equipment around the Robert's woman's house. He wouldn't have been able to go back for it now. There was a stolen cell phone he could use a time or two, if he was lucky.

Maybe he could break into a house to make one call. He didn't know where he was going. He'd know when he got there. He checked his rear-view mirror. He wasn't being followed. His plans had flushed down the toilet. When he found a place to keep the stupid blonde he'd work on a new plan.

The blonde moaned. She must be regaining consciousness. He'd hit her on the head to shut her up. Her bitching had made him want to just kill her now and get it over. That he couldn't do. She was his bargaining chip. She'd draw the teacher and her asshole boyfriend. Douglas would kill them all. He just needed a plan. The woman groaned again. She was waking up.

"What the hell?" Julie's head ached. Her gut hurt like she'd been hit. She had. The monster who'd hit her was driving the car and she was handcuffed to the door armrest. At least Brit and Esther were safe. If he had recognized Brit he'd have just killed her immediately, maybe all of them, then run.

She had to think. Her wallet was still in her jeans pocket. Her tiny cell phone was still in the other pocket. He hadn't searched her while she was unconscious, thank God. That probably meant he hadn't stopped driving since he'd snatched her. Since her phone was turned off it shouldn't alert him that she had it.

"So, you're waking up. Start bitching and I'll put you out."

Her captor glanced away from the road to stare at her. She leveled a look at him but said nothing. He'd pay for this after he paid for what he'd done to Brit.

He faced the road again. "Where are you taking me?"

"You'll find out soon enough." He'd carefully studied the neighborhoods as he passed through. Ahead he saw a For Sale sign. Weeds nearly obscured the yard. He turned into the driveway. No cars in the driveway or the carport. Good.

"Who lives here?" Julie asked, knowing he probably wouldn't tell her, anyway.

Julie's question was met with silence. He pulled under the carport. "Stay here." He opened the car door and left her alone. He disappeared from sight. She immediately struggled with the cuffs. If she could just get to her pocket while he was gone. She stopped her struggle when she saw him moving back toward the car. Shit! The longer she stayed his captive the worse her chances of survival would be. He wouldn't hesitate to hurt her or to kill her once he found Brit and Sam.

He waved a key at her. "Found it in a flower pot out back. We're going inside." He unlocked the door on the passenger side, nearly toppling Julie as she swung out with the door he opened from the outside.

"You ass! That hurt." He unlocked the cuffs on the door, but not before they made her already bruised wrists even more painful. "Damn you!" Julie wanted to smash his face in. He was laughing at her. He was digging his grave deeper. Somehow she'd get loose and she'd take him out!

He yanked her around the front of the car to the yard. Grass and weeds in the backyard were nearly waist high. Walking would have been difficult enough without being cuffed to a man who pulled her as his stride rushed her into a stumbling gait. "Slow down, unless you want to carry me after I break my ankle falling in this jungle. It's scratching my feet and legs."

"Quit bitching, or I will drag you. That would hurt more than just your legs."

She wouldn't make it easy for him. It hurt, but she tried to drag her feet, to make him stumble. She'd seen him stuff the key into his shirt pocket. How could she get it?

The door he approached looked in need of repair. When he slammed his shoulder against the wood the door gave way. Once they were inside the chances of being seen by someone who could help her diminished.

"Gee, nobody home," his voice rang in the nearly empty, finished basement. He flipped a wall switch and light illuminated the area. The air was old, as though the area had been shut up for a long time. "Come on, let's see what else we can find."

He led her up carpeted stairs. Her arm hurt from being jerked the first time he slammed his shoulder against the door, apparently locked from the other side. She struggled with each of his efforts. It gave way after the third slam.

The owners must be fond of mauve. The very air seemed mauve coming through mauve sheer curtains on the many tall windows. Mauve was not her favorite color. Julie could see traffic passing on the road but held no hope anyone would see her or realize her predicament.

The house's odor was as pungent on this floor as it had been in the basement. They wandered from room to room. An occasional piece of furniture had been left behind, chairs, tables, a large desk, a bed. Would he decide to hole up here? Could she get away if he did? Would Sam and Drew or the cops find her before it was too late?

Douglas needed to secure the blonde bitch so he could think. They'd passed a bathroom with no outside windows. He'd lock her in it. He dragged her into the small room.

"I'm gonna unlock the bracelets. Don't fight me so I won't have to hurt you." He blocked the one door to keep her captive. "Sit on the john and stay still." He watched her from the corner of his eye as he removed the key from his pocket. He unlocked the cuff on his own wrist. "I could cuff you to that." He looked toward the lavatory pipes.

"Please," she begged.

"I could cuff you to that, instead." He indicated the shower curtain rod. He enjoyed the fear on her face. He even felt a stirring in his groin. He could imagine her begging him to let her live, promising to do anything he wanted. She had the look of a woman who knew how to please a man. He could even teach her a thing or two. What would she do to protect herself? She was at his mercy. How far would she go to protect her friend?

"Would you like me to leave you uncuffed in here? Would you?" He stroked her arm around the cuff. "Oh, look. You bruised yourself. You could run cold water over it."

He turned the cold water tap. The water ran brown at first, then it cleared. He ran his hand under the water, taking his time rubbing water over the pale skin of her arm. "Doesn't that feel good?" She flinched. He smiled. He hardened more. He cupped his hand again and collected water. "Thirsty?" When he touched his wet fingers to her soft plump lips they trembled. He liked her fear, but this wasn't the right time to let his cock do the talking.

He wanted to enjoy this woman. She could probably be trained to do his will to be obedient. She was nothing like her teacher friend or those other bitches at the teacher's house. They'd let him think they were good. They weren't. He'd have to kill them once he had the teacher and her boyfriend. Maybe he'd let this one live. He felt the calm he needed. Before he explained what he had in mind for her he needed to get away to think.

"I'm gonna take the bracelet off and leave you in here. All the comforts of home, huh? I'll lock the door. Don't try to get away. If you're good, I'll be good to you. But," He paused. "if you make a fuss or anger me, I'll have to punish you. I don't want to, but I will."

He removed his belt, then unlocked the cuff. "I'll use the belt if you make me. Be good for daddy, hmmm?" He wanted to thank the person who had put a bathroom door that swung out. He pulled a heavy battered dresser into the hall to keep his captive inside the bathroom.

***

Brit paced her living room. The computer screens offered no help. Instead, they accused her. She'd let Julie be captured. Maybe she should have let the men handle things. Then she and Esther would not have been here for the attacker to find. They could have let him watch this house 'til he rotted or gave up. Someone would've spotted him eventually and captured him and put him back in jail to stand trial.

Instead, she and Esther had tried to play undercover cops and messed up royally. So what if they had been in control before Julie showed up? Bastard could've taken her. She and Esther were better trained to defend themselves.

The phone rang. Brit listened for the machine to pick up. Detective Briggs was at her side immediately. He listened with concentration as though he could memorize the message and see through the lines to the caller.

Drew 's voice came through, loud and clear. Detective Briggs punched the speaker button so they could both talk to him. "Your neighbor's yard has been swept clear. We removed all signs there was ever an intruder. We should hear something about the trace on the getaway vehicle." He paused. "Brit?"

"Yes, Drew?"

"Are you okay?" His concern was touching but she wished ... she wished she had Sam by her side. Detective Briggs had shown surprising consideration. She almost liked the man. Sam was making arrangements to keep her safe, but she had no intention of sitting still while the men did all the work.

There had to be something she could do. She had every intention of being here when old Douglas tried again to contact her. For some reason she was sure he would, even though she believed he hadn't recognized her.

"Brit? Answer me or I'm coming over there, now. Briggs? What's wrong with her?"

"I'm fine, I was just thinking."

"Well, don't!" Sam ordered. Detective Briggs scowled. "Don't," Drew repeated.

Brit glared at the men, wanting to tell them she wasn't stupid. They thought they didn't need her help. They'd learn.

***

Douglas hated to leave the prime piece of womanhood locked in the bathroom, but he had to think. He checked the kitchen in the deserted house. The soft drinks and beer he found in the refrigerator wouldn't go far, but the cold beer was just what he needed now. He'd leave a thank you note. Ha! Maybe he'd offer a soft drink to the beautiful Julie, but he'd let her stew first.

He found matches in one drawer and a real estate broker's cards in another. The closets were basically empty, but he found a not so clean blanket in one. Hmmm. Someone must expect to return for the furniture. There were phones attached to the walls. No dial tone. He couldn't call out, but neither could Julie.

Settling in a chair by a window, Douglas willed himself to relax. Cars passed the house without slowing down. He checked his watch. Soon he'd need to call the teacher's phone and leave a message. He wanted to let her know he had her friend, if she didn't already. A niggling bit of information hid in his memory, but he couldn't put his finger on what had gone wrong today.

After all his careful planning he'd been bested by two crazy females. All he'd wanted was information. He'd been greedy. That had caused him to lose his vantage point. His bitch of a mother would love that one. She'd never thought he was worth a damn anyway.

Sweet memories of Mama.

"Douglas, you bastard, you can't do anything right." His birth certificate was testimony to his heritage. His father's name didn't match his.

"You can't keep your prick in your pants. I found the dirty magazines in your room. You're just like your good-for-nothing father." He imagined his mother's nagging voice.

She'd slapped him the day he'd finally let her have it. "Well, you never married him and you had me because you screwed a married man. So that must make you a bitch." She'd acted shocked and hit him. She'd probably wanted to for a long time. He hadn't hit her back, but he'd had the last word. "Slut! You made me." The fact that she'd gotten religion in her later years hadn't made his life any easier.

He couldn't dwell on his mother. He'd put her in a nursing home since she'd lost her mind after overdosing on her *medicine.* He'd have to pay her a visit after this was over.

He pushed away the disturbing images. There were mistakes that needed fixing. There was a job he'd botched. There was revenge to be had. Maybe if he'd waited a while longer his prey would've shown up. Maybe he'd have picked up some piece of information that would have led him to the teacher or her boyfriend. He could kill his hostage. Or he could let Julie go and follow her. She could find out where the Roberts woman had gone. Nah. He'd put out his bait and reel his victims in.

First things first. He'd check on Julie then find a phone. He was saving the stolen cell phone for a call later. He needed to ditch this car for another one in case someone had made the one he'd driven away from the neighborhood. He tossed the empty beer can at a corner. He was relaxed and focused. Nothing would go wrong again.

Could there be squatters staying here? Or teens, even? Or could this be a drug drop?

***

Julie washed her face at the lavatory. She'd have to be ready when old Douglas came for her next time. If she could just find something to hit him hard enough she'd stand a chance of escaping.

He hadn't frisked her, thank goodness. She twisted and removed her cell phone from her jeans pocket and opened it. She punched it on. Shit! No signal. How far had they driven? She'd been out of it but for how long?

If only someone had let her know what was happening with Brit and Sam, she wouldn't have panicked at the answering machine message. Well, considering *If only* wouldn't do any more good than *Why didn't I* would.

She slid the small phone back into her jeans pocket. At least she had a toilet and drinking water. Maybe someone would come here and scare Douglas off. Though the place looked deserted, the *FOR SALE* sign would surely attract some attention, although the tall weeds suggested it had been on the market for a long time. The owners hadn't finished moving all their stuff, but maybe they intended for the new owners to trash what they didn't want.

She heard Douglas's footsteps seconds after she'd hid her phone. How lucky was she today? Not at all, it seemed. She sat on the floor beside the tub and rested her head on her knees. *Let him think I'm tired or sleepy.*

"Ah, Julie." He shook his head at her like one would a child. "Aren't you feeling well? I didn't mean to hit you so hard."

He squatted beside her. She tried not to let him see her revulsion when he touched the sore place on her cheek. His hand trailed down her neck to her collarbone. A tremble escaped before she could steel herself against it. God, she hated him!

"Like that, my sweet girl?" he purred. "I know how to pleasure a woman. I'll have to show you later. Your skin is so smooth." His palm slid into her blouse, gliding over the swell on her breasts. She could see he was excited. Sweat beaded his upper lip. His breathing accelerated.

She wanted to vomit. She couldn't. She had to gain his trust. He grinned at the catch in her breathing. "Like it?" he asked. His free hand slowly unbuttoned her blouse. "Lace, I like lacey bras." He slipped the front catch loose.

When his head bent to kiss her nipples she wished for something to hit him over the head. Could she hurt him if she slammed her palm into his ear? He nipped her gently. How far would she have to let him go?

Douglas wanted more than anything to spend the afternoon with this woman. He wanted to show her that he could make her enjoy being with him. It had been a long time since he'd been with a woman he hadn't had to pay or force to be his sex partner. He wished he could lead Julie to a bedroom and lay her on a bed with clean sheets and pillows.

He wished he could do things normally. He'd show her every trick he'd ever learned, and she'd pleasure him. He'd get off without hurting her. She'd get off on him. She'd make him feel like a man, not a monster.

Most of the time he hadn't minded being a monster. Normal sex hadn't done it for him in the past. He'd been aroused only by causing pain and fear in women. For just this once he wanted to make someone like him.

His blood thundered in his head. His erection was painful in a good way. He felt like a normal person, not like the freak his mother had called him.

Reality sank in. He had to get himself and his hostage to a safe place. He'd finish this ill-fated job and take this lovely, perfect woman away with him. He stopped tasting her fragrant breasts and the closeness that threatened to unman him. He cleared his throat.

She mustn't know how she made him feel or she could use it against him. Women were like that.

"I brought you something cold to drink." He picked up the drink can he'd put on the floor so he could touch her. "It was in the refrigerator. I've got to leave to make some phone calls. I'll be back when I figure out where we can go to hide and be safe together. I wanted you the day we met in the grocery store. If I hadn't been so tied up with an assignment I'd have asked you out then."

"You? No way." She scowled at him.

"Looks like fate brought you to me." He stood and took steps toward the door. "Be a good girl while I'm gone, my lovely. Be here when I get back?" He stopped and looked back over his shoulder at her, grinning. His grin creeped her out. "Oh, yes, you don't really have a choice, do you?"

The door clicked shut. She heard dragging sounds and knew he had blocked the door with some piece of furniture. Julie heard another door shut farther away.

She retched into the toilet, heaving until her throat hurt and sides ached. How could she ever have thought this monster was cute? He'd have look totally different then.

Chapter Twenty

Waiting was the hard part. Briggs had called in his report on his car radio. He and Sam and Drew had several guy conversations, the kind that left Brit and Esther out. That was fine with Brit. She and Esther were in the kitchen preparing sandwiches and talking girl talk. Why were women always in the kitchen? Maybe because it gave them something to keep busy. If they had a woman partner would she be relegated to the kitchen?

"How could they forget that I'm in this more than anyone else?" Brit sliced tomatoes onto a plate.

Esther washed lettuce and drained it. "They haven't forgotten. They are just being macho men. They do that to me all the time. It's a man thing."

"Well, I'm the real target and the bastard has my best friend. They needn't plan on leaving me out!" She put cold cuts on a platter.

"Hey, don't feel bad. They won't let Sam go with them when they head out. He's not police, either." Esther smiled at Brit. "Time to call the guys to feed their faces. We don't know when Mr. Drake will call about Julie."

"He'll be out to get to you for tricking him." Brit had to smile at the memory of the stupid man when Esther had hit him where it hurt. She felt her smile droop when she remembered his cruel hands on her breasts. The things he'd threatened to do to her made her throat go dry. Her heart raced. She would see him taken down!

She reached for the ringing phone. "Let the answering machine get it." Sam and Drew, and Briggs reminded from the living room.

Esther and Brit were in the room with the machine by the time her message ended. The anticipation in the room was thick enough to cut.

"Hey, teacher. I've got something you want. You might want to get in touch with me. Oh, that's right. I can't give you a number 'cause I don't want you to find me! Maybe you'll stop playing your stupid games. I'll call again at seven o'clock tonight. If you aren't there, too bad for your friend!"

The dial tone filled Brit's ears.

"Well?" Brit asked. "So, now what?"

"You'll have to be here to take the call and keep him talking," Drew answered.

Briggs looked unhappy about letting Drew do the cop thing. Drew must outrank him somehow. "Yes, Ma'am, I'll be here then, also. If you can keep him talking we might be able to send someone where he is."

Sam put his arm around Brit. "I got the number from your caller ID." He handed the paper to Briggs, who called to the station to check the trace. A pay phone, one of the few working ones in town. Big surprise.

"Why don't we all have something to eat." Esther motioned toward the kitchen. "So, brother." She took Drew by the arm to steer him toward the food. "Have you guys checked out the car tag with the DMV?"

"Still looking. The tag is registered to a man who died more than a year ago." Drew grabbed slices of wheat bread and a knife. "This one is taking a little extra work. Our man is shrewd, a real pro with connections. Seems he spent a lot of time in the prison infirmary." He spread mustard. "Several calls were traced to the pay phone there. He borrowed someone's cell phone, too."

"We alerted all patrolmen to look for vehicles like the one that was parked across the street, but finding it could take a while. He's likely changed vehicles by now."

Brit was quiet. *Where is Julie? How is she?* She'd check Julie's car for her cell phone. Could she possibly have it with her? That would be too good to be true. If she could just let someone know where to find her without getting caught. Her phone was small enough to hide in a pocket. She wouldn't tell the men about her theory yet. She'd just bide her time.

"Something wrong, Teach?" Sam asked.
"No, just thinking." Brit answered, absently.

***

Julie had tried not to anger her captor when he'd returned to free her from the bathroom. She'd barely rewound the toilet paper roll, hiding her first message. Lipstick made a messy writing medium, but she had nothing better. *Please let a woman reach for the paper, a nosey woman who checks everything before using it.*

"You were so thoughtful to bring me something to eat." Julie smiled at the man who had insisted she call him Douglas. *Guess it would get me in trouble if I called him the names I've thought.*

"I couldn't let my lady go hungry, could I?" He looked at her as though he thought she should know that she was his.

He spread a dirty blanket on the hall floor and opened bags of deli food. He fed her slaw and potato salad from the spoon he used. At least that would mean he hadn't doctored it to make her sick or kill her. Probably didn't want her to have even a plastic weapon. She'd have liked to refuse the food. Who knew when she'd be allowed to eat again, if ever?

Douglas wiped her mouth with a napkin then gathered the refuse to take with them and toss somewhere else. No clues, or so he thought.

"Time to go." He allowed her a bathroom stop and a chance to wash her face. He hadn't closed the door but he hadn't stood where she could see him, either.

"Bracelet time." He was gentle with the cuffs this time. "Be a good girl and the trip back to the car will be easier."

She wanted to fight him, to scream and make a fuss. She noticed no one in sight outside. Her heart sank when she saw the vehicle in the carport. The old station wagon looked like it had been in a demolition derby. He removed his cuff to put her inside. He gave her an old sweatshirt to put on, then cuffed her to the door again.

"Careful, now." He shut the door gently.

250

He donned an old sweatshirt like hers. Then he got into the car, sliding behind the steering wheel.

"I know this vehicle isn't much, but no one will notice us. Here, put this cap on." Her cap advertised John Deere. His was a Robins Air Force Base cap. No one would recognize either of them

"We're off." He backed carefully into the deserted street.

He drove carefully and at the speed limit. He ran no yellow lights or stop signs. Old Douglas had been far too attentive for Julie's taste. He acted like he cared about her. He had treated her like a lover. *God! How much will he expect from me when we arrive wherever he is heading?* Julie shivered.

Douglas was looking at her. "What's wrong? Cold?" He turned his attention back to the road. "I could get you a jacket from the back or I could turn up the heater for a while." He leered in her direction. "We'll be someplace safe soon, and I'll warm you."

She squirmed in the seat.

"Julie?" He raised his eyebrow and turned his head toward her. Some people might call him handsome. But his rotten soul shone through. She knew the real man, the rapist.

"It's nothing. I just need to find a restroom, if I could please."

"Now, Julie," His tone was reproving. "You know I can't risk having anyone see us before I finish my business. Besides, it shouldn't take more than twenty minutes more.

"Twenty minutes?" She tried to keep her voice small, almost pitiful. "I'll try to hold it."

She looked almost desperate, like he'd said hours instead of minutes. He started looking for a gas station with outside restrooms.

He made a turnoff from the busy highway. The battered sign read Peach County. They'd be in the boonies soon. The woman was still squirming. He finally spotted an old style two-pump gas station. "Julie, I want to let you go into this restroom, but I can't let you talk to anyone."

"But I promise…"

He eased around to the back of the faded white cinderblock building. If Julie had really been desperate she'd have been more so when they rolled over the broken blacktop lot. The vehicles they'd seen in the front had been old or camouflage decorated. Their owners would probably believe a man should be allowed to jerk a woman around.

Douglas parked the nondescript station wagon out of sight of the front of the station. He cut the engine, then moved so quickly she screamed. The gag he stuffed in her mouth tasted of lint.

She glared at him.

"Sorry, my girl, I can't have you alerting these bumpkins. I'd have to hurt anyone who interfered with us. Even if you tried to be good there is no way you wouldn't be remembered. You're the kind of woman who gets attention. I'll go inside and get the key."

She wanted to cut off the man's balls and feed them to him. She struggled with the handcuffs. They were still securely bound to the armrest. Within a few minutes she saw him walking back toward her. He held the wooden paddle in front of his face, like a trophy. She could read the label easily. He unlocked the rusty looking door. Lad--s had been written with paint but it had worn partly off.

He laughed. "I told the man inside that my wife was sick and we needed to use their facilities. I intimated you were in the family way and not too happy about it yet." He opened her door. She nearly fell out as she followed the handcuffs. Douglas unlocked them. She glared at him, but he practically dragged her to the open door.

Please don't let him follow me inside. He didn't. His bulk blocked the door before he reached over her head and pulled the string to flick on the light. She almost wished he had left her in the dark. The walls were clean, but the sink was stained and rusty. The toilet seat was broken. Douglas slid a knife blade to her neck. "You can take out the gag, but if I hear you yelling for help I'll kill anyone who comes."

She nodded. She wouldn't yell. She had other plans. The off kilter door shut with a bang. His footsteps echoed on the gravel. He must be headed for the phone booth she'd spotted when they drove up.

Slipping her cell from her pants pocket, she punched the power button. Reception. Please let Brit's cell phone be on. One ring. She unsnapped her jeans. Two rings. The third ring.

"Hello."

"Brit," Julie whispered, "we're just inside the Peach county line on Hwy 78."

"Julie! Are you..."

"Brit, please don't interrupt. We're headed east in a battered green station wagon. My cell power is nearly gone so I gotta hang up. He mustn't catch me using this phone or he'll take it away. He said we should be at the farm soon. I don't know any more, not where we were or where he's headed. Bye."

"Be careful, love y..." She heard but disconnected.

Loud heavy footsteps headed her way. She stuffed the phone in her pocket as she heard the key in the lock. She flushed the nasty toilet then washed her hands under the rusty faucet water.

The door opened. Douglas stood, silhouetted in the doorway. She wouldn't be able to make a run for it, but at least Brit could tell the police where she was headed.

"Feel better?" He motioned for her to give him her hands. "Gotta put the bracelets back on 'til we get to the farm."

"Please?" Julie tasted the bile caused by her need to beg this man for anything. She hoped her expression wouldn't give her away. "They hurt."

***

"Well?" Esther gestured as she followed Brit to her computer crowded office.

"I don't believe it. I just don't believe it." Brit reached to a high shelf for a folded, enlarged state map. She unfolded it, spreading it on the floor.

253

"Brit! What are you doing?" Esther turned back to the door. "Sam, come see about your girlfriend. I think she's lost it."

"Peach County. Peach County," Brit repeated like a mantra. Placing her fingertip on Florence she traced the main highway out of town, turning left, then north until she reached Highway 78, leading west.

"Detective Briggs," she called. "Someone get Briggs."

"Right behind you, Mrs. Roberts," he answered, hunkering down beside her. "The cell phone call?"

"Yes, Julie said they're just inside the county line, on Hwy 78." She pointed at the spot where the highway crossed the Peach County line."

"Now?"

"She was in the restroom of an old gas station not two minutes ago."

"Driving?"

"A beat up old station wagon. Headed west."

"Going?"

"He said something about a farm. She heard him coming back and had to break the connection. That's all."

"Let's find 'em." Briggs pushed past Sam and Drew to lean over a computer keyboard. Within seconds he'd pulled up a screen showing a map of Peach County, two counties over. He grabbed his cell phone and punched an icon.

Brit tried to listen to the detective's conversation while explaining to Sam and Esther what she had learned. "Julie is okay, so far.

"Why didn't she call sooner?" Esther asked.

"No signal."

She heard Drew saying something about kidnapping and having called the FBI. "The FBI is already involved," Drew answered. "It's a kidnapping."

"How many people can we involve before we spook him?" Brit asked Drew. "What will happen then?

Briggs answered her question. "He doesn't know we're on to him, does he? We assume he'll call back to try to get you to come to him. He'll surely use Julie as bait."

Sam turned to Brit. "No," Sam said. His quiet voice had a steely edge.

"No?" Brit asked. "No, what?"

"Not again. You're not putting yourself in danger again." Sam's warm hands cradled her cheeks. His eyes were as deep green as she'd ever seen them.

"But, Sam," Her lips trembled. "I have to try—"

Sam's finger on her mouth silenced her. The jolt to her stomach was stronger than any reaction she'd had to him so far. Her heart almost stopped.

"I will not let you put yourself in danger again. I can't take it. I won't allow it, Love. Don't even think about it."

"But—" she tried to explain.

"I know you and the answer is no! No, I won't let you."

She saw red, but he'd stopped any argument. He was trying to show his mastery, stamping his ownership of her heart and her body. He already owned her heart.

She couldn't give in to him. She'd risk her life for her closest friend or for Sam, for that matter. She couldn't let him run her life. She couldn't deny her principles. Sam was too smart to deny that hiding would solve nothing. Someone wanted her dead and could hire another killer and another.

Sam would be safe as long as he held her, as long as they were connected. God, he loved this woman. He could feel her pulling away. His heart nearly choked him. He'd gone too far telling her what to do. She'd probably never forgive him if he kidnapped her and took her away from all this. He was tempted. Who would blame him?

"Sam," Her voice cut through his trance. "I have to do this." He knew it, but he didn't have to agree to it. "If anything happens to my friend because of me I'll have a lifetime of guilt. I won't let that happen." She'd do what she thought was right, even if it meant facing her attacker again. He felt so helpless.

"Brother." Drew and Esther were at his side. "Sammy." Esther's childhood name for him meant she wanted to influence him. So now what? He hadn't the right to tell Teach what to do. He wanted to, though.

Security would need to be invisible but formidable around her. Officer Briggs and Drew were the police, but security was his business.

Brit moved away to confer with the officer. "He said he'd call this evening. All phones are set on caller ID and we have back up from the Peach County Sheriff's Department. They're looking for any vehicle fitting the information Miss. Devereaux gave you. They'll be looking for someone using a pay phone, since it's unlikely Drake would use a phone at the same place he has your friend.

"He might set up a fake site so we'll leave you, then maybe a different set of instructions for you to come alone, but he'll expect Mr. Samuels to be somewhere nearby."

"If anything happens," Sam began.

"We'll be with her every step of the way."

"We were all watching out for her, but we all failed her already," Sam accused. "If we'd been doing our jobs we'd have him and Julie would be safe. What if he beats us again?"

"Not this time," Drew assured Sam and Brit. "We'll take care of you and Julie." He hugged her. "I promise."

"You need to get some rest," Sam moved toward Brit again. "Please?"

"I can't relax." She shook her head.

Esther led her to a glider rocker. "Sit, I'll get us both some tea. I'll sit with you." She started toward the kitchen. "Julie will need you to be alert. Don't move."

Brit sat. Her foot moved the chair back and forth. Letting Sam hold her would have been so much easier than what she had to do. He'd protect her. *I have to do this myself. I have to do this for Julie. Tommy's killer will be caught and punished. The men who want me dead will be caught and put away. Then I can really begin to live. With Sam?*

The soothing movement of the rocker was restful. *Where is Julie? Is she safe?*

***

Julie watched the road, trying to remember landmarks. *Where's he taking us? I hope the information I gave Brit will help. How can I get away without making things worse?*

"You're awfully quiet, Julie dear. Is something wrong?" Douglas's tone was so damned solicitous. *Jerk! Play along, just play along.*

"I'm just tired. The restroom back at the station was disgusting." She shivered and tried to look ill. "I'm still a little nauseous. How much farther?"

"Almost there." He patted her arm. He slowed for a narrow bridge. The th-thunk thrummed in her blood. They turned onto a blacktop road marked by a bent sign on a listing pole. She'd forgotten how loudly the tires sounded on rough blacktop. She felt and heard everything so intently. Who would find her here?

Blacktop gave way to gravel. With each bump she wished she'd actually done more than make her call at the station. How long before her captor would search her and find her phone? How long before he would expect favors for favors?

"You're gonna love this place," Douglas broke into her thoughts. She had to take note of their location. Houses were far apart, mostly back from the road, but at least there were houses. Definitely the boonies!

"Does this place we're going belong to you?" she asked. She couldn't look him in the eye, so she looked past his ear. "I'll bet it's your getaway." Shit! "I mean getting out into the country can be so soothing. You know, away from the hustle bustle and nosey, I mean noisy neighbors."

He chuckled. "It's not the Hilton, but it's nice. There's electricity, hot and cold running water, even indoor bathrooms. Actually, there's a hot tub. We can have some fun there."

Julie cringed at the images caused by that statement. Maybe she could drown him. "We seem awfully far from any place to buy food or supplies."

He glanced at her but had to put his attention back to keeping the station wagon out of the ruts in the rough dirt road.

257

"I had someone put in food supplies. There's wood for the fireplaces, if we need it. Is there something you need?"

"My, ah, tummy doesn't feel so good. Maybe it's something I ate. I hope so. Or I may need some, uh, girl stuff." Julie put a pained expression to go with the blush naturally warming her face. She hoped this man was a cleanliness freak who could be put off by what she would try to make him believe. Lord help her. She'd had enough experience with cramps to know how to fake them. Maybe if he thought she was sick she could take him by surprise.

"Get ready." He seemed excited. A large mailbox marked the drive where he slowed to a stop. The old vehicle rattled while they made their way down the neglected drive. Weeds scraped the sides and the undercarriage. The wood fence was missing paint and several posts. Past a curve, the faded, two story house loomed large and dark, the perfect location for a spooky movie.

Damn, wrong thought for someone in my predicament. The closer they moved the shabbier the house front looked. A separate garage listed to the left, its door hung open and crooked. No one lived here. No one would be here to help her. She'd sorta hoped.

"It just needs a little paint," she offered. "Is it a working farm?" She nodded toward the red barn and two other outbuildings.

His answering smile told her she had said the right thing. *Could this house belong to him?*

Douglas was proud of the farm. As his stupid mother had aged she'd neglected the one thing he'd treasured as a child. This house was a place for him to belong, even if she'd never made him feel welcome in her life or her heart. She hadn't needed to sell his horse, but she had. He'd seen to her bills and given her money. The bitch had been too stingy to take care of his dog, either.

He'd counted on his animals to keep him grounded between jobs. Since he'd had her put away no one lived here when he was working. He'd kept the utilities connected and paid Aunt Viola to clean for him. His only cousin, her son, was the only person who knew who he was and what he did.

"Can we take the cuffs off?" Julie asked. "Please?" She held her wrists out to him. "I can't wait to see your home."

"You won't try to run? I wouldn't want you to get lost in the woods out here." He rubbed the cuff marks left on her wrists.

"Are there snakes?"

"I'll protect you," Douglas postured.

Who'd protect her from him?

Julie followed her captor up cement steps and across loose boards on a large front porch. "We'll use the back porch next time. I can't have you falling through one of these rotten boards, I'll fix them once we've finished our job with the teacher bitch and her boyfriend."

Our job? He's out of his freakin' mind.

He was trembling, his face an angry mask when he finished he sentence. By the time he'd unlocked the door and escorted Julie to a deacon's bench in the dark entry hall he had stopped shaking.

She sat calming herself while he brought sacks from the wagon. He was strung tighter than an archery bow. *Gotta make it work for me. Can't let him lose control and hurt me. God knows he's dangerous. How do I help him along?*

Releasing a long breath, she stood to open the door for him. "I should've helped you. I'm sorry."

"No woman of mine has to carry stuff when she doesn't feel well. I'll get the rest later."

Following him to the kitchen, she tried to ignore the mingling of musty smells and lemon flavored furniture polish. The piney scents of kitchen cleaners nearly knocked her back into the hall. At her first cough Douglas opened the back door and a window.

"Aunt Viola uses enough cleaners to strangle a witch. She believes she's chasing out evil spirits."

Too bad she can't chase out his evil spirit. Julie smiled at his joke.

"Make yourself at home, my dear. We may be here for a while. Just be careful of uninvited guests."

Snakes? She wondered. Mice?

"Hungry?" he asked when he noticed her rubbing her flat stomach. He certainly was. The woman had a body made for worshiping. Once he'd taken care of his business he'd show her about worship.

"Um, not really. But I'll be glad to prepare dinner for you. You've taken such good care of me." Maybe there was rat poison she could cook in his food.

"Not enough time. I'd enjoy a quick snack, though." By the time she'd prepared a quick snack from ingredients in the old refrigerator he'd need to leave. He had a phone call to make and the phone was the one utility he hadn't kept on. Besides, Julie might be too tempted by one. Though she still needed some training, eventually she would be perfect for him.

Julie nearly retched when he gave her a tour of the second floor of the house. One room was set up for sleeping. He ran a loving hand over the polished dresser then over the velvety bedspread.

"Aunt Vi knows how to launder bedclothes fit for a king, soft and fragrant. You'll appreciate the feel against your skin tonight." He caressed her cheek. "You'll enjoy skin against skin tonight. We'll celebrate."

Had she really been a free woman just this morning, her only worry why her best friend had moved without telling her? Even the bare mattress on a narrow bed in a second bedroom looked tempting. The other upstairs rooms were bare.

Each time Douglas touched her she steeled herself against her revulsion. "If you want a shower or a bath just let the water run 'til it's clear. Or I can help you when I get back."

At the door his goodbye nearly undid her. His embrace, his caresses on her breasts through her shirt disgusted her. He actually believed she liked them. When he'd tried to put her hand on his zipper she'd panicked. He'd believed she was shy. She'd touch his privates if she had a hot iron or something sharp. He'd stopped short of an orgasm of his own, barely. For some reason he seemed to put her on a pedestal. She needed to keep it that way.

Once he turned the station wagon around and drove down the rutted driveway she searched for a phone, a radio, any way to get in touch with Brit. Her cell had no reception, and she had no idea how far he'd gone or what he'd expect when he got back here.

***

Douglas couldn't wait to call the teacher slut. She'd better be home to take this call. He'd have to kill the dark haired woman staying in her house to get her attention. Julie was too important to him. He couldn't kill her, but the teacher didn't know that.

He pulled up in front of Aunt Vi's house to use her phone. He had his own key, so he let himself in. She'd be at the American Legion playing Bingo. Good, because he didn't have time to answer dumb questions for her.

He punched the keys on Vi's large number phone.

The teacher had better answer her phone. On the third ring he almost hung up. The voice on the answering machine made him see red. She'd defied him, she'd –

"I warned you! You should have followed my instructions. I'll start killing everyone you love until you finally do as you're—"

"Wait. Please wait. I couldn't get to it fast enough. What do I have to do? Where must I go?" Her voice sounded scared. Good!

"I've got your friend, Julie. She's a great lay!" He hated saying bad things about her. The teacher's gasp and moan were worth it. "She likes sex, doesn't she?"

Mrs. Roberts didn't seem pleased to hear that. Too bad.

Douglas dialed a contact number for his employers. Getting no answer, he dialed another. Still no answer.

Chapter Twenty-one

Bile burned Brit's throat. If that bastard Drake had harmed Julie she'd never forgive herself. She had to keep him talking. She had to make him believe he was in charge.

"Is she all right?" She sounded breathless, even to herself.

"Oh course. She's had a good time, so far." He paused so long Brit had to make herself breathe normally. "I'm taking real good care of her. She tries hard to please. She does like it rough. That woman is a real a wildcat!"

"Please, don't hurt Julie. She isn't the one you want. I am. I really don't understand why you want to hurt me." The fear in her voice was real.

"I've been watching you for a long time. You really upset me when you ran away. That wasn't nice."

"I'm sorry. I was just so scared." She fought the urge to put her hand over her mouth, to chew on her knuckles. "You left such awful messages. How could I come back to my house when you threatened me."

"*Surely* you couldn't think I'd really kill you, Sugar. I was just upset. *Surely* you can understand my position."

I understand all right, you son of a bitch. I don't trust you worth a damn.

"I sent you some really nice things, the food and the flowers. You weren't exactly grateful."

"I know, but I didn't understand what you were doing." She swallowed the lie even as she told it. "I thought you were really trying to kill me."

"Oh, no, my dear, I'd never kill you. I just wanted to scare you. It's so much hotter when there's fear involved."

Hot for you maybe. Hell will be hotter when we send you there.

Sam frowned at her. If his eyebrows had come any closer together they would have crossed.

Her tormenter crooned. "Come save your friend." His laugh chilled her blood.

"How do I know you'll let Julie go?"

"I definitely *won't* let her go if you don't come trade places with her. I didn't enjoy my visit to jail. Those people were so rude to me, uncouth and all. The food wasn't nearly as nice as what I sent you. You owe me. And don't bring that boyfriend."

"Where are you? Can I talk to Julie, just to let her know I'm coming to her?"

"She's resting from our hot sex. You really ready to sacrifice yourself for your friend, are you?"

"Of course," Brit answered immediately. "She'd do the same for me."

"She already did." He chuckled.

"Where is she?" Her insides tumbled. "I can't come to you if you won't tell me where. I could come right now, if you want."

The law enforcement crew and her self-appointed bodyguards in the room telegraphed their disapproval of that suggestion. She rolled her eyes in their direction

"Meet me at the junction of 78 and old Forsyth Road. Come in your Mustang, alone. I'll be there at 11:30 tonight. Don't be late. Pull into the Shell station parking lot. I'll meet you there. Bye, now."

"Wait, don't hang up. How will I find you? Will Julie be there? Damn!" The dial tone hurt her ears. He'd hung up.

Sam enveloped her in his strong arms. "Good girl." He captured her mouth with his own in a bone-melting kiss. *Company be damned.* She kissed him back. After the harrowing call she needed his strength.

"Trace went through. We snagged him," he spoke against her hair as he held her to his strong body. She could hear his heart beat through his shirt. It raced as hers did. Was his reaction to their kiss or fear for her? "He's not even near there."

Drew moved to them. "Aw, Jeez, you two," he muttered. "Get a room, how about it."

Sam laughed. "Wish we could use one of the rooms we have. Or that we could get rid of our company."

Drew shook his head and grinned. His look became serious. "He's not far from where Julie called you. I doubt that's where he has Julie, though. He wouldn't be that careless or stupid."

"I agree," Detective Briggs said. "Diversionary tactic. He's arrogant, but he's a professional. We need to rattle his cage and make him mess up."

"Do you think he'll show up there?" Brit asked.

"I think he's testing you." Briggs typed a message on a laptop computer.

"So, now what?" Brit asked.

***

Douglas had plans to set in motion. He drove to the block down from teacher's house in forty-five minutes. He cut his lights and watched the driveway. A black Ford truck pulled out and headed toward the road out of town. *The bitch called the boyfriend as I'd expected. It's only eight fifteen. Good. The ass is taking the bait. He'll probably go for help and wait for her to show up at the meeting place. The fools had planned to trap old Douglas.*

The familiar jeep raced into the driveway. *"Mr. Play Soldier" is here. Great, the teacher has company. What are the chances the "hot tamale" and the "killing machine" will leave so I can get the bitch alone.*

Had she believed he wouldn't really kill her? He would, with pleasure. This time he'd skip the rape. No need to try to fool anyone. He needed to just do the job and get it over. *My Julie is waiting for me. We can be out of town and on our way out of the country before she learns of her friend's death. I may just have to pass on killing the boyfriend.*

He watched the "war boy" bring his tamale and the tall goddess of a sister out to the Jeep and drive away. Good, nine o'clock. The teacher should be alone, finally! She'd probably figure on leaving by ten thirty. Plenty of time to check things out.

Douglas drove closer to the house and waited.

***

Twenty minutes later Brit sat in Sam's jeep in front of his parent's house.

"Sam, you can't leave me here. What if he calls to see if I've left yet? He'll smell a trap if I don't answer the phone. He could get angry and kill Julie."

"Honey, he won't. Peterson is watching your house. Drew has gone to talk to the woman who lives at the house where the asshole used the phone to call you. We have no way of knowing if she's friendly with him or if she's another of his victims. There must be a reason he felt safe to call from there instead of from a pay phone."

"But, Sam, if he's looking for me in the Mustang, he'll know he's been duped. Then what?"

"I'm gonna stick to you like Velcro! No one'll get near you without going through me. If we have to we'll go to the gas station together. But I don't think we'll have to."

Brit jumped when her cell phone rang. Before she could answer Julie's voice came low but clear." Gotta make this fast. No phone here. Battery's very low on this thing! Old Douglas is out, but I don't know where or for how long. Write this down. I'm in an old house, his mother's. Head out 78 past Three Creek Baptist Church, maybe fifteen miles more at the most."

Brit repeated Julie's words as Sam wrote.

"Watch for a narrow blacktop road with a falling down sign for Bickle Road, I think. It's just after a narrow bridge. The road turns to gravel after maybe three miles. Houses are few and far between. The driveway leads off the road for about a quarter of a mile. There's a large mailbox at the road. Looks like "Drake" was painted on it at one time."

Reception was breaking up. "Hurry!" Brit urged.

"Number 1798, you can see that. Two story, white house, a barn and several falling-down outbuildings. Be careful. He's a looney."

"You be careful! We're coming!"

Reception ended.

Sam grabbed his phone and punched Drew's number. "Julie called on her cell phone. She's okay but she ran out of juice. Get in touch with everyone who needs to know, then head out toward 78 and Peach County. I'm leaving Brit and Esther here at the farm." He read the directions to Drew. "If we're lucky he'll leave early to meet Teach so we can get to the farm before he hurts Julie. See if you can get info on Drakes on Birkle Road in Peach County."

"Sure thing, I'll gather the troops. Be careful and keep your phone on."

Sam had moved around the Jeep by the time he'd disconnected with Drew. He opened Brit's door. She stayed in her seat.

"Come on, Teach. I'll walk you inside and go help rescue your friend."

Brit sat looking at Sam. "I'm going with you."

"Honey, you need to stay here with Esther while I join the men to get this bastard." His callused hand caressed her cheek.

"You said it, she's my friend. She's in trouble because of me and I need to be there for her."

"But he's dangerous. How can I keep my mind on the job of rescuing Julie if I have to worry about you?" Sam ran his hand through his hair. "You are not going to meet him and you're not going with us."

"Sam, the Florence Police, probably the Peach County Sheriff's men, and the FBI, and Drew are all out to capture this man. They have to free Julie, that's their job. I don't see why they can't do their jobs without your help." His expression said it all. He wouldn't miss the chance to play hero.

"If you go, I go." She crossed her arms and stayed in her seat.

"Honey, you'd just be in the way."

"You are so full of —" Her cell phone rang again.

"Oh, teacher? Are you ready to leave and come meet me?" Douglas Drake's voice made Brit's heart stop beating.

"Oh," How had he gotten her here? "Yeah, I'll be leaving in a couple of minutes. I'm looking forward to our meeting."

"You sound funny," Douglas said. "Excited? Scared?"

Brit remembered her calls had been automatically forwarded to her mobile phone. He hadn't found this number, after all. "I was just about to take a quick shower. I'm using my cordless. Maybe I should just skip the shower."

"Don't do that on my account. Too bad I can't watch, isn't it? Well, maybe later. Change of plans. Meet me in the Waffle House parking lot off the exit to 78 on I-475 at eleven."

He hung up. "I think he's suspicious. He just changed the plan. It sounded like he was using a cell phone this time. He must be checking up on me."

"Honey, we're wasting time." Sam put his hands at her waist to help her out of the Jeep. He liked her compact build. He liked everything about her. Actually, he loved everything about her. The one thing he wasn't crazy about was her independent streak. "Come on. I need to see you safely inside so I can go."

"No way! I'm going with you." She drew herself up to her full height, all five feet two inches of seated woman.

Enough is enough. Sam reached across to unbuckle her seat belt. Her hands pushed at his. She didn't even slow him down. He stood on the running board. Her waist was easy to span with his two hands as he lifted her up and over his shoulder. *She'll make me pay for this, but I need to get her inside with the family so I can leave to join the other men.*

***

"Your brother cannot tell me what to do, damn him!" Brit paced the bedroom decorated in a decidedly masculine manner. The sturdy dresser and chest of drawers were simple. The dark smooth wood looked like Rachel still polished it to a sheen when she dusted.

"Who does that muscle-bound jerk think he is?" She stopped to face Esther. "He'll spoil everything if Drake shows up to check on me. We have to help Julie!"

"What?" Esther asked. She rummaged in the closet, then she backed out and placed a couple of bags and something on a hanger on the dresser.

"We could go to the Waffle House early." Brit paced again. "He might show up there. What if he realized I'm not in my house? He's probably watching for me to leave. I should be there. What if he's planning to---"

"Brit, a cop will leave your house in a Mustang in about," Esther checked her watch. "fifteen minutes. If Drake is watching he'll think you're following his instructions." Esther pulled open a dresser drawer, then another and moved stuff around.

"A decoy? Whose idea was that? Why wasn't I told? How did you know?" She watched Esther. "What are you doing?"

Esther turned her face to Brit. Her innocent expression would have made Brit laugh if she hadn't been so mad at the men.

"I listened. It seems they consider you a threat to their attempts to save you, but they didn't consider my interest in helping save our friend."

"So, how do we get away from your family? The *Daddy guard* and *Brother guard* aren't likely to let me leave. Sam gave them instructions to lock me in this room if they had to. They looked like they would."

Brit stopped her tirade when the cell phone chimed again. She cleared her throat and answered it. "Hello?"

"Oh, teacher? Ready? I certainly am. I'd love a pecan waffle, wouldn't you?"

"Almost," Brit answered. She looked at Esther and shrugged. Esther checked her watch again. She held her hands up, palms out and wiggled fingers and thumbs. Ten minutes? "I'll be on my way soon. I promise not to be late."

"Good." He broke the connection.

Esther handed Brit a jacket and a pair of ratty boy style high-top tennis shoes. "They're Sean's old ones. This is the

268

room he uses when he stays here. Mama saves his stuff like she saved all of ours."

"You are a wonder!" Brit snagged a pair of socks as they left Esther's hand in an underhand toss. "Your pushy brother thought he was so smart snatching my shoes." She sat on the edge of the plaid bedspread. If your family hadn't been there he probably would've taken my slacks, too."

"Maybe he wouldn't have left, then."

"Fat chance."

"Maybe Sean's old jeans? Never mind. What you have on is fine. My pants would swallow you, and we'd get caught if I came out of my room carrying clothes. My purse is a different matter." She pointed to the back-pack styled bag." Get a move on."

Brit stood and tested her footwear. The fit wasn't too bad. She took the jacket Esther offered and followed her to the window. Esther pointed to a tree sort of close to the house.

"You want me to what?" Brit asked. Esther was suspiciously quiet. "No way!"

She watched as her leader shouldered the small pack, opened the window, then leapt to catch a sturdy looking branch and swung toward a larger branch. She crawled deftly to the trunk.

Brit closed her eyes and prayed. Sweat broke out on her brow. Her heart raced. She swallowed hard. Then she crouched on the window ledge. Taking a leap of faith, she caught hold of the branch Esther had left. Following Esther's lead, she made her way down to the ground.

Silently they jogged to an out-building. Esther unlocked a door and led Brit to an old, yellow VW Bug.

"Does this thing run?" Brit asked. It looked like a Demolition Derby left-over.

She watched her intrepid companion unlock the passenger door and open it. When the driver's door creaked open she still stood rooted to the ground. Esther slid behind the steering wheel and cranked the relic.

"Coming?"

Brit came to life and scrambled in. She shut the door as the motor raced. Wide garage doors raised as the derelict car approached them.

"Hang on. We'll be discovered in seconds." As she said it, it happened. Porch and yard lights barely beat the men who appeared at the front door. "They'll follow us and they'll warn Sam and Drew. Want to change your mind?"

"Not a chance." Brit fumbled for a seat belt. The shocks, if there were any, were put to the test.

Esther shifted smoothly while pushing the car to racetrack speed. She laughed when Brit hung on to the seat and closed her eyes. There was enough light to tell her they were going too fast for the drive and then for the dirt road they entered on two wheels.

"Sorry there aren't any seat belts, but we never replaced the ones the boys cut up. This baby taught us all to drive. Even Sean learned with her. Daddy and Matt planned to restore her but haven't had time yet. By the time Matt has a kid, if he and Becky ever do, this darlin' will have time to age again."

Brit finally relaxed her clinched fists and tried to breathe normally. "You've been planning our escape." Esther nodded. "How long?"

"Since I was fourteen." She laughed. "Once Sam let me drive a tractor I started plotting ways to sneak out."

"You didn't."

"Sure, I did." Esther downshifted to a stop at the blacktop road. "Drew and I used the same plan when we were grounded. We were only caught half the time until Luke and Daddy put in all the outside lights. They made my goodnight kisses rough on dates, kinda too public."

Brit laughed. "You slowed down on the real road, 'fraid the cops would object to racing speed?"

"Yeah, something like that. So, where to?"

"I think ---" Her cell phone chimed.

"Gonna answer it?" Esther glanced at the clock, which actually worked. Ten after ten o'clock.

"I'm supposed to be on my way to the Waffle House."

270

She checked the messages, Sam's number.

It chimed again. She didn't answer it.

Esther's phone rang. "Yes?" She looked at her companion. "Sorry, we don't need any life insurance." She disconnected. "Daddy and Luke have reported on our escape."

"What did Sam say?"

"You figure it was Sam?"

"I could hear him all the way over here."

"The Mustang has left your house. An older model, green truck pulled in behind it and is following it at a discreet distance. An agent picked up the truck and Mustang at the main intersection and followed them."

"Well, got any bright ideas?"

"I say we keep going. I'm in the mood to kick some ass. We still have at least thirty minutes before you're supposed to meet the man. I say we head for the farm Julie described."

Esther's phone rang again. "Well?"

She shook her head. "Uh-huh."

She glanced at Brit, made a face, then looked back at the road. "Um hm, okay."

She slammed the steering wheel. "No way, Pal."

"Drew?"

"Of course. My brothers are predictable and protective and bossy as hell. They always have been like that. Got it from our daddy."

Brit's phone chimed. She waited, then checked the voice mail. "Brit, I don't want you in danger! Stay clear of trouble. We've covered the Waffle House and the Drake place. There's no way you can help. I'll slip in and sneak Julie out while Drake's away to meet you. You and Esther need to go back home where you'll be safe. Even if he realizes we're waiting here for him, he won't go to our farm. Don't be stubborn."

Esther answered her own phone before Brit finished the message. She held it away from her ear "Please tell my stubborn woman I love you both. Go the hell home! Please, please go where you'll be safe."

"We love you, too. Be careful." Esther disconnected.

271

"I think we need to go to the Three Creek Baptist Church Julie mentioned. We can watch the traffic from there and be near if Julie needs us. Head for 78 and Peach County."

"Look in my pack," Esther instructed. She switched on the inside light. "Check the inside pockets."

Brit opened the pack then unzipped a pocket. "Holy sh-" She pulled out a small pistol and shells.

Esther glanced her way again. "Now the other pocket."

Brit found another small handgun. "Good God, Lady. Are these both yours?"

"Did you forget my brother is a cop. Of course they're mine. For now, one is yours." She paused when she heard Brit's loud intake of breath. "You can shoot, can't you?"

***

Julie searched the house for weapons she could hide. Three dull kitchen knives she stuffed in places in her clothes she hoped wouldn't poke her. The grocery bags Douglas had left held flashlights and batteries.

She grabbed several plastic bags to stuff together for strength and donned the old musty smelling woman's jacket over an old sweater she'd found hanging on a nail in the pantry. She grabbed two water bottles and an unopened pack of crackers and a package of cheese. To those she added a small towel and two forks.

She'd checked the outbuildings for a way to leave, but no old cars or tractors waited. Only in the movies would that happen. The pitchfork would do as a walking stick or as a weapon, if she needed one.

On the way out she grabbed candles and a box of matches. It was dark enough to make walking around scary but not as scary as having Douglas find her here when he returned. Afraid to follow the road, she walked through the wooded area beside the driveway. Praying she wasn't making a mistake, she moved toward the old road, praying night animals wouldn't bother her.

"God, please don't let him find me." She walked slowly until she reached the dirt road. Jogging along the road's edge for a short while, she listened for a car engine. The night was quiet, except for the crickets and night noises. She hadn't heard such quiet since she and Brit had camped out during their teen years. A hoot owl scared ten years off her life.

"I'm not afraid of ghosts," she mumbled as a mantra until she didn't need to think to say the words. She sing-songed under her breath, "Lions and tigers and bears, oh my."

She saw lights coming toward her from the direction of the highway and heard the engine at the same time. Thankful for the trees and bushes lining the road, she scrambled behind cover.

Bats flew from the trees' lower branches overhead, nearly sending her back onto the road. She tried to slow her breathing to normal. The truck was dark inside as it passed. By the time the truck passed she could hear her blood pounding in her ears. The taillights became red pinpoints then faded into the night.

What if that was Douglas? The way he kept changing vehicles she couldn't be sure. She waited until she was sure the driver hadn't spotted her and turned around to come back. She scrambled back onto the road, thankful for her protective jeans.

***

Sam prayed Esther and Brit would go back home where his father and Luke could protect them. Briggs hadn't wanted him to go along but had finally relented when Sam had promised to stay out of the way.

Officer Briggs and his partner would meet the Peach County Sheriff's men, since the house was in his jurisdiction, and go from there.

Drew and an FBI agent had circled the block and followed Douglas and the Mustang. There should be no problem if the women would just stay away.

"Should we have someone stop the VW and detain the women?" Sam asked Drew over his cell phone.

"Who knows where they are?" Drew reminded Sam. "Esther knows these roads like the back of her hands. She could have taken any number of shortcuts to where ever she thinks they need to wait."

"Yeah, I know."

"Did she mention whether she has her guns?"

"No, but you know she would. At least she knows how to shoot as well as either of us." Sam shrugged when Briggs and his partner turned in the front seats to look at him. "I don't know about Brit, though. Damn it!"

The unmarked police car pulled in behind the Three Creek Baptist Church and met a Peach County Sheriff's car. At least they knew where Douglas was, for now. Sam champed at the bit while the lawmen spread out a large paper and pointed to spots on it. Detective Briggs, not a small man himself, was nearly dwarfed by the uniformed County cops. These men must have grown up pulling the plows instead of driving tractors.

When the deputy turned away from the car and spat Sam was sure he was right.

By the time the lawmen separated to their own cars Sam was anxious as an expectant father. Actually, he wouldn't mind being an expectant father.

***

Julie had been walking for hours, or so it seemed. Her watch read ten fifty-five. She'd passed three driveways, but she had no idea how far the houses were from the road. She saw no lights from the road. Would she lose time going down driveways that might be dead ends? She'd take her chances and hope she could see a house from the road.

She gauged her distance at nearly four miles. She remembered at least three more drives and large fields and an orchard between her and the highway.

She'd have to stop unless she could make better time. Lights coming from behind forced her off the road again, behind a pair of large fragrant bushes. What was at that end of the road? The racket of the engine was nearly drowned out by the rattling of the old truck. A flatbed truck. An empty, flatbed truck lumbered slowly past. The windows were down and the driver bellowed a country tune along with the radio. Long gray hair flew behind her.

Julie was surprised when her feet moved her toward the back of the truck and some inner force pushed her onto the flat bed. The truck didn't slow. The driver continued to bellow the country tune off key. Julie flattened herself against hard boards and thanked God for the help. She prayed the odd looking driver wouldn't notice her stowaway.

***

Stupid teacher drives that Mustang like a little old lady. Doesn't she know how to appreciate a fine machine? Wonder if she'd drive differently if she realized this could be her last night to enjoy it? Yep, turn right. How long is she gonna crawl along?

The sooner he met his target at the Waffle House, the sooner he could take her out in the woods and kill her. He watched the classic car ease to a traffic light.

"Damned light's green, keep moving. Ah, shit, yellow. What the Hell?" he muttered. His quarry's exhaust belched out as it zoomed through a red light. Slamming on brakes, Douglas cursed. She can't have done that on purpose.

"What the Hell? She can't know I'm following her." Sweat dampened his shirt. He was muttering again, but who would know? "Can't afford to get stopped by cops. Might be at least one intelligent cop who'd recognize me. Just what I need."

An older, green truck turned in front of his and behind the Mustang that had left him standing. A white rattletrap followed. By the time the light turned green, three vehicles separated Douglas from the teacher's car.

He swiped at the sweat now dampening his upper lip and forehead. *Convincing the teacher to follow me to the deserted shack shouldn't take much effort. She and Julie were friends. Too bad they aren't more alike. Doesn't matter. Killing the teacher's a job. Even this killer has honor. Take a job, do the job. That's been my motto and I'll follow through.*

The white rattletrap finally turned right. Now only two cars separated him from the Mustang and his prey. Once he offed the teacher he could take his lady and leave this country and this job. He'd need to get Julie away before she could hear about her friend's death. He'd have to convince her someone else had done the hit. She'd probably never forgive him for killing her friend.

Douglas almost cheered when the green truck turned off. Ten minutes, at most, and they'd be at the meeting place. "Well, bitch, not much longer." The old excitement seeped into his bones. His breathing quickened. His palms were damp.

Oh, yes, he could do this one last job. He'd collect the final installment from his employers and make a fast getaway. If he couldn't get to them he'd settle for the money stashed in foreign bank accounts.

***

The bed of the old truck rattled, jarring Julie in a monotonous, rocking motion. Lulled to an exhausted trace-like state, she almost missed the right turn onto the highway. Wind chilled her through the sweater and jacket.

Oh, great. What's up ahead? Next stop I get out and try to call Brit. Hope there's a pay phone. Cell battery's gone. How much farther?

The truck slowed. Where? No lights indicated civilization. She glanced at her watch. Only eleven o'clock. She hadn't dozed as long as she thought she had. A right turn had her scrambling to hide under something. There was nowhere to hide. Preparing to roll off the truck bed, she stopped her efforts.

"What you doin' on my truck, girl?" A raspy voice called from the cab. The door opened. The wild haired woman slid from the seat to the ground. "Kinda late at night for a female to be walking on a deserted road by herself."

Julie could only stare at the driver, a woman? Her long, wild, white hair and her hands-on-her-hips stance were the only things about her that gave her gender away. Baggy overalls, work boots, and a battered hat could have belonged to an old man. The voice was kind.

"You don't need to be scared of me." She must have seen more than Julie could. Actually, she looked like the kind of person who might even smell fear. She was close enough now for Julie to see her faded blue eyes, bracketed by a network of lines and dirt. "Somebody after you, child?"

Julie tried to answer but couldn't get past the fear in her throat. What if this strange looking person knew Douglas? What if she was as bad as Douglas? She definitely looked rough. Julie could see her thin lips moving but the sounds coming from them seemed like gibberish. Her head weighed a ton. Her limbs froze. The dark night went darker.

***

Sam waited in the patrol car. The radio squawked messages meant for cops all over Florence, but none addressed his concerns. The detective with Sam who made sure he stayed put spoke to the person on the other end of the radio. Sam listened but only with effort.

Where are Esther and Brit? Haven't heard from them in a while. Can't believe Brit hung up on me. Doesn't she understand I'm trying to keep her out of danger?

How can the cops and I concentrate on saving Julie and capturing Drake if Brit's around. Add Esther to the mix and things will be even more complicated. Now I gotta worry about the woman I love and my sister.

Where the hell are Drake and Drew? Drew hasn't been in touch since he announced his approach to the meeting place, right behind the decoy Mustang and its FBI driver. They should be in the Waffle House parking lot by now. Has Drake discovered their trick?

Why was it taking so long for the Peach County cops to bring Julie out? Lights moved toward Sam and the patrol car. Three men swept their lights back and forth. Men only. Three men had walked down the drive toward the Drake house and three men were coming back. Where was Julie? Surely they would have brought her out if they'd found her. She wasn't walking toward him or being carried.

***

277

Esther pulled her Bug into the graveled parking area of the Triple Creek Baptist Church. A lone light lit the front of the church. No light lit the back. "Now what?" Esther asked.

"We should pull out of the light as far as possible. We'll still see any cop cars coming this way. At least we'll know Julie's safe."

Esther's cell rang only a squawk's worth before she answered it. "What do you mean Julie isn't there?"

"What?" Brit asked, staring at Esther.

"What could have happened to her? Could Drake have an accomplice who moved her?"

"Esther, what's happening? What's he saying?"

Julie made a shushing motion. "Well, you're with the cops. What do they think happened to her? Could they have missed any places in the dark? Maybe she's tied up and hidden." She stopped when Brit gasped. "Sorry."

Esther handed the phone to Brit.

"Sam?" She listened, nodding. "So you found no signs of injury? They checked outbuildings and such? Okay. Me, too. Sam, we're not going home but we'll stay out of the way. Sam!"

"He wants to speak to you again." She handed the phone back to Esther.

"Sam, she'd have come on her own. There was no way she'd have sat around and waited any more than I would have! At least I can keep her out of trouble. Oh, yeah? Heard from Drew and the decoy? Right!"

***

Douglas watched the Mustang. The teacher had parked in a well-lit area. A truck had pulled in soon after he had. No one got out. Odd. Something didn't feel right about the situation.

He watched a hand adjust the rearview mirror of the Mustang. It was time to go to the car and tell the teacher to get into his truck and go with him to see her friend.

He wished someone would get out of the other truck. He didn't need anyone to witness his contact with the teacher. Someone might notice and remember. Maybe it would look like

278

lovers meeting. He opened the door of his truck and sauntered toward the Mustang.

He knocked on the closed window of the driver's side. The woman seemed to shrink away from the window.

"Roll it down," he spoke loudly to get her to hear him. How did she think she would learn where her friend was if she wouldn't talk to him. Her hair hung on the sides of her face. The handkerchief she held to her face like she was crying hid most of her features.

"Open the window and I'll tell you where your friend is. Come on, lady." He wanted to call her the troublesome bitch she was. The window opened a little. "I'll take you to her, if you come with me."

Her voice sounded hoarse, like she'd been crying. He needed to get her in his truck so she couldn't get away.

"I can't get out," she said.

"Why the Hell not?" He needed to calm down so she wouldn't spook. He flexed his fingers to relax. He pasted on a smile.

"Julie's waiting for you. I told her you were coming." He laughed. "If you don't come with me I won't untie her before I teach her how to beg. I've been nice, so far. No blood spilled, no bones broken, yet."

The woman cried into her handkerchief. The bitch was getting on his nerves. He didn't have time for her hysterics.

"Okay, never mind. I'll just go back to her." Maybe she'd follow him. He walked to his truck. He hesitated before opening the door and getting in. He'd really prefer to have her with him. Short of causing a scene, he couldn't force her to get out of her car here. This should have been easier. She insisted on ruining his plans, again. This would be the last time she'd have the chance to mess him up.

When he pulled out of the parking lot onto the road the Mustang followed him. *When I get her away from everyone she's gonna pay for all the trouble she's caused.*

She followed at a safe distance. There were few vehicles on the road. The deserted shack wasn't far. Douglas was nearly

279

beside himself with anticipation when he approached the four-way stop. An occasional car or truck passed or turned onto the road. He'd prefer not to have anyone see his truck and the Mustang turn onto the same road. Of course, by the time anyone could do anything with the information he'd be long gone. But still…

At the four-way stop he glanced behind at the Mustang as she stopped. Behind her was a black truck. It was too dark to be sure, but the damned truck looked too familiar. Can't be a coincidence.

He passed the road where he'd planned to turn. Eight miles later he turned on the road leading to highway 78, toward Peach County and his house. If that damned truck kept with them he'd know he'd been double-crossed. He'd told the bitch not to tell the police. Now what the Hell to do?

***

Julie ached all over. Just turning onto her side hurt. A cool, damp cloth washed her brow. Heavenly. Where was she? Was Douglas washing her face? She trembled. A groan escaped her lips.

"All right, sugar. It's all right. Nobody's gonna hurt you. Me and Ned's gonna take good care of you."

Julie opened her eyes slowly. The face near her own was beautiful with age. Blue eyes crinkled under gray eyebrows. Lines bracketed the old woman's smiling mouth. Soothed by the crooning of the hoarse voice ,Julie closed her eyes for another minute to gather her thoughts.

"Wh-Where am I?" she asked.

A new, deeper voice answered. "Why, child, you're with Wilma and me, in our house. She found you on her truck. You'd done passed out."

The woman spoke softly. "You're all scratched up, like you been runnin' from somethin'. Who's that there Douglas fella? You kept callin' out his name like you was scart of him."

The woman, Wilma, she figured, dipped the cloth into a water basin and washed her arm. It stung only a few seconds.

"I put my special healin' powder in the water. Make it up myself, you know. It'll cleanse your wounds and keep you from gettin' infection."

"So, girl, you gonna tell us who's got you so scared, so we can help?" Ned looked like a hillbilly Santa, with his plaid shirt tucked into overalls. His white beard hid most of the bib. The house was so quiet Julie could hear the loud ticking of a clock.

Wilma held Julie's head up. The rim of a glass felt cool against her lips. "Drink a couple of swallows, child. It's water from our spring out back. I'll get you something more if you drink this first. If you're hungry we can talk while you eat a bite."

"Thanks." Julie was surprised when she drank a swallow then another. "Good water."

Ned and Wilma grinned proudly. "Best water in the state. Man wanted us to bottle it and sell it. We don't sell water! The good Lord give it to us to share. It'd be a sin, like sellin' air."

"Wilma wanted to call the sheriff, but I thought you might be runnin' from the law. You done somethin' wrong?"

"No!" Julie answered too quickly. She tried to raise herself on her elbow, but her head swam. "Please, I need to call my friend and let her know I'm okay. My cell phone ran out of battery power. Do you have a charger?"

Ned patted her hand. "I got chargers for big batteries and a generator, but we got no cell phone. Our son says we oughta have one for emergencies. Maybe we'll get one, one of these days. You can use our phone."

"I'll pay for the call. I think it's long distance."

"Stay put and I'll bring the phone to you." Wilma placed the heavy looking rotary phone on the bed beside Julie. She dialed Brit's mobile.

"Brit, I got away from Douglas and I'm okay," she blurted. "Yes. Go someplace safe and stay there 'til they get the bastard." She paused. Wilma and Ned stared at her.

"What did you say?" Julie yelled into the phone. "You're where? Are you crazy? What if he finds you there?"

She heard Ned comment to Wilma. "Thank her friend's hard of hearin'? She don't haf to yell." She didn't hear Wilma's response."

"You're too close to his house. I don't care where you're supposed to meet him."

She paused while Brit spoke. Her heart beat double time. "But when Douglas finds out you've tricked him he'll come looking for you and for me. Hell, he won't give up. He thinks he's in love with me." Julie couldn't believe what her friend was telling her. It was too bizarre.

"Don't you think he'll be spooked when he finds a small army waiting for him? Okay, let everyone know I'm fine. I'll call the law, if there's anyone available."

Her head pounded. "For heaven's sake be careful! The man's a loony tune who wants you dead."

Wilma reached for the receiver. "I found your friend on the bed of my truck. She's awful scratched up and tired, but me and Ned's takin' care of her. We're not far from where she hitched a ride." Julie hadn't realized she been spotted when she hopped onto the truck. Wilma had known she was there, but she hadn't even slowed down.

"Sounds like you shouldn't be near here. You're hiding behind the church? Honey, that's a favorite place for the shiners to meet their buyers. You don't want to hang around. Let me give you our phone number so you can check on your friend. Then you get away from the church. Got a pencil and paper?"

Julie could imagine Wilma wetting the lead on a pencil. "Okay. Our number's 799-3232. Oh, yeah, 478. Got it?" Julie watched Wilma mouthed the numbers Brit must be repeating back to her.

"She's safe as in her own mama's arms. Sheriff knows us, honey. We're Ned and Wilma."

Julie took the phone back in time to hear another phone ring. She heard Esther's voice, so she figured she'd cut her part short. "Brit, girl, I gotta rest a few minutes and we need to conserve your phone's battery power. And you probably want to hear what Esther's saying, anyway."

All Hell's about to break loose. Hope no one gets hurt.
***

Sam rubbed the back of his neck. Relief that Julie was safe for the moment was overshadowed by the dangers Drake still posed. If he returned home he'd be caught by one of the sheriff's men or an FBI man. Men were scattered strategically around the house and property. Anyone turning into his drive would be stopped. Drew's description of the truck Drake drove should make the job easier. He must be wandering around an awful lot. Either he was leading the Mustang on a merry chase, or he didn't know where he was going. Surely he hadn't made the decoy or Drew following. It sounded like he was moving right into their trap. *Too easy.*
***

"Brit, think we should change locations? If Julie's free, do we need to wait here to see Drake caught? That Wilma person might have a point about this place. Wouldn't it be a kick in the head if we were caught here by moonshiners or drug dealers instead of Drake, especially with the local law so nearby at Drake's.

A siren screamed. Lights flashed a streak past the church. "You don't suppose?" Brit asked. "Naw," she answered herself. "He couldn't be close enough and they wouldn't announce they were after him."

Esther grinned. "It would be funny if he was stopped by a state patrolman for speeding. Boy would he be in deep shit. There is an APB on him, after all."
***

The black truck kept showing up. Douglas had made several turns but couldn't lose him. Someone was following him and the Mustang. He'd make a fast turn and hope the Mustang followed. He wasn't far from the Triple Creek Baptist Church. He'd never killed anyone behind a church before.

Chapter Twenty-two

Sam couldn't believe he and the cops couldn't find Julie. When his cell rang he spotted his brother's number and answered it. "Sam, Drake seems to be heading your way in an old model tan Chevy van, very muddy. License plates too muddy to ID. We followed him from the Waffle House parking lot."

"Any problems?" the patrolman asked Sam.

Sam held the cell phone away from his mouth. "No problems, so far. Drew says they're all headed this way." He returned to his brother. "So, how?"

Drew's voice came through. "The decoy managed to fool him. I'm following from a distance."

The police radio squawked. "Agent Mustang, here." It sounded kinda like code or maybe CB talk. "Following yokel and should meet soon. Someone needs a car wash, a big one."

Maybe Drake has a dirty truck?

"We're waiting dinner since you're not the only one missing. Sis isn't here. We'll watch for you," Detective Briggs answered into the radio. After a quick catch up for his deputy and an explanation to Sam he opened the door of the cruiser. "Gotta pass the word."

That should fool anyone listening in.

Sam rang Esther's cell. "Drew says they're headed this way. Please, go home. You don't need to hang around. Julie's safe, so there's no need for you and Brit to be in harm's way."

"Sorry, brother. Brit says she wants to see the bastard get what he deserves. When you call to tell us he's in custody or dead she'll be ready to leave."

"Damn! Be careful!" Sam hit the door armrest. Headstrong women. God, he hoped they stayed put where they'd be away from the fireworks.

***

Julie sat in the back seat of the oldest Chevy sedan she'd ever seen. "Wilma, I really appreciate what you two are doing."

"Ain't nothin', girl. Sittin' in the back of Triple Creek Church might get your friends in trouble. We need to move 'em. Maybe they'll go on home if they see you're safe. Wouldn't want some 'shiner' or dealer to find 'em. If Luther finds 'em waiting back there he'll think they're settin' a trap and kill 'em."

"Luther? Who's he?" Julie asked.

"Meanest dealer around. He grows his own weed. Makes a tidy profit, too."

***

Sam nearly retched from the pain in his gut. His neck felt like he'd been slammed by a sledgehammer. A cold sweat drenched his face. Brit was in trouble. He answered the cell before the first ring finished. Drew's voice yelled, "All hell's about to explode. Drake's turning into the Church driveway."

The sheriff's car moved ahead of the others. Sam had abandoned his seat belt to lean toward the driver of the police cruiser. Drew hadn't said which church, but Sam knew. How could they have all been so stupid to think he wouldn't have doubled back on them? How could the woman he loved put herself in danger again? Again! And with his sister? At least Drew and the FBI agent were there. But would that keep Douglas from going berserk and creating mayhem.

***

"We've got company," Brit slid down in her seat. Esther cocked her revolver. "There's more than one set of lights." She punched Sam's number.

Before she could get in more than two words he shouted, "You didn't leave, did you? Never mind. Don't answer that. Stay down and be careful. Drake's pulling into the church parking lot."

Brit could hear Sam's commanding voice. Leaning across the floor shift she hissed, "He's here? Oh, God."

"You've got plenty of protection. Don't interfere. Don't show your face. Don't get out of the car and do anything stupid!" He left the connection open.

Brit and Esther peered at the van pulling around the corner. Maybe the VW wouldn't be noticed.

***

Douglas had never been so ready to finish a job. He waited for the rush he had always felt when he moved in for the kill. He was barely behind the church where no one would see him from the road. He had to lure the teacher from her car. Hell, he'd shoot her through the window if he had to. He'd turned his van around to head out quickly. She'd pulled in behind him.

He checked his weapons then quickly opened his door. His peripheral vision caught a glimpse of an old VW Bug. As soon as he was done with the teacher he'd have to make sure there were no witnesses. Soon the teacher would be dead and he could go get his Julie and go away. They'd be together forever. With the money he'd stashed in phony bank accounts he'd never have to work again.

The Mustang lights stayed on. The hairs on the back of his neck stood on end. Something didn't feel right. He could hear his own breathing. The closer he got to the car the stranger he felt. His pistol hung ready at his side. Maybe he should have just planted explosives on the car to blow it up with the teacher in it. Nah! He wanted her to know she was going to die by his hand. He'd have to move quickly, in case company showed.

He knocked on the Mustang window. A bright light shone in his face as he heard the glass being lowered. He averted his eyes, then turned back to see the barrel of a pump shotgun pointed in his face.

"Shit," he blurted. The light nearly blinded him.

"Police, drop your weapon," a woman's voice ordered. "I said drop the damned weapon. Hands behind your head or I'll blow your face off."

Like hell he would. He raised his gun hand, prepared to duck below the window.

"Don't even think about it." A man's voice warned from behind Douglas. "Drop the weapon and move away from the car."

Douglas flinched. Cold hard steel pressed at the base of his skull. He'd kill the bitch and the bastard who interfered. He raised his gun to shoot. "Shit!" The pain in his back made him lose any advantage he might have had. The car door had slammed into him. He fell to his knees. The shotgun pressed into his temple again.

He still had his knife in his boot. The man standing over him looked willing to kill him here, now.

Night sounds surrounded him. Crickets, frogs, cars on the road yards away, another car door opening. *How the hell many people are here anyway?* He looked up. Both gun barrels pressed his temples. He saw a small figure approaching from the direction of the Bug. He managed to move his head to see who approached. *No. No! It can't be.*

The woman coming closer had dark hair, but the face was familiar. He wanted to look behind him. The hot mama who lived in the teacher's house? Yes, but she looked different. Something in her eyes. The teacher?

The teacher couldn't be in front of him and behind him pointing a shotgun at his head.

"Looking for me?" the woman in front of him asked.

He wanted to lunge at her, but the cold, hard barrels dug into his flesh. "Stand up slowly." His arms were yanked behind his back.

Anger shot through him. He had a card to play and he played it. "I still have your friend. I've buried her alive. Unless I tell someone where to find her she'll die. No food, no water, air running out. Her death will be slow and painful. Now get these damned guns out of my face."

"No, you don't have my friend and the guns pointed at you are the law." The crunch of tires announced more company.

287

Brit stifled a laugh when an automotive monstrosity pulled into view behind the captive. Two white-haired people hobbled from the ancient car. Julie followed them.

Julie raced straight to Brit. A roar reached Brit's ears as Julie threw her arms around her. She wasn't sure who hugged the hardest, but it didn't matter.

"Julie, how did you get here? You were supposed to wait for me, dammit! You were supposed to wait!" Douglas shouted.

Drew and the agent restrained the maniac fighting like an animal. More headlights and crunching gravel brought the sheriff's car. Behind it Florence police raced in.

Brit felt Sam's arms around her only seconds after she saw him exit the police car. She barely heard the words identifying the captive as the man who had escaped jail. She heard snatches of Miranda rights and warnings to go quietly while he was led to the sheriff's vehicle.

Sam wanted to hold Brit in his arms forever. He was glad Julie was safe, but his mind was on the woman he loved. He wanted to hold her. He wanted to shake her. He wanted to get her alone so he could assure himself she was unharmed in any way. He wanted to scold her for putting herself in danger. He wanted to kiss her senseless. He loosened his hold to take her face with both hands while his lips touched hers.

No one existed here but Sam and the woman he needed as much as he needed air. He tasted her sweetness. He opened his mouth to take more of her. His hands left her face to pull her into him. She tasted of heaven. He could kiss her forever.

"NOOO," Sam heard Esther yell.

Pain shot through his body as though his instincts were in full force. He groaned. A scream made him end the kiss before a body slammed into him, knocking him to the ground. Searing pain shot through his arm and across his chest. Sounds mixed in his mind while he fought to stay conscious. Gunshots were the last thing he heard.

Gunshots rang out. Brit's shoulder ached. Her attacker lay on the ground. Drew's gun pointed at the bleeding, prone figure. She counted seven guns. Her arm felt heavy. A gun, she gripped a gun. That made eight guns? She had fired her gun. She was vaguely aware when Julie took the gun from her hand

Kneeling, she reached for Sam. In the beams of light from the cars she saw bloodstains spreading across Sam's chest. The coppery scent nearly gagged her. She struggled for control. Yanking her jacket off, she propped his head up. She tried to find the wound, the source of the glistening life flowing from the man she loved. She couldn't lose him now.

"Sam, don't you dare die on me. I need you. Sean needs you. I'll never forgive you if you leave me." Esther and Julie were at her side. Esther offered Brit sterile cloths from her backpack. She found and pressed the wound with both hands across the slash.

Esther's hands joined hers, wiping and pressing cloths. They saturated as soon as they were pressed. Julie and Drew ripped open package after package. Someone handed Brit several sanitary napkins. Sanitary napkins? Couldn't be. The slash seemed to cross his arm and his chest. She'd keep his life from flowing out no matter what she had to do.

"I can't lose another man to that bastard." She thought she heard someone say he was already dead. She didn't even care. She pushed aside a memory of the gun's kick as she'd fired it. She didn't have time to think about it. She felt Sam's body heat. She listened to his labored breathing. Blankets and jackets appeared and covered Sam's body as she worked. She didn't know whose.

She had been vaguely aware when Drew joined their efforts, though she had taken pads from his hands. She knew he spoke to his brother. She knew Esther spoke to Sam. She just shut out everything but Sam.

Screaming sirens and flashing lights broke into the quiet after the gunshots. Efficient EMT'S, three maybe, surrounded Sam to attach IV'S and move him to a stretcher.

Only when Julie threatened to have a paramedic sedate Brit did she move away for the people to do their jobs. She clasped her restless hands to keep from reaching for Sam.

She followed his stretcher into the ambulance. Brit held Sam's hand all the way to the hospital, watching latex gloved hands cleaning his wound and working to keep him comfortable. She prayed. She encouraged. She pleaded with him to keep fighting. Brit bargained with God.

She followed Sam into the hospital, turning loose only when he was rushed into surgery to assess and repair the damage.

***

Mr. and Mrs. Samuels had hurried into the hospital waiting room and embraced Brit and Esther. Esther recounted details of Sam's stabbing and Brit's bravery. Brit filled in with a detail once in a while, but she couldn't concentrate on the conversations. She appreciated the Samuels comforting her when they were worried about their son and brother. The coffee Julie brought her cooled, untouched. Drew disappeared after a nurse assured them Sam was holding his own.

Brit rose and paced. She walked up one hall and down another. It was time to call her parents to let them know it was over. She told them about Julie's kidnapping and Sam's bravery.

"Mama, what can I do?"

"Pray, honey, pray."

"Yes, Mama. I passed a chapel. I'll keep you posted on Sam's condition. When things settle down I'll tell you more details. Julie owes us lots of them when she feels like sharing."

She walked toward the chapel, closing her cell phone. Peace seemed to emanate through its entrance. The quiet, small room drew her.

There, in the dim candlelit corner, she vowed to do anything God wanted of her. Esther joined her to share a few minutes of peace and quiet. "I'll even leave him alone, if that's what it takes. I'll give him up so he can find a woman to marry and be a mother to Sean."

"But, Brit, you can be a mother to Sean. He's so fond of you, already. You can marry my brother."

290

"I can't marry Sam." There was no way Brit could explain the guilt she'd felt when Tommy had died. She'd finally gained control of her life again. Sam could take over her life. She'd have to give up her house, the place she'd bought herself. He loved children and would probably want more. She couldn't give them to him. It would never work.

"Of course you can."

"What?" Could Esther know what she'd been thinking?

"Of course you can marry Sam. He loves you."

"He's bossy."

"He wants to protect you. That's the way the Samuels men are." Esther smiled.

"He's controlling."

"He's strong. You just have to know how to handle him." Esther rose from the bench she'd shared with Brit. "I'll see if Sam's out of surgery or if there is any news."

"Esther, it's my fault he's lying in there. If I'd stayed in the car tonight Sam wouldn't have been trying to protect me. If I hadn't let him kiss me he'd have been paying attention."

"If we'd stayed home we wouldn't have been there for him or the police to protect?"

"See?"

"No, I don't see. That would make it my fault for being there, too. My brother *could have* stayed with us. It *could be* his fault. The bastard who hurt him *didn't have* to attack you. He *didn't have* to kidnap Julie. He *didn't have* to lure you out tonight. *He's* to blame, *not you*." Esther hugged Brit. "I'd never let you near my brother if I thought you'd ever harm him. None of us would. I'll come back after I speak to Mom and Dad."

"I'll go with you." Brit rose. "I'm done here." What more could she offer for Sam's life?

***

At six a.m. shades of pink morning light filtered through her windows to tint her walls. Brit sat at her kitchen table, sipping coffee. She'd showered to wash away the strain of the night, to remove the scent of blood, Sam's blood. After hours of

291

tossing and turning in bed, moving from one nightmare to another, she had given up. She had never seen so much blood.

Images of Sam falling haunted her sleep, waking her to the horror that he could have died without letting her say goodbye.

After Tommy's death she had believed she'd never love again. Did she even deserve to? If she hadn't sent Tommy out to work distracted would he have seen Douglas Drake's truck and avoided being hit? If she'd stayed with Sam's parents like he'd told her to would he have been stabbed?

She didn't like being told what to do. Sam was an in-charge kind of man. They'd lock horns all the time. Their being together wouldn't work. The lovemaking was beyond wonderful, but it couldn't always make up for their differences.

Sam deserved to build a life with a woman who could make him happy, one who could give him children. He was so good with them. Though she and Sam had done nothing to prevent pregnancy, she knew there would be no child from their lovemaking.

After the operation the surgeon had given orders that each family member and Brit could see him in pairs for two minutes. Drew went in with her. He seemed as teary as she felt. She'd never seen Sam look so pale, even against the stark white of his bandages.

"Good job, old buddy," Drew said. Sam's eyes stayed shut, as they had expected. "We got the bastard. Now we can all get on with our lives. I'll call Sean and Adrienne before any news reports can mention the killing. New reporters are waiting downstairs for details. Here's Brit."

She'd held Sam's hand and he'd gripped it, even in his sleep. She'd kissed his lips. She was certain he'd kissed her back. "I love you," she whispered.

Detective Briggs had smuggled her out a back door to avoid the reporters and taken her home in a squad car. He had been so kind after he'd read her the riot act for putting herself in danger. He hadn't mentioned Sam's danger. He hadn't needed to remind her.

He'd seen her inside, checking her house, in case Drake's employers had sent someone to do his job. "You still need to be careful."

The poor man had blushed when she'd hugged him before he left.

***

She'd been home only minutes when the loud jangle of her phone shattered the eerie quiet. She almost let the answering machine take care of the call. Then she'd remembered.

Her message needed changing. She should be safe for now. She wasn't going anywhere. With Drake dead she'd seen no reason to stay away, in spite of Detective Brigg's warning the people who hired him still wanted her dead.

"Brit?" Drew's voice had reassured her. "How about if I bring Monster home?"

"Oh, please. I miss my baby."

"I'm on my way. Thought you'd feel that way." She could hear her pet whine into the cell phone. Slurping noises came through. "Stop that, I'm taking you to your mama. Save your kisses for her, you monster."

"Oh, baby," Brit crooned.

"Just around the corner." Drew laughed. "I'm not dessert, you overgrown mutt." As he ended the connection Brit could hear his truck engine in her driveway. He had made good time after leaving the reporters.

She raced to open her door. A bundle of energy hurtled itself at her. She dropped to her knees then to the floor. She could hear Drew laughing but could see nothing. Her eyes were closed to protect them from the tongue bathing her face.

"Someone will be in to clear out most of the surveillance equipment in the morning," Drew assured her. "Oh, yeah, it is morning already."

"Thank you, Drew. Thank you." Brit held monster's head, rubbing her face against his muscular neck. She pulled away from the enthusiastic doggy hugs to stand.

293

"Gotta get by headquarters, then get some rest. I'll have to be in Atlanta by noon to file reports and question Drake's employers. I think we can convince them we have the goods on 'em and get enough confessions to bury them all. Are you okay here alone?"

"It's my home, Drew. Besides, I'm not alone now, thanks to you." She hugged him.

He was nearly out the door when she asked. "Who actually killed Drake?"

"I don't know." Drew shrugged. "We'll know more after ballistics tests come back."

"I never killed a man before." Her voice shook. "I never even shot any living thing before tonight."

"For what it's worth, I don't think you killed him."

"I'd do it again to save Sam or anyone I love." Her voice hardened. Her eyes stared into Drew's amber ones. "I would!"

Brit planned to get to the hospital. She just had a few things to do first. She watched Officer Briggs and his men remove their equipment. The FBI men and Sam's technician cleared out the rest, leaving only Sam's security cameras.

By afternoon she'd called the hospital twice to check on Sam. She left her house to go to the hospital but detoured by Julie's. Together they watched television coverage of the nightmare. Would making everything so public make Brit safer? Who would dare threaten her now?

Julie talked about the hours she had spent at the police station and with the FBI agents. A certain bar owner had taken her home. Remembering the first night she'd gone with Julie to Mustang Red's made Brit laugh. Julie had been with him on the night Drake had been captured at her home after the second attack. Jessie and Julie seemed so well matched.

The more Brit talked to Julie or Sam's family about him, the more she worried she should just try to stay away from him. It made no sense, but it made all the sense in the world. Her life would be busy without Sam.

***

Sam reached for the consciousness hovering outside his grasp. He heard voices, those of his family and other voices that became familiar as doctors and nurses tended him.

When he could finally make his voice work with his eyes and his brain he asked questions. Everyone came but Brit. Julie and Jessie visited him. From Julie he learned that Brit had meant to visit but hadn't been able to. Esther told him about Brit's fear that she'd put him in danger and nearly cost him his life.

He couldn't believe she'd bargained with God for his life. Not once had he believed he would die. He had to make her understand they had been brought together by a power greater than either of them or any killer.

His premonitions had chosen her and they'd probably haunt him if he let her go. For the first time since he'd believed he loved Sean's mother more than anything, he knew he loved a woman so much he couldn't lose her. Brit and Sean were his life. He had to make her understand.

**

By evening the police had brought the Mustang home and it was back in her garage.

Life was back to normal, but there was no Sam in it. He must have gotten the message when she'd failed to visit him in the hospital or even call him. Each time she'd picked up the phone to call she'd put it down without dialing the hospital number. He hadn't called her, either. She was glad. Explaining things over the phone would have been so difficult.

Her sleep the first night after all the excitement had been filled nightmares. Sometimes she could have sworn she smelled the copper stench of blood after she awoke. Loving someone left a person open to pain and worry! She couldn't risk her heart like that again. She'd learn to live without him, but at least she wouldn't have to wonder when he'd look at her and remember what she had done. She couldn't be the kind of woman who didn't argue or put herself at risk again.

**

Sam heard all the publicity about the shooting and threats against Brit. Newspapers and television channels covered every aspect they could. They even brought up Brit's husband Tommy and every crime he'd been accused of committing. Drew, who had returned to Atlanta, assured Sam there was now enough evidence to put the small town crooks away forever, at least.

Sam trudged from the street and up Brit's driveway, trying to stand straight. His arm and shoulder were stiff. His arm rested in a sling.

Why had the woman stayed away from the hospital? Esther had tried to tell him she didn't feel she would be good for him. Bull! Having her in his life was in his plans, no ifs, ands, or buts about it. She'd agree to marry him if he had to talk to her all afternoon and all night. Sean waited to be his backup, if he needed to. He and his mother had flown into Atlanta and headed straight to the hospital.

Within minutes after Sean's mother had left his hospital room to take Sean home, Sam had been on his way to the nurses' station to check himself out.

By the time Sam was ready to leave, Sean had returned with his car. Adrienne had offered to drive Sam, but he and Sean refused her offer.

He didn't really think of his house as home anymore. *Where Sean and Brit are is home. All I have to do was make her believe it. And I will.*

He knocked, but no one answered.

She has to know I'm here. Monster's raising a ruckus. Her garage door is open and I can see her Mustang. Had everything really started with his following her home after school one evening to protect her?

He looked back at Sean. Sean's nod was encouragement enough. Again she stood at her screen door, looking like a lost soul. He remembered standing on this porch in the dead of night, trying to persuade her to let him, practically a stranger, into her house to be sure she was all right.

She'd looked so vulnerable in her robe that night. In the daylight, wearing faded jeans and a short sleeved sweater, she seemed so small and fragile, especially with one bare foot resting on the other. He could stare at her all day and night and still need to drink in her freshness, her beauty. His heart raced at the thought of having her in his arms as his wife. Once she agreed to marry him he could let his son take him to their house.

He cleared his throat and chanced a tentative half smile. "Gonna let me in, Teach?"

"How'd you get here?" she asked instead of opening the door. "Shouldn't you be in bed?" She glanced at his wounded shoulder and winced as though she felt his pain. She had to feel how much he loved her.

Sam tilted his head toward Sean. "My ride." He shrugged, then wished he hadn't. Shrugging hurt. Probably would for a while.

Brit looked back at him. Even through the screen he could see tears brimming onto her lashes. "It's okay, sweetheart. Just let me in, please."

Her teeth worried her lip as she unlatched the door. She pushed it open. Before he stepped up to go inside she moved to the edge of the step. Her trembling hands touched the sides of his face. "I'm so sorry I put you in danger!"

He groaned with the need to bury his face in the softness of her breasts. She brushed back a lock of his hair but returned her hand to hold his face. He saw her eyes close just before her lips touched his forehead.

Air became scarce. Her scent was exciting, comforting, tempting. He'd know it anywhere.

His mouth opened to let out the breath he'd held. Her mouth touched his and set him ablaze. His uninjured arm slid around her waist, pulling her close. He slipped his tongue past her teeth to caress and taste. Her need, matching his, shot through him to every part of his being. His moans vibrated from his chest. His skin burned from her touch on his face, his neck, his shoulders.

Pain shot through the wounded arm and his chest, making him forget the pain building in his groin, reminding him they stood in her doorway in plain sight of his son or anyone on the street or watching from a window.

"Oh, Sam." She stepped aside but reached to touch his uninjured arm to help him inside. "I'm so sorry I hurt you. I'm so sorry I forgot--"

He stepped inside. "I'm not." He touched a finger to her lips. "I'm not sorry, darlin'. I needed that."

"The pain?"

"The kiss. I need another one." He was gonna need it to get through the discussion ahead.

The large wet tongue washing his hand alerted Sam to Monster beside him. The big dog seemed to sense that he couldn't have handled the usual roughness and play.

"Sam, you need to sit." Brit guided him to a chair. She could see he was in pain. She hadn't planned to kiss him, but he'd looked so good, so much better than she'd expected, considering the way he'd looked when she'd left him at the hospital.

Had she really believed she could let him go? How could she live in the same town, teach his son, live in the same world without showing how much she loved him?

"Sit with me, please?" He pointed to his lap. She gingerly perched on the knee of his uninjured side. "While I was lying in bed without you I had a lot of time to think."

She knew about having too much time to think. Between her nightmares of losing Sam she'd thought about nothing but him and her prayers and promises.

"Everyone told me about what you did. I remembered a scream, pain, then a gunshot. I was drowning in the black void. I heard your voice."

She remembered begging him not to die, ordering him to stay alive. In those moments she'd known she couldn't live if he had died. She'd been in that place before and almost hadn't survived the pain of loss.

Sam's voice was hoarse. "I could never have left you. I plan to marry you and start our family. So—"

"You haven't asked me—"

He grazed her palm with his lips. "Esther told me some nonsense about your having doubts."

"But, Sam..."

"She said I'd need to convince you we were right for each other. She said you can't have kids. You told me about that a lifetime ago and we'll adopt, if we have to. We still have Sean."

"But I've never been a mother."

"Your students love you. Sean promises to try to be good most of the time. At least you missed nasty diaper changing and teething and childhood diseases."

Actually, she'd kinda looked forward to those.

Sam pulled her against his chest. "I want to go to sleep at night with you in my arms. I want to awake every morning with you in my bed. I want to smell your scent on my pillow, on my skin from being so close to you. I want to grow old with you, to look after you and have your love."

"Sam, I'd have done anything to keep you safe and alive. I made promises to God, I prayed. I thought I could walk away. You give orders and I don't follow orders. We'll argue all the time."

"Darlin' I wouldn't love you so much if you were a following-orders kind of woman. I just have to try to keep you safe. I love making up. If I didn't have my son outside waiting I'd show you why we need to get married. I'd call your father to ask for your hand, but he already gave me his blessing before we came back here."

"You what?"

"Your family is grateful to me," He dodged a pretend punch. "and my family loves you. My son says all he asks is that we wait 'til school is out so his teacher won't be his stepmom."

"I think we can arrange that." Brit stood. Then she took his hand to pull him up.

"Is that a yes?" Sam kissed her before she could answer. "I'll take it as one." He kissed her again.

Monster raced back and forth from his mistress to the door and back. "I think he's trying to tell us something." Brit followed her pet to the door in time to see Sean raise his hand to knock on the screen.

"Hi, Ms. Roberts. I'm sorry about what happened to you while I was gone. I wish I'd been here to help," he said.

"Hi, Sean, I'm glad you were safely away from here. I caused your father enough worry."

"Uh, ma'am, have you said yes to my dad yet? The doctor said dad should go home and rest." Sean fidgeted. "If you haven't said yes, could you get on with it. He'll convince you, anyway. I know him."

Sam waited at her side. His good hand rested on her shoulder. "She's gonna marry us."

"I didn't say yes."

"Sure you did. Don't you remember?" He turned her to face him. "I love you. But I need to take more pain medication and rest." He winced. "Come by to see me tomorrow? Don't make me come get you. We need to set dates, shop for rings, plan a honeymoon, decide where to live, and get the mothers together."

Brit smiled. "I thought you'd never ask."

***

Sam awoke as the sun painted his room a pale pink. It sneaked under his blinds and woke him to a beautiful day. He heard Sean moving around quietly. He'd soon leave for school and Sam could have the house to himself when Brit came by. The principal had insisted she take a couple of more days off before returning to school from spring break.

His shoulder and chest burned. Soon the woman he loved would be here. He dozed for an hour, but his excitement wouldn't let him sleep the day away.

After the pain caused by Douglas Drake went away, his love for Brit would be with him forever.

By the time Sam heard the knock on his front door he was as nervous as a boy on his first date. This morning no threat hung over her head or his.

Sam almost forgot to check the peephole on his door. Her beauty took his breath away. When he opened the door the need to touch her was stronger than his need to breathe.

He pulled her into a one armed embrace. The hairs on the back of his neck rose. He felt lightheaded, as though a fist clutched his heart and squeezed gently.

Could he have a premonition coming on? Looking at the woman in his arms he could swear he felt an extra heartbeat. Somehow he knew. This might be the first of many *good* premonitions. He hadn't noticed a good one before. Maybe he hadn't been paying attention.

She would make a wonderful mother. Should he tell her what he felt or wait for her to learn by conventional methods? He'd enjoy his information for a while. The wonderful secret nestled in his heart.

"Let's talk about a wedding. I'm in the mood to get married soon, really soon."

Follow Mary on Instagram marymarvella
https://www.amazon.com/Mary-Marvella/e/B008E1SJ32

https://goodreads.com/author/show/4909455.Mary_Marvella

https://www.facebook.com/ARomanceCaper

www.MaryMarvella.com

https://www.facebook.com/mmbarfield

https://www.facebook.com/pages/Mary-Marvella-

Author/121044561311561

http://pinkfuzzyslipperwriters.blogspot.com

Follow Mary Marvella on Twitter @mmarvellab

http://amzn.to/22t6vOC

BIO Mary

Mary Marvella has been a storyteller for as long as she can remember. The arrival of the book mobile was as exciting as hearing the music of the ice cream truck.

Retired from teaching classic works of the masters, Mary plays let's pretend with her characters. She presents editing workshops, edits, coaches writers, and tutors one-on-one.

Mary has published novels, novellas, and short stories. Her genres include paranormal romance, romantic suspense, women's fiction, and sweet romance.
Georgia raised, she writes stories with a Southern flair.

Books by Mary Marvella
Non fiction:
https://www.amazon.com/Weeding-Garden-Your-Manuscript-Marvella-ebook

Novels:
Cheerleader Dad Sweet Romantic Comedy
Margo's Choice Women's Fiction

The Gift Women's Fiction
Haunting Refrain Romance, Reincarnation
Protective Instincts Book 1 of The Protection series, Romantic Suspense
Protecting Melissa Book 2 of The Protection series Romantic Suspense
The Cost of Deception Book 3 of The Protection series Romantic Suspense

Novellas:
Christmas's Best Bet, Humble Pie Mainstream Fiction
Forever Love Romance with Reincarnation and ghosts

Short Stories:
The Christmas Promise Mainstream
Matt's Christmas Angel Sweet Romance

Soon
Her Deception Mainstream Suspense

Anthologies:
Finding Love's Magic
Thanksgiving Road
Of Mountains and Mysteries
Legends of the Dragon
The Rise of the Phoenix
A Cup of Love
Haunting Tales of Spirit Lake
A Stone Mountain Christmas

Made in the USA
Columbia, SC
24 April 2024

34845378R00181